INTERLANDER

by Thomas Ward

Arcadia

MMX

Chapter One
Dr. Hilary Lynch

What kind of individuals are emotionally and mentally fit to walk in two worlds? And how does one set about discovering and recruiting such people?

Once the gun smoke of 1989 had cleared, these questions presented themselves to the Interland Security Service with considerable urgency. I quickly understood that my long association with Sebastian would not be enough to guarantee the Service's constitutional position. As guardian of the new sophiocratic state, Seb had a wide range of interest groups to satisfy, and it was inevitable that the loyalty of old colleagues would be taken for granted and their interests overlooked. The Service, I realised, was on its own and, given the planned expansion of the enclosure, it needed to recruit in earnest if it was to maintain its position and privileges within the new government.

In my own mind I was clear from the start that potential recruits should be very bright indeed. Our work is so extremely delicate and so complex that it would be downright dangerous for us to carry any deadwood. But I also knew that simply being intelligent was not going to be enough. We needed young people with a degree of daring and native cunning—which isn't quite the same thing as intelligence—as well as endurance and a certain quality of dreaminess or playfulness. I still find this last quality difficult to define, although I believe I know it when I see it.

More than this, however, I came to understand that we needed people who were, at some fundamental level, unhappy. I have written elsewhere that the experience of crossing the boundary is profoundly liberating, and so it is. But it is not only liberating. To slip between worlds day after day, to form relationships within the enclosure, to feel the full spectrum of human emotions within these relationships and yet to know that these feelings are at best only half real: experience has taught me that these things are simply not possible for people who are basically at peace with themselves.

We certainly weren't looking for bores in the Service—we all still enjoyed our drink and our parties too much to want to be saddled with a lot of misery guts—but we didn't really want ordinary, happy people, either.

Fortunately, a means of selecting suitable candidates quickly presented itself; in fact, it was staring us in the face. Unfortunately, I may not speak or write of it publically.

Dr. Hilary Lynch. *Soul Freedom,* Chapter 8

Chapter Two
Professor Randall's Proposition
Cambridge, 1972

Dr. Hilary Lynch was glad of the dark. As the lights dimmed she pushed her spectacles up her nose, arranged her face into an expression of polite attention and relaxed. She sipped her gin and tonic and half-listened as Professor Randall talked about experiments, progress, blind alleys, funding, deadlines, gas. And she half-watched the images that the professor projected onto the wall above the fireplace: a little boy with half his face missing; a young woman with what appeared to be scales instead of skin; an elderly gentleman with a large hole in his chest, lined with brass. It was glorious to be so close to the professor like this, listening to his lovely, buttery voice, glancing at his shaded profile, and knowing all the while that he could hardly see her dreadful bulk. The professor's hands were especially delightful. They moved swiftly and sinuously over the projector, snapping out the used slides and discarding them, then selecting new ones and slipping them quickly into the machine so that the picture sequence was seamless. Occasionally, the professor's hands drifted upwards to push his thick hair back from his eyes, making it stand up messily on his forehead like a child's. Hilary stole another glance at him and sighed as she re-lit her pipe. She sipped her drink and thought hard about the professor's hands, blushing scarlet in the smoke and shadows.

"You all right, Hillers? You look a bit shaky, old girl. Gin not taken you badly, has it?"

"This was from Dr. Marcus Gormley, Hilary's long term colleague. An extremely thin man, his head was turned sharply towards Hilary in a way that reminded her of a small, unsavoury bird, something with hollow bones and sneaky, watchful eyes.

"After all, you're a woman of a certain age," Marcus went on. "Not sure how wise it is to be hitting the sauce this early in the afternoon, even if it is to ease you through a department meeting. Might want to slow down a bit."

Marcus sipped from his own glass and smirked at Hilary across the gloom.

"Thank you so much for your concern, Marcus," Hilary said severely, "but I'm absolutely fine—a bit chilly, is all. Cambridge in February is hardly the warmest place in the world, is it? Which is no doubt why you're insulating yourself with such a thick layer of port."

The professor's eyes flickered anxiously between the pair of them.

"Look, I know it's a bit cold. I'm sorry. But I'm nearly done, so, you know, let's not fall out. I wanted to show you my camp stuff as a way of properly introducing myself, I suppose, and also because I've an idea that it might offer a way forward for the department."

Hilary poked at the bowl of her pipe with a shaking finger.

"You can take as long as you want as far as I'm concerned, Sebastian," she said casually. "It's just Mendel and me at home this evening and I doubt he'll miss me very much, if truth be told. And I can put up with a bit of cold. Let's face it, I've got a fair bit of insulation myself. I'm all yours."

"Yes, you fire away, Seb," Marcus agreed. "You're the boss, after all. And your camp work was very highly regarded over here, as I'm sure you know. You take your time, young man. Hilary and I will do our best to behave, won't we, Hillers?"

The professor smiled shyly and ruffled his hair, causing Hilary to stir softly.

"Thanks, Marcus. Thanks, Hilary. Thanks both of you for indulging the new bloke. And I suppose you're right—my camp stuff did go down fairly well, although, ironically, by the time my research was complete, I had almost entirely lost interest in the material I was meant to be studying."

Marcus spluttered into his port.

"What on earth do you mean?" he twittered. "Your gypsy work made your reputation, man. I've no doubt it won you the post here, for one thing."

"Yes, I know, Marcus, and, believe me, I'm not ungrateful for the reception it's had. It's simply that by the time my five years were up I was far more interested in the *structure* of my work than I was in the experiments themselves. And actually, I think it's the structure of the stuff that might have some bearing on our current situation."

"I'm not entirely sure that I follow you, Sebastian," Hilary said.

"Sorry, Hillers, I don't mean to be mysterious." The professor stared into his drink and swirled it around in his glass. "Look, it's obvious to all of us that our subject is engaged in a fight for survival. My predecessor here just about kept things going, but that's pretty much all he did, isn't it? And in saying that I'm not criticising the man. I regard it as a considerable achievement, given our situation. I suppose that, ideologically, we still represent the victors to the vanquished, and that's always going to be uncomfortable. Let's face it, the calibre of our students is appalling; our funding is dreadful; and, apart from a few lucky so-and-so's like yours truly, we never get the chance to work with any flesh-and-blood subjects. The general view in the common rooms is that Anthropology and Posthumanism is dying on its Teutonic arse. I've only been back in the country for six months and that much is clear to me already."

"Just the way things are," said Marcus gloomily. "The university regards us as a bunch of Kraut sympathisers. Doesn't matter how often I remind people that I fought at Canterbury." He shrugged. "I'm afraid it's just how things are."

"Well, it's how things are *at the moment*," Hilary said, rather more earnestly than she had intended. "But it's certainly not how things have to be. I came into A and P, many bloody moons ago admittedly, because I actually believed in the subject. You know … I thought that I'd be able to *do good* in Anthropology and Posthumanism. I hope that doesn't make me sound like a hopelessly naïve old boot, but it's true." She gulped her drink. "I mean, obviously, working in A and P means making tough decisions about some people—your own camp work proves that, Seb. But still, back then I honestly thought we could be proud of what we do, despite the German link and the New European Order nonsense and what have you. To be honest, I still *do* think that… you know, I… I believe in *Sophia* and *Know Thyself* and *Humanity Refashioned* and whatnot…'

Hilary tailed off and stared at the wall. Marcus smirked, while Professor Randall studied Hilary in the semi-darkness. Eventually, he said, "I've never thought of you as naïve, Hilary, nor as an old boot, come to that. We don't talk much about things like motives, do we? It's too personal, I suppose, but perhaps we should. For the record, I also believe in the nobility of *Sophia* and *Know Thyself*. But we have to face facts: the subject *is* associated with Germany in the British mind and so we have no money, no decent students, no credibility and no opportunity for hands-on fieldwork. And I'm afraid things are going to stay that way until someone comes up with a significant proposal to reinvigorate our field. With that in mind, I'd like to show you a few more pictures, if I may. Help yourself to another drink whenever you fancy one."

The professor's sideboard was well stocked with bottles. Marcus poured himself another glass of port while the professor clicked a new rack of slides into the projector. A cluster of wooden huts viewed through wire flickered onto the wall above the fireplace.

"Right, you know already that I was lucky enough to be granted an initial group of 400 Romanian gypsies as my research base."

"Because you were good at kissing backsides in Berlin."

"Well, I was prepared to take full advantage of the German connection, yes, Marcus, and I make no apology for that. But I can assure you I drew the line at actually kissing anything German. Now in the course of my studies, the figure fluctuated a bit; there were some babies born, some adult additions, and obviously we lost a number of subjects through the work itself, but the total number never sank below 350 and never rose above 550. And there was a core group of about 200 that was unchanged throughout the time I was working. We were privileged to have 150 acre compound constructed specially for us in the forest about two miles from the main camp, where the subjects were split into three distinct settlements. They had living blocks, wash blocks, kitchens, workshops, leisure facilities, gardens and so on. It wasn't exactly luxury, I admit, but it was decent enough. I insisted on that because I needed the subjects to be reasonably happy and compliant. The Lithuanian guards used to complain that my gypsies had better accommodation than they did. Admittedly the Lithuanians are absolute buggers for grumbling, but they may have had a point. We set the compound up pretty well."

The professor continued to work the projector and a sequence of images of life inside the compound appeared on the wall. There were pictures of the subjects eating in communal dining rooms, playing football, hanging out their washing, dancing, fighting, even making love.

"To begin with," the professor went on, "the compound was guarded as securely as the main camp. There were watchtowers every 300 yards along the perimeter, regular dog patrols, tremor sensors for tunnels and so on. But we found that the security gradually became redundant, until in the end we just had seven men covering the whole site, and they used to spend most of their time watching dirty films in the guard hut. In fact, work at the compound came to be seen as a soft option, it was often used as a respite for the poor chaps who'd been on oven detail over in the main camp."

"So what are you saying?" Marcus asked. "Did the subjects just resign themselves to their fate? I saw something similar with new bugs in the military; to begin with, they'd cry blue murder every time they got so much as a slap, but eventually..."

"Actually it's rather more interesting than that. What seemed to happen was that the subject group began to lose any interest in the outside world at all. More than that, they almost seemed to lose any strong feeling of the outside world's *existence*."

"What, do you mean they just forgot about it? Seems a bit unlikely, Seb!"

"No, I didn't say they *forgot* about it. I said that they seemed to lose any *strong feeling* for it, which is rather different. Of course, they knew perfectly well at some level of their consciousness that there *was* a world beyond the wire, but they gradually lost interest in it, until it simply didn't feature in their day-to-day thinking. We helped to curb their wanderlust with some bits and pieces we put in their water and a preliminary surgical adjustment. The details are all in the notes. But, still, the change in the subjects went beyond anything we could have expected." The professor's voice purred with delight. "I was able to observe them spin a tight web of meaning around themselves so that their feeling for reality effectively petered out at the compound perimeter. *I watched them make a world, Marcus.* Can you imagine what an extraordinary privilege that was, professionally speaking? Now, admittedly, the gypsies are a fairly insular and superstitious bunch, but even so, it was remarkable to see how desperate they were to keep their spooky little world intact. Do you know, towards the end when we were getting pretty slack about security, the compound fence collapsed at one corner. Before we had a chance to get the maintenance chaps up from the camp to sort it out, the subjects repaired it themselves with bits of old furniture and chicken wire. *They actually repaired their own prison.* It really was the most extraordinary thing to watch. I only wish I could have kept the compound going after my research was formally complete to see how things developed."

"Not possible?"

"Not a chance, Hillers, sadly. I had been given leave to work with my subjects for four years and four years is precisely what I got. I tried appealing to Berlin but it made bugger all difference; every one of my gypsies went up the chimney precisely on schedule. The Germans are nothing if not efficient, but you don't need me to tell you that, of course."

The professor chuckled and clicked off the last picture. He unplugged the slide projector and the hum that it had been making died abruptly.

"Of course I was left wondering," he went on casually, "what might have happened if it had been possible to keep the compound going indefinitely."

Hilary shifted awkwardly in her seat and scratched her chin. Marcus finished off his port in a single mouthful.

"Cards on the table time, Seb," he said gruffly. "What is it you've got in mind?"

"Well, suppose we could duplicate the compound experience here in Britain," he said slowly. "Think about it; we would only need a relatively small area to begin with, which we could secure and protect just like my compound was protected. And we'd adjust the subjects in the same way my gypsies were adjusted. Then we could observe the process that I saw begin in the camp at close quarters. And we'd have a pool of compliant subjects for research, without any of the fiddly bureaucratic business about seeking their permission or honouring their European Rights or what have you." The professor's eyes darted from Marcus to Hilary and back again. "It would be like empire days all over again, except no one would have to go traipsing off to bong-bongo land in a pith helmet to get any field-work done. Our subjects would be right on our doorstep. The opportunities for study would be almost limitless. And also..."

"Oh, come off it, Seb!" Marcus interrupted. "The logistical problems, the legal problems, the security problems would be immense. Also, I don't honestly see that locking up a bunch of British people is a good way to endear us to our fellow countrymen, which is what this is supposed to be about. No, your enthusiasm's commendable and your imagination certainly bloody is, but the whole idea's completely impossible."

"It's certainly very difficult, but I don't think it's impossible. If I did, I wouldn't have suggested it. For one thing, I still have contacts in Berlin who could help us with the legal side. Providing we picked an area where the people were mostly corrupted Caucasian, say category B's or C's, I think we'd be able to swing it, constitutionally speaking. We're still part of the New European Order after all, if only just. As you say, security would be a problem, but I don't believe it's insurmountable. Actually, with your background, that might be an area you could help with, Marcus. And as for anyone objecting to our *locking people up*, as you put it, well, I don't accept your terms. The whole point of what I have in mind, if it works, is that the residents in our enclosure *won't want* to be anywhere else. We can hardly be accused of denying folk their freedom if they're all perfectly happy and don't *want* to go anywhere, can we?"

Hilary felt vaguely there was something she should say about this, but she wasn't quite sure what it was. She opened her mouth to speak, but the professor went on quickly, "And anyway, if we promote the project carefully and make it clear that this is a home-grown *British* project, designed to benefit *British* people, increasing *British* prestige abroad, then people might be a lot less bothered than you imagine. One of the oddest things about the compound was that off-duty staff from the main camp used to come up to watch my subjects in their spare time, as if we were running some sort of soap opera. We had a network of concealed cameras and microphones inside the compound that were originally meant for security purposes, but they ended up being used recreationally. People loved catching up on who was sleeping with whom; who was cheating whom; the feuds that went on between the different settlements; their business dealings, and just about everything else, really. I didn't object because the phenomenon fascinated me. By the end I spent almost as much time watching the watchers as I did observing the subjects themselves. I don't see why something similar shouldn't be possible here, *if* we decide to go ahead, that is." The professor sighed. "Look, I know that I'm new and young. If you think the idea's bonkers, then for goodness' sake tell me and I'll forget the whole thing. But listen, this is the definition of Anthropology and Posthumanism from our founding charter at the university in 1886. This is what our forebears thought our subject was about, and it's really rather salutary." The professor pulled a notebook from his inside pocket, opened it and cleared his throat.

"Taking as its twin mottos Sophia—wisdom—and the Delphic Oracle's command to Know Thyself, the discipline of Anthropology and Posthumanism finds its object of study in humanity itself. Its practitioners seek to understand the human animal in its social, psychological, biological and chemical aspects in order to refashion it in a nobler form, free from the tyrannies of ignorance, superstition and nature itself. We seek to recreate humanity as its own artifice and possession."

The professor snapped the book shut and tucked it back in his pocket. He gripped Hilary's arm. "You see, we're bloody important in A and P; at least, we're supposed to be. We're about *achieving* things, *changing* things. We're not supposed to be a joke." He grinned. "But you don't need me to tell you that, either. Look, the lecture's over. I ... well, I just think that if we pursue my idea we might make some real progress at last. That's all I wanted to say."

Hilary gasped. Desire rippled through her like pain from the professor's touch. And there was another emotion as well—something powerful and startling that her mind couldn't quite catch hold of. She cast around desperately for something to say.

"Yes, Seb," she began, "I...look, what you say sounds reasonable enough in th...theory. Well... I mean, it's more than reasonable; potentially, I suppose, it's brilliant. But this is Great Britain in the 1970s we're talking about. People here aren't like Romanian gypsies; they're *connected*. They're not primitive and superstitious; they're *modern*. You can't really hope to cut a group of them off from the rest of us."

The professor released Hilary's arm and stood up. He strolled to the room's north-facing window and peered into the drizzle, the dusk silhouetting him like a gloomy halo.

"On a good day you can just about make out the tower of Ely Cathedral from here," he said softly, "the ship of the fens. What an extraordinary feat of engineering that is when you think about it. It's a perfect square, you know, built without any external support and visible from 40 miles away—and constructed with nothing but ropes and pulleys."

"Yes, Seb," said Hilary. "I'm sure that's true, but..."

"Extraordinary imprint on the landscape. Extraordinary. And on history, of course. Oh, I don't doubt that an awful lot of people will have died in the construction—stonemasons and labourers and so on, you know, *ordinary* people. But then, they had their priests to bless and bury them, didn't they? And they died in an extremely good cause. It's a wonderful achievement. Really it is... I don't think anyone would dispute that."

"Yes, but Sebastian..."

The professor span round.

"I grew up in the fens," he said. "Neither of you knew that, did you? Well, I did. And it's one place that isn't very *connected*, Hilary. You take my word for it; it's not damn well connected at all—or *modern*. If you'd spent 18 years living in the middle of a potato field you'd know what I mean. Some of those bloody farmers would make my gypsies look sophisticated and cosmopolitan, really they would."

For a moment nobody spoke. Then Hilary said in a quiet voice, "Ok, Sebastian. Ok. Why don't you tell us exactly how this might work?"

Chapter Three
Hilary's Dreams

The meeting had gone on for a very long time. The professor had treated his colleagues to a simple tea of cold sausage, bread and cheese, washed down with more port and gin. As the dark afternoon had drifted into evening and then into night, he had directed them through a pile of large-scale maps and aerial photographs and a thick sheaf of legal documents. Marcus and Hilary had become excited as the feasibility of the professor's scheme dawned on them, and then grown somber as the alcohol finally turned them serious and the enormity of what they were planning sank in. By the time the meeting broke up in the early hours, they had reached agreement that the professor would fly to Berlin as soon as possible "to kiss bits of the appropriate Germans," as he put it, and to see precisely how much support the plan would have. After that, they would meet again to review the situation. By then, Hilary's eyes were red and itchy with smoke, and she was unsteady on her feet as she struggled down the uneven staircase away from the professor's rooms.

Despite the late hour and the light rain, a few students were still meandering around the college's main court. Hilary was cheered to see how little attention they paid to the European Martyrs' Memorial that was bathed in bright light at the east end of the court, next to the porter's lodge. By rights all college members and visitors should have paused at the memorial in silence whenever they entered or left the college, but nowadays hardly anybody seemed to bother. Hilary was glad to see that the Union Flags at the monument's four corners were also being ignored; they hung limp and unimpressive in the floodlit drizzle so that the thick, black swastikas at their centres were almost completely invisible. As Hilary watched, an attractive young couple began chasing each other around one of the flag poles, laughing and shouting as they went. Eventually the woman grabbed the man and shoved him against the pole, kissing him in between fits of giggles. That was what youth was supposed to be about, Hilary thought approvingly, being beautiful and in love and not giving a hoot about stupid things like flags or the European Martyrs—much, much better than in her own day. She moved on unsteadily across the court, her head bent against the rain.

When she reached her rooms Hilary ran a comb quickly through her grey bobbed hair and changed into her nightie. She lay on her bed with the lights off, smoking her last pipe of the day and scratching Mendel softly between the ears.

"The professor and I are going to be seeing rather a lot of each other, my sweetness," she whispered. "Jolly big project in the offing, you see. We're going to save the department and the nation, and the world, too, come to that. We're going to refashion humanity together in accordance with the founding principles of Anthropology and Posthumanism. Got to get it right, obviously." She giggled contentedly. "He's got such wonderful hands, Mendel, so quick and strong—rather like your hands would be if you had hands: quick and strong, like a surgeon or a knight."

Still giggling, Hilary knocked out her pipe and moved Mendel gently to one side of the bed so that she could slide under the covers. For a while she drifted contentedly around the edges of sleep, imagining a wonderful future in which she and Professor Randall toured the world together, giving lectures in the ways of Sophia and generally saving the nations from their superstitions and folly (without exactly willing it, she imagined that Marcus would conveniently die, leaving her and the professor to spread the gospel of Anthropology and Posthumanism alone). Finally she slept, but even then Professor Randall haunted her dreams. In a jumble, she recalled the tone of his voice as he spoke about his research in the camps; the earnest way he rubbed his eyes as he pored over the maps and photographs; the delightful golden colour of his skin in the lamplight; and, best of all, the electrifying desire that had run through her as he had gripped her arm. Desire and... *something else.* There had been another feeling when the professor held her, something unexpected and disturbing—not love, not admiration, not joy. Something quite, quite different; but what? Hilary's sleep grew fretful; her breathing quickened, and her body grew hot and sticky. And then, at the outer edge of her dreaming, where her mind grew light and free, she briefly recalled and understood what the other feeling was: it was fear—cold, dreadful fear. She twitched and cried out at the realisation, then rolled over onto Mendel, sending him squirming to the floor. She did not wake up, however.

Chapter Four
Birthday Boy
London, 2065

The morning sun woke Sam Moorcroft up early on his 16th birthday. He had the sensation of drifting upwards towards a bright light through a swirl of dark, last-minute dreams, and then his eyes opened, and he found himself lying in his bed feeling hot and muddled. He realised after a moment that he also felt happy without quite knowing why, and then he remembered what day it was, and a satisfied smile crept across his face. He pulled himself up in his bed and yanked the enhancement clip from his temples. For a moment, Sam's thoughts became disjointed and fuzzy as the charge faded from his brain, and then they clicked sharply into focus and he lay back with his hands behind his head thinking about all the things he could do today that he couldn't do yesterday.

At 16, Sam could join the army and smoke; he could ride a motor scooter and get a job; travel abroad on his own; have sex; visit Ely; buy fireworks; have a soul-augmentation with his parents' consent; and own a tortoise or a terrapin or something similar. Sam reflected on his new possibilities for a moment: obviously his mum would kill him if he even looked at a cigarette or a motor scooter, and to be honest he didn't fancy fireworks, tortoises, soul-augmentations or getting a job, and he was too weedy for the army. But that still left sex, foreign travel and Ely as real options, which was quite a lot to be going on with. Sam's smile broadened as he remembered that he was going to take advantage of at least one of his new rights that very morning. He wriggled, flung back his duvet and jumped out of bed. Then he stood and stared at his 16-year-old self in the long bedroom mirror.

The reflection that stared back at Sam had rather a long nose, a mop of brown hair that flopped meaninglessly over his forehead and a sprinkling of spots on both his cheeks. His shoulders were round and feeble-looking and the rest of him was skinny apart from his stomach, which bulged over the top of his pants like a pale balloon. He frowned at his reflection and did his best to straighten himself up, sucking in his stomach and twisting and turning to get the best possible view of himself. As he did so, his thoughts drifted of their own accord to the other part of his birthday plans, the part that he hoped would happen that evening. A deep blush spread across his face so that his spots temporarily vanished. He stepped closer to the mirror, breathing deeply right up against the glass so that it misted and blurred, imagining that *she* was opposite him with her lips almost touching his, instead of his own reflection. After a minute his mum's voice drifted upstairs, shouting something to his dad about supervising the drones with the spinach, and Sam felt suddenly ridiculous. He blew a raspberry at his reflection, wiped the glass with his fist and quickly pulled on his jeans and a shirt. He had a very brief wash and went downstairs for his breakfast.

Sam's brother Roger and his girlfriend Jen were already in the kitchen when Sam arrived. They were both students at Cambridge where Roger was studying History and Jen was studying Anthropology and Posthumanism. At the moment it was the holiday, however, and they were staying at the Moorcrofts' and working in the family restaurant. This wasn't a good arrangement as far as Sam was concerned; when they weren't at work the pair of them spent most of their time arguing about politics in loud, self-assured voices or kissing embarrassingly in the sitting room. This morning they had both been out for their early run and were now tucking into cereal and fresh coffee with the daily papers spread out like a lake on the kitchen table. They were still wearing their Randall College Rowing Club tops and looked flushed and athletic. The cardiovascular chips that they both had implanted in their wrists were beeping impatiently. Sam noticed Roger's hand resting on Jen's naked thigh, occasionally squeezing the smooth flesh gently and deliberately, just like he had seen his mum squeeze aubergines at the market.

"Hooray for the birthday boy," Roger called out cheerfully as Sam walked in. "I hope your willy grew an inch in the night, Sam. That's what's supposed to happen when you're 16."

Sam frowned without replying and stuffed some bread in the toaster. Jen slapped Roger affectionately on the arm.

"Don't be bloody stupid, Roger. Happy birthday, Sam, many happy returns and all that." She paused. "Well, aren't you going to get Sam his present?"

"Sam doesn't mind waiting, do you, Sam? I'm training him to understand that all things come to those who wait."

Jen hit Roger again and he groaned and stretched lazily before staggering to his feet and trudging upstairs. When he had gone, Jen said, "I know he can be a bit of a prat, but he really is fond of you, you know. He always speaks very fondly of you when you're not actually here. And I know he's pleased to be taking you to Ely."

"Yeah, yeah, he's all right," Sam mumbled.

"And this Rachel who's coming with us? Is she actually your girlfriend? I mean, she obviously likes you. She's round here quite a lot, isn't she? What's actually going on between the pair of you? I've been dying to ask all summer."

Sam felt himself blush again. He pulled his toast out of the toaster, buttered it quickly and bit it, chewing it over and over until it became a slimy paste in his mouth.

"God no, she's not my girlfriend," he said eventually. "She's just my friend, really, probably my best friend. But… but, I mean, she's friends with all of us. My mum's known her mum for ages. They were pregnant at the same time, so I've known her since we were babies. But she's not… she's not my girlfriend."

Sam trailed off as Roger strode back into the kitchen. He was smirking.

"Sam's sort of sexless, aren't you, Sam?" he said as he tossed a neatly wrapped parcel down next to Sam's plate. "Poor, lovely Rachel hangs around with her tongue practically hanging out but his loins just don't seem to stir—remarkable for a chap of his age and vigour."

"Shut up, Roger," Sam said furiously.

"Yes, you can be bloody boring sometimes," said Jen, sounding properly cross this time. She picked up the parcel and handed it to Sam. "Here you are," she said. "I hope you like it and I hope we all have a great day together up at Ely. We should do if your brother can restrain himself from being an idiot for a few hours."

Sam crammed the rest of his toast into his mouth, and then wiped his fingers on a tea towel and unwrapped his present. It was a book—not a digipad or a pamphlet, but a proper old book, the sort with a cover made of woven cloth and board, and with the words printed on yellowing, slightly uneven pages. Sam had to squint to read the tiny gold writing on the spine: *Soul Freedom – Dr. Hilary Lynch.*

"It's a joint thing from Roger and me," Jen said. "I know it probably seems really small, but it's not in print anymore, so it was quite tricky to track down. It's not listed or anything, of course, but it's not exactly *approved of*, either. I only got it through someone at college."

"Yeah, well, thanks. It's… it's great."

"I don't know if you'd heard of Hilary Lynch; not many people outside the Project have nowadays. She's got, well, *issues* about some aspects of the Project and sophiocracy as you'll see, but she's excellent about the very beginnings of the enclosure and about Randall himself. The book's not actually finished because she keeled over with a heart attack and died before she got it done. It's still a remarkable read, though. Well, anyway, when Roger said you were thinking about going up to Ely for your birthday it seemed sensible to get you something to do with the Project—but not the tourist crap you can buy anywhere, something intelligent."

"I did tell Jen that it might be a mistake to get you something intelligent, Sammy," said Roger through a mouthful of cereal. "But she insisted. Women can be stubborn creatures, as you may or may not find out for yourself one day."

Jen glared at Roger, but before she could say anything Mrs. Moorcroft strode into the kitchen with Mr. Moorcroft bobbing along in her wake, and as always when Sam's mum entered the room the conversation immediately died out of respect.

Sam's parents could not have been more different. Angela Moorcroft was a large woman whose considerable bulk was contained today as always in a spotless white chef's jacket. She wore wire spectacles, and her hair was pulled back viciously from her face in a tight bun. She was carrying a leek as if it were a cosh. Arthur Moorcroft, on the other hand, was slight and balding. His skin had a greyish tinge, and he always had an anxious and disappointed expression on his face, as if he were expecting the worst and seeing it happen at the same time. He smelt complicated: of half-cooked food, and aftershave, and pipe tobacco.

"Happy Birthday, Sammy," said Mrs. Moorcroft as she dropped a kiss on his head and wiped some butter off his cheek in one graceful movement. "What's that you've got?"

"It's just my present from Roger and Jen." Sam passed the book to his mum who poked her glasses down her nose and peered at the spine. After a moment she flipped it open.

"Oh, it's to do with Ely, I see." Mrs. Moorcroft put the book back on the table and wiped her hands slowly and deliberately on her chef's towel. "Probably better if you don't leave that sort of thing lying around in the kitchen, Sam. It's bound to have germs on it, a dusty old book like that."

Jen coughed over her cereal and turned pink. When she had recovered, she said smoothly, "And as I was saying, Sam, it's quite a rare text, but if you enjoy it, I can get plenty more material about Ely through contacts at college, even some of the older, out-of-print stuff. Just let me know if you're after anything in particular and I'll ask around. Now what time did you say we'd be at Rachel's?"

"About half nine."

Jen glanced at her watch.

"Well, in that case, Roger and I had better get moving. Come on, alpha boy, let's go and get changed."

Roger groaned and stretched again, glancing at his slowing CV chip as he did so, before following Jen out of the room. Mrs. Moorcroft stared at their retreating backs over the top of her spectacles.

"She's a cool one, isn't she? Perhaps a bit too cool for her own good."

Mr. Moorcroft smiled mildly and picked up the copy of *Soul Freedom*. He opened it and his eyebrows twitched.

"She's g…good in the restaurant, though, and she seems f…fond enough of Roger. Oh yes, h…happy birthday, Sam," he added, almost as an afterthought.

"Well, we'll see about her and Roger, won't we; it's early days." Mrs. Moorcroft smoothed the non-existent creases in her top. "Now then, Sammy, go upstairs and get your coat. I'm not having you catching a cold just when you're old enough to start doing a bit of proper work."

Sam groaned.

"But Mum, it's August."

"I don't care what month it is. The wind comes whistling across fens straight from Siberia. If you're going to waste the day gawping up at Ely you can at least make sure you're warm."

"But it's quite a long way from Siberia to Ely, Mum; surely the wind warms up a bit over Poland and Germany. Holland's pretty warm. Anyway, Jen says that almost everything's underground at the Project nowadays. It's all done by holograph, so it's out of the wind."

Sam glanced at his dad for support, but Mr. Moorcroft was reading *Soul Freedom* intently and seemed oblivious to the discussion.

"There's no use looking at your father, Sam; he agrees with me, don't you, Arthur? DON'T YOU, ARTHUR?"

Mr. Moorcroft glanced up and nodded vaguely. He shut the book and handed it to Sam.

"You see, your father agrees with me. Now go and get your coat."

Sam trailed back upstairs and into his bedroom. He pulled his duffle coat out from the wardrobe and then sat on his bed and opened the copy of *Soul Freedom* at the first page. The little book was satisfyingly heavy to handle and gave off a wise, dusty smell. Sam lifted it to his nose and breathed deeply. Then, without really planning to, he began to read.

By my reckoning only God and Sebastian Randall have ever made a world and neither of them was particularly concerned to describe the process—at least, not accurately in God's case and not publicly in Sebastian's. As I edge closer and closer to oblivion, however, it seems increasingly important that the story of the Ely Project and the sophiocratic state is passed on as truthfully as possible to the next generations, so that whoever comes after us may consider Sebastian and his great achievement in their proper light. Given that no one else from the very early days of the Project seems to be bothered about providing a true record of events, I thought I may as well have a go myself. Goodness only knows if I'm up to the task; I am well past my intellectual prime (such as it was) and I haven't written anything more complex than an elementary security briefing or a shopping list for years. Still, I feel an obligation to do the best I can. If some of the factual details are shaky it's because the gin and the passing years have finally poisoned my mind, caveat lector.

Obviously, I cannot describe the actual genesis of the Project in the mind of our illustrious founder and national guardian. I know that he was inspired by his work in the camps and I believe that he was driven by a combination of his own ambition and his commitment to the ideals of Anthropology and Posthumanism. More than that I cannot say. I intend simply to tell the story of the Ely Project from the first moment of my involvement with it until my final and definitive resignation, which at the time of writing is yet to come.

I first encountered the Ely Project on Friday 14 February, 1978, when I was working as senior lecturer in Anthropology and Posthumanism at Cambridge University. It was one of those grim, late winter days Cambridge seems to specialise in, when all the zip and fun of the Winterval festival is long gone and you are left with a seemingly endless stretch of cold and darkness, without any obvious sign that Spring is on its way. The sky is constantly grey, one's hands seem to be permanently chapped and everyone's noses drip like leaky taps. For those of us lucky enough to work with him, however, the bleakness of the season was more than offset by the fiery brilliance of our head of department, Professor Sebastian Randall. Seb had only been in post for six months that February, but he already had a reputation as a hugely gifted young man in a hurry. The events of that afternoon were to show just how richly deserved that reputation was. They would also change the history of the world and with it the course of my own life.

My colleague, Dr. Marcus Gormley, and I were invited to Sebastian's rooms in what was then Jesus College for our six-monthly department meeting. This was Sebastian's first six-monthly since he took charge of the ship and I think he felt that

*it was high time to take our feeble little department in hand.
It's difficult to credit today when ...*

There was a soft knock on the door. Sam looked up, startled, and then, without quite knowing why, flipped the book shut and stuffed it under his pillow before calling out for whomever it was to come in. Mr. Moorcroft slipped into the room and shut the door behind him. He stood for a moment without speaking, looking awkward.

"Ah S...Sam. I, er, just w...wanted a quick word," he stuttered eventually. He didn't look at Sam as he spoke, seeming to be deeply interested in something just above and beyond Sam's left shoulder. "I, er, w...well, I wanted you to know how sorry I was that I couldn't c...come with you today. Obviously, it's your b...birthday and it would have been nice to go to Ely with you, but it can't be helped, I'm afraid. It's just one of th...those things."

"That's all right, Dad, I know you've got the restaurant and stuff."

"Oh y...yes, the restaurant. Yes. There is that, of course. It's just I would have liked to c...come with you if I could."

Sam shrugged.

"You and Mum have paid for it all, so thanks for that anyway." He wondered what to say next. His dad showed no sign of leaving; he just stood there with his hands flapping at his sides like dying fish. After what felt like hours a car horn honked in the street, making them both jump. Much relieved, Sam grabbed his coat and stood up.

"That'll be Roger and Jen," he said. "I'd better get going if we're not going to be late for Rachel."

As Sam was reaching for the doorknob Mr. Moorcroft suddenly grabbed his wrist. Sam winced at the strength of the grip. His dad's hand was very firm and very cold. Mr. Moorcroft chewed his lip anxiously; he still wouldn't look at Sam.

"I hope you have a gr...great day, Sam," he said softly. "I'm pleased you want to go to Ely, actually. It's a g...good present. I'm glad you want to see the Project. But whatever you do when you get there, don't forget that they are *human b...beings* inside the enclosure, will you? You really mustn't forget that, with all the play-acting and silliness and what have you. Remember that they're *human b...beings*. I mean it."

"Of course I won't forget it, Dad," Sam said lightly. "I know they're human beings, that's obvious isn't it? I mean, what else could they be?"

Mr. Moorcroft nodded slowly and relaxed his grip.

"Good. Well, you get off th...then and have a great day. Give my love to Rachel." Suddenly Mr. Moorcroft smiled crookedly. "And don't forget to put your c..coat on if that Siberian wind begins to bite."

"Yeah, ok, Dad," Sam said and grinned. He dashed out of the room and ran downstairs, rubbing his wrist as he went.

Chapter Five
Welcome to the Ely Project

"You are absolutely the hardest person I know, Sam, to buy presents for. And that includes my great, great granny, and she's 106, twice augmented, and blind and deaf. Honestly, I mean it, you're impossible. You just don't *do* anything."

Sam grinned and ripped open the card that Rachel had given him. It was a digi-download token for £80 with a painting of a river on the front. Rachel shrugged helplessly.

"It took me half an hour just to pick a card and even then I don't think I chose a particularly good one. Can you try and make it your mission this year to get *interested* in something, just to make present-buying easier? Anyway, what else did you get?"

"I got a rare book about Ely from Jen and Roger and today is my present off Mum and Dad. Apart from that I just got download tokens."

Rachel grinned.

"You see, you're useless. Anyway, happy birthday, come here." She leant across the back seat of the car and kissed Sam gently on the cheek. Sam smiled shyly and turned red.

"Sam's not really interested in specific *things* like hobbies, Rachel," said Roger from the driver's seat. "He prefers to contemplate *everything*, don't you, Sam? It's kind of a mystical thing; it's what makes him such stimulating company and such a profound source of wisdom. A mundane hobby would be rather beneath him."

Roger turned round and winked at Rachel. As he did so the traction pad fitted to his temple throbbed red and the car sped forwards. Rachel giggled and Sam did his best to ignore his brother. He concentrated on trying to nurture the warm feeling where Rachel's lips had touched his cheek. Gradually the sensation faded. Sam touched the spot softly and peered out the window.

They had been travelling for over 40 minutes and had long since left London behind. As they headed northeast the land had gradually emptied of human habitation and had become flatter and flatter until the road seemed to drift along in a vast, green emptiness, echoed above by the sky's unbroken blue. Only the monorail interrupted the monotony of the view; it snaked high above the road, criss-crossing it lazily every few miles. From time to time Sam glimpsed silver monotrains whistling along the tracks, little more than shimmers of speeding light in the high morning sun. The landscape made him feel lonely even though he was sitting in a car with three other people.

"How much further?" he asked abruptly. Jen swung round from the passenger seat.

"We're practically there. Another ten minutes at the most. The tower you can just about see in the distance is the Sophiocratic Temple at Ely; that's the old cathedral of the Nazarene cult, of course. It's land-locked by the Project now, if that's the right word. Loads of important Project people live in the old city, but you can only reach it underground. And there are actually Project installations just over there to our right."

Sam swung round and looked the way Jen was pointing.

"I can't see anything."

"Well, you wouldn't. Old Randall loved his fenland views so he had everything to do with the Project landscaped to make it pretty much invisible. You're just a few miles from the largest social experiment in history, arguably the most significant human development since our thumbs turned round, and there's nothing whatsoever to show for it. It's extraordinary, isn't it? It's called the lie of the land. You get the same thing on the other side, within the enclosure. But that's for security reasons, of course. Not even the temple tower is visible to the subjects."

Just then Roger's traction pad glowed again as he directed the car off the motorway. They sped down a slip road that curved sharply to the right, and then passed through a short tunnel. When they came out the other side they were at the top of a steep descent into a parking bay. Sam gasped; there were thousands of cars in the bay as well as hundreds of coaches.

"I see what you mean," he said. "Randall really was a clever bloke, wasn't he? You know, to have made all this invisible."

"I don't think there's much dispute that Sebastian Randall was a clever man, Sam," said Roger dryly.

"Yup, and there are seven other bays the size of this one," Jen said. "And the monorail station, of course."

"God, eight bays, all like this. Eight bays! I didn't realise it was going to be this big. That's loads of people. Thousands and thousands of people."

"Remember what I was saying, Rachel?" Roger said as they sped down the slope. "There's a real wisdom about my brother, isn't there? Can't you just sense it?"

At the bottom of the slip road a path of blue lights illuminated automatically to guide them to a parking space. When they had parked they took what they wanted from the car: a pile of downloads for Jen, a notebook for Rachel, a couple of bottles of beer for Roger and nothing for Sam (who decided to leave his coat in the boot), and locked it. Then they headed for the north end of the bay where a crowd of several hundred milled around a row of 20 gleaming brass and chrome lift terminals. Every minute or so the doors of one of the lifts would slide open and the crowd would jostle forward and pack it to bursting point. Eventually a few unlucky people were shoved away from the entrance and the doors would slide shut.

Sam could hear lots of shouting, some of it very rude, and even snatches of song coming from the crowd as they approached. Many of the people were dressed in enclosure-style clothes: rough, dull-coloured breaches and jerkins for the men and embroidered blouses and long skirts for the women. A number of them were carrying bundles: picnic hampers, bulky brief cases, holograph recorders and even a few crude musical instruments. Some people also carried brightly coloured banners proclaiming them to be members of local Ely groups which were twinned with settlements inside the enclosure.

"Something you might want to bear in mind as first-timers," Jen said softly to Sam and Rachel as they drew near to the lifts, "is that an awful lot of the people who come to Ely regularly are absolute morons. I'm not being disloyal saying that; I love the Project, I really do. I've been coming myself since I was 16 and Mum and Dad used to show me holographs of Ely even before that. I want to make a career here, for goodness' sake.

But it's a fact that a lot of visitors who come here recreationally are the kind of people you'd cross the street to avoid." She sighed. "They're all rather, well, they're just…'

"They're common," Roger said bluntly.

"Well, yes, I know it sounds awful to say it, but yes, they are. Most of them either belong to those dreadful fen-watching groups and just come for the pretending and the fancy dress and the gossip, or else they're sad old men with dirty raincoats and a pile of disgusting holograph discs about fenland farm maids or whatever. Not everyone's like that, of course, but I'm afraid a lot are." She frowned and shook her head sharply. "It's very sad, because none of that's really what the Project's about at all."

Jen stopped talking as they reached the edge of the crowd. They waited until the lift nearest to them arrived, and then she and Roger shoved their way quickly towards the open doors, with Sam and Rachel trotting behind them. Without quite knowing how he had got there, Sam found himself sandwiched between a woman with a very red face, who was wearing a cream smock that showed off most of her breasts, and a fat man who smelt strongly of alcohol and was carrying some sort of guitar. There was the usual scuffle at the front of the lift as the last hopefuls were pushed aside, and then the doors hissed shut. With lots of shouting and cheering from the passengers, the lift began its descent. As it did so advertisements for various Fruit of Sophia were played through the lift's loudspeakers:

Drink and be merry and then stay merry with the super-soaker synthetic liver!

Standard Six drones—because you're worth more than housework!

The Soul Saviour Seven new generation enhancement clip—with settings for joy, peace, innocence, humor and concentration, self-mastery has never been easier. What's your excuse?

The passengers continued to chat and laugh as the lift descended, apparently oblivious to the advertisements. Behind Sam, the fat man reached out slowly and pinched the red-faced woman's bottom. She squealed and leapt in the air, landing heavily on Sam's foot.

"You're a roight dirty rouge, you are, Master William," she roared in what was obviously a fake accent (and Sam could see she was trying not to giggle at the same time). "I'll set my Jack on you if you keep pesterin' me. I'll 'ave you before the magistrate at Cromer. You see if I don't."

The man just grinned at her and reached into his inside pocket, retrieving a silver hip flask.

"You ain't never complained before, me sweetheart," he said slurrily, "leastways not when your Jack's off at market." He took a long swig from the flask and then passed the drink across to the woman, winking at Sam as he did so. The woman smirked at him and took a large mouthful herself before passing it back. Across the lift, Jen grimaced at Sam and rolled her eyes.

Very soon the lift came to a halt and the doors slid open. White light streamed inside making the chrome gleam like sunshine, and with it came a roar of thousands of excited voices. Some subtle change in the lift's pressure or perhaps the slightly echoing sound of the crowd gave Sam the impression of being in a very large enclosed space, very far underground. A man and a woman in bright blue uniforms with white braid across their chests and firearms on their hips were waiting just beyond the doors; they swaggered forward and the man raised his arm for everyone's attention.

"Ladies and gentlemen, welcome to the Ely Project," he said gruffly. "You will be processed as quickly as possible. Before that, however, I am required to remind you that once you have passed through the Eden Gate you are on sovereign Project territory, governed by bylaws 1 to 863 of the Guardian's Office. I am specifically required to remind you that any violation or attempted violation of the Project boundary is a felony carrying the maximum penalty of chemical curtailment under bylaw 36. If you attempt to compromise the boundary you will be restrained using lethal or non-lethal weapons." The man patted his holster casually. "Now are there any questions?"

No one in the lift spoke.

"Good, 'cos it's too early for shooting people. Now out you come and have a nice day."

Sam shuffled out of the lift with the rest into a large enclosed area with whitewashed walls. Ahead of them there was a high steel barrier inset with turnstiles, metal detectors and payment booths, above which the words *Know Thyself* were displayed in enormous, flickering pink neon script. A holograph of Sebastian Randall's head floated above everything, staring down at the new arrivals. The whole area was staffed with dozens more of the people in blue uniforms. Sam shoved himself forward to catch up with Jen and Roger.

"Who are they?" he asked, nodding at the guards.

"Bullying idiots," Roger replied softly, "otherwise known as the Boundary Security Corps. They're designed to put the fear of God into the proles. But for goodness' sake, Sam, do take them seriously. They have a reputation for being rather trigger happy if people bugger about near the boundary. I'd hate to deliver a 16-year-old corpse to Mum and Dad this evening. I think it would take the shine off your birthday a bit, don't you?"

"They *do* have a job to do, Roger," said Jen stiffly. "The BSC are responsible for the entire boundary, Sam. They make sure no one goes in who shouldn't and no one from the other side comes out. Once we're through the Eden Gate," Jen nodded at the steel barrier ahead of them, "they're responsible for every aspect of law enforcement. The civil police and the army have no jurisdiction inside the Project."

Sam studied the two Boundary Security Corps officers discreetly as they jostled past. The woman was standing with her hands on her hips staring hard at the visitors' faces, while the man casually tossed a black truncheon in the air and caught it again without looking at it.

"Are they the ones who actually, you know, *cross over*?" Sam asked quietly.

"God no," Jen answered. "You're thinking of the ISS, the Interland Security Service. They're completely different. They're much more sophisticated, for starters, and they're completely independent of the BSC and just about everyone else. They're rather mysterious, to be honest; since 1989 they've more or less done their own thing. Actually, if you're interested in the ISS, there's quite a bit about them in *Soul*

Freedom; Hilary Lynch was heavily involved from the beginning. But you won't ever see them, Sam. They only work inside the enclosure; they're not in the least interested in the likes of you and me."

Chapter Six
Sir Douglas Latch

The lift had carried Sam and the other visitors deep underground, but the network of installations that made up the Ely Project went much, much deeper and spread out erratically, like ants' workings, under the entire area of the enclosure. At the deepest level of the Project's administration, miles from the lift and the Eden gate, there was a low corridor of unpainted concrete, reinforced with rusty iron hoops. The corridor smelt damp and earthy and echoed with distant whispers and footsteps. It was lit by bare, bright lights encased in steel cages that made your shadow slouch and jump at you from front and back as you walked along.

At the end of the corridor there was a battered wooden door leading to a small office in which an elderly man was slumped in his chair, snoring loudly. He was extremely thin and rather short with a dead straight, slightly cruel mouth and a mane of wild white hair. He was dressed in black trousers and a grubby black open-necked shirt adorned with epaulets bearing four silver stars. The buckle on his scuffed belt was also silver; it took the form of two faces looking in opposite directions, surrounded by a holly wreath. The man was seated at a large rosewood desk on which there was a computer terminal, a jumble of papers, a pipe resting in an ashtray, a red leather-bound book and a chipped mug that was half full of very expensive port. The only other furniture in the room were three battered armchairs arranged around a fireplace, where a pair of logs smouldered lazily. The room's walls were lined from top to bottom with shelves of little red books identical to the one on the desk, each of which had a date on its spine. Only a large portrait behind the desk was permitted to interrupt the arrangement of the shelving. It was of a stoutish, elderly woman with thick glasses who wore her iron-grey hair in a severe bob. She cradled a cat tenderly in her arms and gazed out into the room with a weary expression on her paunchy face.

The man, whose name was Sir Douglas Latch, had been asleep for quite some time, long enough for his computer to doze off with him. Its screen saver had activated and now the screen was filled with the same two-faced figure that graced his belt buckle, across which the words *In duobis mundis ambulare* floated gently from right to left in gothic script. They were followed by the English translation: *To walk in two worlds.* When he was awake and sober Sir Douglas sometimes worried about the presence of the translation, regarding it as a sign that standards were slipping. He felt certain that the woman in the portrait wouldn't have tolerated anything as crass as a translation of the Latin. ("Postulants should *know* Latin, and if they don't know it they should bloody well *learn* it, and if they're too thick or too lazy to learn it, well then the stupid so and so's shouldn't be bloody postulants!" etc. etc.)

A loud knocking caused the sleeping man to stir. He reached out clumsily across the desk and knocked over the mug. Port slopped across the papers.

"Wotsit, eh, oh bugger, bugger, bugger!" he exclaimed as he tried frantically to mop up the spill with the corner of his shirt. The knocking came again.

"All right, all right, come in, blast you, but I hope for both our sakes you've got something interesting to tell me, whoever you are. If all you have is some whinging bloody missive from the Guardian's Office or a boring balance sheet or something similar, you might want to bugger off now before I actually discover who you are."

The door opened and a young man stepped briskly into the room. He was dressed in the same black uniform as the older man, except that his was considerably cleaner and his epaulets only had one star on them. Also, his belt buckle was brass instead of silver.

"Tony, dear boy, how lovely to see you," the older man purred in a suddenly friendly voice. He gave up on the spilt port and slumped back in his chair, reaching for his pipe as he did so. "I know I can rely on you to provide me with a bit of fun, old chap...'

"I certainly hope so, Sir Douglas."

"Yes, well, so do I, because if you've brought me something dreary, I swear I'll have your liver for a pin-cushion and your kidneys for paperweights. Please don't imagine I'm joking. I was on the other side until some stupid time this morning, drinking rather more than is good for me, to be honest. So I'm afraid, dear boy, that you don't find me in the best of moods. Now what is it you wanted to tell me?"

The younger man took a deep breath.

"Arthur Moorcroft's sons have just been processed at the Eden Gate."

Sir Douglas's head jerked upwards. He stared hard at Tony while he poked around in the bowl of his pipe with a biro lid. Eventually he said, "Have they indeed? Young Arthur's sons, well, goodness me. To think he has children old enough to visit the Project. Are they alone?"

"No, Sir Douglas, they're with a couple of females of approximately their own ages. I've got the bumph here."

The young man handed Sir Douglas four slim buff files. The older man opened them and flicked through them, his lips moving quickly as he read.

"Now that's interesting. It's young Samuel Moorcroft's 16th birthday today. What are we to make of that, do you suppose?"

"Um, I hadn't actually noticed that, Sir Douglas."

"Of course you hadn't, Tony. That's why I have you as my adjutant, to miss crucial details and make me look good. But what does it mean that Samuel should choose to visit the Project on the first day that he is legally entitled to? The very first day." Sir Douglas frowned and sucked on his pipe.

"He certainly seems keen to get here, sir."

"Very astute, Tony."

The older man leaned forward and tapped quickly on his computer keyboard. A series of motion pictures of Sam, Roger, Jen and Rachel leaving the lift appeared on the screen. Both men studied them in silence for a moment.

"Samuel has rather a nice, sensitive face, wouldn't you say?" the old man murmured. "You can see the father in him, I think—something about the eyes. Less of his mother in evidence, thank goodness. Do you suppose that this, what's her name … Rachel Fairweather, is his girlfriend?"

"I don't know, Sir Douglas, although I believe the older one, Roger, is definitely in a relationship with Jennifer Catesby. They're up at Randall together."

"Yes, I read that, too, Tony," the old man said dryly. He tapped the keyboard again and Roger and Jen loomed large on the screen. They were being searched and retina-checked at the Eden Gate.

"Actually, I know of Miss Catesby's family. They're four generations of Ely loyalists; I believe an ancestor did something frightfully brave in 1989. And now Rachel is reading A and P at Randall; she's just about as committed a sophiocrat as one could wish to meet—not that I *do* wish to meet committed sophiocrats, of course. I see from the file that she's already applied to work at the Project after graduation and I've no doubt, given her background, that her application will be successful. Mark my words, in three or four years time Miss Jennifer Catesby will be striding down some dreary corridor in the administrative block with a deeply significant file to do with budgeting clutched in her mitt and a smug grin on her face. You see if she isn't. And she'll be thinking piously about *Know Thyself* and the glorious possibility of *Humanity Refashioned* as she trots along, silly girl."

The old man made quotation marks with his stubby fingers as he mentioned *Know Thyself* and *Humanity Refashioned*. The younger man shifted uncomfortably.

"What about the older boy, Sir Douglas?"

"Yes, what about Roger? The first fruits of dear Arthur's loins, no less." Sir Douglas tapped the computer again and cropped Jen out of the picture. Roger filled the entire screen.

"As you'll have seen, he's reading history and has no known political commitment. He rows a lot. In fact, I believe I saw him in the Randall boat that bumped Caius last May, although at the time it didn't click who he was. Typical boring sportsman, I'm afraid. You can see it in his face, can't you, full of vigour and healthy good humour, and just a little bit gormless. No, no, I think it's young Samuel who interests me. Come to Ely on the first day he legally can. Significant, wouldn't you say?"

The older man leant back in his chair and knocked out his pipe. He refilled it, keeping his sharp, blue eyes on the computer screen all the time. Roger was handing over his currency card to a BSC officer at the Eden Gate and then he and the rest of the group were ushered through to the other side.

"What would you like to do, Sir Douglas?" the younger man said. "Shall I put out a code blue on the whole group?"

The old man frowned and glanced at his watch.

"I think that's rather too much, too soon, Tony, don't you? No, I'm going to keep an eye on them myself. What I want you to do, dear boy, is to run along to the mess and get me a full breakfast and another bottle of port, the '82 if they have any. Then you can get on with cancelling whatever it was that I'm supposed to be doing today. I don't care what you tell people, as long as it's not the truth, of course."

The younger man turned to go. Then at the door he span round.

"So you're unavailable all day, Sir Douglas?"

The older man rolled his eyes.

"Of course I'm going to be unavailable. I'm going to spend the next several hours getting drunk and watching young Samuel Moorcroft enjoy his birthday treat. It might be rather a fun day. Actually I may need you later on to arrange some special privileges for Master Samuel, if I do decide to go blue. We'll see how we get on." Sir Douglas tapped the keyboard again and the image of Sam was projected from the screen to form a three-dimensional holograph on his desk. He tapped it again and the image rotated through 360 degrees. Sam was now on the far side of the Eden Gate and looking about him. His eyes sparkled with wonder and his mouth was hanging open. The older man chuckled and murmured to himself, "That's it, Samuel, you have a jolly good look round. You know, I think you might enjoy your day with us. I really do. It's the blood, you see, dear boy. No one ever bloody believes me, of course, but I swear it's in the blood."

"Will that be all then, Sir Douglas?" the young man asked from the door.

"Oh God, you're not still here are you, Tony?" Sir Douglas said wearily.

The younger man frowned and slipped quietly out of the room.

Chapter Seven
Like a Whole World

Sam gazed and gazed around in wonder. Beyond the Eden Gate the underground chamber broadened into an oval. Sam had no idea exactly how big it was but he reckoned that you could fit at least six football pitches into it with room to spare. The chamber's walls soared upwards to a vaulted ceiling where images of the sun and clouds moved gracefully against a background of shimmering blue. As Sam watched, astonished, the roof darkened as the sun apparently set on the left of the chamber, and then it grew bright again with a collage of stars and a whisper of new moon. These moved sedately around the great arch until they began to fade as the sun rose again on the right. Then the pattern repeated itself.

There were four balconies running round the chamber's walls, on which Sam noted restaurants, bars, holographics and old-style cinemas, book shops, camera shops, craft shops, clothes shops selling fenland garments, off licences, food shops selling delicacies from inside the enclosure, and much else besides. Hundreds of people jostled around the balconies carrying shopping bags, or else lolled against the balcony rails outside the cafes and bars, munching takeaway food and swigging from bottles. People waved and shouted at one another around the chamber, although to Sam it seemed impossible to hear what anyone was saying above the general clamour.

And the ground floor was even busier; thousands of people bustled about singing, chattering, laughing and arguing. There were dozens of banners of local Ely groups visible around the chamber; their members clustered around them in ragged, excitable bunches. Many of them were dressed in enclosure clothes and a number of them were apparently quite drunk.

BSC officers patrolled the area in pairs looking tough and sullen, fingering their pistols or truncheons as they went. Sam noticed that people drew back and quietened down as they approached, taking care not to meet their eye. There were also the inevitable groups of drones gathering litter and wiping floors, as well as harassed-looking tour guides leading parties of excited visitors from shop to shop. Sam also noticed a number of men and women in grubby green uniforms selling newspapers. They wandered through the crowd with their piles of papers draped over their arms, vying with one another to attract custom:

Murder in Walsingham. Read about the Walsingham murder.

New observation network in Upper Fillington: opening next week.

New-moon sex pics from Morgrave festival – see 'em all

Exclusive pics of the Walsingham Murder. See it as it happened.

Sam felt a sharp tug at his sleeve. It was Rachel, looking wide-eyed and exited.

"Well, what do you think of it then, birthday boy?" she said.

"It's incredible, isn't it? I had no idea it was as big as this. I mean, I knew from Roger that it was pretty impressive, but this is … well, it's … it's the biggest thing you could imagine, isn't it?"

"Yeah, I know, it's more than I was expecting as well. And this is just the Oval Chamber! I mean, you learn all about Ely and sophiocracy while you're growing up and obviously you know it's *important* and *big* and everything, but then you get here and … and it's like a whole world."

Sam glanced up at the ceiling where another starry night was falling. He felt a rush of excitement.

"It's not just *like* a whole world, Rache," he said breathlessly. "It *is* a whole world."

Just then a pair of BSC officers swaggered past. Rachel moved back until they had gone and then drew close again. She touched Sam's hand.

"Yeah, well, thanks for inviting me. It's great to be here. It's the sort of thing you have to *see*, isn't it?" She grinned and nodded to an old man in a long raincoat sitting alone on a nearby bench. He was fiddling angrily with a portable holograph machine. "Just keep me safe from the horrid pervy men with the dodgy holographs that Jen was talking about, ok?"

Sam smiled but before he could answer Jen and Roger appeared. Jen had bought a copy of the Ely Project newspaper and was flicking through it quickly.

"It's called *The Insider*," she said without looking up. "Ninety percent of it is tourist crap, but it's worth getting for the listings at the back. They tell you about any exhibitions and new stuff in the enclosure." She glanced up. "Did you have any idea what you might want to do today, Sam? It's your birthday, after all."

Sam looked muddled.

"Well, not really, I just wanted to see it, really, you know, see *inside*. I … I hadn't thought much about what we'd actually do."

"Bloody hell, little brother," Roger said. "There are over three hundred installations here, as well as God knows how many museums, holographics and exhibitions. This is the beating heart of sophiocracy. It's the belly of the beast. You can't just *see it*; you've got to make some choices. Didn't you think even a little bit about where you wanted to go?"

Sam shrugged and Jen folded up her copy of *The Insider* decisively.

"Well, look," she said, "Stanmore's got a good double pub which might be fun for lunch and there's a new exhibition there as well, called *Deviancy and Dysfunction*, which I wouldn't mind having a look at. And it's a decent installation for a first visit anyway, a fair bit going on up top but not too busy down below: just the pub, a couple of bookshops and a delicatessen, if I remember rightly, so it's not overrun with tourists and gawpers. Does that sound ok, Sam?"

"Yeah, ok. Sounds all right. Whatever, really. I just want to see inside."

Roger grinned and rolled his eyes while Jen stowed her copy of *The Insider* in her bag.

"Good," she said. "Stanmore it is. It's only three minutes by minirail. Follow me and make sure we keep together."

Sam hadn't noticed the minirail terminal when they had arrived. It was on the opposite side of the Oval Chamber from the Eden Gate and was entered by turnstiles watched over by a pair of bored looking BSC officers. There was another holograph of Sebastian Randall mounted on a dais immediately outside the entrance; he was seated at a substantial desk, frowning and studying a sheaf of papers, occasionally running his hand absent-mindedly through his hair so that it stood up untidily from his forehead.

"There he is, Sam, the father of the nation," Roger whispered as they shuffled through the turnstiles. "Working tirelessly to ensure the success of the sophiocratic experiment. Doesn't it make you proud to be British, eh?"

"I've always thought he was a pretty good-looking bloke when he was younger," Rachel said. "I mean, you can sort of see why people followed him, can't you?"

"I think people supported him because of his *ideas*," Sam said stiffly, "not because they fancied him."

"I *know* that, Sam, I was just saying that he looks like he's got, you know, *charisma* or something. He's an attractive man, that's all."

Sam frowned but didn't reply as Jen led them into the station.

They walked down a small staircase, along a tiled corridor and out onto a platform next to the minirail tube. There was a short queue ahead of them which shuffled forward every two of three minutes as an empty minicar shot out of the tube-end. A uniformed attendant and a drone loaded each car with a party of visitors and then it moved off with a soft whooshing noise and a blast of dry, hot air.

"Where yer all off to then?" the attendant asked when Sam's group reached the front of the queue.

"A four-car to Stanmore, please," Jen answered. "Been busy today?"

"It's been pretty hectic, love, but not many for Stanmore. The murder over at Walsingham has pulled in the crowds and then there's a sex thing on at Ditchingham, and the wrestling at Watton fayre has got a lot of 'em excited an' all. Stanmore should be pretty quiet; get you there in a jiffy, this time of day."

"Excellent," Jen said as another empty car whizzed out of the tunnel. The man held it steady on its air rail while the four of them scrambled in, and then the drone leant over and helped them arrange their belongings and fasten their harnesses. He made soft sucking noises as he worked and had specks of dried saliva glued to the corners of his mouth.

"I'm not keen on having drones this close to me, to be honest," Rachel said under her breath as he fumbled with her straps. "I know it sounds silly, but I always think that they are *thinking about me.*"

"Well, you won't have to worry about that up at Stanmore," Jen said. "They don't let them get anywhere near the surface in case it triggers some sort of deep genetic memory and they start freaking out or make a dash for it or something. I don't know if it makes much sense, really. To me it's always seemed more like superstition than science, but that's what they do."

The drone slid the car lid shut and then withdrew and picked his nose while the attendant punched a control pad on the platform wall. The car rose and shivered as the air rail swelled beneath them, and then they were propelled forwards at incredible speed into the blackness of the tube.

To Sam it seemed more like three seconds than three minutes later that they emerged into the bright light of Stanmore minirail station. The car hissed to a halt and another uniformed attendant slid the top open and held the car steady as they climbed out onto the deserted platform.

"Right," the man said. "You're at Stanmore; I hope that's where you was after. The lift at the end of the platform takes you right up into the installation. We're open until four, although I doubt you'll wanna' stay that long. You ain't exactly chosen the most exciting settlement, I'm afraid."

"We know, that's why we're here," Jen said crisply. She turned her back on the man and led them smartly down the platform and into the lift. When the doors had slid shut she said, "Stanmore's part of the original enclosure so a lot of the tourists and lower level staff think it's rather primitive. I believe it's still got some old real-space observation posts, but they're not open to the public any more. Obviously we'll be visiting by holograph booth." She paused and Sam heard the beep of her cardiovascular chip speed up. "And, unlike some people, we'll be visiting for *proper legitimate* reasons, not just to watch stupid fighting or stare at fenlanders having sex."

"Speak for yourself," Roger said, winking at Sam and Rachel. Jen glared at him and the beep from her wrist grew even faster.

"I bloody well will speak for myself, Roger," she began. "I'm sick of..." Just then, however, the lift doors slid open and they were confronted with yet another BSC officer—a young woman with a machine gun.

"Ok guys, welcome to the Stanmore installation," the officer said. "You are presently 80 meters below the enclosure. You'd never get up to the real-space settlement even if you wanted to, but I still have to remind you that any violation or attempted violation of the Project boundary is a felony carrying the maximum penalty of chemical curtailment. If you attempt to compromise the boundary you will be restrained using lethal or non-lethal weapons. Are there any questions?"

"None at all, officer," Jen answered.

"Good. Have a nice day." The officer stood to one side and gestured them out of the lift with her gun.

After the Oval Chamber, the Stanmore installation felt rather cramped. Sam estimated it was about a hundred metres long by fifty wide and as high as a normal two storey house. One of the longer sides was dominated by the timber frontage of a pub called the King's Head, which leaked the warm smell of beer and food, as well as a hum of conversation, into the installation plaza. The other long side was taken up with a posh-looking food shop called "Enclosure Savouries", and two bookshops. One of these was modern, its window crammed with hand-held digi-texts and bright advertisements for current downloads. The other was cramped and old-fashioned, stocking a mixture of digi-texts and old style paper pamphlets and books. One of the shorter sides was taken up with the lift and a small BSC guard post while the other was filled with rows of chrome egg-shaped pods. There were a few visitors wandering between the shops, and a solitary paper seller slumped on a bench, munching a chocolate bar. Jen gestured towards the chrome pods.

"Right, what I suggest we do is go and have a couple of hours in the holograph booths straight away and then meet back in the double pub for lunch at 12 o'clock. Does that seem sensible? And if anyone's had enough of the Stanmore before that," she glanced at Roger, "there's always the shops to visit or you could hop on the minirail and go on somewhere else, as long as we're all back here by 12."

Roger tapped his bag so that the beer bottles inside clinked.

"Don't worry about me. I'll be able to entertain myself around Stanmore for an hour or two."

"Well, don't let the BSC catch you taking beer in," Jen said severely. She turned to Rachel and Sam. "Ok, the booths are pretty self-explanatory; just follow the instructions and then relax and enjoy yourself. And look … I know it might be difficult, but do try and remember the principles of sophiocracy while you're inside. It's really *not* about prying or anything sordid, it's about trying to understand how human beings tick so that we can change ourselves for the better. Obviously, that's principally about the Fruit of Sophia: stuff like drones and alphas and enhancement technology and whatnot. But if you let it, it works on a more personal level as well. The enclosure isn't just a pool of spare parts and subjects for experiment; it's also a kind of mirror. Try to keep that in mind." She blushed and grinned. "Oh God, do I sound really awful and pretentious?"

Roger squeezed her hand.

"No, you just sound like what you are—a true believer. And that's probably better than being cynical about everything. Come on, let's go, and I promise I'll be careful with my booze. I won't disgrace you."

Chapter Eight
Stanmore

Five minutes later Sam was sitting in a large leather chair in one of the holograph booths, with a black joystick sticking up between his knees. He glanced round and waved at Rachel just as the door of her booth slid shut, and then pressed a button on the arm rest of his chair to close up his own. All the sights and sounds of the installation were immediately cut off; the only light came from the greenish glow of the computer screen and the illuminated keyboard in front of him. Sam leant forward and studied the text that had appeared on the screen.

Know Thyself
Welcome to the Stanmore installation. Stanmore was included in the initial enclosure of 1978 and was a key site in the Project's scientific research for 11 years. Following the Revolution of 1989, however, and the subsequent expansion of the enclosure, Stanmore became less central to the Project's main academic thrust, allowing a quieter, more settled life to evolve. The result is a peaceful, friendly settlement that is popular with the discerning Project visitor and with the enclosure's junior research cadets.

Stanmore is twinned with the Pennine town of Hebden Bridge, and the Hebden Bridge Ely group, although rather small, maintains strong and enthusiastic links with the settlement.

We hope you enjoy your visit to Stanmore. Please select from the following options:

1. Past Times in Stanmore.
Traces the proud history of Stanmore from the Norman Conquest until the 2nd War Between Brothers. (Contains some re-enacted material and some-flat screen footage that has been digitally inflated.)

2. Stanmore and the Enclosure.
Examines the recent history of Stanmore within the Ely Project.
Includes archive footage of the Guardian visiting the settlement
and operational shots of the BSC.

3. Deviancy and Dysfunction.
Doctoral Research by Jasmine Baraclough of Durham
University. Ms. Baraclough uses Stanmore as a base for her
enquiry into the bio-social and psychosexual structure of
criminality in young men between the ages of 16 and 25.
(Contains some explicit language.)

4. The Settlement Today
Real-time visit to Stanmore.

Sam used the joystick to maneuver the cursor to option four
and pushed the switch at the top forward. Immediately the text
dissolved and a map of Stanmore appeared on the screen with a
new message beneath it.

Know Thyself
1. Your real-time visit to Stanmore will extend as far as
the boundary indicated in red on the map above. Within
that territory all routes, homes and public spaces are
legal and accessible for visitors.

2. Please use the joy-stick to pilot your visit. Your
position is indicated by the blue cross on the map. You
can increase the scale of the map by moving the top
switch of the joystick forward and decrease it by moving
it backwards.

3. In the unlikely event of emergency operations being
undertaken in Stanmore, the holograph presentation will
terminate and a blue warning light will flash in the top
portion of the screen. You must immediately leave the
holograph booth. DO NOT attempt to re-enter the
settlement until advised that you may do so by Project
staff.

4. If you feel nauseous or develop a headache in the course of your visit, leave the settlement for a while. If your symptoms persist, consult Project staff.

6. Please click HERE to commence your real-time visit to Stanmore.

Sam clicked where he was instructed and the text immediately dissolved as the map expanded to fill the screen. For a moment nothing else seemed to happen and then Sam became aware of the muted sound of children shouting. The sound seemed to be coming from somewhere deep inside his own head; it grew steadily louder and clearer until it was possible to make out particular voices. Then, without knowing when it had appeared or where it came from, Sam realised that the chamber was full of hazy bluish light. Gradually the light thickened and twisted into ghostly forms: people, buildings, carts, round lumps that might have been baskets or barrels. The shapes began to fill up with colour and shift into their proper perspective until eventually Sam found himself sitting, completely unobserved, in the middle of a market. He glanced at the computer screen and saw that a blue cross had appeared on the area marked *common* on the map. Below the map a line of text read:

The common provides free grazing land for geese and sheep belonging to the citizens of Stanmore. It hosts a market each Saturday and the village fayre every midsummer.

Sam rotated the joystick and the scene span round. The market was quite small, perhaps a dozen fixed stalls as well as a few people selling lace, shoelaces or sweets from large wicker baskets that they carried on their hip. The children that Sam had heard were about 10 or 11; they were chasing from stall to stall wildly shouting and laughing. As Sam watched, one of them, a little girl in a patched dress, turned three cartwheels in front of the cake and bread stall, causing a customer to stumble backwards and drop her change. While the stall holder was distracted, two more of the children helped themselves to treacle tart and lemon meringue pie off the other end of the stall and then the whole group sped off screeching with laughter.

Sam pushed the joystick forwards and moved slowly through the market, arriving at a stall that was covered in the fresh carcasses of small animals and birds. Round about the stall were the baskets that Sam had seen; they held living pigeons, squirrels and what looked like large mice. The rich, warm scent of wild animal filled Sam's nostrils. He sniffed and twitched his nose, trying not to sneeze, as a woman arrived at the stall and peered into the pigeon basket.

"I'll give yer five bob fer a brace of them pigeon an' not a penny more," she said bossily to the stall holder.

"I can't do it fer that, Pauline, yer know that," the stall holder replied." "They're fattened up fer three month at me own table. Thems practically pets. I'll do 'em for seven and six, but that's it."

The woman straightened and grimaced.

"Six bob, Larry, or you can forget it."

The stall holder held the woman's determined gaze for a moment and then sighed.

"All right then, Pauline, seein' as it's you. Six bob. But don't you go telling no one."

Sam pushed the joystick forward again and moved off across the common just as the stall holder and the woman were beginning to argue over the price of rabbits. He arrived at a road that marked the edge of the market. It was busy with pedestrians, horses and carts and a few ancient bicycles, and was lined on both sides with a mixture of shops, pubs and houses. The buildings were all made of slate and timber and had a ramshackle, chaotic look about them: roofs sloped at irregular angles, doors and windows tilted, walls bulged alarmingly. Sam turned right and drifted along the road, sometimes dodging the traffic, sometimes pushing straight through it, making it vanish in a blur of blue light, until he came to a large flint building that dominated the street. It had a tall spire at one end and was marked outside by a large cross with a wooden man hanging from it. There were bundles of holly and fir mounted on the crucified man's hands and feet, and next to him an elderly man in flowing scarlet robes was addressing a crowd from a low platform. The blue cross on the map was now hovering outside a building marked *temple*. Beneath the map a new block of text had appeared:

The Stanmore temple has been a place of worship for over 900 years, mostly under the control of the Nazarene cult. Since enclosure the indigenous cult has been incrementally developed into the Sacred Wheel tradition by the Project's Religion and Spirit Department. Wheel worship is today practiced in its various forms throughout the enclosure. At Stanmore the cult is complimented by devotion to the Green Man.

Sam pushed his joystick further forward to move himself through the crowd until he had a good view of the preacher. The man was probably in his late sixties, although it was difficult to tell because, like all the other enclosure people, he was completely un-enhanced. He had white flowing hair and a beard that reached down to his waist. His voice was deep and melodic and as he spoke he gestured extravagantly.

"I say it again, people of Stanmore, if we neglect the Wheel of Being we will pay bitterly in our hearts and in our homes. This is old wisdom, my children: there is night and day, summer and winter, seedtime and harvest, birth and death and birth again." The speaker pointed to the man on the cross. "All of these spin with the Wheel. All of these turn and turn about and turn again.

"How then shall we be faithful to the Great Wheel? How shall we preserve the spinning and turning of our own brief lives? People of Stanmore, the answer is simple: we must make our hearth offerings with the turning day, we must honour All Hallows, Christmas and Beltane with ready wills, we must be regular at the temple and we must pay our tithes to the priesthood with gladful hearts."

The softest murmur of discontent ran through the crowd at the mention of the tithes. At this the preacher's face became very grave; he flung his arms high into the air so that his robes fluttered in the breeze. His voice rose:

"My children, how it pains me that you should be so stiff-necked and stubborn. I ask you, my dear ones, to consider, who is it but your priesthood who labours for you each day at the altar, offering the sacrifice of thorn and blood? Who but your priesthood holds the boundary in their constant prayer to check the darkness of the beyonds? Who keeps the demon from our gates? Who was it healed your old cow when she had soft pad, Reuben Crowfoot; or called your geese back from the outside wind, Mistress Lowell? Is it too much, then, to ask that you honour your priesthood, your guardians, with some small token of your gratitude? For if you do not pay your tithe, my children, and how it hurts me to say this, you will pay in other ways. This is the nature of the Wheel. We reap what we sow."

The preacher's eyes wandered sorrowfully from face to face in the crowd, causing people to drop their gaze and shuffle uncomfortably. For a disconcerting moment Sam felt that the man was staring straight at him, but then his gaze swept past and, much relieved, Sam swung the joystick around and made his way back towards the street.

Deep under the dark fenland earth, Sir Douglas Latch sat alone in his office peering intently at the miniature holograph image of the Stanmore preacher as it played across his desktop, gesticulating wildly. The figure's voice squeaked into the room through the computer's speakers.

"My children, the way of the Wheel is the way of sacrifice and of joy, of woe and of restoration, of tithing and of return. This is old wisdom, my dear ones; learn it and know peace. What we give, so we shall receive. Does the farmer earn a crop without offering his seed to the earth? Does the miller gather flour without offering his corn to the stone…"

"Does the greedy old priest get hold of his cash without boring the balls off everyone?" growled Sir Douglas. He jabbed the keypad, making the sound cease and the figure vanish. Then he lit a cigarette.

"If anything's going to put young Master Samuel off Ely, I fancy it's the likes of Reverend bloody Smythe," he murmured to himself. "And the only old wisdom that bugger's interested in is the wisdom of fleecing his dear children for his beer money and his lady friends."

Sir Douglas sat back and smoked in silence for a few moments then hunched forward and jabbed at the keyboard again. Sam appeared on the screen. He was sitting in the fuzzy gloom of the holograph booth with his eyes flickering from side to side in excitement. The tip of his tongue was poking out between his lips and he was grasping the joystick so tightly that his knuckles were white. Sir Douglas poured himself a mug of port and sipped it as he smoked, never taking his eyes off the screen.

"I spoke too soon," he said eventually. "It seems Reverend Smythe has not quite broken the spell, has he, Samuel? Thank goodness for that."

He poked the keypad and Sam disappeared. He jabbed it again and after a moment a voice crackled into the room.

"Did you want me, Sir Douglas?"

"Ah Tony, dear boy, yes I did. Young Samuel Moorcroft and his gang are down at Stanmore, where I believe there are still some real-space observation posts."

"Yes, Sir Douglas."

"If memory serves they're half-abandoned, although I think the BSC may use them for storing their pop guns or something. Anyway, I'm keen that Samuel should get a look at them under a code blue."

There was a brief silence.

"How would we actually do that, Sir Douglas?"

"We'd begin by using our brains." Sir Douglas lit a fresh cigarette from the stub of the old one. "Look, we know that Jennifer what's-her-name, Catesby, the older boy's girlfriend, is at Randall reading A and P, and that she's up to her well-bred ears in sophiocracy. Correct?"

"Correct."

"Good. So it seems reasonable to assume she'll know people in the Project who might be able to claim access to areas that are normally off limits. Just dig someone appropriate up, arrange a *chance* meeting, brief the BSC and get Samuel up top for a good look round. Make sure he goes on his own though, I don't want his meditations interrupted by that ape of a brother."

"Um, yes, but, Sir Douglas, the BSC might not be too keen."

"And what on earth has that got to do with anything?" The old man's voice rose in irritation. "YOU ARE AN INTERLANDER, TONY. A NON-COMMISIONED INTERLANDER, BUT STILL AN INTERLANDER. WHO CARES WHAT THE BSC MIGHT THINK? Just let them know what you want doing and then make damn sure they do it. And if they look like they might want to cause problems mention my name, is that clear?"

"Perfectly, Sir Douglas."

"Thank God for that." Sir Douglas's voice was suddenly friendly again. "Look Tony, I know that you mean well. Perhaps next week if we're both free we could cross over together and have a spot of lunch and some drinks somewhere pleasant. Somewhere with young women and music. Would that be nice?"

"Yes, Sir Douglas."

"Splendid. Now be brave and get on with your job."

Sir Douglas leant forward and jabbed at the keypad, then drank the last of his port. He stood up and walked unsteadily to the book-lined wall, running his thumb along the books' spines and squinting at their dates as he went along.

"Arthur Moorcroft, now let me think," he murmured as he worked his way along the shelves. "Must be 20 years ago, at least. No, bugger me, it's more like thirty. Thirty years since I met young Arthur. I rather think I'm getting old."

Eventually Sir Douglas found the book he was looking for. He pulled it off the shelf and flicked through it where he stood, occasionally pausing to read a passage in detail. The muscles of his jaw tightened as he read and the veins on his neck stood out like cords.

"Thirty years since I met him," he murmured, "and 20 years since he betrayed me. And now I get to meet Moorcroft junior ... something rather and circular and pleasing about it all, really." The old man giggled. "The way of the Wheel and so forth. Perhaps that old goat Smythe is onto something after all."

Chapter Nine
Real-Space

Sam was the last of the group to arrive at the King's Head for lunch. He found Rachel, Jen and Roger sitting at a table near the door together with two skinny men who were playing cards. There didn't seem to be a lot of room left for Sam but Jen glanced up from the menu she was reading and smiled.

"Don't worry, Sam, they're holographs. They disappear if you sit on them."

Sam studied the two men carefully; they looked real enough in their grubby fenland clothes and broad brimmed hats. Both were intent on their game; neither of them spoke much but occasionally one would sip from a large tankard of beer and belch softly.

"Hurry up and sit down, Sam," Rachel said. "They're disgusting. This one keeps burping in my face."

"Are you absolutely sure they're holographs?"

Roger leant forward and punched one of the men firmly in the chest. He flickered briefly and then vanished.

"Yeah, they're definitely holographs," Roger said. "The whole point of a double pub is that everything looks as authentic as possible. This place is an exact replica of the King's Head up in Stanmore. Whatever's going on up there in real-space gets projected straight down here. It's quite clever, really."

Sam looked round the pub. It seemed very busy indeed at first glance, but if you looked closely you noticed that lots of the customers had a habit of vanishing whenever they were bumped into. As Sam watched, a group of women tourists settled themselves around a good-looking fenland man at a table near the bar. One of them kept pretending to kiss him, making him disappear and reappear over and over again, while the others giggled. Eventually the holograph stood up to go and another of the women made a wild grab for his waist so that he vanished permanently. The whole group hooted with laughter.

"Didn't your mum ever tell you not to snatch, Silvia?" one of them asked. "Them as snatch never get."

"But he loves me, I know that he loves me," the other woman replied. She giggled and sipped her drink. "Did you see his thighs when he got up? Like bloody tree trunks. Beautiful."

Sam turned back to his own table in time to see one of the card-playing fenlanders spit towards the floor. The gob of spit vanished before it hit the ground.

"God, that is so gross," Rachel said. "Sit on him, Sam, or I'm going to put my bag on him."

Sam lowered himself carefully onto the seat and the man vanished. Roger looked over and smiled.

"From your bewitched look, little brother, I'd say you had a good time up at Stanmore."

"I thought it was fantastic," Sam said slowly. "I didn't expect it to seem so *solid*. I mean, I know it was all holographs but everything still seemed complete and … and different." He shrugged. "It was fantastic."

Jen put down the menu and smiled at him.

"It *is* an incredible achievement, isn't it? I've been hundreds of times and I still find it inspiring. Honestly, I never, ever get bored of it. Each time I come I see something new. Oh yes, Sam, I nearly forgot."

She reached into her bag and pulled out a thin, glossy booklet which she passed to Sam. It was entitled *Deviancy and Dysfunction* and had a picture of a crossbow and a pile of gold coins on the front.

"It's the brochure for the new exhibition," she said. "Call it a supplementary birthday present. I visited this morning and I must say it's very impressive. They've set up a smuggling gang in a network of old abandoned barns outside the village and used them as a framework to study anti-social behaviour and criminal tendencies in young men. It's astonishing how tiny genetic recrafting in the subjects can make absolutely enormous changes in their behaviour. And you can follow most of it by holograph. It's an excellent piece of research. Really detailed and …"

"Yeah, yeah, yeah, that's all very well," Roger cut in, "but I'm going to get a bit deviant and dysfunctional myself if we don't eat soon. What are you having?"

"Oh, I'm having the eels," Jen said.

Sam wrinkled his nose.

"Do they really eat eels, then?"

"Where do you think the word Ely comes from?" Roger said. "It's the isle of eels. Eels are the big thing in the fens. You've got to have them when you visit the Project. It's a must."

Rachel looked at him suspiciously.

"Are you going to have them then?"

"Of course not, Rachel, they taste like crap. I'm going to have a burger and chips. I'm just keen that Sam should enjoy the whole Ely experience."

Jen groaned and rolled her eyes while Sam and Rachel studied their menus.

"I'll have eels as well, but with chips," Sam said eventually.

"I'm going to have chicken," Rachel said. "But I might nick one of your eels if they don't look too horrible, Sam. Shall I go and order?"

"Yeah, ok," Roger said, handing over his currency card. "Mum and Dad said they'd pay for lunch. But don't waste your time trying to get served by the fat barman with the purply veins all over his nose. He's a holograph. I spent ages waving my card at him when I was buying the drinks. Eventually I tapped him on the shoulder and he vanished. I felt a bit of a prat."

Rachel nodded and squeezed out of the table. Sam was discreetly studying her hips and legs as she maneuvered her way to the bar when a confident voice sounded across the pub.

"Jen Catesby."

Sam swung round and saw a young man in a smart suit pushing his way towards them, vanishing holographs and elbowing his way past tourists as he went. Jen was smiling at him uncertainly.

"I thought it was you I saw coming in," the man said as he pulled up a stool and sat down at the table. "I don't know if you'll remember me; I'm Henry Conway. I was two years above you up at Randall, doing A and P. I left last year."

"Oh yes ... yes, I do remember you," Jen said after a moment. "Didn't you present a paper on mental-uploads or digi-consciousness or something like that at the college Ely group? I remember thinking how cutting edge it all sounded."

The man smirked.

"Yeah, that's me. I'm still punting around the same old stuff, I'm afraid." He gestured to a plastic photo pass dangling round his neck. "But at least I'm getting paid for it now. I'm a grade three Project cadet working over at Swaffam on pretty much the same material."

"So what is it you actually do that's so cutting edge?" Roger asked. Henry stared at him.

"Sorry, do I know you?"

"This is my boyfriend, Roger," Jen said quickly. "You might remember him from college."

"Actually, I'm not sure I do. Are you doing A and P?"

"Good lord, no," Roger said. "I'm afraid I'm just not A and P material. I'm reading history."

"Good man. It's a solid sort of subject, isn't it? I'm not sure how much future there is in the past, but there we are. To answer your question, the stuff I'm involved with is to do with uploading the entire structure of human consciousness: memory, will, understanding and so on, so that it can be downloaded into another body or even into a sentient robotic system." Henry sighed theatrically. "It's hard going to be honest and we seem to be wading through dozens of bloody subjects, particularly kids, but it's also very exciting." He leaned across the table and lowered his voice. "Apparently the Guardian himself takes a personal interest in our work."

"Doesn't seem that exciting to me," Roger said. "I wouldn't fancy hanging around for ages as a computer program. Imagine if you got an itchy leg or needed to pee or something. It'd be purgatory, wouldn't it?"

"You can laugh if you want," Henry said coldly. "The fact remains, what I'm doing is just the last stage of what's going on already, what sophiocracy's all about." He gestured to Roger's CV chip, its glow clearly visible through his thin cotton shirt. "I see that you've got a cardiovascular chip. I bet you also use an enhancement clip most nights and you've probably considered synthetic organs; for all I know you've already got them."

Roger shrugged.

"Thought so. And you'll use drones at college, and possibly at home as well. And if they're reasonably up to date they'll all have titanium alloy jointing and quantum processing units."

"I'll take your word for it. What's your point?"

"I should think it's pretty obvious, even to an historian. All these things were developed within the Project through work on our subjects; they're all Fruit of Sophia, right? And all of them are designed to liberate us from our bodies to some degree; at least that's how we see it down at Swaffam." Henry's eyes gleamed with enthusiasm. "Well, don't you see, the work we're engaged in is simply completing the process. It's meant to free us from these grunting animals that we're attached to so that we can be what we really are at last. We can be pure self-possessed minds; or spirits, if you prefer. Don't you understand, it's sophiocracy taken just about as far as it can go."

"Personally, I quite like being attached to a grunting animal," Roger said.

"Now why doesn't that surprise me?" Henry turned back to Jen. "Anyway, what are you doing here? Is it business or pleasure today?"

"Both, really. You can't ever visit the Project without working if you're involved in the subject, can you? But today, I'm mostly here because it's Sam's birthday. Sam is Roger's brother."

Henry swung round to look at Sam. Sam watched as he arranged his features carefully into a smile.

"Excellent, what a great birthday treat. Are you having a good day with us, Sam?"

"Yeah, I am. I visited Stanmore this morning. It was good."

"Good for you! It's not a bad little settlement, is it? There was some top notch work done here in the early days, actually."

"Not just in the early days," Jen cut in. "I went to *Deviancy and Dysfunction* this morning and it was excellent."

Henry smiled and shrugged.

"Oh yeah, the smugglers. Actually, I was saying to Jasmine only last week that I thought she'd put in some really solid work there. A bit old-school for my taste, but well researched all the same." He stood up. "Well, anyway, thanks, but I won't stay for a drink. I only dropped by to pick up some goat's cheese from the deli. Stanmore's fantastic for the stuff, I'll say that for it. Nice to have met you all."

Henry nodded at them and turned to go. Suddenly, he turned back.

"You know what? It occurs to me that it might be nice for Sam to have a real-space peek into the enclosure. A bit of an extra treat for his birthday. There're some original observation posts out in the wilds at Stanmore and I could probably wangle a visit if he'd like that."

"Gosh, what a fantastic opportunity," Jen said. "Could you really swing it?"

"I would have thought so. I've got a few connections. I'm afraid I could probably only get the birthday boy himself up there, though. The BSC aren't keen on groups of people traipsing around in real-space, obviously."

"That's quite all right, Henry," said Roger smoothly. "Obviously I'm dreadfully disappointed that I won't spend part of the afternoon looking at a field but I'll get over it. I think we all will." He turned to Sam. "Well then, do you fancy it, little brother?"

"Yes," Sam said. "Yes, actually, I'd like that a lot."

"Great, well I'll meet you by the holograph booths at two o'clock. And I hope that I'll have rather more to show you than a field."

Henry smiled briefly at Sam and Jen, and then, ignoring Roger, pushed his way bossily towards the door.

As he left the pub Jen and Roger spoke at the same time:

"What a stroke of luck."

"What a complete arse."

Sam was worried that Rachel would be annoyed about his visit into real-space. After all, she was his guest and he was effectively abandoning her. Also, he assumed she would be jealous. Who wouldn't be jealous of such an opportunity? He spent the first part of the meal fretting about how to broach the subject but in the end Roger did the job for him.

"So, Rachel, if Sam's going wandering around in wonderland this afternoon and Jen's off to the archives, what are you planning to do?

"What do you mean?" Rachel said. "What's Sam doing?"

Sam took a deep breath.

"A friend of Jen's has offered to take me up into real-space, just for a bit. He came over when you were ordering the food. But I'm afraid only I'm allowed to go, sorry."

Rachel shrugged.

"Oh, that's fine, Sam. I promised my mum that I'd get her something woolly and ethnic; you know how keen she is on enclosure knitwear. I was going to have a proper look round the Oval Chamber."

"I may as well come with you," Roger said. "I feel like I've pretty much done Stanmore."

Rachel smiled at him and hooked her hair back behind her ear.

"Ok, if you don't mind hanging around a few clothes shops. You can keep the pervs away."

"Of course, always glad to be of service to a lady."

"Good." Sam said quickly. "That's good, then."

"Yeah," Rachel said, "and you can tell me all about your adventures up top this evening."

The mention of that evening made Sam blush. He ate the rest of his food as quickly as he could and then hurried out of the pub and walked over to the holograph booths. Henry was already waiting for him; he was hopping from foot to foot impatiently and had a tough-looking BSC man with him, carrying a machine gun.

"This is Sergeant Hargreaves," Henry said as Sam arrived. "Any boundary visit has to be accompanied by BSC, I'm afraid, even if it's the Guardian himself going up there. But don't worry about him, he's under my authority."

The sergeant bridled. Ignoring Henry completely, he addressed Sam.

"Now then, young man, you obviously know some pretty important people to get a privilege like this, but that doesn't mean you get to break any rules, you understand? We're going to be right on the boundary. *I'm* responsible for what goes on up there, so I'm obliged to remind you that compromising or attempting to compromise the boundary is a ..."

"Yes, yes, yes, never mind all that," Henry cut in. "Sam's very well aware of it all, aren't you, Sam? No one's going to compromise anything, Sergeant, you have my word. Could we just get going please?"

The sergeant flexed his fingers against the stock of his gun but didn't say anything. He turned sharply on his heel and led them through the lines of holograph booths.

"Now then, Sam, I hope you're feeling fit," Henry said, "because we've got to do a fair bit of climbing. I'm afraid there are no lifts up to the top here. You're really going to be seeing the old Project this afternoon: before holographs, before minirail, before the revolution, back to the very earliest days."

They arrived at a steel door set in a dirty brick wall in the deserted, shadowy space behind the holograph booths. The BSC sergeant glanced from side to side then turned the door's rusty handle and leant heavily against it. After resisting briefly it creaked inwards into pitch blackness. The sergeant reached inside the doorway and a weak light flickered on, illuminating a bare brick corridor. Sam gasped.

"Isn't it even locked?"

"Yeah, I know, it's shocking, isn't it?" Henry said as he pushed past Sergeant Hargreaves into the corridor. "But here's a trade secret, Sam: the boundary is such a tremendously dominating reality in peoples' minds that it doesn't really need a lot of physical defending. To be honest, a determined boundary breaker could get across relatively easily in any number of the older installations. The BSC are a deterrent more than anything else these days—at least on this side." He strode down the corridor a few steps and kicked a piece of blackened brick into the gloom. "Bloody hell, this is practically archaeology. I believe your brother would actually be quite at home here. Come on, let's get going."

Henry and Sergeant Hargreaves competed subtly to take the lead as they walked along the corridor so that their pace kept increasing. After 20 minutes Sam was practically jogging to keep up when the corridor tapered to an end at a rusty spiral staircase. Henry jumped onto the bottom step ahead of the BSC man.

"Right, Sam, it's 863 steps to the surface, if memory serves. Because we don't know what's happening up at the top or the quality of the boundary lock, we're going to have to keep quiet on our way up, just as a precaution. Have you got any questions?"

Sam shook his head. Henry nodded, then set off up the staircase, followed closely by the sergeant and then by Sam. The steps disappeared through a narrow hole in the ceiling and continued upwards through a tube of black brick. The only light came from the BSC sergeant's torch and Sam soon felt disorientated and sick. He kept his hands as well as his feet on the cold metal steps as he climbed and made a point of not looking down. It was a relief when he finally arrived at a narrow wooden platform illuminated by two more dim lights. He pulled himself unsteadily to his feet and Henry gestured to him to be quiet.

"Sergeant Hargreaves has to go out first and have a scout around," he whispered. "He'll let us know when he's checked that the coast is clear."

There was a steel door on the right of the platform with a large metal wheel mounted on the front. The sergeant slung his gun over his shoulder and leant hard on the wheel, turning it clockwise. It squeaked and then span quickly though his fingers; as it did so the door slid forwards.

"Probably months since anyone's bothered to come up here," the sergeant grunted, peering distastefully at the rust stains on his hands. He swung the door open and Sam just had time to glimpse another, identical, door beyond before the sergeant stepped inside and swung the first door shut again.

"Boundary lock," Henry whispered. "Keeps light and sound out of the observation posts. The design's practically out of the ark, it's all light portals these days. But these old things still work reasonably well."

Sam couldn't think of anything to say so he stood in silence with his hands in his pockets, staring at the floor. He glanced up a couple of times, and each time he was disconcerted to find Henry peering at him slyly. The third time it happened Henry smiled at him.

"Have you got any special connection with the Project, Sam?" he asked casually. "You know, have you got any family link or anything?"

"Not really. My mum worked here for a while doing catering for special exhibitions. But that was years ago and she doesn't really approve of the Project anymore. Jen comes here quite a bit, of course, but she's not really family; at least not yet."

Henry frowned and nodded, looking puzzled. He didn't say anything else but continued to glance curiously at Sam in the silence. It was an uncomfortable feeling and Sam was glad when the wheel on the door span again and Sergeant Hargreaves poked his head back through the opening.

"Right then, it's as quiet as the grave. You can come straight through."

Sam and Henry stepped into the cramped chamber between the two doors and Sergeant Hargreaves closed the first one behind them. He shuffled past them and span the wheel on the second door until it swung open, flooding the chamber with pale sunlight. He lowered his machine gun and stepped outside. Henry and Sam followed him.

Sam found himself in a narrow trench reaching well above his head. It had duck boards on the floor and a narrow step running along each side. There was a strong breeze and a few spots of rain in the bright sky. The contrast after the artificial light of the Project was breathtaking. Sam closed his eyes and inhaled deeply.

"Obviously it would have been roofed over in the old days," Henry said, indicating a few pieces of broken wood that were lying around in the bottom of the trench. "That was when Stanmore was a busy research centre of course. Nowadays hardly anybody comes out this way, so when the roof collapsed they just left it."

As he was speaking Sergeant Hargreaves opened a sliding door in the trench wall and began poking around inside a cupboard.

"We've still got BSC stores up here, though," he grunted. "Flares and ammunition and suchlike. I've been briefed to check them while I'm up here. My superiors didn't want it to be a completely wasted trip."

Henry climbed up onto the step above the sergeant and peered down at him.

"You do whatever you want, Sergeant, I'll let you know when we're done. Why don't you get up on the viewing step, Sam, I'll show you the sights."

Sam clambered up a short ladder onto the step and looked around. In front of him there was an expanse of flat reed beds, criss-crossed by raised paths. This ended in a slight rise crested with a few trees about a mile and a half away. Beyond the rise Sam could make out a plume of bluish smoke drifting into the sky. In the opposite direction, the reed beds extended as far as Sam could see; only a pair of ruined cottages on the horizon broke the emptiness of the view.

"Right then," Henry said. "The smoke you can see comes from the furthest west of Stanmore's outlying farms. I believe it's occupied by some mad old cow who does a nice job of scaring off anyone who might take it upon himself to wander out this way. Apparently, the locals have got her down as a witch, and they're probably right. The mound itself is artificial, of course; it's the lie of the land covering this observation post. Stanmore proper is about a mile further to the east. There's nothing at all beyond us to the west until the boundary two and a half miles away, so everything over there is dead land as far as the subjects are concerned. There are a few inactive BSC posts scattered about, but that's about all. Nothing round here is under holograph coverage, incidentally. For that you need to go into Stanmore itself. Then there's blanket coverage as you'll know from this morning."

"What happened to the people in the cottages?"

Henry shrugged.

"Displaced at the time of the original enclosure. Probably moved into Stanmore proper; they had fewer options for dealing with people in those days than we do now. Anyway, the coast is about five miles away to the east. There are some lovely beaches which must have been helpful for Jasmine's smuggling thing. And then five miles along the coast to the south there's Limeport, which is a grade two settlement. It's something of a local metropolis; a lot of Stanmore folk will go there from time to time for the market. I don't know if you saw the market in Stanmore this morning, but it's pretty basic. There's a big entry point just outside Limeport, which is regularly used for possessions, and you've also got access from the sea, of course, which is handy if things get hairy..."

Henry kept talking, describing the history of the settlement, the local geography and the Project arrangements, but Sam wasn't really listening. As he stared around at the reed beds, the ruined cottages and the distant plume of smoke, and felt the weight of sky stretched above him, he was overtaken by a strong feeling that these things were not as alien to him as they should have been. If he had not actually seen them before, then at least he could remember, from a long time ago, how it *felt* to see them. If he was not quite at home in that curious landscape, neither did he feel entirely foreign.

It was an unsettling feeling—exciting, but unsettling. Sam shivered and dug his fingers into the damp earth at the top of the trench. He pulled up a handful of soil and cradled it tenderly in his palm.

Chapter Ten
Strong and Unexamined Affections

"Honestly, it's different when you're inside the enclosure in real-space, Rache. You can touch things and they don't disappear. You can feel the sun and the wind. Everything's well ... *real*."

Rachel frowned and licked a blob of jam off her finger.

"Yes, but what did you actually see up there?"

"Just a sort of marsh and a couple of ruined houses, but that's not the point. You're actually looking at the real thing, not at holographs. Think about it, if I'd got out of that trench and kept walking I'd eventually have met a real fenlander, somebody whose thoughts and ideas are completely different from mine, who feels differently, and knows different things—like someone from outer space or something."

"Well, I'm glad you didn't get it into your head to go walkabout, Sam. I wouldn't want to see you chemically curtailed. Let's face it, you're dozy enough as it is."

Sam grinned and sliced a piece of cheese off the block on his lap. He smeared it with pickle and stuffed it into his mouth.

They had been home for about half an hour. When they got in they had discovered a scribbled message from Mrs. Moorcroft demanding that Roger and Jen should get down to the restaurant "asap if you want to hang on to your jobs," so the pair of them had got changed quickly and hurried out. Left on their own Sam and Rachel had collected food from the kitchen and settled themselves outside under the Moorcrofts' old apple tree for a picnic.

Sam shifted his back against the tree trunk and tilted his face towards the evening sun. He felt calm and delighted with everything. The visit to Ely had been far more exciting than he had expected, especially the complicated feelings that had flowed through him as he had stood in the observation trench and held the soil from the enclosure in his hand. He knew beyond doubt that he would go back to the Project again and again: to visit the double pubs by himself; to go wandering through the settlements one after another by holograph; and perhaps, if he was lucky, to get another glimpse into the real-space enclosure. The Project was like an enormous book, or an enormous library of books, that he could study at his leisure for years and years to come, and the thought was magnificent. But for now he was content to lay his ideas concerning Ely to one side. The Project was the sort of thing that was so big and important that it would stay alive in your mind somewhere even if you weren't actually thinking about it. And anyway, now it was time to put the other part of his birthday plan into operation.

"Do you want to share a bottle of wine, Rache?" he asked suddenly. Rachel looked at him astonished.

"Sam, your mum knows exactly how much wine she has. If you nick a bottle she'll know straight away that one's missing."

"So what if she does. She won't know it's me who's taken it, will she? She'll probably think it's Roger and Jen. They're always taking wine and food and stuff from the restaurant."

"Yeah, but eventually she'll ask if it was you and you'll own up straight away, just like you always do."

Sam stood up.

"Well, ok, so what if she does find out? I'm 16, Rache; I don't always have to do what my mum says."

Rachel grinned.

"Sam, are you suddenly getting all rebellious? How exciting."

"Look, do you want some wine or not?"

"Yeah, ok, it'd be nice, actually."

Sam nodded and headed back to the house. Rachel called after him, "Just make sure your mum knows it was you who nicked it, alright?"

Sam padded quickly down to the cellar and grabbed the bottle of red wine that he had selected the day before—a dusty, posh-looking one that, according to the label, came from "vineyards of the well-established Burgundy enclosure, where the vintner's ancient art blends seamlessly with the sophiocratic ideal." He took two glasses and a corkscrew from the kitchen and went back outside feeling guilty and determined and faintly ridiculous all at once. At the back door he paused: Rachel was still sitting under the apple tree with her shoes kicked off and her legs stretched out in front of her. Her hair had fallen loose again and she kept running her hand through it absent-mindedly, making it ripple and shimmer in the sunlight. Her eyes were shut against the brightness and Sam could just make out her dark eyelashes fluttering against her skin. He closed his own eyes and tried to reconstruct her face in his imagination. He could manage the basic shape and the colour but, just like the million other times he had tried, as soon as he began to fit in any of the features the whole thing shimmered away like a reflection on rippling water. It was stupid; there wasn't a single face in the world that he thought about more often and yet there wasn't another that he found so impossible to remember. Opening his eyes again he found Rachel staring at him and smiling.

"Well, come on then, rebel boy, don't just stand there," she called. "Now that you've done the dreadful deed we might as well enjoy our ill-gotten gains."

Sam gulped and marched across the garden. He sat back down next to her and wedged the bottle between his knees to open it. He filled one of the glasses and handed it to Rachel, then filled the other one for himself. Rachel lifted her glass towards him.

"Well, Sam, cheers. Congratulations on getting to 16, only four and a half weeks after me." She sipped her wine. "And thanks for a great day. It was brilliant."

Sam drank some wine and half closed his eyes, feeling himself pleasantly caught between the heat of the sun outside him and the complicated warmth of the wine inside. He took a second sip and then a third and a fourth, and then he said as casually as he could:

"I wonder if they fall in love inside the enclosure in the same way we do?"

"I think breeding and stuff's pretty strictly controlled, isn't it? Jen said that they sort out birth control through things they put in the water and if there's a couple they want to mate for alphas or drones or whatever, they see to that through drugs as well."

"Yeah, yeah, I know, but once they've done all that, I wonder if the fenlanders actually *feel* love in the same sort of way we do."

Rachel shrugged.

"Why are you suddenly so interested in this, Sam? Did you see someone you fancied up in Stanmore? Please don't tell me you're going to turn into a sad old man with a crush on some enclosure teenager with pink cheeks and big boobs. I know we've been friends for a long time but there are limits."

"No, nothing like that. I was just wondering if love felt the same everywhere."

A small, private smile played around Rachel's lips. She took a big gulp of wine.

"I don't think love even feels the same way in the same person, to be honest. I mean, I certainly love different people in different ways. I think most people do, don't they?"

"Yeah. Yeah. I suppose I do too. Um … what sort of ways do you mean?"

"Well look, I love my mum and dad in a sort of irritated, grateful way. They annoy me like mad, but I can't imagine them not being there and I care about them loads, obviously. And I love my friends in a more relaxed, fun sort of way, I suppose. Like I actually enjoy being with them, which to be honest I don't always with my mum and dad. Then I love Hamlet in another way. I love him because he needs me and he never ever does anything horrible to me."

"But Hamlet's a dog."

"Doesn't mean I can't love him. And then of course there's proper love, being *in love* with sex and everything, and I think that's different again."

Sam gulped his wine and inched closer to Rachel. She glanced at him and grinned.

"I think being in love is always pretty complicated. I think it's probably just as much horrible as it is wonderful, even though no one ever says that. And I think that the horribleness of it is worth it because it feels so fantastic. And actually, Sam, yes I do think it must be similar wherever people feel it, even inside the enclosure, because I think it's kind of vital to who we are. Oh yeah, and it makes you do stupid, irresponsible things that you wouldn't normally approve of; but somehow if you're in love they're not stupid or irresponsible anymore."

Sam nodded.

"And what about you and me, Rache?" he said slowly. "What … what … sort of cat…category are we in?"

Rachel turned to him and for a moment her face slid into a kind of softness that he had seen before when an animal or a child was ill.

"Oh Sam, you're my oldest friend in the world. I think you probably know more about me than anyone else, including my mum and dad. I absolutely cannot imagine you not being around and I feel completely comfortable with you, so yes, I do love you. In fact, I love you a lot."

Sam was silent. He refilled his wine glass with shaky fingers and stared at the grass. Rachel carried on:

"God, I feel weird saying that. But perhaps it's the sort of thing people *should say* occasionally. And I've had a bit of wine so I'm afraid I'm going to keep going. After all, it is your birthday. I love you, Sam Moorcroft, because you're sort of vague and unfinished, and because you just drift around without bothering much what people think. I love you because you're shy and kind, and your mum still buys all your clothes and makes you look nice in them. I love you *because you're my best friend*. But obviously I'm not *in love* with you, Sam; you don't have to worry about that."

For a long time Sam peered intently into his glass without speaking. Finally he said softly, "Yeah, yeah, obviously."

Rachel took another big sip of wine and topped up her glass. She went on, "I mean, in some ways it would be convenient if we were in love with each other, wouldn't it? It would all be really easy. But I think one of the awkward things about being in love is that it can happen between completely inappropriate, mismatched people. It's not easy. It's not *meant* to be easy. Do you know what I mean? The papers are full of married men who've run off with their secretaries or women who have sex with their son's teenage friends and get semi-curtailed for it. Even those saddos up at the Project who get all funny over Enclosure girls. They're all in love in a way, even if it seems a bit, you know, distasteful. The point is you can't always control who you fall in love with. It's *not* always convenient." She paused. "Are you all right, Sam? You look a bit pale. The wine's not disagreeing with you, is it? I don't want to have to explain things to your mum if you end up covered in puke."

"No. No. I'm fine," Sam said in a small, dry voice. "I … er … I read a thing the other day about men who actually do it with drones."

"Yeah, well, that's just gross, obviously. But you get my point. Being in love and sex and everything is so bloody complicated. In the end I think you've just got to be honest with yourself, work out what you want and then get on with it, and try not to hurt people too much as you go along."

"Yeah, I suppose so," Sam said quietly.

The pair of them talked for a whole hour, until the dancing shadows cast by the apple tree lengthened almost to the house and a cool wind put goose bumps on their bare arms. In fact Rachel did most of the talking, becoming flushed and excited as she warmed to her theme and the wine had its effect. Sam mostly just agreed with her; he feared that his voice might crack if he attempted too long a sentence of his own. And even as he was agreeing, he grew increasingly bewildered by the strange, animated girl who shared the wine and the tree trunk with him. Rachel had become *different.* She felt differently from him and knew different things. And although she loved him, she was definitely not *in love* with him because love wasn't meant to be easy or convenient. You just had to get on with it, didn't you? It was just so bloody complicated, wasn't it? Sam could only nod and agree. He felt disconcerted and miserable as the day settled itself softly into dusk.

Eventually Rachel glanced at her watch.

"Bloody hell, Sam, it's nearly nine. I'd better get going. Do you want some help clearing up?

"No, it's ok. I've … I've got plenty of time. You get off."

"All right. Just make sure you stuff that wine bottle to the back of the recycle bin, ok? With a bit of luck your mum might not spot it for a week or two."

Sam shrugged.

"I'll probably tell her. You're right, I always own up to stuff in the end. I may as well get it over with."

"Oh, Sam," Rachel said, "I really do like you a lot, you know." She leant over again and kissed him gently on the cheek. Sam looked away quickly.

"That's twice you've kissed me today."

"Yeah, well, it is your birthday," Rachel said as she scrambled to her feet. "Don't worry, I won't make a habit of it. And I'm sorry if I've bored the arse off you going on about love and sex and everything. I've been thinking about it recently, that's all."

"You haven't bored me," Sam said as he got up and followed her into the house. He opened the front door for her in the hall and she squeezed him briefly on the arm.

"Well listen, thanks again for a great day. I'll call you tomorrow maybe."

"Yeah, ok. I'm supposed to be starting work in the restaurant in the evening but I'm in before that."

"Right."

Rachel turned and walked down the street. Sam watched as she hurried across the road to avoid a squad of drones on litter duty and then vanished round the corner. He closed the door and stood in the cool silence of the hall for a few moments with his head bowed, and then went back out to the garden and gathered up the picnic things. He washed and dried the plates mechanically and put the leftover food away, then trailed upstairs and flopped down on his bed.

He was surprised at how little he actually felt. There was a numbness inside him as well as a vague, uncomfortable feeling that he might have made himself look stupid.

"But really, I didn't say anything awful," he murmured after a couple of minutes. "It's not like I actually told her that I loved her or anything. It's all ok, really. It's all still normal."

Even as he spoke them, however, the words sounded phony, and suddenly Sam just wanted to forget everything and be comforted. He pulled on his enhancement clip and turned the dial to maximum, enjoying the pleasant liquefying feeling that immediately swamped his thoughts. After a moment he rolled over dreamily to face the wall and as he did so his head struck something hard under his pillow. He reached up and his fingers closed softly over his copy of *Soul Freedom*. Retrieving the little book he juggled it clumsily for a moment while his anaesthetised mind struggled to identify it in his memory. Finally he turned the clip down a couple of notches.

"Oh yeah, yeah, that thing off Jen and Roger," he slurred. He opened the book at the first page and scanned through the text to find the place he had got to that morning. Then, curling up like a child, he began to read where he had left off.

Myself and my colleague Dr. Marcus Gormley were invited to Sebastian's rooms in what was then Jesus College for our six-monthly department meeting. This was Sebastian's first meeting since he took charge of the ship and I think he felt it was time that he took our feeble little department in hand.

It's difficult to credit today, when Anthropology and Posthumanism has transformed itself into the sophiocratic system and become the ruling principle of two thirds of the globe, but in those days the discipline was regarded with distaste by most British people. The subject had been born in the age of empire and had flourished after the Second War Between Brothers by quickly making its peace with the new German establishment. The Germans handed over bundles of cash and created numerous interesting research opportunities, and in return A and P people smiled politely, crossed their fingers and affirmed the great intellectual calibre of our new overlords. If the money was right, some academic or other could always be relied upon to spout off about how closely the New European Order corresponded to the ideal of Sophia. It was embarrassing to have to hand out honorary doctorates to bone-headed thugs in jack boots, but the embarrassment was something that A and P people could learn to live with.

With time, however, the force of the New European Order began to wane in Britain. In retrospect this should not be a surprise; most normal people get fed up pretty quickly with endless saluting and marching, not to mention countless films about the glories of the 1,000-year Reich (mostly screened on Sunday afternoons when, let's face it, all one really fancies is getting sloshed and putting one's feet up with an old Jane Austen video). No tyranny lasts forever and gradually the New European Order met greater and greater resistance, both passive and active. As the NEO gently fell apart, so Anthropology and Posthumanism began to lose credibility in academic life and respectability in the country generally. It was this situation that Seb Randall was determined to rectify.

In the interests of honesty I should make it clear that at the time of the meeting I was a committed, if rather jaded, practitioner of Anthropology and Posthumanism. I sincerely believed that if humanity could direct the light of reason into that swirl of chemistry and alienation which are its core, the path would be set for our race's transformation into a new breed of intelligent, healthy, beautiful, peaceful beings. I believed that my involvement in A and P was a fundamentally moral undertaking and I believed myself to be a clever woman well deserving of her place in the subject's vanguard. Also in the interest of honesty, I should perhaps admit that I was deeply attracted to Sebastian himself. In many ways he seemed to embody the perfected humanity that I was striving for, a prototype of the brave new world I believed I would help him to create. Perhaps if I had found some way of speaking frankly to him—or to anybody—about my feelings, I would have had my emotions under tighter control and been rather more probing when he outlined his extraordinary plans. I have often noticed that people who are under the influence of strong and unexamined personal affections can act in very peculiar ways.

The reader should keep this in mind and try to be generous to an old woman who is perhaps rather less clever than she once imagined and who never reached the promised land of beauty and wisdom that she once dreamt about.

Sam let the book slip from his fingers and closed his eyes. Part of what he had just read reminded him of something, something recent and important, but he wasn't sure what. He groped around in the sweet ooze and flow of his mind to try and remember what it was, but the thought eluded him. Finally, he grinned at the silliness of worrying about it, or about anything at all, and reached again for the dial of the enhancement clip. He turned it back up to maximum. The charge dug deeper into his brain and within moments he was sound asleep.

Chapter Eleven
Sometimes You Have to Face Things

Sam had only been working in his mum and dad's restaurant for four weeks but he already recognised *the crisis*. It came at about nine o'clock every Friday and Saturday evening (Sam only worked weekends) when the restaurant was full of people at different stages of their meals, all demanding starters, mains, desserts, wine, cigars, or their bill—and demanding them immediately. If you listened carefully when the heavy service doors swung open you could hear snatches of the diners' orders to the harassed waiting staff, "Could you try and track down that bottle of claret, please? We ordered it a good 20 minutes ago; it's not really acceptable to have to wait this long."

"We asked for pan-fried *enclosure* vegetables, young lady. Now these leeks have clearly never been anywhere near Ely. Look at them, they're bloody anaemic?"

"Quick love, where's the toilet? I'm bursting."

The atmosphere in the kitchen was pretty frantic at the best of times, but during the crisis it became positively violent. Mrs. Moorcroft stood, pink-faced and furious, at the hot plate, grabbing the new orders as they came down from the restaurant and bellowing instructions around the kitchen. Junior chefs slid about frantically at her command with piles of raw vegetables or simmering saucepans cradled to their chests, shouting and swearing at anyone who got in their way. Things got spilt and people got scalded or cut. Sam had twice seen punches thrown during the crisis; he made sure that he kept himself tucked away behind the huge sink until the busiest period was over. He worked washing pots with Froggy, one of the restaurant's two drones; the pair of them seemed to have reached a tacit agreement to keep as low a profile as possible.

Tonight, however, the crisis seemed to be worse than ever. Mrs. Moorcroft's cheeks were purple and there were four pools of spilt sauces dotted around the kitchen, making it treacherous underfoot. Also the noises from the restaurant were more raucous than usual; Sam had heard swearing and cheering, and even the sound of glass being smashed. He and Froggy were working as quickly as they could but the pile of sizzling pans and dirty plates on the working surface next to them never seemed to get any smaller. They had already had three saucepans thrown back at them—one of them narrowly missing Sam's head—because they hadn't got them properly clean.

Like most drones, Froggy was peculiarly sensitive to atmosphere and now, as the kitchen became chaotic and aggressive, Sam was conscious of him getting tense. From time to time he would run a sudsy hand anxiously across his bald head and down onto his cheek, leaving trails of bubbles across his face. Then he would frown deeply and make a frightened squeaking noise, glancing nervously at Mrs. Moorcroft and hopping from foot to foot so that Sam began to worry that he would slip over. When he had finished dancing around he would work with renewed vigour for a few minutes before repeating the process.

About half an hour into the crisis, the drone suddenly twitched and dropped the frying pan he was scrubbing into the sink so that it splashed water all over the floor. He crouched down behind the work surface and closed his eyes, sticking one finger in his ear. Sam glanced up to check what was bothering him and saw Jen bursting through the service doors looking flustered. She and Mrs. Moorcroft eyed each other suspiciously.

"Any sign of those entrées for table four?" Jen asked breathlessly. "They're getting rather impatient up there."

Mrs. Moorcroft wiped her forehead with a towel and peered at the line of orders arranged on hooks in front of her.

"Not a chance, Jen. The order only came down a couple of minutes ago. It's going to be 20 minutes at least. Tell them that they'll just have to wait."

"I think the order came down at least *ten* minutes ago," Jen said, reddening. "It's really awkward to keep putting them off, you know. Can you please try and get a move on?"

Mrs. Moorcroft shoved her glasses up her glistening nose and pointed a stubby finger in Jen's face.

"Listen, young lady. First of all, you don't talk to me like that in my own bloody kitchen. Secondly, although you might not be aware of it, swanning about in the restaurant in your pretty little frock, we are actually rather busy down here. So why don't you go back through those doors, smile sweetly at table four and explain that they might have to wait for a minute or two, all right?"

The noise in the kitchen died away as Mrs. Moorcroft spoke. Next to Sam, Froggy was rocking backwards and forwards on his haunches and humming tunelessly to himself.

"All right, Angela, if that's what you suggest, I'll give it a go," Jen said. "But don't be surprised if you end up with injured waiters and a trashed restaurant. You see, table four happens to be taken by a party of alphas."

"Oh, for God's sake, that's all we need," Mrs. Moorcroft said softly. "Who let them in?" She stood with her hands on her hips, swallowing repeatedly so that the layers of fat on her neck flexed and sagged alarmingly.

Sam tucked himself further behind the sink and wondered how long it would be until he could go home. The presence of alphas in the restaurant would explain the smashed glass and the swearing, and might mean very serious trouble indeed. Alphas were one of the major Fruit of Sophia; they were genetically crafted purpose-breeds who were ordered by those few parents who could afford them from the Department of Enclosure-Advanced Fertility. Sam was hazy about the science involved—although he had read somewhere that it took up to 25 enclosure fetuses to manufacture a single alpha—but like everyone else he knew only too well about the finished product. Alphas were physically beautiful and extremely bright, but they were also incredibly arrogant. In Britain, they tended to go to three or four of the country's best public schools and then on to a couple of well-known alpha colleges at Oxford and Cambridge. They were only supposed to marry and reproduce with other alphas in order to preserve the excellence of their genes. When they weren't propagating themselves, younger alphas banded together into dining clubs, complete with fancy uniforms and passwords, and got appallingly drunk in unsuspecting restaurants. Often the places they visited had to be closed for several weeks afterwards while the damage was repaired. Sam wasn't surprised that Jen was worried; alphas could turn violent if they didn't get the first class service they believed was their birthright. They always paid hefty sums in compensation afterwards—they could afford to—but still…

"Well, who let them in?" Mrs. Moorcroft demanded again.

"I think it was Roger who actually took the booking. But it wasn't really his fault; they booked in as the Bethnel Green Aqualung Society. He couldn't have known who they were."

"Well, he might have bloody guessed there was something odd about it. Bethnel Green's hardly overrun with enchanting coves and freshwater bloody lakes, is it? Anyway, where is he when we need him?"

"He's got the night off. He's gone to see a friend over in…' Jen began, but Mrs. Moorcroft interrupted her.

"Yes, all right, I don't actually want to know where he is; I'm just annoyed that he's not here to help." She frowned and rubbed her face again with her towel. "All right, here's what we do. First of all, you go up there and apologise for the delay. Be extremely polite but don't let them see that you're afraid or we've had it, understand? While you do that I'll ring the police and let them know that we may have a problem. How many of them are there?"

"Twelve."

"Twelve! Bloody hell fire! Well look, give them four bottles of house red by way of an apology for the wait and then … oh God, leave this to me."

While Mrs. Moorcroft had been speaking, the serving doors had swung open again and one of the alphas had strolled into the kitchen. He was well over six feet tall, blond (Caucasian alphas were nearly always blond) and extraordinarily handsome. His well-muscled frame was encased in a bright blue tailcoat from which a froth of lace erupted at the neck. He peered around the kitchen disdainfully.

"Good lord, aren't people pathetic," he drawled. "Actually working in a hell hole like this, I mean, who'd do it? Honestly?" He sighed theatrically and lit a cigarette, shaking his head in disbelief. "Now then, may I ask who's in charge here, please?"

"That's me, young man," said Mrs. Moorcroft grimly. "You

shouldn't really be down here, you know."

"I shouldn't really be down here." the alpha squeaked in a fair impression of Mrs. Moorcroft's voice. "The point is, *I am* down here and there's not an awful lot you can do about it, is there?"

"Not an awful lot, no. But look, if you go back to your table, we'll get your entrées to you as soon as we can. I'm sorry about the delay; we'll make you the priority."

The alpha scooped a couple of pieces of lamb's liver from one of the plates waiting to go to the restaurant and shoved them into his mouth. He licked the sauce off his fingers and belched loudly.

"Too right you'll make us a priority. The thing is, my dear, we should have been a priority from the moment we walked in. My friends and I don't take kindly to waiting while a load of slug-heads get served ahead of us, do you understand? So what I suggest you do is sort our food out straight away and then bring it to our table personally with a public apology for the delay. In fact, why don't you bring it to us on your knees? That way you might just have a bit of restaurant left tomorrow morning."

Mrs. Moorcroft nodded but before she could answer, the door from the meat store swung open, banging against the wall like a pistol shot. Mr. Moorcroft walked into the kitchen. He was carrying a meat cleaver, still pink with blood. Next to Sam, Froggy emitted a piercing squeal.

"Some sort of pr…problem, Angela?" Mr. Moorcroft asked softly as he approached the alpha.

"Not really, Arthur, no. This gentleman's food has been slightly delayed but we've sorted it all out now. He's just about to go back up to the restaurant."

"Excellent. I tr…trust you've impressed upon him that it's highly improper for him to be down here in the first place and that if h…he or his associates behave inappropriately a..again we'll have to ask them to l..leave."

Mr. Moorcroft planted himself in front of the alpha and smiled up at him pleasantly. The alpha swayed and moved his lips silently for a moment. Then he said, "Now look here, you short-arsed, slug-head little oik. As I was just explaining to fat face here…"

Before he could get any further, Mr. Moorcroft slammed the flat of meat cleaver hard against the alpha's cheek. He held it there, pressed into his flesh, while animal blood dripped over his chin and down onto the ruffles of his shirt.

"It has always amazed me how so much time and m…m…money is put into making you people such perfect physical and mental specimens and y…yet no one ever bothers to teach you elem…entary manners," Mr. Moorcroft said. "So regardless of what you may have been discussing with my wife, l…let me make a few things clear. First of all, you are going to go back to your table and y…you will not come back into the kitchen again. Secondly, you will wait in turn for your food l…like everyone else. Thirdly, if you or any of your associates threaten any of our st…staff or customers, or break as much as a single wine gl…glass, I will personally do you gr…grave harm. Do you understand?"

Mr. Moorcroft's face twisted in loathing. He moved the cleaver so that the blade pressed harder against the alpha's flesh.

"Do y…you understand?" he asked again.

The alpha dropped his cigarette onto the kitchen floor. He nodded quickly and backed away from Mr. Moorcroft before turning on his heel and slipping back through the service doors. The kitchen was absolutely silent.

"Sorry about the his…his…histrionics, everyone," Mr. Moorcroft said quietly. "I don't think they'll give you anymore bother, Rachel, but if they do pl…please let me know immediately."

Rachel nodded and followed the alpha back into the restaurant. Mr. Moorcroft turned to his wife.

"Are you all right, Angela?"

"Yes, thank you, Arthur. More or less. At least I am now." Mrs. Moorcroft reached out and squeezed her husband's wrist. "Now then, have you done those cutlets that I asked you for? We'll be needing them in a minute?"

"Yes, y…yes they're on the side in the cold store," Mr. Moorcroft replied meekly. "You can have them whenever you w…want."

Mrs. Moorcroft nodded, shoved her spectacles back up her nose and consulted the row of orders.

"Right then, everybody, the party's over. Let's get some work done, shall we? I need three T-bones, two rare, one medium; four mixed veg, two organic enclosure, two just organic; and four new spuds in butter. And let's get a move on; we've lost a lot of time."

Gradually, the sounds of chopping and stirring picked up again around the kitchen. Mr. Moorcroft collected a tray of cutlets for his wife and then wandered over to the sink and handed Sam the cleaver.

"Sorry to m…make more work for you, Sam, but could you give this a r…rinse please."

"Yeah, course dad. Um … are you ok?"

"Fine, thanks."

"I've never seen you do anything like that…'

"I'm f…fine, Sam, really."

As Sam rinsed the cleaver, Mr. Moorcroft crouched next to Froggy. The drone was curled up in a ball and mumbling to himself, his clothes soaked with washing up water.

"He doesn't like it when it gets tense," Sam said. "He's a good worker, though."

"Yes…Yes, I know, Sam."

Mr. Moorcroft wiped the drone's face gently with his handkerchief and smoothed down his shirt before helping him to his feet.

"Don't worry. You're fine n…now. It's all over now," he murmured. He turned to the pastry chef who was working nearby.

"Are y…you busy, Billy?"

"Fairly, Mr. M. Why do you ask?"

"Could you spare a couple of m…minutes to take Froggy here to his pod. He's a bit up…upset. Give him his injections and fluids and then put him on the cl…clip and see if you can settle h…him down for the night."

The pastry chef looked doubtful.

"I think the boss likes him to stay to the end of service, Mr. M."

"Don't worry, I'll ex…explain to Angela."

"Fair enough."

The pastry chef put down his mixing bowl and dusted his hands off on his apron. He came and took Froggy's hand.

"That's right, you go with Billy," Mr. Moorcroft said. "He'll l...look after you."

Still shaking, the drone allowed himself to be led away through the kitchen's back door. Mr. Moorcroft turned back to Sam, rolling up his sleeves.

"Sorry, Sam, I've robbed you of your col...colleague just when you're busiest. The least I can d...do is replace him for a while."

"Don't you have to do your meat stuff though, dad?"

Mr. Moorcroft plunged his hands into the sink and fished out the frying pan that Froggy had dropped.

"It's all done. I'll let you in on a little s...secret about catering, Sam. Most of the time kitchens don't really have to be as h...hectic as they seem." Mr. Moorcroft smiled crookedly. "I think it's fair to s...say that some people rather relish the tension. Unlike poor old Fr...Froggy."

Sam and his dad worked alongside each other in silence. Mr. Moorcroft worked incredibly quickly, scraping and rinsing pots vigorously until the veins bulged in his thick wrists. After ten minutes he tossed the heavy pan from the deep fat fryer onto the draining board as if it weighed almost nothing and said, "Actually, S...Sam, I've been meaning to have a chat with you, for a wh...while."

"Yes, Dad."

"Yes. Um, it's your m...mum who's, um, worried about you, actually."

"What's she worried about now?"

"She thinks that you've been a b...bit odd since your birthday. Actually, she's worried that E...Ely might have unsettled you somehow."

"How could Ely have unsettled me?"

"Well, y...you've been a bit distant and...'

"I'm always distant. Roger's the chatty, normal one, remember."

Mr. Moorcroft frowned.

"Well, there's your r...room as well."

Sam shrugged and dumped a pile of clean cutlery into the draining basket. After a moment, Mr. Moorcroft went on, "Look S...Sam, I'm pleased that you're interested in Ely, honestly..."

"Yeah, you said that before."

"It's tr...true. But there's a good way and a bad way to be interested in it. You shouldn't g...get obsessed."

Sam shrugged again.

"Your mum also th...thinks you may have fallen out with Rachel."

"What makes her think that?"

"Well, you hardly see her anymore. It does seem that you go out of y...your way to avoid her sometimes."

Sam scrubbed ferociously at a saucepan that was sticky with creamy sauce and bits of burnt chicken. He used a knife to work the pieces of meat loose and then scooped them together into a soggy mass and dumped them into the dustbin under the sink.

"We're busy, Dad. It's sixth form. There's loads more work this year and we're in different classes for everything. We just don't see as much of each other."

"Are you really throwing your...yourself that much into your schoolwork?" Mr. Moorcroft asked. Sam didn't answer and for a while they worked in silence again. Then Mr. Moorcroft dropped his scrubbing brush onto the side and leant on the sink, staring at the grey water.

"L...look, Sam, I appreciate that neither myself nor your m...mother are particularly approachable. I wish we were different, but we're n...not. But, having said that, I hope that if something was really bothering y...you, either about Ely or about ... well ... anything else, that you'd feel able to s...say *something* to us."

Mr. Moorcroft paused. There was an ugly scar on his upper arm, the result of carelessness with some hot fat years before. He scratched it sharply so that it glowed red.

"Sometimes you just have to *face* things, Sam," he said gently. "I know it's d...difficult, but sometimes you just have to. Even unpleasant, difficult things."

Chapter Twelve
Rachel

Sam pondered his dad's words as he cycled home from work an hour later. It was probably true that he had been a bit distant with his family recently, and he had certainly been spending a lot of time alone in his bedroom. And his mum was right—of course—it was because of Ely. The truth was that since his birthday Sam had become a voracious reader for the first time in his life, spending long solitary hours working his way through dozens of pamphlets and digi-downloads about the Ely Project. He had begun with the booklet that Jen had given him about the *Deviancy and Dysfunction* exhibition at Stanmore, and when he had finished that he had taken his birthday download tokens to an Ely shop just off Fleet Street and bought a selection of digi-downloads about everything from the first days of the enclosure to contemporary Project life. He had used his wages from the restaurant to add to his collection, buying a new stack of downloads and pamphlets each week. He read everything at great speed, garnering as much information as he could about how people in the enclosure actually lived: how they spoke, what they ate, how they courted and married, how they earned their living, etc. He scribbled notes in the margins of the pamphlets and books as he went along, marking significant pages with luminous plastic tags. He also printed out sections of the digi-downloads that seemed particularly important and stuck them on his bedroom wall. His room had quickly become something of an Ely shrine, the floor stacked with piles of Project literature and the walls plastered with printed sheets illustrating contrasting architectural styles across the Project or tracing the development of the enclosure courtship patterns after the expansion of 1989.

Sam could not have explained why he found the Project so fascinating. He knew that when he was reading or daydreaming about Ely, he felt happy. He knew that the very fact of the enclosure's existence bought him a mixture of exhilaration and peace. Beyond that he was content to leave his motives unexamined.

Obviously, it was a lie about working hard at school. He had chosen English, History, Economics, French and Anthropology and Posthumanism AS level, as well as taking compulsory courses in Sexual Health and the Principles and Development of Sophiocracy. In truth, however, Sam contributed very little to any of his subjects. Not even the A and P and sophiocracy courses fired his enthusiasm. Who could really get interested in questions such as, "Outline the development of longevity technology in the 2030's with special reference to the undertaker project at Swaffam," or "Heinrich Himmler laid the egg that Sebastian Randall hatched. Discuss," when you had felt the cool air of the enclosure catch at the back of your throat, when you had actually grasped a fistful of damp soil from beyond the boundary in your hand? Sam did enough to get by at school, but that was all. He sat quietly in his classes and spent his lunchtimes and free periods in the library reading a download or pamphlet that he had brought from home.

A soft rain began to fall and Sam pedaled harder through the quiet streets. It would be good to get back home, strip off his smelly kitchen clothes, have a shower, and go to bed. And it would be particularly good to read a bit of *Soul Freedom* before he went to sleep. Sam grinned at the prospect. The little volume was the one Ely book that he hadn't read quickly. It was too good to be hurried; it felt peculiarly personal and important, and seemed to demand reverence and restraint. He had grown genuinely fond of Hilary Lynch, relishing her honesty and enjoying her distinctive version of Project history that was sarcastic and sad and delighted by turns. He took ten minutes each day to read a page or so of the book carefully and affectionately, savouring every word.

There was a squad of drones in high-visibility jackets gathered around an open manhole at the top of Sam's street. They were much earlier models than Froggy, with characteristically over-large heads, thick lips and pinched noses. There were two females amongst them, Sam noticed, indistinguishable from the rest except for the black-rimmed spectacles that were fixed to their heads with wire (early model female drones always had bad eyesight for some reason). As Sam approached, one of the males stumbled forward to get out of the way and tripped over the curb. For an awful moment it looked as though he might fall down the manhole, but then another of them—a female—extended a muscular arm and yanked his collar. The male squealed and as Sam sped past he just had time to see the female pull him to herself and stroke him reassuringly on his rainy cheek. It was rare to see that sort of thing with drones, even early models. Sam made a mental note to mention it to Rachel as evidence that drones weren't all horrible or sinister. Then he checked himself and freewheeled for a moment while a sick feeling rose and fell in his throat. He wouldn't be mentioning the drones to Rachel for a while; in fact, he wouldn't be mentioning anything to her. The pair of them were hardly speaking.

His mum was mostly right about that, too. Sam and Rachel hadn't fallen out exactly, but since the conversation under the apple tree he'd found that he had run out of things to say to her. And it wasn't just that she clearly didn't love him, or fancy him, or whatever, in the way he would have liked. As Sam had thought about what she had said that night it seemed clear to him that she had shifted right out of the world they had shared for as long as he could remember into a more complicated and risky world that he didn't understand. What was it that she had said? *You've got to work out what you want and then just get on with it*—something like that. What was that supposed to mean? What was it that you just got on with? Sex, presumably. But if it was sex, how were you supposed to work out what you wanted before you got on with it? And how were you supposed to get on with it if the person you wanted to get on with it with didn't want to get on with it with you?

To begin with, Sam had tried to keep things as normal as possible between the pair of them. But after a couple of awkward conversations when he had ended up tongue tied and queasy, he decided it was easier to avoid her. At first, Rachel had made an effort to keep in touch with him, but then she had seemed content to drift away. That should have been a relief, of course, but it wasn't.

And it wasn't a question of not facing the situation, either, Sam reflected, despite what his dad had said. The situation with Rachel was fundamentally unfaceable because it was mysterious, and it was mysterious because Rachel herself had suddenly become mysterious. That much at least was clear to him.

Sam was still thinking about these things and frowning to himself when he arrived at his house. He dismounted his bike and pushed it along the side passage to the back garden. Here he had to turn right and cross the patio, past the sitting room, to get the bike to the shed. It was always tempting not to bother, of course, but his mum would kill him if she came home and found it left out in the rain. As he trudged past the sitting room window a tiny sound, something between a moan and a whimper, caught his attention. He glanced through the gap in curtains and immediately wished he hadn't. The only light in the room came from the electric fire but its warm glow was sufficient to make out Jen and Roger entwined on the floor. Roger was lying over Jen in such a way that her face was obscured but Sam could clearly see her bare shoulder. Her blouse was discarded on the sofa. He felt himself blush in the darkness.

"They shouldn't bloody do that," he murmured fiercely. "Anybody could walk past, the neighbours or anything. It's ridiculous."

At that moment, almost as if he could hear him, Roger turned and looked towards the window, revealing Jen's face as he did so. Except that it wasn't Jen's face. It *should* have been Jen's face because it was the face that had just been kissing Roger, but it wasn't. *Of course it wasn't*; Jen was still working in the restaurant. Sam felt sick.

Rachel mouthed "Sam' as she scrambled to cover herself with her blouse. Sam couldn't believe how thin her arms were or how strange it was to see them joining her shoulders without the benefit of any clothes. He found himself leaning close to the window so that his breath frosted it. He wiped it clean with his cuff and stared stupidly as Roger pulled on his underpants and strode towards him. Behind him Rachel pulled her blouse on properly, fumbling with the buttons, then grabbed her knickers and skirt and dived out of the room.

"Sam, what the hell are you doing here?" Roger demanded when he had yanked the window open.

"I ... I live here," Sam said stupidly.

"Yeah, but I thought you'd be busy at the restaurant for hours. I booked a party of alphas in tonight."

"What, did you book them on purpose then?"

Roger reddened.

"Yeah, well it's difficult to get any privacy in this bloody place, isn't it? I've been struggling all summer, in case you hadn't noticed."

"You booked *alphas* on purpose?"

"Yes, Sam, I did. Because I wanted to be undisturbed, all right? So how come you're back so early?"

"They weren't much trouble in the end. Dad dealt with them." Sam swallowed hard. "That was Rachel you were with, wasn't it?"

"Yeah, yeah it was. I'm sorry, Sam, but it was. Look, hang on there for a minute and I'll come out. It doesn't seem right to have this sort of conversation through a window."

Roger pulled the window shut with shaking hands and picked up his clothes before leaving the front room. A few minutes later he emerged from the back door fully dressed, carrying two glasses. He handed one to Sam.

"Here you are, drink this. It's whiskey. It might make you feel better."

Sam took the glass and sipped it. The drink was sharp and strong, and made his eyes water.

"Where's Rachel?" he asked when he had swallowed it all.

"She's gone home. It seemed sensible that I should talk to you first. She feels awful."

"I'm not surprised. What about Jen?"

Roger sighed.

"Look, Sam, this must be a horrible shock. I can't believe we were so careless. I'm truly sorry. And so is Rache. She really cares about you, you know. She hates the thought that you might be, you know, upset."

"What about Jen?" Sam said again.

"Sam, I'd love to explain everything to you about myself and Jen but I can't because I've made promises to keep some important things private. But you'll just have to accept that things are complicated between us. They've always been complicated. I *am* fond of her but our relationship isn't quite what it seems, although she doesn't know that, and she mustn't know it. That is very, very important." Roger cleared his throat and went on awkwardly. "And the thing with Rachel just sort of happened, I'm afraid. It turns out that she's liked me for quite a while and I admit that I'm not particularly good at holding myself back in that sort of situation. It's only been going on for a few weeks, since just before your birthday, actually. That's all."

Sam's mind froze. He felt his chest tighten and his eyes burn. He saw again Rachel's naked arms and then her fiddling with her blouse buttons, and for the first time in his life he found that he could recount every detail of her face perfectly. He began to shake.

"I feel sorry for J...Jen," he croaked. "I think it's a load of crap about pr...promises and secrets. I think you just thought y...you could have two girls at once and you jumped at the chance."

"Sam," Roger said gently, "look, I understand that you have, you know, *feelings* for Rachel. You've bloody grown up with the girl, haven't you? I'm really sorry about everything, honestly. What you've just had to go through is awful. I mean it; I can't imagine what it must be like. And what's going on between me and Jen is pretty awful as well, and I admit that I'm responsible for most of it. But I'm afraid you're just going to have to deal with it all, Sam, because awful things happen sometimes." The tenderness in Roger's voice acquired a hard edge. "Dealing with awful things is part of being an adult. And I can't let you ruin things by blabbing to Jen. For all sorts of important reasons I just can't let you. I *won't* let you, Sam, do you understand?"

Sam forced himself to look up and meet his brother's gaze and, meeting it, felt the hatred unfold inside him gently like the unfurling petals of a poisonous flower. He wiped the rain and tears from his face with the back of his hand.

"I won't t…tell Jen," he said shakily. "But I think you should."

Roger shrugged.

"That's up to me, isn't it? Look, do you want to come in for a cup of tea or another whiskey or something?"

"No thanks. I think I'll just go for a walk. Try and s…sort myself out a bit."

"But it's chucking it down."

"I don't care. I … I just don't want to be inside."

"Ok. Well, take care and don't go too far. I'll put your bike away for you, how's that?"

"Thanks."

Roger shrugged.

"Least I can do under the circumstances."

For a wild moment Sam considered going round to Rachel's house and quizzing her. Some desperate, miserable part of him wanted to know everything about her relationship with Roger: how long, precisely, it had been going on; what they said to each other; what they did to each other; what it *felt like* when they were together. But it was late and he was wet and dressed in his kitchen clothes and, anyway, he was probably the last person in the world she wanted to see. Instead, he walked quickly through the rain, unaware of his direction, or the time, or of anything much except the urgent need within him not to be still. While he kept walking the image he had seen through the sitting room window remained unfocussed in his mind. Whenever he slowed or stopped, however, his memory took form and colour and then Sam felt he would collapse with unhappiness.

Eventually, well after one in the morning, when he was wet through and his face was sticky with tears, Sam found that his path had taken him back to the end of his own street. He trudged back to his house, slipped through the front door and crept upstairs. Clearing a small space among the tottering piles of pamphlets and papers in his room, he dumped his wet clothes in a heap on the floor. Then he flopped naked onto his bed and pulled on his enhancement clip. As his thoughts began to soften and blur he reached under the pillow—the action was almost reflex by now—and retrieved his copy of *Soul*

Freedom. As always, the little book felt pleasant and soothing to his touch. He flicked quickly to the place he had reached the previous day and began to read. He had gotten as far as Chapter 3, the opening of the enclosure.

... after that it was simply a matter of slipping a few interesting things into the fenlanders' water supply and tinkering with their heads a little to take the edge off their curiosity. We were obviously able to draw on Sebastian's earlier camp work to complete this side of things and soon the boundary was effectively secure from the inside.

There remained, of course, the issue of guarding the boundary from without. This work was overseen by Marcus Gormley, who did something brave during the Second War Between Brothers and was therefore judged to be well placed to mount the necessary security operation. He recruited a bunch of handsome ex-soldiers and local toughs, dressed them in ridiculous blue uniforms and silly hats, and authorised them to shoot anyone who tried to penetrate the enclosure. This was the beginning of the Boundary Security Corps, and I have to say that, despite the absurd outfits, they did an excellent job. Marcus himself was in his element; he was soon styling himself "Colonel" and spending his days whizzing around in a jeep with a pistol on his hip.

During this period my own responsibilities concerned the management of the enclosure itself. Under Seb's supervision, I recruited a dozen of our best young A and P graduates and used them to enter the enclosure for the purposes of monitoring the natives, maintaining appropriate chemical levels in the water and removing subjects for adjustment or experiment (the research output of Anthropology and Posthumanism was expanding exponentially with the new source of subjects). These 12 were the nucleus of what was to become the Interland Security Service. They were an outstanding team and from the start I encouraged a rather relaxed atmosphere amongst us. We all drank quite a lot and socialised together, which made sense given the demands of the job and the extraordinarily sensitive nature of the work we were undertaking. Truth be told, we regarded ourselves as something of an elite within the

Project from the beginning and we soon became extremely close. For me personally this was a very happy, fulfilled period, perhaps the happiest time of my life. Consider: I was engaged in significant work with regular access to Seb Randall (which mattered to me very much at that point), and I was working with tremendously bright young people whom I liked and respected. I might have been old and fat and ugly, but I was old and fat and ugly and important. And I was surrounded by clever and attractive young people who liked and respected me for who I was.

Things were by no means perfect, of course. From the beginning of the Project we faced significant domestic opposition and were constantly engaged in a propaganda battle that would occasionally flare into violence. There were also the inevitable jurisdictional tussles between different groups associated with the Project, notably Marcus and myself. The fact is the two of us had never particularly liked each other during the lean years at Cambridge, and success only sharpened our animosity. I suppose he felt—correctly—that I was a bit smug about the quality of my own operation compared with his band of yobs. For my part, I thought his whole military manner was ridiculously affected, and I was concerned that he might take more power for his people than was appropriate. With Marcus, as far as I was concerned, it was always a bit quis custodiet ipsos custodies.

When the complexity and unpleasantness of daily life threatened to become overwhelming, however, I had the glorious option of retreating into the enclosure world for an hour or so. This I did often, either alone or with colleagues from my own unit. Often I would simply walk along the narrow fenland footpaths listening to the birds and enjoying the warmth of the sun on my back (the sunshine always felt warmer within the enclosure—I don't know why). Occasionally, I would visit one of the enclosed settlements in some guise or other and enjoy a drink and a chat with the locals. There was— and is—a real feeling of liberty to be had in crossing over that I can scarcely describe. Let me say simply that each trip across the boundary felt like a minor rebirth. Things felt peaceful and possible when I was on the other side...

Sam slammed the book shut and pushed it back under his pillow, then ripped off his enhancement clip and lay back with his hands behind his head staring at the ceiling. After a couple of minutes he leapt off the bed and began weaving his way up and down his bedroom, still naked, in between the piles of Ely literature. His exhaustion was completely forgotten and the sadness of the evening was suddenly outflanked by dangerous and extraordinary possibilities. Except, Sam told himself, they weren't really possibilities because what he was thinking about was completely and utterly impossible. In fact, it was more than impossible; it was unthinkable. Absolutely unthinkable. Every reasonable and obedient part of his mind told him so. And yet… And yet… he was thinking it. His heart beat quickly and delicately as Hilary's words danced and looped around his brain: *There was a real feeling of liberty to be had in crossing over. Each trip across the boundary felt like a minor rebirth. Things felt peaceful and possible when I was on the other side.*

A great and irresponsible joy gathered within him and he found himself shaking and laughing as he paced the room. Steadying himself, he gathered up a number of Ely pamphlets and downloads from the clutter on the floor and loaded the downloads into his digipad. He grabbed a pen and notebook off his desk, then sat on the edge of his bed and began to read, making hurried notes as he did so.

Chapter Thirteen
Interrupted Breakfast

Sir Douglas Latch was enjoying an early breakfast of eggs and kippers in the mess of the Interland Security Service, central region. His rank obliged him to sit by himself at the high table, surrounded by the splendid silver place settings that were already arranged for that evening's dinner. Irritatingly, as far as he was concerned, a single candle had been lit for him, making the silverware sparkle richly in the dimly lit room. A low murmur of conversation arose from the two dozen interlander officers who were breakfasting alone or in small groups at the long wooden tables beneath him. The officers all wore the same black uniform as Sir Douglas himself and like Sir Douglas they wore it carelessly, even scruffily. Shirts were untucked, buttons were left undone, belts and shoes were scuffed and worn. This was in marked contrast to the impeccably turned out stewards who drifted up and down the room in white jackets and trousers, serving food, coffee and stronger drink. Three large cats also meandered slowly between tables searching for scraps from the breakfasters. The peaceful scene was overlooked by portraits of senior ISS officers past and present that lined the wood-paneled walls. Pride of place above the high table went to the same picture of the elderly woman that graced the walls of Sir Douglas's office. Next to her was a smaller portrait of Sir Douglas himself, of which he was deeply embarrassed. He was glad that he couldn't actually see it from where he was sitting.

Sir Douglas was chewing his second kipper when a rich, jolly voice rippled up to him from the foot of the high table steps.

"Ah, Douglas, good to see you, old chap. Mind if I join you?"

Sir Douglas rolled his eyes in frustration, but he managed a thin smile at the newcomer.

"Not at all, Timothy; it's always lovely to see you. Sit yourself down. I can heartily recommend the kippers and the eggs but not the toast this morning, I'm afraid. They get this new stuff straight from Fakenham which crumbles as soon as you put a knife to it. It's tasty enough but it's just not meant for toasting."

The newcomer clambered up the steps and planted himself opposite Sir Douglas. He patted his bulging stomach.

"Right you are, Douglas. I shall have a word at the next householder committee meeting. You can rely on me."

"I'm sure I can rely on you to sort out the catering, Timothy."

Timothy smiled and clicked his fingers. An elderly steward stepped smartly to his side.

"Can I help you, sir?"

"Yes, I rather think you can. I'll have some fruit please, then scrambled egg and kippers. And tell me, do we have any squirrel in this morning?"

"I believe so, sir."

"Excellent. I'll have a little of that as well, grilled please, but for God's sake tell chef not to overdo it. Oh, and some coffee, of course, and perhaps a chocolate milkshake as well. Have you got all that?"

"I think so, sir."

"Excellent. Well, off you go, then."

The steward glided down the steps and Timothy licked his lips contentedly.

"I got a taste for squirrel when I was based up near Lincoln in the 40's. They cook it with fennel and something else up there, but I never quite worked out what the something else was. I've never had it half as good outside the enclosure."

"True of so many things, Timothy, I'm afraid."

"True enough. True enough." Timothy frowned and explored the inside of his right ear with a plump little finger. "You weren't around last night, Douglas. I wanted to speak to you about timings for Saturday's possession over at Bletchenam, but when I rang your office I kept getting put through to that rather bovine brass-buckle you retain as your adjutant, and all he would tell me was that you were unavailable. He wouldn't tell me why or where you were, cheeky bugger."

Sir Douglas continued eating in silence while Timothy eyed him speculatively. Eventually he said, "I checked the operations lists of course, and you hadn't crossed over. And you weren't in the mess because I came and had a look myself."

Sir Douglas poured himself a large glass of claret and sipped it carefully.

"If Tony didn't tell you where I was that *may* have been because I had instructed him to keep mum. I don't call that bovine; I call it doing as you're told."

"I see. So you were somewhere secret, were you?"

Sir Douglas sighed.

"Oh, I may as well tell you, I suppose; you'll find out soon enough anyway. I was up in town at the Guardian's Office for a security briefing. There you are, Timothy, you've winkled it out of me with your extraordinary powers of interrogation. Congratulations."

Timothy arched an eyebrow.

"A security briefing at the Guardian's Office, eh? How thrilling. And tell me, is there anything in particular on the horizon, security wise? Anything that affects the Service, I mean?"

"There would hardly be any point in me attending the briefing if it didn't affect the Service, would there? If you must know," Sir Douglas leant across the table and dropped his voice so that it was barely audible. "If you must know, we are about to be put on the alert against a code red boundary breach, expected in the next six to twelve months."

Timothy's mouth dropped open.

"Good Lord, are we really? What, is this the fen-lib people again?"

"Yes, I'm sorry to say that it is. As usual, MI5, Special Branch and the BSC are all playing their silly power games and refusing to pool information properly, but this time they do seem genuinely nervous. I gather that we more or less know the who, but not the when or the where. It's the gallant young men from Cambridge again, I'm afraid."

The two men sat back in their seats as the steward arrived and unloaded Timothy's food. Timothy dismissed the man with a curt nod and leant forward again.

"Always bloody Cambridge, Douglas. Why should Cambridge produce all the rebels; do they put something in the water there? It's Randall's own town, for goodness' sake."

"I've wondered about that a lot myself. It's a real mystery, isn't it? Of course I can only speculate about the bloody place. But, for what it's worth, I suspect the rebel nonsense was originally just a case of posh youngsters showing off, and then, over time, it's hardened into a Cambridge tradition, like May balls and puking in the Cam." Sir Douglas lit a cigarette and frowned. "You know, romantic young men sitting round open fires, getting sloshed on college port, singing old rebel songs from the eighties and spouting off about freedom and justice and all that nonsense. How else are they going to fill their time at Cambridge, for God's sake? Then occasionally, I suppose, they get fed up with all the talking and decide to do something brave to make themselves feel daring and noble. So they attack the Project and get themselves shot, any survivors are curtailed and that's it for another generation. Except, of course, that we in the Service have to work our arses off repairing the enclosure afterwards. This will be my third major rebellion, you know, if it happens. It's frightfully boring."

Just then Tony entered the mess. He glanced around hurriedly and smiled with relief when he saw Sir Douglas. He bustled over.

"Ah, Sir Douglas, I'm jolly glad that I've found you. Something's come up that I believe you might want to look at."

"Something fun, would you say, Tony? I could do with a bit of fun this morning."

"I believe so, Sir Douglas. Well, sort of fun, anyway. Well, you might think it's fun. Um, Samuel Moorcroft has just been processed at the Eden Gate."

Sir Douglas stood up immediately, leaving his food unfinished.

"Timothy, you must forgive me, but I'm going to leave you. I would be grateful if you'd keep quiet about the matter we were just discussing, at least until it's public knowledge. I believe the briefing's going to be published in Friday's weekly operating notice, so even you should be able to keep your gob shut until then."

Timothy was busy gnawing the flesh off a squirrel bone and so was unable to reply. He waved at Sir Douglas who nodded briskly and marched out of the refectory with Tony trotting beside him.

"Is he alone?" Sir Douglas asked as they entered a lift in the mess lobby. Tony pressed the lowest button and they sank downwards at speed.

"Yes, Sir Douglas, at least he was alone at the Eden Gate, and I've checked; there's no record of any family member or known friend in the Project today."

"Excellent, Tony. You know, I really do believe you're improving. Now then, where was Samuel heading? Do we know yet?"

"Thank you, Sir Douglas. Yes ... um ...' the younger man pulled a small notebook out of his breast pocket and consulted it. "He went shopping briefly in the Peasants' Boutique on the third oval, where he purchased two pairs of britches, three shirts, two jerkins and some boots. He had them wrapped up; he didn't wear them. After that he called at a chemist and bought first aid materials, and then he seemed to be heading in the direction of the minirail...."

The lift halted and the doors slid open. The two men marched out. Sir Douglas drew sharply on his cigarette and threw the butt onto the concrete floor.

"You say that he *seemed* to be heading towards the minirail?"

"Yes, Sir Douglas; the last I saw he was going in that direction, but then, you see, I remembered that I should probably tell you that he was here, so I wired him as a code blue and came straight to the mess. I'm afraid I didn't see where he ended up."

"Good of you to think of me," Sir Douglas said dryly. "Interesting that Samuel should be buying fen clobber, isn't it? I hardly see him as a fancy-dress merchant."

"Nor do I really, Sir Douglas."

"And he's alone. That might mean something or nothing, of course, but I would say at least that it's promising."

"Yes, Sir Douglas, and um ... well ..."

"Don't go bloody shy on me, Tony, what is it?"

"Well, I might be wrong, but to me he seemed a little, well, *agitated* at the Eden Gate."

Sir Douglas lit another cigarette and smoked in silence as they walked.

"Young Samuel looked agitated, did he?" he said eventually. "Well that's extremely interesting, isn't it? Really, extremely interesting."

The two men didn't speak after that. They marched quickly to a minirail platform where a car was immediately made available. After a five-minute ride they disembarked and walked along a short corridor before taking another lift to the lowest levels of the Project. Finally, they descended a rough wooden staircase and arrived at the concrete corridor with steel supports that led to Sir Douglas's own office. At the end of this corridor Sir Douglas placed his eye briefly against a small pad mounted on the doorframe and the door swung open. He strode to his desk, lighting another cigarette as he sat down, and switched the computer on. He jabbed at the keypad impatiently. The screen flickered and Sir Douglas stared at it intently.

"Tony, dear boy, I do believe you're right. Samuel does look bit out of sorts doesn't he? And he was going to the minirail station, so you were right about that as well. He's just arrived at Stanmore, in fact." Sir Douglas glanced up at the younger man. "You really *are* improving, Tony. And Timothy was telling me how loyal you were to me last night when he was trying to find out where I'd got to, so well done for that as well. I know I don't always show it but I am jolly grateful for all you do for me, you do know that, don't you?"

Tony flushed with pleasure.

"Yes, Sir Douglas, thank you."

"Good, now close the door and shut up. I want to watch this."

Sir Douglas sat and smoked, his eyes fixed on the computer while Tony hovered by the door. On the screen, the figure of Sam, carrying two heavy shopping bags, was being searched by a BSC officer at the lift in the Stanmore installation. When he was allowed to pass he disappeared into the King's Head and then reappeared a few minutes later carrying a bottle of lemonade and a sandwich. Sir Douglas nodded approvingly.

"That's right, Samuel," he said softly. "Keep it natural, dear boy, keep it natural. After all we don't know who might be watching, do we?"

Sam strolled around the installation looking in shop windows until he arrived at the rows of holograph pods. Here he stopped and looked quickly in both directions before moving swiftly between two of the rows and on into the gloomy space beyond. Sir Douglas breathed in sharply as the cameras followed Sam to the steel door in the wall. He looked round again more carefully and then dropped his bags and turned the handle, pushing against the door with his shoulder as he did so. The door didn't move.

"Did we get that door oiled?" Sir Douglas murmured. "We should have got the bloody thing seen to, Tony. It took that BSC oaf all his strength to shift it and Samuel's hardly a big chap, is he?"

On the screen Sam leant more heavily on the door but it still refused to shift.

"Damn. Damn. Damn," Sir Douglas whispered. "Come on, Sam, you're breaking the law for God's sake, you might put your back into it."

Sam stared around wildly and then stood back and threw himself against the door. For a moment, it looked like nothing had happened and then a line of deeper blackness appeared between the door and the black brick of the wall. Sam pushed the door open and then grabbed his bags and darted into the deep darkness, pushing the door shut behind him.

Sir Douglas leant back in his chair and smiled. He lit a fresh cigarette from the one in his hand.

"Tony, it is my sad duty to inform you that Samuel Moorcroft has just breached the boundary. Put it on the wire immediately, please, that our code blue has gone green, notify all fixed posts in the central region, then get a couple of duty men up into Stanmore. Oh, and you'll have to speak to the BSC, of course, to get the Stanmore installation closed to the public immediately."

"Do you think he'll go straight in then, Sir Douglas?"

"No, I think he'll hide in those old lockers until tonight.

That's what I'd do. But I could be wrong, and I'm not taking chances. For various reasons Samuel's rather special, Tony; I don't want to bugger this up."

"Very good, Sir Douglas."

Tony turned and marched out of the room leaving Sir Douglas staring at the steel door on his computer screen.

"You beautiful boy, Samuel," he whispered. "You beautiful, beautiful boy. Now then, let's see what you've got planned for us, shall we? Let's see what games we can play together!"

He was silent for a minute, and then he giggled softly.

"Lord almighty, whatever are Mum and Dad going to say, Samuel?" he said. "Eh, beautiful boy, what are they going to say? Eh?"

As Sam shoved the door shut he knew that his life had changed forever. He was now a fugitive and a criminal, facing chemical curtailment or worse if he was caught. The thought made him shiver in the clammy darkness of the tunnel and he felt the hairs rise on the back of his neck. He rubbed his aching shoulder and fought to control his nerves. The point was surely not to dwell on what would happen if things went wrong but to concentrate step by step on making sure that things went right. After all, arguably he had already got through the most dangerous part of his adventure by slipping through the door unobserved. No one knew what he had done or even suspected him of anything, that much was obvious. If they did, he would already be lying flat on his back with a hypodermic needle in his neck and paralysing drugs seeping into his brain. That hadn't happened. He was surviving. With luck and careful planning, he would continue to survive.

He didn't dare switch the lights on in case they triggered an alarm, so, gripping the handles of his bags, he began to walk cautiously into the pitch blackness of the tunnel. The sound of his own footsteps and the rustling of the carrier bags against his legs echoed nastily around the bare brickwork until he began to imagine that there were other people walking in step with him on either side, waiting to pounce on him at a moment of their own choosing. He veered from left to right to check he was alone and twice banged into the tunnel wall, jumping back in alarm and dropping his bags as he did so. He had to sink to his knees and fumble around for his belongings in the dust and broken brick before he could continue.

After a while Sam lost any sense of time and direction, and began to wonder if he had accidentally turned through a door that he had not noticed on his first visit, and was now hopelessly lost beneath the Project without any hope of finding his way out. It was only with great effort that he kept placing one foot in front of the other, breathing the cold air in quick, ragged gasps as he did so.

Just when he had convinced himself that he had definitely taken a wrong turn, Sam's foot struck something hard. He reached out slowly and his hand touched the grainy coldness of the spiral staircase. He clung to it tightly for several seconds while his heartbeat returned to normal and then he began to climb, counting the steps as he went. It was hard work dragging his bags after him and by the time he reached the top he was breathless with exertion. He crawled onto the wooden platform and worked his way carefully around the edge on his hands and knees, running one palm along the wall as he went. Finally, his fingers met the slim crack which indicated the door of the boundary lock. He levered himself to his feet and yanked sharply on the lock wheel, causing it to squeal shrilly. The noise made him jump and tumble backwards, and for a couple of minutes he stayed stock still, crouched on the floor, listening intently to the silence while the blood pounded in his ears. When he was satisfied that no one had heard him, he hauled himself back to his feet and turned the wheel until the door swung open. He gathered his belongings and crept into the lock, pulling the door shut and securing it behind him. The wheel on the outer door of the boundary lock turned more easily. He mustered his courage and span it, pulling the door open as he did so.

Suddenly, Sam felt the shock of wind and sunlight on his face and his ears were full of the distant sound of birdsong. He stood quietly, adjusting to the brightness and the delight of the fresh air, before stepping out of the boundary lock and pulling the second door closed behind him. He moved quickly along the trench to the first of the BSC lockers and levered its door open just enough for him to squeeze through. He clambered inside and tugged the door shut, then crouched, blinking, in the semi-darkness.

The locker smelt musty, of old wood and earth. Thin strips of daylight spilt in through cracks in the planking walls, revealing cobwebby crates stacked on each side. These were stamped with black labels: *Assault Ammo—Non-kill; green netting; smoke; restraint bags.* By shoving several of the crates to one side Sam cleared an area that was just large enough to lie down. He flicked away some mouse droppings and lowered himself to the floor, wrapping himself haphazardly in his coat. Then he lay still and tried to consider the last half hour of his life.

Beyond the most basic level, however (he had broken the law in the most serious way imaginable; he now had no choice but to go on; he hoped everything would be all right), Sam discovered that he couldn't settle the facts of the last thirty minutes into his brain. His mind resisted the enormity of what he had just done. The peculiar feeling settled upon him that his ordinary life was going on as normal at home with a normal, obedient Sam going about his normal business. The boy in the locker was nothing but a rebellious husk of himself, stepped out of his own life, secret and hollow, hidden away in the forbidden earth. The feeling made Sam dizzy, and he giggled at the oddness of it. Rolling over, he tucked his hands behind his head and traced the haphazard journeys of dust motes as they drifted in and out of the thin beams of daylight.

Chapter Fourteen
Fight

Sam opened his eyes and was immediately wide awake. He stretched his legs as far as he could and listened carefully. The locker was completely silent. Shuffling to the door, he placed one ear against the wood and listened again before tugging it open a couple of inches and peering outside. Judging by the fading light it was about 7 p.m., which meant that he had been in the locker for almost nine hours. He rubbed his eyes and ran his hand through his hair, then gathered his bags and crawled out into the trench.

When he had retrieved his first aid kit, map and notes from his coat pocket, he stripped off his old clothes and stuffed them back into the locker behind a pile of crates. He pulled a pair of britches, a shirt, a jerkin and the boots from his bags and put them on, storing the rest of his purchases in the locker with his old clothes. He glanced down at himself and frowned; the whole outfit looked much too clean and new. Gathering handfuls of earth and grass from the trench wall he rubbed himself with soil and then examined his outfit again. The result wasn't particularly convincing—the clothes now looked like brand new garments that had got dirty—but it was the best he could do. He climbed up to the observation step and looked around cautiously. When he was satisfied that the coast was clear, he clambered out of the trench and stood up slowly on the parapet.

He needed to head approximately northeast, but obviously had to avoid the little hillock with the old woman's cottage behind it. One of the raised paths that crisscrossed the marshy ground seemed to head roughly in the right direction. Sam folded his map and tucked it away inside the unfamiliar folds of his jerkin and then, as an afterthought, shoved one of the shopping bags in as well. He breathed in a lungful of the sharp evening air and shivered violently. Then he turned his back on the fading sun and began to walk.

* * *

On the hillock, the old woman observed Sam's progress carefully through a brass telescope. She was crouching in prickly grass behind a tree with her tatty skirts gathered up round her waist and a clay pipe clamped between her teeth. As Sam picked his way along the path she jotted some lines quickly on a notepad without taking her eye off him and then folded the telescope away and tucked it in her pocket. She rolled silently away from her hiding place and down the bank and then clambered to her feet and dusted herself down, pulling bits of grass and briar from her clothes.

"I'm getting too bloody old for this malarkey," she murmured, stretching so that her joints cracked. She re-lit her pipe and puffed at it aggressively, making the bowl crackle. Then she marched into the nearby cottage.

As she bustled through the door, the woman disturbed a large white cockerel that had been pecking half-heartedly at the doormat. The bird shrieked and flapped at her, and then scuttled outside as she swung a muddy boot at its head.

"Go on, bugger off," the woman murmured as she hurried to the hearth. Here a soot-blackened cauldron was suspended on three chains above a pile of ash. She pushed it to one side and kicked the third brick from the left on the hearth floor, causing a portion of the brickwork to creak and then swing away from the wall. The woman bent down and reached a bony arm into the cavity, retrieving a slim document folder, a radio set and a handgun. These she took to the battered table in the centre of the room and sat down.

A ginger cat leapt out of the shadows onto the woman's lap as soon as she settled herself. She stroked him lovingly while he circled round, clawing at her skirts.

"All right, Ludwig," she breathed. "I love you, too, you handsome fellow. You can stay there if you like, but you must be good and quiet while Mummy's on the phone, understand?"

As if in answer, the cat curled itself into a tight ball. The woman leant forward carefully so as not to dislodge him and flicked through the folder. When she had found the page she was looking for, she read off a series of numbers and punched them into a keypad on the radio set. A moment later, the radio spluttered into life and a bored-sounding voice said, "Good evening. This is the *Refugium Peccatorum*. Please state your name, location and this week's password."

The old woman squinted at the file again and leant forward, speaking into the radio's microphone.

"Good evening, *Refugium Peccatorum*. This is ISS agent Starling, currently stationed at central region fixed point 21 B. That's point 881 on the standard Service positioning system. I am speaking from the station. And this week's password is *pigs ear*. Goodness knows who invents these ridiculous things but there we are."

"Could you spell the password please, Agent Starling?"

"You spell pig's ear as it sounds: papa, india, golf, sierra; there should be an apostrophe between the g and the s, incidentally, but there isn't. New word: echo, alpha, romeo."

There was a short pause and then, "Thank you, Agent Starling. What can I do for you this evening?"

"I have an urgent message for the Sheriff of Nottingham concerning his code green, item number 136 on today's wire. Could you put me through to him? And could you do it quickly please? I have chickens to feed."

"Please stay on air, Agent Starling," the voice droned. "I'll connect you as quickly as I can."

"Well, you might at least try and *sound* a bit urgent, you bloody useless brass-buckle," the old woman murmured, but the line was already dead. Two minutes later it crackled again and Sir Douglas Latch's voice oozed out of the radio.

"Alice, my dear, always a pleasure to hear from you; lovely that you should get in touch, absolutely lovely. Now then, old thing, what have you got for me about my little code green?"

"Good evening, Douglas," the old woman replied briskly. "I trust you're well; you certainly sound it. Your subject exited BSC post J-18 at 1857 hours. He was dressed in enclosure costume and was heading north by northeast along dyke path 642-681 on the Service positioning system."

"Excellent, Alice, absolutely excellent. Thank you so much. Wonderful that I can depend on you. Now then, old girl, could I ask you to maintain your post for the time being? We're not absolutely sure where the subject might be heading yet, you see, and as so little of the land round you is holographed we're having to do things the old-fashioned way. I know it's a ball-ache my dear, but I don't think we have any option."

The woman sighed and reached across the table for a scuffed pewter hip flask. She unscrewed the top and took a mouthful.

"I was afraid you were going to say that. It's cold up there, you know, and uncomfortable. I'm getting creaky."

"Aren't we all, my dear? Listen, when this code green's out of the way you must come over to the mess, and I'll buy you dinner and lots of lovely drink by way of a thank you. We can reminisce about the old days and get so drunk that we end up wetting our pants and scandalising the postulants. How does that sound?"

"It sounds absolutely divine, Douglas. You always knew how to show a girl a good time. It still means I've got to spend a cold bloody night on the hill, though."

"Can't be helped, old girl, I'm afraid. But seriously, you must come over for some nosh when we're done. It would be splendid to see you."

The old woman drank from the hip flask again and wiped a sheen of liquor from her lips. She stroked the cat absent-mindedly.

"I'm not sure that I really belong in the mess anymore," she said slowly. "To be perfectly honest, I think I'd be a bit of an embarrassment. I think I'm about three quarters native these days. I'm happiest with my chickens and my goat, if truth be told."

Sir Douglas giggled softly.

"Goodness me, how somber you sound, Alice. I swear that you become more and more like Hilary every day. Look, my dear, it's up to you; if you do fancy a meal, contact me through the *Refugium*. But you'd better do it sooner rather than later because a little bird tells me we're all going to be rather busy before too long. And in the meantime keep your eye out for my dear little code green, whose name, you may be interested to learn, is Samuel Moorcroft."

"No relation to Arthur?"

"His son. And you can see it in his eyes as well. Rather

sensitive. Nice."

"Good God, no wonder you sound so bloody happy."

"Exactly, my dear, so wrap up warm and get back on your hill. There's a good girl."

"All right, Douglas. You can rely on me."

"Excellent. Sheriff of Nottingham out."

"Starling out."

In his office, Sir Douglas clicked a button on his keyboard, and the line went dead. He slipped out of his black uniform jacket (the room was extremely warm, thanks to the fire that was roaring in the grate) and studied the large map that was open on the desk in front of him. Then he pressed another button and spoke quickly into the computer's microphone.

"Tony, shut up and listen. I've just had Agent Starling on, and she reports that young Samuel has left the trench and is heading north by northeast, so it looks like he's making a go of it. I haven't got a clue where he might be heading yet, but it doesn't matter, I'm going to get on with the paperwork anyway. While I'm doing that, I'd be grateful if you could advise our duty men in Stanmore. Then a plate of chicken livers and leeks from the mess, please, Tony, and a pot of coffee. And then you can knock off, dear boy; I daresay you could do with a break."

Without waiting for a reply, Sir Douglas clicked the keyboard to disconnect the line. He filled and lit his pipe and stared at the opposite wall for a moment or two. Then he flexed his fingers and leant forward to type.

The Department of Boundary Security -
Active Transgressions Unit

Dear Mr. and Mrs. Moorcroft,
It is my duty to advise you that your son, Samuel Henry Moorcroft, has been apprehended by officers of the Boundary Security Corps while attempting to breach the boundary of the Ely Project, at Ely.

Violating or attempting to violate the Project boundary is a felony under bylaw 36, governing the Ely Project, for which the maximum penalty is chemical curtailment. Samuel has been detained and is currently helping officers of the Boundary Security Corps with their enquiries. He is fit and well and is cooperating fully with the authorities. His file will be sent up to the Guardian's Office for adjudication within the next six months.

Unless and until you hear again from this department, you must make no attempt to contact your son by any means. No member of your family may visit a Project enclosure, either at Ely or at any other location in this country or abroad. Failure to comply with this instruction will result in your own detention and could compromise Samuel's case.

Thank you for your co-operation in this matter.

Sir Christopher Hogg
Permanent Secretary
Department of Boundary Security -
Active Transgressions Unit

Sir Douglas printed the letter and signed it lavishly as Sir Christopher Hogg. He sat back in his chair and read it through, chuckling and puffing at his pipe as he did so. Then on impulse he leant forward and appended the letter in his own hand:

He's doing awfully well. You should both be very proud.

As the day faded, Sam hurried along the thin track, skirting the hillock and pushing on into the empty country beyond. Thick black water sucked and lapped against his route on either side, and swarms of tiny insects fretted around the clumps of reeds that poked through the marshy surface. Twice Sam saw creatures slip from the bank into the water and swim quickly away at the sound of his approach. Occasionally, he stopped and consulted his map and his notes, and then checked his position against the landscape's shallow contours. He lengthened his stride after each stop; it was important he reach his destination before the light went completely. The place he was looking for would be easy to miss in the dark.

After about 20 minutes, Sam came to a division in the path.

He took the right fork and continued quickly. Here the water gradually rescinded from the raised track, and then turned into a series of separate ponds. Eventually the land dried out completely and the track broadened to become a small road, the sort of thing you could easily take a pair of horses along, two abreast, or ride a couple of motorbikes down. Sam stopped and pinched himself; he mustn't think like that. No one would ever ride motorbikes along this particular path because there was no such thing as motorbikes on this side of the boundary. They had been phased out together with cars, gas and electricity, firearms and modern clothing in the first 20 years of the enclosure. That was the period the textbooks referred to as the *collective regression*. He would have to be very careful; it was going to be very easy indeed—dangerously easy—to forget where he was and what he had done.

After another half hour's walk Sam spotted the place he had been looking for. It was a tumbledown barn to the left of the main path, reached by a narrow track that was menaced on both sides by clumps of gorse and hawthorn thickets. He dropped to his knees behind a tree stump and observed the place carefully. There were windows mounted high on the side of the barn that faced him, but no door. Sam was expecting that; he knew from his reading that the building's only entrance was on the other side, facing south. Part of the roof on the right had collapsed and hadn't been repaired; that was no surprise, either. The *Deviancy and Dysfunction* booklet explained that the smugglers who used the barn had deliberately left it damaged to make it look abandoned and unwelcoming. Sam had to admit that their ploy had worked; the building was certainly bleak. He was relieved to note that it was also in complete darkness. He knew from his reading that the area was so marginal and the barn so forbidding that the smugglers didn't bother with a watchman to guard the place. The landscape did their work for them.

Still, he wasn't going to take any chances. He emerged slowly from behind the tree stump and approached the barn bent almost double, taking advantage of whatever cover was provided by the bushes. When he reached the building he flattened himself against its back wall and worked his way along it sideways, as he had seen soldiers do in old films. Slipping silently round the corner, he continued in the same way along the side wall and then slid around the next corner. The barn door was now immediately in front of him. It was shut, but Sam could see the heavy rusted lock lying open above the catch. He took a last quick look round and then rushed to the door and leant hard against it, depressing the latch as he did so. It swung inwards, emitting the gritty, creaking noise of wood working against wood. He stepped inside and pushed the door shut behind him.

The barn was gloomy and cool and smelt of damp, with bits of broken, rotten wood littering the floor from the collapsed ceiling. There were some crates stacked at the far end that looked promising, but before Sam could investigate them, a rustling noise in the corner made him glance round. Through the gloom, he could just make out a creature curled on a pile of dirty sacks. It was stirring, obviously disturbed by his arrival. Without taking his eyes off the shadowy form, Sam took a step backwards towards the door. Then he froze. He felt his neck and face turn hot as the thing stretched and stood up, revealing itself to be a boy of about his own age, perhaps slightly younger. The boy scratched himself between the legs and shook his head, as if to clear it of sleep. He had matted hair and quick darting eyes, and his tunic hung open, revealing a sinewy torso that glowed ghostly-pale in the semi-darkness. He looked rough and dangerous. He scowled at Sam and stepped forwards so that he stood in one of the pools of light that spilt into the barn through its ruined roof. Then he reached slowly behind his back and pulled a knife from his britches.

For a strange moment, Sam felt the urge to communicate with the boy, to make a link between them, perhaps to explain himself and draw the terror from the situation, but there was no time. The boy continued towards him, moistening his lips with his tongue and weighting the knife gently in his palm, his eyes holding Sam's unblinkingly.

Sam stepped back again and, feeling ridiculous as well as terrified, raised his fists to defend himself. As he did so the boy's faced twitched; he covered the remaining paces between them in a single flowing movement and brought the knife up quickly towards Sam's chest. Sam swung a fist at him wildly and felt his knuckles jar against the boy's wrist; he lashed out again and managed to punch the boy hard in the side of the head.

The boy grunted and stepped back and for a moment Sam felt a rush of elation. The feeling was short-lived, however. The boy deftly switched the knife from his right hand to his left and then lunged again, towards Sam's neck. Again, Sam managed to deflect the blow, this time by grabbing the boy's wrist. The boy was strong, however, much stronger than Sam. He pushed the knife on towards Sam's chest as Sam fought desperately to shove the blade downwards and away. Locked together, they staggered around the barn, scuffling in and out of pools of light and shade, so close that Sam could smell the earthy, unwashed smell of the boy's skin and observe the jagged edges of his bared teeth. Eventually, the boy's greater strength began to tell and he slowly forced the tip of his knife into Sam's tunic and down towards his waist.

When Sam heard the faint ripping sound of his clothes tearing, he panicked and kneed the boy as hard as he could in the groin. The effect was immediate; the boy staggered backwards and sagged to the floor, dropping the knife as he did so. Sam also lost his balance and collapsed against the barn wall, his arms flailing for support. His hand closed over a smooth wooden pole—a pickaxe handle or something similar—and he leant on it heavily, gasping for breath.

"I'll fix you. I'll cut you up," the boy hissed as he reached for his knife and began to lever himself back to his knees. Sam lifted the piece of wood above his head and advanced on him.

"Look, just stay where you are and put the knife down. Or I'll hit you. I will. I'll hit you if you don't stay where you are. There's no reason for us to fight. I … I don't want…"

Before Sam could finish the boy lunged at him again from the floor, the knife pointing straight at his stomach. Without thinking about it, Sam swung the wood at him as hard as he could, striking him squarely on the side of his skull. There was a dull thud and the boy yelped and sagged back to the ground, dropping the knife again as he did so. A thin stream of spit leaked from his mouth onto the dusty floor.

"Look, I'm sorry, I didn't mean … You know I didn't mean to hurt you," Sam babbled. "But you were going to stab me. I really think you were going to st…stab me, so, you know. So … what else could I do? I didn't want to hurt you but you had a kni…knife."

He threw the piece of wood away into the shadows, then retrieved the knife and advanced on the boy, holding the point shakily towards his neck. He knelt down and put his face close to the boy's. His breath was quick and shallow, and his eyelashes fluttered against his grimy skin. Sam patted his cheek a couple of times with the blade of the knife and then, satisfied that he really was knocked out, clambered back to his feet.

As he got up, Sam heard a soft drip and then a moment later he heard another. He glanced down in time to see a dark liquid splash on to the boy's face. As he peered up towards the ceiling the drip came again, this time splashing on the floor next to the boy's ear. Confused, Sam looked down and then up again and as he did so, the thought occurred to him that whatever it was, the liquid wasn't coming from the ceiling because his own body was positioned between the roof and the places where the drips were landing. As the fourth and fifth drips splattered against the floor Sam's hand reached slowly for his own chest. His tunic was sticky and warm to the touch, and when he withdrew his fingers and examined them, the dark red colour was unmistakable, even in the fading light.

There was no pain at first. Sam opened his tunic and examined the wound. It was quite long, stretching from just below his shoulder to the bottom of his ribs, but it didn't seem particularly deep. He took his sticking plasters from his tunic pocket and stuck eight of them in diagonal crosses over the gash to keep it closed. Then he took a piece of bandage, folded it double and smeared it with antiseptic before laying it over the length of the wound and securing it with more plasters. Some blood immediately leaked through onto the bandage, but not much. Relieved, he refastened his shirt and jerkin and slipped the knife carefully into his belt. Then he examined the barn.

Sam knew from his reading that the smuggler gang used the place to store both money and goods, but it was only the money that he was after. It would be far too suspicious if someone of his age tried to sell contraband goods around the enclosure settlements, and anyway, despite his reading, he didn't really know how you would go about it. He approached the crates at the back of the barn and pulled one off the top, wincing with the first shock of pain as he did so. He used the knife to prise the crate's lid off and the rich scent of tobacco assaulted his nostrils. Replacing the lid as best he could, he moved on down the stack. The second crate he opened contained bottles, the third kitchen knives and the fourth some sort of spice that made Sam sneeze violently. By now the wound was throbbing unpleasantly, and he could feel a film of sweat forming on his back. He slumped down on some loosely packed bails of straw next to the crates and thought about what to do next. His whole plan for surviving within the enclosure depended on his stealing enough money from the smugglers to get by, at least to begin with. It was difficult to see how he would manage otherwise.

The bale was much less comfortable than it looked, with hard lumps just beneath the surface. Absentmindedly, Sam pushed his hand into the straw to remove the worst of them and his fingers closed on something that felt like leather. Intrigued, he worked the object loose from the bale and examined it. It was a crudely-made purse, secured at the top with a length of twine. Sam sliced the twine with the tip of the knife and upended the purse. Thick gold coins tumbled onto the floor of the barn.

This was the first time Sam had seen money, apart from in downloads and old films, and for a while, his curiosity got the better of his relief. He picked up one of the coins and studied it, turning it over and over in his palm. There was a picture of a man's head on one side and some sort of fish surrounded by interwoven flowers on the other. The little disc was pleasingly heavy and chunky. Unlike a flimsy currency card, it actually *felt* wealthy. He could imagine carrying a bag of these things around and feeling as if he owned something real and powerful.

A soft groan interrupted Sam's thoughts. The injured boy had rolled onto his side and his mouth was opening and shutting painfully, like a fish gasping for air. Startled, Sam quickly gathered together the spilt coins and put them in his pocket, then set to work pulling apart the remaining bails and loading his shopping bag with the rest of the purses. Five minutes later he stole past the boy and slipped out into the night with the knife tucked into his belt and the laden shopping bag slung over his good shoulder.

Chapter Fifteen
Stranger on the Road

Sam didn't notice the glint of reflected moonlight on the top of the hillock as he trudged back along the path towards the BSC trench. The pain from his wound and the discomfort of the heavy shopping bag meant that he didn't notice very much at all. He clambered awkwardly into the trench and retrieved the rest of his new clothes from the locker, changing into a fresh shirt and jerkin, and then climbed back out and continued on his way. He followed the same path in a gentle ark for another three miles until he arrived at a proper track, which he calculated to be the main route into Stanmore from the east. He drew back a little until he was out of view of the road and crawled into a small hollow beneath a hedge. When he was satisfied that he was out of sight, he settled himself as best he could in a position that wouldn't hurt his shoulder and lay still, clutching his shopping bag close to his chest all the while.

The morning dawned cold and bright. When Sam woke up, his wound was throbbing painfully and he felt edgy and light headed. That would be because he had spent two nights without the enhancement clip, as well the aftereffect of the fight and going for too long without food. He would have to get used to life without the clip, but obviously food was vital. He would lose his strength completely if he didn't eat soon.

He removed one of the purses from the shopping bag and put it in his pocket and then shoved the bag and the rest of the money as far as he could into the hedge where he had slept. He crawled out of his hiding place, stretched and rubbed himself down, then walked stiffly back to the road. He placed a pair of large sticks at the roadside, making a rough arrow that pointed towards the hedge and looked around to fix the spot in his memory. When he was certain that he would know the place again, he turned west and headed down the road towards Stanmore.

To begin with, the track was bounded by rough, uninhabited country, dotted with ruined buildings, and the hedges on either side were lively with the rustlings of wild animals and birds. This was as Sam expected; he was still too near the boundary for the area to sustain a human community. Gradually, however, signs of human habitation began to appear: ramshackle farm buildings, small plots of cultivated land, a scarecrow. After a mile or so Sam came to the first obviously inhabited house. It was set a little way back from the track with black smoke pouring from the chimney and a disheveled bay horse tethered on the rough land in front. As he looked up at the building, he saw a woman drawing the curtains in an upstairs room. She glared down at Sam suspiciously making him look away and continue quickly down the road.

Shortly beyond the house, Sam heard a scuffing noise on the path behind him. A moment later a man's voice called out cheerfully, "Now then, young fella, yer up early."

Sam swung round. The man who had spoken was only three or four paces behind him. He was short and fat with a red face and a tangle of grey hair hanging loose down to his shoulders. There were wire glasses perched on the end of his bulbous nose and the butt of a homemade cigarette clenched between his teeth.

"I ... I beg your pardon."

"I was remarkin', young fella, how early an hour it is to see someone of your age up and about. To my way of thinking a young lad like you should be dozin' this time of day. Or else ensconced with a lady friend in some quiet spot." The fat man winked and threw his cigarette onto the ground. He looked Sam up and down. "Still, perhaps it's mischief-makin' you're up to, and old Pereduke should mind his own business. Perhaps that's why yer out so close to the beyonds without so much as a charm to keep the demon away. Who else would be out here save mischief-makers, I wonder, 'cept for the poor buggers who actually have to live here, of course."

"Oh no," Sam said quickly. "I'm not making mischief or crime or doing anything like that. Um ... my name's Mick, Mick Randall. I'm not from round here. I didn't realise that I was so close to the beyonds."

"Well, you are, young fella."

"Ah, well, I didn't know. I'm from Walsingham, you see.

My dad's a leather merchant there. Or at least, he was."

Sam stopped speaking abruptly. The fat man was busy rolling a fresh cigarette. He licked the paper and glanced up at Sam.

"What do you mean *he was*?"

"He's just died," Sam said slowly. "He just died of, um, bowel-gripe. It's a horrible disease. I don't know if you've ever seen it, but it makes you go all thin and yellow. You can hardly eat or drink or speak or anything before you die. You just have to lie on your side hanging onto your guts to stop it hurting too bad. It's awful."

"I'm sure it is, young fella."

"Yeah, it is, and that's not all. My older brother inherited my dad's business, all of it. All I got was a bit of money to set myself up somewhere. That's how inheritance is organized in Walsingham, in case you didn't know."

Sam winced inwardly. The last sentence sounded like what it was: a bit of information he had picked up from a digi-download. He thought quickly and went on, "I *was* going to stay in Walsingham, of course, because that's where all my family are, but three nights ago my brother and I got drunk and had a row about the inheritance. I said he should make me a partner in the business, but he just laughed at me. Then, when I wouldn't let it drop, he lost his temper and hit me. We had a fight and, even though he's older, I was getting the better of him. But then Roger—that's my brother's name, by the way, and he's a complete idiot—he grabbed one of my dad's leather knives and slashed me with it. I was lucky he didn't kill me, actually."

Sam slipped out of his jerkin and undid his shirt. He peeled back the bandage so that the wound was visible. It seemed to have become redder overnight. The fat man whistled softly.

"Cor bugger, that's a nasty cut an' all. So why didn't you report this brother of yours to the magistrate then, young fella? I reckon he would have been thrown in the clink for summat like that and then maybe you'd get your dad's business after all?"

"Well, that's the awkward thing," Sam said as he re-fastened his clothes. "Roger's married to the magistrate's daughter. Well, not actually married, he's *engaged* to the magistrate's daughter. He's not quite old enough to be married yet. At Walsingham, we don't tend to get married until our late twenties. But the point is that he and the magistrate are very close; in fact, some people are already saying Roger might become magistrate himself one day. They don't know what he's really like, of course. Well, anyway, after the fight Roger went running straight off to the magistrate to tell his tale and, as a result, the magistrate said that if I didn't leave Walsingham immediately, he'd have me arrested for attacking Roger, even though it was him who started it. So I got my little bit of money and left in a hurry. I didn't even have time to pack any clothes. Or ... or a charm. I just went. I was hoping to spend some time in Stanmore to see if I can find any work. If nothing suits me, I'll go on to Limeport."

The fat man drew on his cigarette and peered intently at Sam.

"That's all very well, but it still don't explain to Pereduke what you're doing so close to the beyonds. Don't you 'ave no fear of the demon over in Walsingham? Or do you reckon you're too posh for the bad fella to bother you?"

"Ah ... Ah, yes. Well, you see, last night I got lost on the little marsh paths you have round here. We don't have them round Walsingham because it's a completely different landscape; it's quite hilly over there. Rolling country. Farm land and so on, you know. I had planned to get to Stanmore yesterday, but it got dark and I ended up going round and round in circles. Eventually, I slept under a hedge." Sam indicated his disheveled clothes. "As I said, I had no idea I was so close to the beyonds. Sounds like I've had a bit of a lucky escape."

The fat man frowned and Sam wondered if he was going to believe him. The story had seemed plausible enough when he had worked it out in his bedroom, but in the telling it sounded farfetched and, even to his own ears, his voice sounded wrong—*posh,* the man had said. To his great relief, however, the fat man smirked and then smiled broadly.

"Well, I reckon Pereduke's already glad he met you, young Mick Randall. You've made my day entertainin' already. And if you don't mind, I'll accompany you into Stanmore, seeing as it's where I'm goin' anyway. I reckon if you stay close by, my old charm should protect the both of us from demon mischief."

The man patted a large wooden cross that was dangling round his neck on coarse string. It was engraved with swirling line patterns and crude animal designs, and had a dried ear of corn pinned to its centre.

"It's a fine piece, ain't it, young 'un? I reckon the bad fella will think twice about havin' a go at us with this to keep us safe. Still, it doesn't pay to hang about. Let's look sharp, shall we?"

For the first part of their walk, Sam was ill at ease in Pereduke's company. There was something slightly mocking in his manner that made Sam wonder if he entirely accepted his story. Gradually, however, Sam began to relax. The other man seemed disinclined to question him further about his background, and, as they drew near to Stanmore and began meeting people on the road, it occurred to Sam that he would attract less attention arriving in the settlement with someone local.

The pair of them reached the milestone, which Sam recognised as marking the old parish boundary as well as indicating the area that was now covered by holograph. Here they caught up with a plump middle-aged woman who was herding a dozen geese into the settlement with the aid of an old birch broom. Pereduke flicked his hair back from his face and smiled at her as they approached.

"Good morning, Molly, and how are them birds of yours this morning?"

The woman nodded politely.

"Not so bad, thank you, Mr. Pereduke. We lost three in the end to that snot-sneezin' business. But them that are left seem to be recovered well enough, by the Wheel's turning."

"Well, I'm glad to hear it. I think the Wheel owed you 'alf a turn at least, with the luck you've had lately. Now then, will you meet a friend of mine? This is Mick Randall. He's come to visit us from Walsingham way, looking for work. You might mention 'im to your Thomas, if you think of it. I reckon the young 'un could help him out if he's looking for an extra pair of hands up at the mill. Mick's an old hand at mill work, ain't you, Mick?"

"Um yes, that's right," Sam said quickly.

The woman looked Sam up and down doubtfully.

"I'll do that for you gladly, Mr. Pereduke."

"I'd be obliged, Molly. Tell your Tom from me that he's a good worker 'an all."

"I will do that, Mr. Pereduke."

The woman shuffled uncomfortably while the geese hissed and pecked at each other round her feet. Finally, she said, "But now I'm afraid I've gotta get on if I'm gonna get a good spot up on the common."

"Of course you must. Don't let old Pereduke keep your geese from their grazin'. You get on yer way."

The woman nodded again, then drew her long muddy coat around herself protectively and bustled her geese on up the road into Stanmore. Pereduke licked his lips as he watched her go.

"There's a backside for you, Mick Randall," he murmured. "Pereduke 'as some fond memories of that particular backside, let me tell you. Here's a tip for yer: if you do get yerself a spot of work up at Tom Drake's mill, try and get it on a day when Tom's away. Like as not you'll be grindin' more than corn, young fella, before the day's out. If you've a mind, that is."

With that he elbowed Sam jovially in the ribs and then marched off towards the centre of the settlement. Sam hurried after him.

Although it was still early, Stanmore was busy. Children were chasing and shoving one another on the way to school; shopkeepers were fastening back their shutters and arranging displays of their wares—vegetables, pots and pans, linen, toys, medicines—on trestle tables in the street; a number of people were driving geese, goats or sheep along the uneven pavements. Strong, alien smells assaulted Sam's nostrils from the piles of fresh food at the roadside (vegetables were much smellier and dirtier here than at the market his mum went to) as well as from the open bins in front of the houses and the piles of animal droppings that were left in the road.

As he followed Pereduke onto the high street and up past the common, Sam began to recognise the roads and buildings and even some of the people from his holograph visit to Stanmore. He found himself constantly astonished and delighted at the solidity of things. As he explained much later to his debriefer, it felt as if he had somehow stepped into one of his own daydreams and magically clothed his dreamland in flesh and bone and stone.

Even as he was delighting in the realness of the town, however, one part of Sam's mind was uncomfortably aware that deep below them the day's first visitors would be arriving at the Stanmore installation and perhaps settling themselves into holograph pods. It was eerie to think that tourists could actually be passing themselves through him right now as he had passed through the Stanmore residents a few months before. When later, Sam described the feeling, his debriefer sighed wearily.

"And yet you *still* didn't think anyone would identify you, Samuel? That seems a little foolish, frankly. I'm rather disappointed, dear boy."

"There was too much happening," Sam said defensively. "With Pereduke and the buildings and everything, I just didn't think about that. I was in another world, don't forget. *I mean literally.* Anyway, my arm hurt."

Pereduke seemed to be a well-known figure around the settlement. He greeted most of the people they met and introduced Sam to a number of them. Within ten minutes he had enquired after the possibility of accommodation for Sam from five people as well as seeking work for him with a thatcher, two farmers and a carpenter, each time promising that Sam had relevant experience in the field. Sam noticed that he always received respectful, if non-committal, replies. If he was talking to a woman, Pereduke invariably made some comment about their body or their performance in bed after they had gone.

"Ah yes, Pereduke has his appetites, young fella," he leered at Sam after an attractive blonde woman had left them. "And they don't seem to be getting no weaker as he gets older, neither. That's the worryin' thing." He glanced at his watch. "But for now it's the appetites of his stomach rather than the ones in his loins which is pesterin' him. What do you say,

Mick, before we part our ways, would you join me for a bit of brecca?"

"Yeah, that would be good."

Pereduke nodded and continued down the high street towards the western end of the settlement. Here the temple dominated the town, although today the building looked dull and uninspiring with its doors closed up and no sign of the scarlet-robed preacher. As Pereduke hurried past he reached up to the statue of the man on the cross and lightly touched its toe, then touched his hand to the cross around his neck. He turned to Sam and winked.

"Got to keep my charm topped up, 'aven't I, young 'un? Old Pereduke spends a fair bit of his time out and about near the beyonds himself, and it doesn't do to be running out of power out there, does it?"

"No, no, I s'pose not."

"Right, so think of that next time you go wanderin' about by yourself at night! Now then, here we are."

They had arrived at a small café three doors down from the temple. It had a brass engraving of a teapot swinging creakily above its door, beneath which Sam could just make out the etched words: *The Fat Kettle*. Its windows were made of lots of small diamond panes of glass, all of which were covered with a thick layer of dust. The cream paint on the window ledges was blistered and peeling. Pereduke smacked his lips enthusiastically.

"Best bit of brecca in whole of Stanmore, no contest," he murmured before pushing the low door open and ducking through it. Sam followed him inside.

The café had only seven tables, squeezed so closely together that there was barely room to move among them. All of them were unoccupied except for the one furthest from the door where a young woman sat alone. Pereduke nodded sharply at her as he walked in but for once received no response. He shrugged and made his way to the table by the hearth where he selected two logs from the pile next to the grate and placed them on the smouldering fire. Settling himself into a chair, he banged loudly on the tabletop with the salt cellar. An elderly man poked his head through the grimy curtain behind the counter.

"Fire's almost out, George," Pereduke called. "Poor do on a cold morning. Now then, Pereduke will 'ave the full platter, please, and so will my young friend here." He turned to Sam. "Come on then, sit yourself down then, young fella. Yer making the place look untidy, hoverin' around."

Sam squeezed through the tables and settled himself opposite Pereduke. Meanwhile, George disappeared back behind the curtain and banged pots around loudly. A while later he reappeared.

"What'll you be wantin' to drink then?" he asked.

"Coffee and gin, please, George," Pereduke answered without taking his eyes off the fire.

"And your young friend?"

"The same." He glanced at Sam. "Gin all right for you, young fella?"

"Yeah, fine."

"That's the ticket. You'll be needin' something to warm your cockles after all your misadventures, I shouldn't wonder."

Pereduke leaned back in his chair and set about rolling another cigarette. He lit it and inhaled deeply.

"I reckon you made a wise choice comin' here, Mick," he said. "Providin' we can find you somewhere decent to lay yer head, of course. Stanmore's a nice quiet town. The people is decent enough, there're plenty of ladies to keep a young fella entertained, and we're out of the way like, so we don't get too much bother from the beyonds, neither. Not if we're sensible." He glanced up at Sam. "Do you get a lot of trouble from the demon over in Walsingham?"

Sam pretended to adjust his bandage to give himself time to think.

"We get some each year at the spring equinox. I mean, who doesn't? There's always some brain fever and the sickness and so on. But we don't do too badly, our priest is top notch, he keeps the land well-covered and generally the Wheel turns for us. At least it has recently."

"Ah yes, yer priest, I wonder if old Pereduke knows of him. What's his name then, this top notch priest of yours?"

Sam was saved from answering immediately by the arrival

of the food. George limped out from behind the curtain and placed plates of bacon, eggs, black pudding, liver, tomatoes and some other dark meat that Sam didn't recognise in front of both of them, together with two sets of grimy knives and forks. Without speaking, he limped back to the kitchen. Sam wracked his brains, aware that Pereduke was watching him intently. Just in time the name came to him.

"His name's Reverend Coran."

Pereduke smiled and shook his head.

"Never heard of 'im. But then why should I? Never been to Walsingham in my life. No one round 'ere goes wanderin' that far afield. You'll be somethin' of a mystery man, young Mick. Now then, don't let yer breakfast go cold. George's platter is a thing to be wondered at." He jabbed his fork at the mysterious meat. "He does his tiggy-winkle with ginger. Soft and tender like nothing you've never had before. I swear it."

Pereduke ate with great concentration, seeming to be temporarily oblivious to Sam's existence. This suited Sam very well. He set about his own breakfast enthusiastically, relieved that he didn't have to answer anymore questions. Presently, George limped out of the kitchen again and placed two steaming mugs of coffee and two small glasses of purplish liquid in front of them. Sam sipped at the thick, grainy coffee, enjoying the scorching feeling in his throat and stomach. Following Pereduke's example, he waited until he finished eating before he tried the gin. It had a fruity, expensive flavour unlike anything he had tasted before and it made his face flush. The fumes filled his nose and throat, and then his whole head, relaxing and emboldening him.

"Um, Mr. Pereduke," he said, "what do you actually *do*?"

The other man looked up from the cigarette he was rolling.

"What does old Pereduke do? That's a good question, young 'un. There's not many here in Stanmore who would think to ask summat like that." He stared at his unlit cigarette thoughtfully. "I ask questions, is what I do, Master Mick. I ask questions and then I make connections and I arrange meetin's. And somehow or other I manage to turn a shilling. Most of all, I s'pose I try to have a bit of fun." Pereduke giggled and lit his cigarette. "Yes, I do try and have a bit of fun. And I reckon you an' me might manage to 'ave a bit of fun together once you get yourself settled in digs somewhere." He smoked contentedly for a moment while he stared into the fire. Then he thumped the table with his clenched fist. "By the Wheel's spin I'm turning into a stupid fat old man, ain't I? Why didn't I think of it before? We might have the solution to yer accommodation problem staring us in the face and I never even thought of it. '

He pushed his lank hair back behind his ears and heaved himself round in his chair to face the woman who had ignored him when they arrived.

"Smith," he called out. "Smith, never mind your moody mopin'. You get yourself over 'ere, young lady."

Chapter Sixteen
Lodgings

Sam had forgotten about the young woman in the corner. Now, as she stared moodily at the pair of them, he realised that she was younger than he had thought, perhaps a year or two older than himself. She had a frank, open face with a sprinkling of freckles over a stubby, upturned nose; her auburn hair was tied back in a ponytail. Pereduke giggled and slapped the table impatiently.

"Bugger me, she's a feisty one, ain't she, Master Mick? Don't be looking at us like as if we were two bits of horse turd, young lady, get yourself over here. Old Pereduke's got a bit of business to discuss with you."

The woman, or girl, or whatever she was, stood up and trailed slowly over to them without a word. She stood next to the table, pointedly not looking at either of them while Pereduke ran his hand quickly over her lower back and bottom.

"Smith, I reckon you've turned yerself into something of a beauty while old Pereduke's back's bin turned. One minute yer a little ginger kid with nowt about you to turn a man's head, and the next yer a lovely lady without me ever noticin' the change." He turned to Sam. "Have you never noticed how it's always that way with the late ones? Yer take yer eye off them for a minute and then the next time you spot them they're all bum and boobs and blushing and whatnot. Often enough they're worth the wait an' all." He licked his lips delightedly and grinned at the girl. "Now then, Smith, to business. This 'ere is Mick Randall. He's a close friend of mine who happens to be lookin' for somewhere to lay his head for a week or two. Maybe longer. I was wonderin' if yer mother still has that top room spare above the shop. I dare say she could use a bit of extra, and young Mick here ain't a poor man."

The girl glanced suspiciously at Sam.

"The room's free, Mr. Pereduke. We got rid o' that cutler two weeks ago because he got behind."

"Excellent. Well, may I suggest you take young Mick 'ere

home to meet yer mother and see how he measures up. He won't be no trouble, I can guarantee it. Who knows, maybe it'll be nice for you to have a chap yer own age about the house."

Pereduke winked at Sam. The girl ignored him and shrugged.

"I'll take 'im to see her if you want, Mr. Pereduke."

"Thank you, Smith. Pereduke is much obliged to you, my dear." He glanced at his watch. "But now I'm afraid I have to be off. I gotta' see a man about a dog. Master Mick, it's been a pure pleasure."

Pereduke heaved himself to his feet and extended his hand. Sam took it.

"Um, yeah, well, thanks for your help, Mr. Pereduke."

"Don't mention it. I've a feeling you might make life entertainin', and Pereduke's always on the lookout for a bit of that. Any problems I might be able to help you with, you can find me 'ere most lunchtimes and in the King's Head most nights."

He pumped Sam's hand, making him wince with pain, nodded curtly at Smith, and then reached into his pocket and dumped three silver coins on the table.

"Right, Pereduke's away," he said and squeezed his way to the door and out into the street. The girl watched him go and then slid quickly into his place and gulped down the mouthful of gin that was left in his glass. She looked up at Sam.

"What did you two 'ave for breakfast?"

"Um, two platters, I think he called them. With coffee and gin."

The girl thought for a moment and then took one of the silver coins from the table. She spat on it and slipped it into her pocket, replacing it with two copper coins of her own.

"Silly idiot always tips too much," she said. "He likes everyone to know how rich he is, see."

She looked up at Sam and noticed him frowning and massaging his shoulder.

"You all right?"

"My shoulder hurts. I, er, had a fight and it got hurt, well, slashed, actually. I'll be ok."

"What, are you a fighter then? Are you trouble?"

"No, not at all. Honestly. It was a fight with my brother. It, er … it won't happen again."

The girl seemed to relax a little. She had incredible eyes: vivid green and restless with a truthful, challenging look about them. Sam felt uncomfortable lying to her.

"You don't look like much of a fighter," she said, "and yer don't really sound like one, either. Me and my mum own a potioners so, if we decide to take you, I might be able to sort you something out for yer shoulder." The girl nodded at the front door of the cafe, "Is 'e a friend of yours then?"

"Not really, I only met him this morning. Um … He's been helpful though."

"He's not helpful to no one save himself, that one. All he does is play with people. He'll be playin' with you jus' like he plays with everyone else. Jus' you wait and see." The girl spat into the fire as if she was clearing the taste of Pereduke from her mouth. She turned and stared levelly at Sam. "Still, if you've only known 'im a few hours, you can't be that infected with 'is horribleness yet. Come on, Mick Randall, let's get you home. You look like you could do with a bit of a kip."

Suddenly her face broke into a shy smile, wrinkling her nose and revealing a wide gap between her front teeth.

"And to be honest, you smell like you could do with a bath an' all."

Sam followed the girl out of the shop and along the narrow streets. He walked two paces behind her, making no effort at conversation, concentrating mostly on ensuring that no one bumped into his arm. The girl walked quickly with her head down, twice shoving children into the gutter when they blocked the pavement in front of her. After a couple of minutes she turned into the narrowest street Sam had yet encountered in Stanmore. The houses were only a dozen feet apart and their upper floors overhung the lower, so that it would be possible for people to lean out of the upstairs windows and shake hands across the street. The road was cobbled, although Sam noticed that a number of the cobblestones were missing, giving the roadway a depressed, unkempt look. Murky water trickled in rivulets down the edge of the pavement.

"Here we are, then."

The girl had stopped outside a narrow shop about halfway down the street. The bulging overhangs on both sides meant the building front was in deep shadow.

"I know it ain't much, but it's dry and it's quiet. Now listen, I'll go in first and tell me mum that yer comin'. She's got nerves, you see, she don't like surprises. Are you sure you ain't gonna flake out?"

"Yeah, yeah. I think so," Sam said through gritted teeth. "Why?"

"You've gone all pale and shaky."

"My shoulder's hurting a bit more, that's all. I probably just need a rest. I'll be all right when I lie down."

The girl nodded and slipped inside while Sam examined the shop front. A wooden sign above the door displayed a faded picture of a snake entwined with a pestle and mortar, around which were carved the words: *Smith's Potioners - Licensed Apothecaries to the Magistrate since 1752.* The shop's single window was stacked high with small pale porcelain tubs and brown bottles with labels such as *Rose Balm* and *Kidney Fluke.* Sam was studying the stacks of medicines when the girl reappeared.

"In you come then. Jus' say hello to me mum, then I'll take you straight up to yer room. Don't mention that yer hurt or anything' like that. She's not good with them sort of things. Have you got yer money with you?"

Sam nodded and patted his pocket.

"Good. Well, it'll cost yer three shillings a week to stop here. And for that you get yer breakfast, yer tea and a half-bath every other day. And we'll do yer washin' for you an' all. Does that suit you?"

"Yes, that's fine, whatever."

"Good, but don't bother me mum with the money. I'll see to all that when we get upstairs."

The girl reached out and smoothed down the collar of Sam's jerkin and then stepped back and surveyed him critically. Apparently satisfied, she held the door open for him to enter the shop.

Inside was dark and cold with a sharp smell of chemicals lingering in the air. More bottles and packages of medicines were piled on shelves on either side of the shop floor, while facing the door there was a high, dark wood counter with a brass till mounted at one end.

"So yer the new lodger that our Louise has picked up, are you?" said a feeble voice. Sam looked around and spotted a frail woman perched behind the counter, next to the till. Her face was very pale with the skin drawn tight and smooth over the bones. It was surrounded by a halo of frizzy grey hair. Her head wobbled from side to side as she spoke.

"Um yes, my name's Mick Randall. It's nice to meet you." Sam bobbed his head in greeting.

"I hope she knows what she's doin', that's all. Not sure you look old enough to be seekin' lodgings. Reckon you might turn out to be troublesome, eventually."

"Nonsense, Mother," said the girl. "Mick 'ere is warmly recommended by Mr. Pereduke 'imself. He's from a good family over Walsingham way. He's a nice lad; he won't give us no bother."

Sam smiled and nodded again, concentrating on maintaining a cheerful expression. The pain from his arm made it difficult not to grimace.

"Ah well, if Mr. Pereduke approves of 'im I suppose he must be respectable enough. Don't know how we'll find time to keep 'im fed and do his bits for 'im mind, not with all this to run."

One of the woman's stick-thin arms appeared suddenly from behind the counter and gestured shakily around the shop.

"I'll look after 'im, Mum, there's no need for you to worry."

"Well, you'll 'ave to, Lou. I'm sure I won't have time. I can't be doing everything now, can I?"

Without bothering to reply, the girl led Sam up three steps to the counter. She lifted a section of the countertop on its hinges and opened a small door into the private area beyond. Sam followed her through and waited while she closed the gateway up again.

The floor behind the counter was covered in a layer of yellowing newspaper. The girl's mother, Sam could see now, was sitting on a high stool with rows of tiny green bottles arranged in front of her. These she was filling full of brown powder using a small brass funnel. As Sam watched, she took a pinch of the powder from the tin box at her side and breathed it sharply up her right and then her left nostril. She paused in her work and her eyes filled with tears; then she wiped her nose with the back of her hand and continued to fill the bottles, wobbling rather less than before. The girl said softly, "I think you've more or less passed the test. Come on, I'll show you up to yer room."

She led Sam through a narrow door behind the counter, across a corridor, through another door and up an uneven flight of stairs to the top of the house. Here she showed him into a large room containing a double bed, a simple wardrobe, a desk and a chair. There was a fire set in the hearth and a sink in the corner with a cracked mirror above it. The mirror was propped up on two rusty nails. The room's ceiling bulged alarmingly and slanted almost to the scuffed floorboards. The only decoration was a chipped statue of a crucified man with leaves sprouting from his hands and feet that hung above the bed and a faded rag rug in the centre of the floor. While the girl busied herself plumping the pillows and turning down the grey blankets on the bed, Sam examined the view from the room's two windows. The smaller overlooked the street they had just left and afforded a perfect view of the flaking yellow plaster of the wall opposite, and the larger looked out onto a small yard where a pair of cats were squabbling over the contents of an overflowing dustbin.

Sam sat down heavily on the bed while the girl yanked the larger window open.

"The last fella we had in, the cutler, he was disgusting. He hardly washed or anythin' and the whole room ended up stinking of him and his 'orrible polishes. I've aired it as best I can but you can still smell 'im a bit. Anyway, I know it's basic but we keep it clean and we'll feed you well. Will it do?"

Sam nodded. The pain from his shoulder was coming in dull waves and he was suddenly extremely tired, making speaking difficult. Without really thinking about it, he swung his legs onto the bed and lowered himself gingerly onto the pillows. His eyes began to close.

"Hey, you hang on a minute." The girl's voice yanked Sam's drifting consciousness back to his body. "Don't you go dyin' on me. Not yet anyway. I need some money off you first."

Sam opened his eyes and found the girl standing over him with her hands on her hips, chewing her bottom lip. He groped in his pocket and pulled out one of the coins he had stolen from the barn. The girl took it and stared at it wide eyed.

"I ain't got no change, you know."

"It's all…all right." Sam flapped his hand weakly and his eyes began to close again. The girl shook him gently awake.

"I said I ain't got no change and this'll cover yer rent for 'bout six months. Are you sure you ain't got nothin' smaller?"

"No … nothing … smaller … sorry."

The girl spat on the coin and rubbed it quickly on her skirt, then put it in her pocket.

"Now look 'ere, Mick. I'll let yer off yer bath till you've had a kip. The room smells bad enough anyway. But I can't let yer sleep before I've 'ad a look at that shoulder of yours. It might be going sinful on you, see. It might need a bit of ointment or summat."

Sam nodded and tugged at his jerkin but found that his fingers had become too weak to manage the fastenings. The girl sat down on the bed next to him and gently moved his hands away before undoing the cords and the buttons herself. She folded back the jerkin and the shirt and then peeled off the bandage. She sniffed disapprovingly.

"Is this what yer wound dressings look like where you come from?" she asked.

"Yeah, m…mostly. Where I come from. In W… Walsingham."

The lips of the wound had become pink and enflamed and the surrounding flesh had turned grey. The girl traced her finger tenderly along the length of the cut, murmuring softly to herself as she did so. Then she stood up and removed the little statue of the crucified man from the wall and pressed it over the wound. She picked Sam's hand from the bed and placed it against the statue, holding it in place.

"You've gotta stay still and peaceful, Mick, and think about the Green Man turning injury into life and blessing, you understand? I'm gonna go and get summat that'll clean it up. I won't be a minute."

She left the room quietly, leaving Sam pressing feebly against the statue. It seemed only moments later that the door opened again and she came back in, carrying a tray of pots and bottles—except that when she lifted her head to look at him she turned out not to be the girl at all. It was Roger who was striding confidently into the room and he wasn't carrying a tray anymore; instead, he had a carrycot tucked under his strong rower's arm. Sam recognised the carrycot from his mum and dad's old holograph prints; it was the one that had held him when he was a baby. He felt himself stiffen with anxiety; it wasn't right that Roger should be holding *his* cot. Somehow it wasn't *safe*. He tried desperately to reach out to grab it back but as he did so the figure blurred and changed again, this time into Rachel. It was Rachel as Sam had seen her through the sitting room window, pale and anxious as she fumbled to do up her blouse buttons. Sam felt tears prickle his eyes and he struggled off the bed towards her. He had almost reached her when suddenly the floorboards between them bucked like a ship's deck, then swelled, and all at once Rachel was miles and miles and miles away. She smiled softly at him across the divide and then she also began to change, this time into Sam's dad—except it wasn't quite his dad because the figure was hollow, almost translucent, with blurry edges. He carried a bloodied meat cleaver and was stuttering and spluttering to Sam as he had done on the day of his first Ely visit.

"D...don't forget that they are human beings inside the enclosure. You r...really mustn't forget that, S...Sam."

Sam shrank in revulsion from the figure and as he did so it changed yet again, this time into the crucified man with leaves sprouting from the wounds in his hands and feet. As Sam watched, the leaves multiplied and thickened, and then twigs and branches appeared amongst them. These snaked round the figure until he was encircled in a wheel of foliage. The strange tree-wheel then began to turn, gently at first and then faster and faster so that leaves span off it like sparks off a Catherine

Wheel. The crucified man rotated with it, and as he did so he grew rapidly old, his skin cracking and wrinkling like bark, his hair thinning, his beard turning long and grey. When the man was almost a corpse the wheel stopped and began to spin in the opposite direction, and as it did so the ageing process was reversed so that the figure became young and agile-looking. And then, when he was practically a boy, the wheel reversed again and the man began to age once more. The process continued and accelerated until the foliage became a green blur and the crucified man flashed from youth to old age and back again in a matter of moments. Sam felt sick. He clutched the blankets and cried out. Gradually, from near at hand, he became aware of a woman's voice singing softly:

Child of the Wheel, heed its turning.
First there's summer; then comes snow;
First there's seed time, then the harvest;
Bring in weal and cast out woe.

Child of the Wheel, mark its turning.
First comes living; then comes death;
Morning time, then peaceful evening;
Strengthen blood and strengthen breath.

The words were pleasant and cooling as they dripped into Sam's mind. He felt himself calm down and the nausea lessen. As he calmed, the crucified man faded, until there was just a trace of spinning green to mark where he had been. Eventually, even that dissolved into the ordinary light and shadow of the attic, and there was only the girl from the shop, sitting on the bed next to Sam. She was smearing ointment over his wound with a look of intense concentration on her face, singing softly as she did so. The chipped statue of the crucified man lay on the pillow by his head.

"Welcome back, Mick," the girl said quietly. "I hope when this stuff gets into you you'll sleep a bit sounder. It's called self-heal, it's an evenin' remedy. It's meant to get right into yer insides and calm them all down."

Sam smiled weakly, bathing in the sudden tranquility of the

attic. His wound didn't seem to hurt particularly anymore. In fact, he couldn't feel it at all; there was just a kind of blankness stretching from his stomach to his neck. He understood that the girl's presence was strong and kind and good. Roger, Rachel and his dad wouldn't trouble him while she was there, he was sure of that. For the first time since he had left home, he felt himself relax. He curled up on his good side and slept peacefully.

"Bring in weal and cast out woe," Sir Douglas Latch exclaimed in disgust. *"Strengthen blood and strengthen breath"*. God almighty, Tony, who wrote this crap? You know, I think I actually prefer the old Nazarene prayers; at least they had a certain dignity about them."

Standing beside Sir Douglas's desk, Tony shrugged.

"I think those chants are actually pretty old, Sir Douglas. They're from just after 1989, I believe, the first corruption of the cult."

"Well, whenever they were written, they jolly well need revising. Have you ever read Hilary on the enclosure cult, by any chance?"

The younger man shook his head.

"Well, you should; it's most amusing. She's utterly bloody scathing about the chaps in charge of the corruption post-'89, precisely because the stuff they came up with was so dreadful compared with what it was supposed to be replacing."

"I didn't think she wrote positively about anything much after 1989, Sir Douglas."

"With good reason, Tony," Sir Douglas said severely. He poured himself a mug of port and sipped it thoughtfully. "But actually her religious writing after '89 is rather more complex than her other post-revolutionary stuff, more nuanced, one might say. In fact, there were odd, scandalous rumours that she may have had Nazarene sympathies herself."

Tony looked appalled.

"She didn't, you know, *believe* anything, did she, Sir Douglas?"

"Oh dear, I've offended the tight-arsed little sophiocrat in you, haven't I? No, dear boy, you can relax. Of course she didn't believe anything. She was a scientist, for goodness' sake. If the rumours are true she just admired the Nazarene cult from afar, for aesthetic reasons mostly. I think she thought it was all rather beautiful, that's all. So don't worry, there's nothing for you to get upset about."

Sir Douglas pushed a button on his computer keypad and the small holograph figures of Sam and Smith that had been projected onto his desk shrank back to become a two-dimensional image on his computer screen. He pushed the button again and the screen went blank.

"Well, Tony, I think we can congratulate ourselves. Young Samuel has found himself a reasonable billet and, providing Smith doesn't kill him with her potions, she should make a decent little friend for him while he's inside. Wouldn't you say?"

"I suppose so, Sir Douglas. Are they going to sleep together?"

"Haven't decided yet. Sam looks as if he could do with a little bit of loving, doesn't he? Might help to shift that earnest bloody look off his face. But of course one mustn't let one's heart rule one's head in these matters; there're always other things to consider. We'll just have to see."

The younger man nodded.

"Very good, Sir Douglas. Do you want me to put anything out on the wire?"

"Yes, do. For now, just hold him at code green and bung a fire wall around him. A full briefing can wait for the weekly operating notice. Oh yes, and I'd like to sort out some work for him as well, but we can look at that tomorrow. Try and get here as early as possible, there's a good chap."

"Yes, Sir Douglas. Will that be all, then?"

The older man lit a cigarette and inhaled deeply, studying the younger one through the smoke.

"Yes, I think so. Thanks for all your help. And look here, just because you're a brass-buckle, it really doesn't give you any excuse for slacking on your reading, do you understand? Study your Hilary, Tony; after all, from a certain point of view, she was the very first brass-buckle, wasn't she?"

"Yes, Sir Douglas."

"I mean it, you know. I don't want to see you dry up. I've seen it too many times with you non-commissioned chaps and it's really very sad. Do try and make time to read and try to stay *excited*."

"Yes, Sir Douglas."

"Right. Well, off you go, then."

Chapter Seventeen
Further Away than Walsingham

Smith leant heavily on her pestle and crushed a mound of fennel seeds in the bottom of the copper pan, releasing a sickly, aniseed scent into the darkened mixing room. She took three leaves of lemon balm from the dried plant that hung above her head and sliced them quickly on a stained chopping block before dropping them onto the ground seeds. Next, she measured two level spatulas of black powder from a squat bottle and tossed them into the mixture, and then removed a small saucepan of simmering milk from the stove and emptied it into the pan. She reached for a slim copper disk and slid it over the top of the container and then shook the mixture vigorously for as long as it took her to recite three times: *A wheel, a wheel of roses, A pocket full of posies, The turning wheel and blessings, Will sure confound the demon.* Then she set the copper, still covered, on a tripod above a lit candle and waited.

The trick with self-heal was to make sure no light got to it while the ingredients were being mixed, and then to be certain you left it for long enough on the flame after jittering it. Too much light would pollute the darkling energy of the remedy, weakening its effectiveness; too short a time on the flame would unsettle the whole ointment and could give the patient a nasty rash or worse. Smith was an experienced potioner, however, she wouldn't be making any mistakes.

While she waited, her thoughts turned again to her patient, the strange boy who had been sweating and mumbling in the attic room for a whole day. There were lots of things about him that didn't make sense to Smith, and that worried her. She considered her world precarious enough without peculiar lodgers unsettling it even more. She had her mum to think of, and the shop, and what people were saying in the town. And behind everything else there were the dark things about her dad to consider, things that lingered at the very edge of her thought, preventing her from relaxing. She couldn't afford to let her guard drop.

It was true that the boy didn't look particularly dangerous in himself and his money was good—in fact, it was very good—but still, he was an unknown quantity, and that was worrying.

Smith chewed her lip and tried hard to be logical. The facts about the boy were these: he had turned up with Pereduke and Pereduke had said that he came from Walsingham. On its own that meant absolutely nothing. Pereduke was a liar; he would make up anything if it suited him and sometimes he'd make things up anyway, just for fun. You couldn't openly doubt him, of course, but you certainly couldn't trust him, either. It was true that the boy himself had confirmed Pereduke's story, but how much did that mean? Smith had never been to Walsingham and she didn't know anyone who had, but she knew it wasn't *that* far away and various things about the boy suggested he wasn't local at all. There was the sharp, careful way he spoke, for instance, as if all his words were clipped off at the end with scissors; the short, neat haircut; and, most baffling of all, the extraordinary clinging underpants she had discovered when she stripped him for bed after he had passed out.

Despite her anxiety, Smith grinned at the memory. She had never seen a garment like them. They were striped, vivid green and red and they clung to him tightly like a stretchy second skin so that when she had first seen them she thought for a moment that he didn't have any privates. It was very, very peculiar.

She peeped under the brass lid and was enveloped in hot, sweet steam. She stirred the ointment briefly with the spatula. It was thickening nicely. Another few minutes and it would be done.

The question was, if the boy wasn't from Walsingham, where was he from? And what had brought him to Stanmore? There was the knife wound to think about and also the knife itself, which Smith had found tucked into his britches. It didn't look like the kind of thing you'd use to slice food or whittle wood; it was short and ugly, and smeared with blood. And there was also the Royal Crown he'd given her in rent, as casually as if it were sixpence, as well as the 14 more coins she had discovered in his pocket. The boy was extremely rich but he didn't look rich and he didn't act rich. What could that mean?

Smith had considered briefly—she *had* to consider—whether the boy was somehow connected to the demon. Reverend Smythe said there were people who lived right at the edge of the beyonds and gave themselves over to act as a sort of bridge between the beyond world and the proper, living world of men. The demon fed itself on the life and happiness of these poor souls and used them for practical tasks like intelligence-gathering in the settlements and murdering people who strayed too far into his territory. If the boy were one of these people it would perhaps explain the knife and the wound and the money (Reverend Smythe taught that the demon paid handsomely), and perhaps also the boy's strange way of speaking. The boy didn't *look* like that sort of person who consorted regularly with the demon, however. Such people were supposed to be cruel and scornful, with souls that had shriveled up to the size of an apple seed. The boy didn't seem like that at all. Smith reckoned herself to be a good judge of character and she thought the boy looked quite kind. There was something bubbling fiercely inside him, like a remedy that had been left on the candle for too long—she could see that, too, but that didn't make him evil. Of course the demon was deceitful—everyone knew that—but the boy *seemed* sincere. When she had ventured into his room to feed him a little soup or wash and dress his wound he had whimpered and held onto her hand tightly in a way that didn't feel in the slightest bit wicked. Also, if he *was* a human bridge between the demon and the world of men, why did he wear such peculiar underpants? It didn't make much sense.

Smith peeked under the copper lid again and gently stirred the remedy. It was the consistency of fresh yoghurt, which meant it was done. She lifted it off the flame and decanted it carefully into a porcelain tub, scraping the last drops in with her spatula, and then blew out the candle and left the mixing room. As she approached the shop, she heard the clink of glass and porcelain and the sound of nursery rhymes being hummed tunelessly. That was good; it meant that her mum was dusting the stock, which meant she was happy today. Not wishing to disturb her, Smith crept quietly past the shop's internal door and went upstairs, taking care to unsettle the remedy as little as possible. As usual, she went straight into the attic room without knocking, but then she stopped in her tracks. The boy was out of bed and standing at the window, draped in one of the blankets.

"I take it yer feeling better then," she said.

The boy turned round and smiled shyly.

"Yeah, I feel more than better, actually. I feel really alert and sort of sharp like I haven't for ages. How long have I been asleep?"

"Just less than a day. How's yer shoulder?"

Sitting down on the chair, the boy lowered the blanket sufficiently to expose the wound. The cut was now only a thin red line and the flesh on either side had returned to a normal colour.

"It feels tingly but kind of healthy at the same time. It doesn't really hurt anymore."

Smith knelt next to the boy and studied the cut carefully, running her finger quickly along its length.

"I reckon the worst of the sin's all drawn out. But I'm gonna give it another three treatments jus' to be sure. I don't want you dyin' on us and causing us problems with the magistrate. Shut yer eyes and think of the Green Man again."

Smith scooped a dollop of the ointment on her index finger and glanced up at the boy. Suddenly she burst out laughing. The boy looked indignant.

"What's the matter?"

"What 'ave you got yer face all screwed up like that for?"

"I was trying to imagine the Green Man, like you said."

"You look like yer on the toilet."

"Oh. Well, I suppose that must be what I look like when I try to imagine things. I ... I mean, does it matter?"

"Not really. I'm sorry. I'll jus' have to try not to look at you. Try again."

Keeping her eyes fixed firmly on the wound, Smith began to work the ointment carefully into the cut. After a moment, the boy said, "Thank you, by the way—for looking after me and everything."

"Didn't have a lot o' choice, did I? How does it feel now?"

"Cold, all over my shoulder."

"Good. Well, stay still 'til I'm done."

Smith kept applying the ointment, murmuring to herself as she did so. Then she said abruptly:

"Where are you really from, Mick Randall?"

"I'm from Walsingham. My brother inherited all the money off my dad and we had a fight. He's engaged to the magistrate's daughter...so I had to leave...and then I got lost..."

The boy's voice trailed off as Smith looked up at him. She kept rubbing the ointment into his chest, swirling it round in tight circles over the wound, pushing steadily into his flesh.

"I said, where are you *really* from?"

For a long time the boy didn't say anything at all. His eyes darted to and fro to avoid Smith's gaze. Finally, he said softly, "I'm from somewhere a lot further away than Walsingham."

Smith nodded and rubbed the last of the ointment into the boy's shoulder. She licked her finger clean and stood up.

"Pull the blanket up and I'll take you downstairs for that bath. I'll get you yer clothes an' all. They've all been washed."

She walked to the door with the boy following. With her hand on the doorknob she turned to face him.

"Have you got anythin' at all to do with the demon or anythin' evil out in the beyonds?"

"No, nothing at all. Nothing at all. I promise."

"Or with anythin' else that could hurt me or my mum, or even upset my mum?"

"No. I...I'm from quite a long way away, like I said, but I just want to live here for a bit, that's all. I don't know anything about demons or anything else. I'm ... well ... I'm just me. Honestly."

Smith frowned and stared at the boy for a long time.

"You don't look wicked," she said finally, "but you don't quite look ordinary either. I 'spect we'll see about you in time."

The boy smiled awkwardly and Smith led him out of the room.

* * *

Sam followed the girl down one flight of stairs and along the narrow first floor landing. He felt vulnerable after his confession and faintly ridiculous wrapped only in the blanket. He hoped that the girl's mother wouldn't appear, and was relieved when they arrived at the bathroom. The girl removed a copper of hot water from the stove in the corner and emptied it into the deep bath that was freestanding in the centre of the room. She replaced the copper on the stove and worked the hand pump above it until it was full again. She dumped this cold water into the bath as well and then replaced the copper on the stove and sloshed more water into it, leaving it to heat. Finally she took a handful of herbs from one of the glass jars that lined the room's only shelf and threw them into the bath, turning the water green and filling the room with a sharp, leafy smell.

"That'll help to keep yer blood good and pure."

"Thanks."

"Now I'll leave you to it. You can put as much water in as you like for today with no extra charges. Leave the door open a bit though, so I can slip yer clothes in."

"Ok."

"The soap's down there." The girl indicated a block of stuff that looked like lard, sitting on a chipped saucer next to the bath. "You can use as much of that as you like as well."

"Ok. Thanks."

"Right, see you in a bit."

The girl went out leaving the door ajar and Sam unwrapped the blanket and dropped it on the floor. He sat naked on the edge of the bath while the copper warmed up and then, when it began to steam again, he emptied it into the bath. He lowered himself carefully into the half-full tub and soaped himself vigorously. When he had scrubbed and rinsed himself twice he lay back in the warm water and closed his eyes.

He couldn't make up his mind how worried he should be that he told the girl the truth about where he came from, or, at least, where he *didn't* come from. Obviously, it wasn't ideal that she should know that his cover story was false, but he got the impression that it would have been more dangerous to have tried to lie to her. Also, there was a solidness about the girl that reassured Sam. She had the same tough look as his mum, of someone who was used to making difficult decisions and standing by them. He had the feeling that once she had made up her mind to take him on board she wouldn't readily betray him. Anyway, Sam thought as he stretched pleasantly, there was nothing he could do now if she did. He was completely in her hands.

Sam's peace was interrupted by a knock at the door. He jumped and squirmed round in the bath.

"Who is it?"

"It's me," the girl's voice answered. "I've got yer clothes. Also, there's someone downstairs to see you."

"There can't be. I don't know anyone here yet."

"You do. You know Pereduke, which means you know most of Stanmore. It's Tom Drake wantin' to know if you fancy a bit of work at the mill. He's talking to me mum in the shop, which means she's telling 'im about how much dustin' she's done today and he's standing there gettin' cross and wishing he'd never bothered callin'. You'd better get a move on."

"Ok, right. I'll get out."

Sam pulled himself out of the bath and stood dripping on the wooden floor.

"Right, well, here are yer clothes, then," the girl's voice said. She began passing him the items round the bottom of the door and Sam crouched down to collect them: shirt, jerkin, britches, socks. All of them were washed and ironed, and smelt of something sweet and spicy that Sam couldn't identify. Finally she passed Sam the knife, hilt first.

"You'd do well to leave that here. It don't look like an ordinary working knife."

"It isn't," said Sam quickly. "I won't carry it around."

"Yeah, and there was quite a lot of money an' all. I've put it in the strong room for now. You don't want too many people knowin' you've got all that."

"Ok, thanks."

"And you might be needin' these."

The girl passed something that looked like a folded

tablecloth round the door. Sam shook it loose and was astonished to discover that it was a pair of underpants. They were plain white and enormous, reaching down to his knees.

"These aren't mine," he said. "I think they might be a bit big. I … er … I don't think they'd be particularly comfortable, to be honest."

"It doesn't much matter whether they're comfortable or not. You jus' wear them, you understand."

"I … er … I think I'd rather wear my own."

The girl jerked the door open suddenly making Sam tumble backwards. He sprawled on the floor holding the pants tightly against his groin.

"Now you look," she hissed, "most people round 'ere don't notice much about anythin', right? They don't ask questions. As long as they've got work and food and a bit of beer and baccy at the end of the day they're happy. So you should be able to get away with your tale about Walsingham and yer wicked brother, and no one will be any the wiser. But if you go around with yer pockets clanging with Royal Crowns or with a blood stained knife stuck in yer britches, or wearing pants that look like you haven't got any private parts, people are gonna get suspicious, ain't they? And then you'll bring trouble to me door, and I can't afford to have that, Mick Randall or whatever yer name is. Do you understand?"

Sam nodded.

"Yeah. Yeah. Ok. I'll leave the money here and I'll … I'll wear the underpants."

"Good. It's good someone gets the use of them again. Oh yeah, you'll be needin' this an' all." The girl passed a large towel to Sam. He grabbed it, taking care to keep himself covered up with his other hand.

"Thanks."

"That's all right. Now hurry up and get dressed before me mum drives poor Tom Drake out of his mind. I'll wait for you in the shop."

Sam toweled himself down and then dressed and made his way downstairs. The girl's mum was wandering around the shop and pointing at things with a feather duster, keeping up a commentary as she did so. The girl was leaning against the counter studying her thumbnail and frowning. A large man in dusty britches stood in the middle of the floor twiddling his broad brimmed hat impatiently.

"And you see, this 'ere is our little stock of lime-wort, which is good for women in their fifties with their feet, in'tit Lou? Well, I say for women, it certainly works best for women, but men can use it an' all—although it only tends to work well for men if they're water signs. You know: Pisces, Cancer and er ... er...'

"Scorpio," the girl mumbled.

"That's right Scorpio. Pisces, Cancer and Scorpio. But anyway, the thing is, we don't tend to shift a right lot of it, do we, Lou? I mean the shop's a bit out of the way, as you know, so we don't sell a *lot* of anythin', but we *really* don't sell a lot of that lime-wort. So, of course it gathers dust dreadfully. Well, you can see the shape of the lids, they're a regular dust trap, ain't they? But I give it a good going over this mornin' and it looks...'

The girl glanced up and noticed Sam.

"Um, Mum, Mick the lodger's 'ere now."

"Oh yes. The young man's 'ere for you now, Mr. Drake. Anyway, I've got me lime-wort nice and clean, as you can see." The girl's mum subsided and the man nodded at Sam.

"Now then, young man. Mr. Pereduke tells me you might be lookin' for a spot of work?"

"Yeah. I mean, if there's anything going."

"Well, actually, there might be a bit of summat up at the mill. Anderson, my regular lad, has to go to Limeport for a couple of weeks and it's gonna leave me short. If you don't mind getting a bit dusty..."

"He's gotta be careful with his chest though, Mr. Drake," the girl broke in. "He's had it cut and it doesn't want overworkin' yet."

"I'm not gonna break his back for him, Smith, don't you worry. He doesn't look like he'd be fit for hard liftin' or anything like that. No offence, young man, but I speak as I find. No, he'll just be raking chaff off and fixin' things up the pulleys and suchlike. Reckon you can manage that?"

Sam nodded.

        Interlander

"Right. Well, I'll pay two shillings for the first day and we'll see where we go after. Does that suit?"

"Yeah, that's fine. When do you want me to start?"

"Seven o'clock tomorrow. You'll finish at four. We're just off the path at the end of Brewer Street, but I expec' young Smith will be able to give you proper directions."

The girl nodded and the man extended his hand. When Sam took it, it felt like sandpaper wrapped round warm stone.

"Good. Well, I'll see yer tomorrow, Mick. We'll set you on and see how you go."

Suddenly the girl's mum twitched.

"If 'e's startin' at seven and working through 'til four someone will 'ave to make his sandwiches for him, won't they Lou? Won't they, eh? I jus' don't reckon I'm gonna have time. Not before tomorrow anyway."

"Don't worry, Mum; I'll sort that out," the girl said.

Tom Drake rolled his eyes and slapped his hat back on his head. He nodded to the girl and her mother and marched out the shop. There was a large pair of dusty footprints where he had been standing. The girl's mum opened her mouth in alarm.

"Don't worry, Mum; I'll sort that out an' all," the girl said quickly.

Chapter Eighteen
The Reckoning

Not even Sebastian Randall could prevent birds from flying across the boundary. Had there been one perched on the tatty sign of *Smith's Potioners* as Sam was meeting Tom Drake, and had it been disturbed by Tom Drake slamming the shop door harder than was necessary as he left (hard enough to make Smith's mum twitch and fret a little, which was what he intended), and had it then flown south west from Stanmore, it would soon have reached the discreet installations that marked the great division between sophiocracy's two worlds. Had the creature kept going, buffeted and carried by the cold Siberian wind, it would eventually have arrived at Cambridge, where perhaps it would have recovered from its long and forbidden journey by resting on the handsome, wrought-iron side gate of Randall College. Just beneath the gate, as it happened, another meeting was taking place.

"You definitely told him three o'clock?"

"Of course I told him three o'clock. Trust me; he'll be here in a minute or two. He's a dependable guy."

"He's never struck me as particularly dependable. We're not playing games here, you know. The organisation doesn't play games."

"Trust me, he'll be here."

The first man pursed his lips in irritation and glanced at his watch. He was the older of the two, in his fifties perhaps, with a narrow, anxious face and thinning, reddish-grey hair. He was dressed in a tweed suit and an academic gown. The second man was in his twenties. He had gentle, distracted features and was dressed in an old overcoat and a tatty cap, pulled low over his eyes. For several minutes neither of them spoke, and then a van approached them at speed down the deserted lane. It screeched to a halt next to the gate and the driver leapt out. He was also in his twenties and fit-looking, dressed in a tracksuit.

"Where the hell have you been?" demanded the older man. The driver held up his hands.

"Yeah, yeah I know. Look, I'm sorry. I got delayed. I've ... well, to be honest, I've got family problems. I got away as soon as I could."

"You need to sort your priorities out, young man. What we're engaged in here is considerably more important than any bloody family problems. Do you understand?"

The van driver shrugged.

"Yeah, of course I understand. Like I said, I'm sorry."

The older man glanced nervously up and down the lane. There was no one to be seen. The only sound was the wind rustling through the ivy that coated the high college walls.

"Right, well, let's get loaded up, shall we?"

A large military duffle bag and a wicker crate were tucked in the shadow of the gatepost. The two younger men heaved both of them into the back of the van, the crate emitting a chorus of unhappy squawks as they did so. The van driver slammed the back door and locked it, then turned to the older man.

"I think we're ready."

"About bloody time. Are you clear about the instructions?"

"Absolutely."

"And you're not going to be distracted by your trouble at home and mess everything up?"

"No."

The older man nodded curtly. He turned to the other man.

"I'm not going to ask you if you're clear about what you're supposed to be doing because I know that you are. I'm just going to say good luck."

"Thanks."

"Do you have your pill?"

The young man nodded.

"Good. I hope to God you that don't have to use it. But if you do, make sure that you do, if you know what I mean." The older man paused and chewed his lip. He looked hard at the other two. "Well, this is it then. Both of you, until the reckoning."

"Until the reckoning."

"Until the reckoning."

All three of them shook hands and then the two young men climbed into the van (Tracksuit took the driver's seat) and it moved off down the shadowy lane. The older man watched it go, frowning, then slipped through the gate and trudged wearily towards the college, his eyes cast to the floor. He had sent brave young people into danger many times over the years but he had never yet reconciled himself to it.

He wilfully ignored the blackbird that was singing its delight over the scene from the top of the college gate. He was a good man engaged in appalling work; if too much beauty or joy slipped into his heart, he knew that he would find it impossible to do the dreadful things that needed to be done.

As they drove off, the only subject the two young men wished to discuss was the operation that lay ahead of them. According to the strict protocols of the organisation they worked for, however, this topic was absolutely forbidden. It lay heavy between them as the van made its way slowly through the winding Cambridge backstreets and so, despite the fact that they knew each other well, their conversation was stilted and awkward. As they turned onto the motorway, Overcoat glanced across at his companion.

"What was the bother at home?" he asked. "Nothing too serious, I hope?"

"I'm afraid that's another of those things we can't speak about," Tracksuit replied. "It's all to do with sex and family and people seeing things they weren't meant to see. Suffice it to say that I've behaved like an absolutely selfish arse with rather drastic and unforeseen consequences. I don't feel at all good about it."

Overcoat frowned.

"Are you sure you've behaved selfishly? You've never struck me as particularly selfish. As an insensitive, randy oaf, maybe, but not selfish. You're certainly not being selfish now."

"I'm not sure it makes any difference. I'm not sure if doing something good in one area of your life makes up for being a bastard in another area—especially if you're being a bastard to people you're supposed to love. I might be doing good at the moment, but I'm sort of doing it in the abstract, aren't I? I think it's probably pretty easy to work for the good of humanity, but it's a damn sight harder to be good and kind to people you can actually see. Do you know what I mean?"

"Not really."

Tracksuit grinned.

"That's because you're thick. God, what a pair. A thicky and, what was it you called me, an insensitive, randy oaf? The organisation's really scraping the barrel with us, isn't it?"

Overcoat also grinned, then closed his eyes and tried to sleep.

The van headed swiftly north and then east, arriving at dusk at a small seaside town where the houses tumbled down a steep incline to the harbour and the smell of salt and ship's diesel tanged the air. They parked next to the harbour master's hut and walked along the quayside to a blue boat on which a man was vigorously mopping the deck. The boat had obviously once been a fishing vessel but both it and its solitary seafarer looked much too smart to be engaged in the fishing trade. The man glanced up as they approached.

"Can I help you at all?"

"My friend and I were hoping to make a short voyage," Tracksuit replied. "By our reckoning you might be just the chap to help us."

"I see. Well, if that's what you reckon, come aboard." The man's voice dropped. "But I was told you'd have luggage."

"We have. It's in our van."

"Well, go and fetch it then. The sooner we're on our way the better, frankly."

The two men walked quickly back to the van and unloaded the crate and the duffle bag. They heaved them onto the boat and the boat owner lowered them into the hold with a pulley and secured them with leather straps (the crate squawked indignantly while this was going on). He scrambled back to the deck, bolted the hold shut and turned to his passengers.

"It's probably better if you two go below. I'm not expecting company but you can't be sure and neither of you particularly looks like a sailor. No offence, gentlemen, but I prefer to minimise my risks. There's food in the galley if you're interested."

"Fair enough; you're the boss," Tracksuit replied.

The two young men descended a gleaming brass ladder into a low room, equipped with a stove and a row of cupboards and drawers. There was a wooden table bolted to the floor at one end of the room, with benches fixed on either side. Overcoat removed his cap and slid along one of the benches while Tracksuit began working his way through the cupboards.

"So, let's see what we've got. There's cheese, bread, some sausages, a bag of oranges..."

"Useful to keep the scurvy away."

"Exactly, shipmate. Tea, coffee, oh God, horrible powered milk, pasta and what's this? Hello, a pack of cards. Fantastic."

Tracksuit sat down opposite overcoat and shuffled the cards expertly, making them flutter from one hand to another.

"What games do you know?"

"Dunno really. Snap?"

"Snap! Nothing else? Bloody hell, it's going to be a long trip."

Just then the boat's engine emitted a low growl and the small room began to vibrate. The two men glanced at each other.

"Well, this is it," Tracksuit murmured. "We're really going, aren't we? Are you, you know, ok?

"I'm perfectly ok," Overcoat replied. "I've been waiting for this moment since I first understood anything about our wonderful government. My dad was killed fighting for the organisation, I don't know if you knew."

"No, actually, I didn't know."

"Well, he was—when I was ten. Sorry, I don't mean to be melodramatic, but you see, it means that I'm quite ready for anything. I'm ready to die if necessary. Honestly, I feel peaceful."

"I wouldn't worry about sounding melodramatic. We're in a pretty dramatic situation, aren't we?" Tracksuit paused, and when he spoke his voice was brittle and strained. "And for what it's worth, my own dad was ... well, *harmed* by the Project. I found some letters about Ely when I was 15 and suddenly everything weird about him and everything stupid and dysfunctional about my whole family made sense. That's when I decided to get involved."

Overcoat reached out and touched Tracksuit's arm.

"You're not a bad person, you know," he said. "Whatever you think; whatever you've done at home; whatever anyone saw that they weren't supposed to see. You're not bad; you're good."

The two men played first snap and then, under Tracksuit's tutelage, whist and rummy as the boat eased its way through the North Sea. When night fell they cooked and ate a simple meal, and then dozed in their seats. Shortly before midnight, the ship's owner came down the ladder.

"About ten minutes, gentlemen. I'll be stopping a mile off shore, as per the contract. You have a calm sea, and I don't envisage any problems."

"Thank you," Overcoat mumbled. When the boat owner had gone, he clambered out from behind the table and undid his coat buttons.

"Right then, you'd better frisk me."

Tracksuit stood up and ran his hands through the other man's pockets, then patted down his legs and arms and checked the folds of his clothing. Finally, he leant close to his companion and sniffed his armpits and his mouth.

"Yeah, you stink; you'll do. Come on, let's get back on deck."

The two men climbed back up the ladder and discovered their crate and duffle bag already stacked by the starboard bow. The boat owner slid open the wheelhouse window.

"The little rower's in the stern. Give me a moment, gentlemen, and I'll lower it for you."

The boat's engines cut out and a sudden clatter indicated that the anchor had been dropped. The wheelhouse door opened and the boat owner emerged, still pristine in his sailing whites. He led the other two to the back of the boat where a small rowing boat was fastened to the deck. The two men watched as the boat owner swung it out over the sea on a wooden beam and then lowered it onto the dark water. He descended a short ladder and held the rowing boat steady.

"Look sharp, gentlemen. Go and get your stuff."

The young men collected the crate and duffle bag and manhandled them with some difficulty into the rowing boat. Overcoat scrambled in after them and the boat owner climbed back onto the deck.

"I take it you're the rower," he said to Tracksuit.

"I am."

"Have you done much of it?"

"A bit, at college."

The boat owner looked doubtful.

"You might find it rather different on the open sea, but anyway, too late to worry about that now. There's a compass in the prow. You need to go due west to hit the agreed landing point. I'll be here for three hours as per the contract. After that you're on your own. There are naval patrols at dawn and I can't afford to take risks."

Tracksuit looked closely at the boat owner for the first time. His brown hair was greased close to his scalp except for a few strands that fell loose over his forehead. His eyes were quick and sly. He did not look in the least like the sort of person you would want to trust with your life. As if sensing Tracksuit's thoughts, the boat owner said, "You need have no concerns about me honouring the agreement. I gave my word to your people; you can trust me."

"I don't give a toss about your word," Tracksuit murmured. "I think I can trust you because my organisation has paid you handsomely to do a job and because we know where you live and where your children live. Do you understand me?"

The boat owner opened his mouth to speak and then closed it again. He nodded quickly.

"Good. I'll see you when I get back."

Tracksuit lowered himself into the rowing boat. Overcoat pushed off clumsily and they struck out for the shore. For a few minutes neither of them spoke. The only sound was the regular beat of the oars and the water lapping against the hull.

"You know what I wish?" Tracksuit said eventually.

"No."

"I wish we didn't have to deal with such sleazy bloody people. It's so difficult to keep the justice of the cause in sight when you have to negotiate with squalid little men like that boat guy. I say negotiate; I suppose I mean threaten, really."

Overcoat shrugged.

"If you wanted to associate with respectable people, you should have got yourself a different hobby."

"I also wish I was coming with you, to be honest."

"Well, all being well you'll be back in a few months and then you can stay for as long as you want."

Tracksuit strained at the oars, making his muscles ripple. He glanced up at the stars.

"Of course. The reckoning, you mean."

"Something like that."

"Do you really think...?"

Overcoat smiled.

"Oh, I try not to think anything much," he said. "I'm thick, remember."

Chapter Nineteen
Mill Boy

The morning after his conversation with Tom Drake, Sam was woken by a loud banging on his bedroom door. He rolled over and covered his head with blankets but the banging came again.

"What ... what is it?" he called out feebly.

"It's six o'clock. You gotta get up, Mick Randall. You've gotta go to work today, remember?"

"Oh yeah. Thanks. Ok. I'm ... er ... I'm awake now."

"Good. Get yourself washed, then come down to the kitchen. I've got yer breakfast on."

"Thanks," Sam said again. He swung his legs over the side of the bed and ran his hand through his hair, then pulled on his shirt and britches and went to the bathroom. He splashed water on his face and cleaned his teeth with a wooden toothbrush and cream from a tub labeled *Dandelion Tooth Scrub - Gritting and Shine*. When he was done he went back to his room to finish getting dressed and made his way downstairs.

The girl was standing at the stove frying eggs and bacon.

"Hello, mill boy," she said. "How's your shoulder?"

"It's fine. I haven't really thought about it for a while."

"Good, I'll give you one more lot of self-heal this evening, then yer done." She nodded to a tin on the table. "That's yer lunch. I've done you pigeon sandwiches with a couple of boiled eggs and a slice of seed cake. I think that'll do you."

Sam sat down at the table and yawned. He tapped the tin.

"I thought the arrangement was that my rent just covered breakfast and tea. Shouldn't I be paying extra for this?"

"We always say that to new lodgers so they don't start takin' advantage. But really, if we've got bits and pieces left over, it's silly not to use 'em up, isn't it?"

The girl maneuvered two eggs and three rashers of bacon onto a plate, together with a slice of bread, and placed it in front of Sam. She went to the dresser and collected a butter dish and a knife and fork. She handed these to him also.

"How do you know I'm not going to take advantage?" Sam

asked. The girl stared at him for a moment.

"I just do. I think yer a liar, Mick Randall, and I think yer sort of complicated and probably unhappy. But yer not the kind who takes advantage. I can tell that."

The girl stood over Sam with her hands on her hips and watched him as he began to eat, then she returned to the stove and boiled water in a blackened kettle. She made a mug of coffee and set it on the table with a jug of milk. She looked hard at Sam again and then reached into the pocket of her apron and pulled out a small brown bottle and a pen knife. Carefully, she unscrewed the top of the bottle and tapped it into her palm. A small brown lump, something like the ginger Sam had seen in his mum's restaurant, fell into her hand. She laid it on a saucer and cut off a thin slice which she handed to Sam.

"What's that?"

"It's tallis root. Swallow it. It won't do you no harm."

"What does it do?"

"It sharpens the wits. I've got a feeling that if you're gonna survive and keep yer story straight, you're gonna need a bit of help to think clear and quick. That's all."

Sam peered at the bit of root.

"It's all right, I promise yer. I take it a bit most days meself."

"Why do you need to?"

The girl shrugged and laid the wafer on the table next to Sam's cup.

"I just do. Look, it's there. Take it if you want it, leave it if you don't. It doesn't matter to me one way or the other. I just think it'll help you, that's all."

Sam picked up the piece of root and sniffed it, then placed it on his tongue and swallowed it with a mouthful of coffee. He ate the rest of his breakfast quickly and took his plate over to the sink, where the girl was stirring large, bluish leaves around in muddy water.

"Leave yer plate there," she said. "I'll do it later. Now then, do you know where yer going?"

"Not really."

"Didn't think so. You turn right out of the house, then left at the top of the street onto Fightin' Cocks Lane. Follow that all the way along to the milk booth and then go left again. That's Brewers' Lane. You go along there to the sheriff's lock-up, which is a small square room with bars on the windows, and jus' next to that you'll see a little footpath. Follow that for about half a mile and the mill's on yer left. It's a big thing with sails; you can't really miss it. And don't forget your lunch."

Sam picked up the tin and pulled his jerkin on. The girl watched him.

"You don't look too bad in that that jerkin, actually. Matter of fact, you look sort of trim."

"Um, well, that's good. Thank you."

"Yeah. Well anyway, yer dinner's at seven. Don't be late or I'll give it to the cats."

The girl turned back to the sink and continued stirring the leaves.

"Right. Bye then."

"Bye, Mick Randall," she said without looking round.

Sam walked briskly through the streets and found the footpath without difficulty. It snaked through some allotments for a short way and then ran alongside a stream that drifted lazily along its channel, higher than the path itself. After ten minutes he spotted what he supposed must be the windmill. It was a large box-shaped building made of bleached, overlapping boards, and it had four sails, like the sides of paper kites, turning slowly in front. As he approached, Tom Drake ducked out of the door to meet him.

"You've turned up then," the miller said, wiping his hand on his apron and offering it to Sam. Sam took it.

"Yeah, I have. Like I said, I want to work."

"Aye, and I don't suppose Smith would 'ave let you stay in bed anyway. She's never struck me as the sorta person who'd put up with laziness." The miller frowned and nodded. "And a good thing, too. Now listen, young Mick, let's forget what the old rogue mighta told me, 'ave you ever actually done a day's work in a mill?"

"Um, no."

"Have you ever been *inside* a mill?"

"No. Sorry. But I've read about them, I think."

The miller rolled his eyes and wiped his face with a grimy handkerchief. The sweat mixed with a layer of dust to leave smears of pale paste on his cheeks and forehead.

"He's a lyin' beggar that one, in't he? Not that I'd tell 'im that, of course, but he is. Well anyway, Mick, thanks for bein' straight with me, but you can forget what you might 'ave read. First thing I'll do is show you round so you can learn how a real mill works, then we'll set you on and see how you do. It ain't rock science, to be honest. Now, you just be careful with the sails when we step inside. They look flimsy enough but they can be very unforgivin', believe me."

The miller turned and moved swiftly back between the rotating sails and on through the mill's low door. Sam stood still, counting the gaps between the sails' passes and then dashed after him. He stumbled into the cool darkness of the mill and found the miller chuckling.

"Well done, young Mick. It gets easier to judge as you get used to it. At least they let you in though, that's the main thing. They say sails that don't like a man will kill 'im before they let him inside their mill." He gestured round the dark room. "Anyway, this is where the corn gets stored immediately as it comes in. It's important to stamp the sacks as soon as they arrive so we know whose is whose. People get funny about that sort of thing. Then the sacks get hoisted by that pulley there up to the sortin' floor. You any good with heights?"

"Not too bad."

"Good, cos you'd make a poor sorta miller if you weren't. Bung your lunch up on that shelf, out the way of the mice, and we'll go for a climb."

The miller kept up a commentary on the mill's workings as he led Sam up increasingly narrow ladders and through smaller and smaller trap doors. In places they had to squeeze past powerful cogs or duck between juddering ropes and chains so that Sam feared his clothes would get snagged or torn. Everything creaked and sighed and shook so that he began to imagine he was shuffling around the warm innards of a living creature. Tom Drake's comment about the sails not liking a man didn't seem entirely fanciful.

Finally, the miller flung open a tiny trap door in the side of the building and the sunlight burst in, illuminating a rectangle of dusty air. He grunted and sank to his knees to crawl through the opening. Sam wriggled through after him and pulled himself to his feet on a small platform that was set at the top of the mill, just behind the sails.

"Ain't a bad view, is it?" the miller asked. "I reckon it's one of the best perks of the job, is this. There's not many folk can see as far as me."

Sam nodded. The landscape was green and largely empty, crisscrossed by ditches that gleamed golden in the morning sunlight. There were hamlets and villages dotted here and there, and around them the darker greens and browns of cultivated fields and allotments. On the far horizon Sam could just make out the smudgy blue of the sea. The pair of them stood in silence while the miller filled his pipe. The only sound was the steady hiss and crump of the turning sails.

"It's funny," Sam said eventually, "I didn't really notice that it was windy until I saw the sails moving."

"Ah, well, it's a strange day when there's not a bit of breeze up here," the miller said. "It's called the outside wind, is this; it's constant all year round and as cold as a witch's arse in winter. You can just about feel a touch of summat chill in it now, can't you?"

Sam nodded, and then he said slowly, "Where does it come from?"

"Where does what come from?"

"The cold wind. The outside wind. Where does it start?"

The miller sucked at his pipe and blew smoke towards the horizon.

"Well it just comes from outside, don't it? It's *beyond*, Mick. Reckon that's all you can say, really."

"But it must actually *start* somewhere. And it must *go* somewhere as well, mustn't it? Where does it blow to in the west after the beyonds?"

The miller's thoughtful eyes turned dark and dull, and his face became expressionless. For a full minute he smoked his pipe in short, mechanical puffs, without speaking and then he made a small noise—halfway between a grunt and a sob—in the back of his throat and his face clicked back to life. He knocked out his pipe on the platform's balustrade.

"Well, come on then, young 'un. We can't just stand around chattin' all day like a pair of old women. Let's get you started. D'you smoke one of these things, by the way?"

"No."

"Fair enough. But if yer ever tempted, just remember young man, never inside the mill. You set the flour on fire and you'll see the air burn like the flames of hell. I did it once and I was lucky that I only lost my eyebrows. Now let's get going."

Despite the cramped conditions and the dust, Sam enjoyed his day's work. It was pleasant to labour in the strange, creaking building with its healthy smell of flour and warm wood, aware always of the gentle presence of the miller as he clattered around above or below him. Sam mostly worked on his own, heaving sacks of corn across the storage area and fixing them to the pulley, to be yanked up to the sorting floor. Alternatively, he would answer the miller's bellowed instructions to fetch him a spanner or a mallet, or to untwist a rope, or clean the teeth of a cog that had become jammed. He ate his lunch on the balcony with his legs dangling into the emptiness and the outside wind cooling his sticky face, and then worked on through the afternoon until the fine strips of sunlight that slipped into the mill began to dim. Eventually the miller's voice sounded down to him, "That's us done for today, Mick. We've earned our corn, I reckon. Now then lad, have you got time for a quick one?"

Sam glanced at his wrist where his digital watch used to be, but before he could say anything the miller squeezed through the trapdoor above him and slid down the ladder. He wiped his hands on his pinny and handed Sam two small copper coins.

"There you go, young man. And there are another couple of them for you an' all, if you decide to turn up again tomorrow. Now then, what time did she say you gotta be home?"

"My dinner's at seven."

"Well, then, you've got plenty of time for a pint. Listen, Mick, you don't want to be gettin' home too early, or else she'll only find more jobs for you to do around the place. I've been married for 14 years; jus' you take my word for it."

The pair of them walked slowly along the footpath. Sam was a little stiff, but the ache in his muscles pleased him, leaving him satisfied and peaceful. The miller was mostly silent, concentrating on his pipe, but occasionally he would point out a rabbit or a heron, or comment on some detail of the landscape. They wound their way back through the allotments and then on through the streets until they arrived at the King's Head. The miller opened the door for Sam and followed him inside.

"You been 'ere before?" the miller asked.

"Um, no. I don't think so. Well … well not really … No … Definitely no'

"Aye, well it's a nice enough boozer. Lots of the lads'll come in here for a quick one after work. Helps put off the evil hour when you 'ave to face the family. Matter of fact, there's few of them in already, look."

The miller pointed to a small knot of men and boys who were standing near the bar. Above the hum of conversation, Sam could hear a familiar voice from the centre of the group.

"You can say what you like, Arthur. I'm just tellin' you what I've heard, which is that if you do that, your buttocks will definitely go blue. Now I ain't saying it's *true* necessarily, but it's certainly true that I 'eard it."

There was a chorus of laughter from the group. The miller frowned and slapped his hat, sending a fine shower of dust to the floor.

"Looks like your mate's in, Mick," he murmured. "Ah well, can't be helped."

Before Sam could answer, Pereduke's voice rang out again.

"Mick, good to see you fresh from yer labours. Straight from the house of bread into the house of ale. Well done, young fella! Now get yerself over 'ere and get a pint down you. You too, of course, Master Drake. Get them a couple of pints, could you Bobby Ploughman? Here's the wherewithal. Now then, I'm grateful to you for givin' Mick his chance, Master Drake. How did he do?"

"Very fair, I'd say, Mr. Pereduke," said the miller without much enthusiasm. "Very fair indeed, matter of fact."

"Excellent. Pereduke never doubted it, not with the lad's

background."

A pint of beer was pressed into Sam's hand. He sipped it and was surprised how refreshing he found it. He took a larger sip and then a gulp. Pereduke beamed.

"A good thirst on you, lad. Excellent; that's what Pereduke likes to see. And how are you getting on with Smith? Is she warmin' yer cockles for you, young fella? Tell uncle."

"Um yeah, she seems nice enough and my cockles are fine, thanks," Sam said. He was pleased when a few of the men around him sniggered. Pereduke laughed heartily and blew some of the froth from his beer onto the floor.

"I'm glad to hear it, Mick. But if you'll take a bit of advice from old Pereduke, you won't hang around there. It's the redheads that have got all the fire and the filth inside 'em, you see. Just what you need, young fella. She'll set you right, will young Smith, if you let her. Take it from a man who knows these things."

"Actually, I prefer them dark ones, Pereduke..." said a lively-faced young man next to Sam. Pereduke held up his hand to check him midsentence.

"Enough of that nonsense, Davis Roof. Dark ones, indeed! That's just because you're the son of a thatcher, ain't it? It stands to reason you don't feel relaxed 'less yer around big tangled piles of black thatch and suchlike. Go on, admit it to old Pereduke; it's true, ain't it? Me and Mick on the other hand are men of taste and refinement, ain't we Mick?"

The group of men laughed again and Sam laughed with them. When his pint was empty another appeared in his hand. He drank this one more quickly than the first, and when it was empty Pereduke slapped him on the back.

"Good on you, Mick, that's what old Pereduke likes to see. Let me get you another one in, young fella."

"But I owe you for one already," Sam protested. "I've got money. I should buy you one back."

"Oh, you owe me for a lot more than just beer, young un," the older man growled amiably. "The way I see it, you owe Pereduke for yer lodgin's and yer labours, not to mention all the lovin' yer gonna get from young Smith." Pereduke held Sam's elbow and leaned close to him. His voice dropped so that only Sam could hear him, "But don't you worry 'bout all that, Micky; I reckon you're gonna pay old Pereduke back more than adequately with all the fun you're gonna bring him. Matter of fact, I reckon you're gonna pay him back a dozen times over, at least."

"Yeah, yeah, maybe," Sam said quickly. "Maybe I will. But I'm gonna start by buying you a drink."

Chapter Twenty
The Trader

Sam's first strange days in the enclosure turned into weeks and then the weeks turned astonishingly into a month and then into a number of months. And then Sam stopped thinking about it. He no longer ticked off significant dates in his head or marveled that he had survived a new experience without giving the game away. At times he almost forgot that there *was* a game to give away. He began to settle into enclosure life, or perhaps it would be truer to say that enclosure life began to settle into him.

His hair grew long and shaggy until one evening Smith sat him down in the shuttered shop and tackled it with a large pair of scissors that smelt of her herbs and chemicals. She left him with a neatened mop that fell well below his collar but was cut back sharply from his forehead.

"I swear by the Wheel, you look like you were born 'ere, Mick Randall," she had said when she was done. And later, when Sam examined himself in the mirror, he saw it was true. And it wasn't only his hair that made him look like a native. Under the influence of Smith's cooking his stomach soon bulged, enclosure-style, so that bits of pale flesh peeked through the gaps between his straining buttons. Pereduke noticed, of course, and ran his hands over Sam's stomach one evening in the King's Head.

"Ah, that Smith's lookin' after you all right, Mick," he had leered. "She's fattenin' you up for the slaughter, young fella. You trust old Pereduke, that's what she's doin' all right."

One day when he was getting ready for bed, Sam had also discovered muscles on his arms. They weren't much—nothing like Roger's rowing muscles or the smooth, hard muscles on an alpha—but they were muscles nonetheless, and the next morning he had made a point of showing them to Smith when they were alone in the kitchen. She had poked one of them sharply and giggled.

"Well, you ain't exactly gonna win the Log Heave at the

Midsummer Fayer, but there's summat there, Mick, that's true enough. You keep on workin' and one day you'll turn into a great strong man so that I won't even recognise you myself."

Sam did keep working. When he had completed his two weeks in Tom Drake's mill he went on to get casual work in the farms, wood yards and workshops that dotted Stanmore and the surrounding area. After a month or so he was surprised and gratified to learn that he had built up a reputation as a reliable worker. He didn't need the money, of course, but he had to be seen to be doing something if his cover story was to stand up and, anyway, he enjoyed working alongside the solid, kind Stanmore men and earning a coin or two from them at the end of the day.

When he wasn't working, Sam was never bored. The King's Head was lively most evenings. There were games of dominoes or cards, as well as songs about women who proved false, or cows that would give no milk, or witches who stole children away, or young men with broken hearts who went wandering into the beyonds and were never seen again. Sam loved the pub's atmosphere and the music, not to mention the drink, and he quickly became a regular.

There were also the Sunday ceremonies to enjoy, when the temple was jammed with people, and clouds of incense hung in the air so that you felt dizzy with the heat and sweetness of it. When Reverend Smythe had concluded the day's rites, the congregation would burst out of the building and wander down the main street to the common where they would flock around, chatting and smoking, before drifting off into the pubs or into one another's homes for games of backgammon and chess.

One day in January, the dykes around Stanmore froze completely and it seemed to Sam that the whole settlement buckled on heavy skates made of wood and bone, and raced along the glistening channels for hours until the sun sank over the beyonds and the wind cut the skaters' cheeks like knife blades, driving them inside for toast and damson brandy. Then there was the day in March when the Petersons' youngest son got engaged to a girl from Little Rutting and Sam joined 20 or so of the young men of Stanmore to build the couple an extension on the side of the Peterson family home. They began digging the foundations by torchlight before dawn and had to relight the torches at the day's end to nail the final roof slates into place and splash blue paint on the last few planks of clapboard. When the work was done, Jack Peterson provided roast pig and beer, and the young men of Stanmore got drunk and became sentimental about friendship and the end of their boyhood. And Sam, with his aching limbs, blistered hands, and full and bulging stomach, almost believed he had grown up with them. He found himself looking forward to the day when his friends would help him build a house for himself and his sweetheart, whoever she might turn out to be.

Only Roger's ghost continued to yank Sam's thoughts back across the boundary. He always came in the early mornings, catching Sam halfway between sleep and waking. He would speak tenderly but forcefully as he had done on the night that Sam had caught him with Rachel ("I can't let you ruin things by blabbing to Jen … I *won't* let you, Sam, do you understand?"). On these occasions, the hatred rose fresh and strong in Sam's stomach. He would throw himself out of bed and pace the bedroom until it was time to go down for breakfast. Sitting at the battered kitchen table, chewing toast or pickled eels while Smith bustled around, it was easy to calm down and let the thoughts of his brother slip once more from his mind.

Smith herself was invaluable as Sam's mentor during his first months in the enclosure. There was also Pereduke, of course, coming and going in the streets and pubs of Stanmore, acting as his unofficial patron. But he didn't entirely trust Pereduke, and anyway, it was Smith who knew the truth that he was not from Walsingham. Sam's candor had created a bond between the pair of them that was strengthened as Smith guided him patiently through the potential pitfalls of enclosure life. At the end of his first month in Stanmore, Sam left the settlement early in the morning and retraced his steps to the hedge where he had hidden the rest of his stolen Royal Crowns. He dragged them out of their hiding place and brought them back to the shop where he handed them over to Smith to be kept in the strong room. Her eyes had widened with astonishment when she saw how much money he had, but she had taken the bag of coins from him without a word. After that, if Sam ever found himself short of money, Smith would simply change one of the Royal Crowns for him from the shop's takings. She also washed his clothes, changed his bed, cooked his meals and twice a week slipped him a sliver of tallis root with his breakfast, "To keep head good and clear, Mick-from-Walsingham," she'd say with a sly grin. "I'm not having you making an arse of yerself and bringin' trouble to my door."

Sam slowly came to appreciate Smith's strength and her gentleness with her mum, and he grew to admire her forthright face that crumpled suddenly into gap-toothed giggles when something amused her. From time to time, when he had nothing to do, he would seek her out in the kitchen or in the shop and sit chatting with her about nothing in particular until she eventually lost patience.

"You ain't pretty enough to be an ornament, Mick," she would snap. "And you ain't quite witty enough to be entertainment neither, so you might as well make yerself useful." And then Sam would find himself with plants to chop, or shelves to stack, or a floor to clean, with Smith supervising.

Or perhaps he would find himself sent on an errand as he was one afternoon in April, seven months after he had arrived in Stanmore. He had been sitting behind the counter in the shop watching Smith tidy and rearrange the stock. The trap door to the cellar where the stores were kept was propped open and a number of half-empty boxes were stacked around the shop floor. Smith worked incredibly quickly, her whirring fingers sliding bottles and tubs of ointment into place like pieces of a puzzle, frowning with concentration all the while. Now, as Sam watched, she slid a tub of rose-heart wart relief into its correct position next to a jar of weasels' livers and then froze. She thumped her forehead with the palm of her hand.

"Damn and blast it. I forgot about that bird-trader. What hour is it now, Mick?"

"About half past five."

"Damn. He said he were gonna go at six and he isn't a regular one, neither. I don't know when he's gonna come back round. I wanted to get a pair of his woodcock. Really fat they were, almost twice as big as Toby Slaughter has."

Smith looked round at the half empty boxes of stock and still-muddled shelving and sighed.

"I can't leave it like this, can I? You'll 'ave to go, Mick. Sorry, but you'll 'ave to."

"Oh God, must I?"

"You must if you want to eat summat decent tonight and tomorrow."

Sam groaned and slid off his stool while Smith rummaged in her pocket.

"Here's fivepence, that'll be more than enough."

"There's really no need. I don't mind…"

"Go on and take it. I don't want charity."

Sam took the coin and slipped it into his pocket:

"Good lad. Now, he's right outside the King's Head. You'll see him easily enough with his baskets. And don't get yerself too distracted with beer afterwards, neither. I want them woodcock for tonight, remember."

"Yeah, yeah, I know. You can rely on me."

Smith stared at Sam severely for a moment and then her nose wrinkled and she grinned.

"Yeah, well, there's lots I could say to that Mick Randall from Walsingham, but I won't. I'll be charitable and hold my peace. Now go and get me them birds."

Sam walked quickly to the pub and spotted the trader next to the door. He was perched on a hand cart surrounded by stacks of wicker crates. Pereduke was at his side with a pint of beer clenched in his fist, and the two of them were talking animatedly. As Sam approached Pereduke swung round.

"By the wheel, if it ain't young Mick Randall. Splendid. Splendid. Slipped away for a pint or two before yer tea, have you, young fella?" The old man cocked his head to one side and peered at Sam inquisitively. "Pereduke thinks that's very wise."

"Not really," Sam said. "I've just come for a couple of his woodcock. She sent me."

"She's a smart young miss, that one. This 'ere fella does the cheapest and fattest birds I've ever known. Out of this world they are, Micky, quite out of this world. No wonder poor old Toby's spittin' feathers today." Pereduke slurped his beer and chortled. "You'll stop for a drink though, Mick, old Pereduke insists. As you can see, I'm havin' one of my humorous days. You wouldn't want to miss out on Pereduke's wit now, would you?" He turned to the trader. "And I dare say you'll 'ave one an' all."

Without giving either of them a chance to speak, Pereduke swilled the last drop of his beer onto the road and bustled back into the pub leaving Sam and the trader alone.

"Was it two woodcock?" the trader asked. He was younger than Sam had been expecting. In his twenties, perhaps, with gentle blue eyes and a wispy beard that seemed misplaced on his smooth skin. Sam had never seen him before.

"Yeah, please."

The trader opened the small wicker door on the front of one of his crates and reached inside for the birds while Sam inspected the rest of his stock. Under Smith's instruction, he had learnt a little bit about bird flesh.

"How much are those pigeons in the bottom crate?" he asked.

The trader stood up with a woodcock in each fist. He handed one to Sam while he wrung the other's neck, then took the other back and killed it also.

"They're a special consignment for someone," he said. "I'm afraid they ain't for sale."

"My money's good as anyone's'

"I said they ain't for sale."

Sam and the trader eyed each other uneasily until Pereduke returned carrying three pints of Badger's Snout ale. He gave one to Sam and held on to the trader's while he wrapped Sam's woodcock in paper.

"Where are you off to next then, young man?" Pereduke asked.

"Walsingham, I reckon," the trader said. He handed Sam the woodcock. "I normally get up there this time of year. There's good money to be made up in Walsingham in spring."

Sam felt the sunshine turn cold around him. He struggled to swallow his mouthful of beer and found that the glass was shaking. He was aware of Pereduke watching him closely.

"Well, that's a coincidence, ain't it, Mick?" Pereduke said

levelly. "If you know Walsingham I suppose you'll know the brother of young Mick, here. Roger's his name. Roger Randall. A leather merchant and a thoroughly nasty piece of work, by all accounts."

The trader drank deeply from his pint, surveying Sam over the top of his glass. He wiped his lips on his cuff.

"Well now, as a matter of fact, I reckon I do know this fella's brother," he said quietly. "He has his funny ways all right. But to be fair I wouldn't have said he were nasty all through."

Pereduke's eyes flickered between the two young men. He giggled and slapped the trader on the back.

"Well, as to that, young man, I don't suppose either you or me is best placed to judge. Don't take offence mind. Old Pereduke was only reportin' what he's heard."

"I take offence from no man," the trader said easily. "It doesn't do in my business. And especially I don't take offence from a man who buys me beer." He turned to Sam, "Now then, mate, the reckonin' for those two is fourpence half penny."

Sam stared at the man stupidly.

"Sorry, that's w…what I owe you is it?"

"That's right, that's the reckonin'."

Sam fumbled for Smith's coin and passed it to the trader with a trembling hand.

"Thankin' you." the trader said. He handed Sam his half penny change and began to stack his crates onto the cart.

"Well, gentlemen," he said when the cart was loaded, "thank you for your hospitality and your custom. I've had a good day amongst the fine folk of Stanmore, but now I must wend my way. A trader's lot, I'm afraid."

"Of course you must, young fella," Pereduke replied. "Never let it be said that old Pereduke kept a man from his trade. You get off down the road and may the Wheel circle you with peace and prosperity."

The trader inclined his head to accept the blessing, tipped his cap to Sam and pushed his cart off down the main street towards the common. Sam and Pereduke watched him until he turned out of sight.

"A bit of a queer fella altogether, Mick, don't you think?"

Pereduke murmured. "Not quite one of us, I'd say. Look, he hasn't even finished his drink."

It was true. The trader's pint glass was in the gutter where his cart had been, still half full. Pereduke picked it up and emptied it in one mouthful.

"Never trust a man who leaves his beer, Mick," he said when he was done. "If you don't remember anythin' else old Pereduke teaches you, I'd ask you to remember that. Now come on inside and have another one in civilized company. Them woodcock ain't gonna turn bad if you stay ten minutes."

The trader pushed his cart across the common and on out of Stanmore to the east. When he had gone a mile past the parish marker stone, he glanced behind him along the deserted road and shoved his cart up onto the rough verge, hiding it behind a hedge. He sat down with his back resting against the cart wheel and reached under his tunic to remove a leather purse that hung around his neck. From this he retrieved a scrap of paper, a pencil and a tiny brass cylinder. He rested the paper on his bent knee and wrote quickly.

23 April. Stanmore. Here we have a settlement mired in contentment, quite useless for our purposes. Recommend holograph surveillance be discontinued with immediate effect. Also, either we have agents here, or the opposition has. If the former, it would have been nice to be briefed. The need to know business can be taken too far! Next stop Walsingham. UTR

The trader rolled up the strip of paper tightly and slipped it into the brass cylinder. He stood up and opened the door of one of his crates, removing a pigeon. He slipped the brass cylinder gently into a pouch that was already fitted to the bird's leg and then held the creature high above his head for a moment before flinging it into the air. The pigeon climbed quickly in the afternoon brightness and completed three sweeping circles before heading west.

On impulse the trader raised his arm and saluted the bird as it shrunk into nothingness, then he pushed his cart across the rough land and back to the road. He glanced behind him again and, seeing that the road was still deserted, continued on his way.

Chapter Twenty-One
Pereduke's Message

The encounter with the trader left Sam uneasy. He slept badly and became distracted and careless in his work. (He was helping to repair a wind-damaged barn at the time. It was work that required a certain degree of attention, as his employer was quick to remind him.) Eventually, he decided that he should consider the matter alone and at length, and so the next day he left the potioners' shop before breakfast and walked to Tom Drake's windmill. Since Sam had first worked for him, the miller had always been obliging with the loan of his balcony when Sam wanted to be by himself, and now Sam sat there again, frowning, with his chin resting in his cupped hands. He chased the scene with the trader round and round in his mind, trying to pinpoint what it was exactly that had disquieted him. There was the obvious and worrying fact the man knew Walsingham, of course, or at least that he *claimed* to know Walsingham. But he had also claimed to know Sam's brother, or rather Mick's brother, which was ridiculous. So did that mean the man was lying about Walsingham as well? Or did he know, perhaps, that *Sam* was lying but had deliberately chosen not to give him away? And there was something else about the man, something to do with his attitude and his manner, that didn't feel right, but what was it? He had looked like a trader and spoken like a trader. And while it was strange that he had refused to sell Sam his pigeons, such things were not unheard of. Perhaps he did have a special order to fulfill. Sam replayed the conversation by memory over and over again, fretting to recapture every detail of the trader's expression and tone. As he did so, he munched distractedly on a chicken leg that he had stolen from the kitchen that morning. He had gnawed it almost to the bone when the trapdoor opened and Smith's bright red head poked through.

"I *knew* I'd find you mopin' around up 'ere," she grunted triumphantly as she squeezed through the opening. "Maggie Meat-Pies saw you headin' down Brewers' Lane and I jus' knew you'd be comin' up 'ere. Then downstairs I saw Tom Drake and he says you come here a lot, just to stare at the sky and scratch yer arse, I s'pose."

"Bloody hell, can't I keep anything secret?"

"Not from me you can't, Mick Randall. I believe I know most of what 'appens round Stanmore." Smith grinned and fished around in her skirt pocket, handing Sam a scrap of folded paper. She settled herself next to him on the edge of the balcony. "Anyway, I've got this for you from his lordship. He was showin' off at the milk booth when I was out shoppin'. He asked me to pass it on to you."

Sam unfolded the note and recognised Pereduke's sprawling handwriting:

Dear Mick,

I hope you are well and you ain't smarting too bad about that thrashing I gave you at doms. You keep practising and you could make a good player in time. Perhaps even good enough to match old Pereduke himself.

Anyway, I ain't writing to gloat—Pereduke's never been much of a one for gloating. The fact is, Mick, I've got a bit of business to put your way. It could help you turn a shilling for a month or two. I still have a few matters to sort out, but if you're interested, could you meet me for a quick one in the King's Head on Sunday morning? That's assuming you're fit for anything after the fun of the festival, of course.

I'm sending this note with the lovely Smith (whose backside gets more and more delightful every day, Master Mick; if I were a younger man, I reckon you and me could fall out over that particular backside.) I hope it's all right for her to have it and you don't mind your landlady knowing your business. Let's face it; she's bound to read it, even though she promises she won't. She's a woman after all.
By the Wheel's spin, etc.,
Pereduke

Sam folded the note up and tucked it away in his jerkin.

"Are you gonna meet 'im, then?" Smith asked.

"Yeah, I suppose so. If he can offer me a bit of work I

shouldn't turn him down, really. Anyway, I don't want to upset 'im; he's always been kind to me."

"No one ever wants to upset Pereduke. But you be careful with 'im, Mick. He ain't a good person."

A gust of wind whistled round the balcony, making the sails flap and creak angrily. Sam shivered.

"I know he isn't *good* exactly, but I don't think he means to do me any harm. He's helped me out up to now, hasn't he? Anyway, what's the festival he mentioned?"

"Oh, it's just Beltane, isn't it? Didn't you 'ave that where you come from?"

"No, like I told you it's all different where I'm from. What's Beltane like?"

Smith tightened her shawl around her shoulders and smiled.

"It's just about the best festival, I reckon. It's all about the Green Man wakin' himself up after his winter sleep. In the temple story he shakes the dust out of his hair and gets met by all his lovers in his bedroom-garden, but they don't recognize 'im because he's got young again through his restin' while they've grown old and ugly in all the cold and hardship of the winter. So he jus' leaves 'em, doesn't he? He doesn't even let 'em touch him. He jus' leaves 'em weeping in the garden and strides off over the countryside to find himself new lovers for a new year. And as he goes, he wakes all the fields up as well, with his stompin' and his singin'." Smith turned to look at Sam. "You know that sorta wide awake feelin' you get when you notice the evenings gettin' lighter or you see the first geese flyin' in from the outside sea, or you see the early blackcurrant blossom? Do you know what I mean?"

"Yeah … well … yeah. I think so."

"Well, that's the Green Man waking up inside you, isn't it? And that's sort of what Beltane is."

"Ok, but what actually happens?"

"First of all there's a big service in the temple, starts at noon and goes on for about three hours, sometimes more. That's when Reverend Smythe actually wakes the Green Man up on his altar wheel …"

"I thought you said that the Green Man wakes up *inside* you," Sam cut in. Smith looked puzzled.

"It ain't that simple. The Green Man's sort of inside you and outside you at the same time. Don't you know anythin'?"

"No, I told you, I don't know anything at all. It doesn't seem to make much sense."

"It isn't supposed to make sense, Mick. It's supposed to be *true*."

"I don't think I see the difference, but carry on."

Smith frowned and chewed her lip.

"Well, when the service is done everyone tips out of the temple and we all follow the Green Man round the village carryin' bits of whitethorn. Reverend Smythe goes first, of course, and then…"

"What's the whitethorn for?"

"Dunno, it's jus' what we do. I think it's something to do with beating the demon away for the year. Then in the evenin' all the whitethorn gets burnt up on a big bonfire on Sheedy Hill. That's to welcome the sun back after the winter and bind him up to the Green Man again. The sun's the Green Man's cousin or his brother or somethin' like that. Anyway, it was the sun that woke 'im up in the first place."

"Is there any nice food?"

Smith burst out laughing.

"I swear, you think with your great big guts, you do, Mick Randall. Yeah, course there's food. There's loads of it and plenty of cider to drink an' all. But that's not the main thing, even for a fat pig like you. It's a very powerful festival, is Beltane, a good time for mixing early-day remedies like sour-sweet and easter-wort. My mum always does that the evening before, and it's also good for …"

Smith trailed off. Sam glanced at her and was surprised to see that she was blushing.

"What else is it a good time for?"

"Well, right at the end of the festival, just before sunup, young people are meant to jump across the last bit of the fire with their lovers and then …well…"

"What?"

Smith shrugged.

"Well, then they're meant to go off and have it off somewhere. It's all to do with the Green Man wakin' and the whitethorn and all that. It's all part of the same thing." Suddenly she levered herself to her feet. "Anyway, Mick Randall, I've delivered my message. I can't be lazin' here with you chattin' about nothing all day. I've got to get back and get on with some work. Jus' you make sure you shake all that flour and dusty crap off yer feet before you come home, or my mum will kill you, and afterwards I'll kill you too."

"Yeah, ok."

"And don't you go stealin' no more of them chicken legs neither, else I'll stuff chicken bones in yer bed and slip giblets in yer socks and how will you like that, eh?"

Sam slowly shook his head.

"What makes you think I stole…"

"I told you, Mick, there ain't much I don't know about what goes on in Stanmore, let alone in my own kitchen. I'll see you later."

And with that she wriggled back through the trap door and disappeared. Sam watched her go, still shaking his head, then tossed the chicken bones over the side of the balcony and stared into the emptiness.

There were the remains of two quail on Sir Douglas Latch's plate and an inch of port left in his mug. He was sitting at his desk frowning at a memo when there was a knock on the door.

"Is that you, Tony?" he called out.

"Yes, Sir Douglas."

"Well, in you come, then. Don't hang around, there's a good boy."

The door swung open and Tony marched into the room, carrying a large plastic box. He stopped when he saw the older man.

"Aren't you a bit warm, Sir Douglas?"

Sir Douglas looked at him blankly for a moment and then smiled.

"Oh, I see. Actually yes, Tony, come to think of it, I am. I'm bloody warm. Just got back, you see, and I haven't had time to change. Things are rather busy."

"Busy, Sir Douglas?"

"Yes, old thing, the clouds are definitely gathering. I have a very bad feeling about this code red, I don't mind telling you." The old man picked the memo off the desk and flapped it vaguely. "This is the most recent briefing from MI5, courtesy of the Guardian's Office. It's really very unsatisfactory. The fen-lib people have their chaps inside the enclosure, as you know. We're expending a lot of time and effort tracking the little buggers, but apparently nobody yet knows how they're sending information back to their associates."

"Nobody, Sir Douglas? Don't they have, you know, planes with radios and things to take care of all that?"

"The Air Force are doing the best they can, apparently, but so far to no avail. Obviously, they can't fly too near or too low over the enclosure. Also, it doesn't help that their stuff is so bloody antiquated." The old man shook his head and lit a cigarette. "Did you ever read Hilary on *Sophia and Science*, by any chance?"

"No. I … er … think I must have missed that one, Sir Douglas."

"You do surprise me. It's a good paper, deals with the collapse of the non-human sciences with the triumph of Anthropology and Posthumanism after '89. Hilary argues that taking humanity itself as the primary subject of human enquiry results in a certain loss of creativity and inquisitiveness in other areas. As we deepen our *lust for control*, as she puts it, so we lose our *thirst for wonder*. And sometimes, as in our current difficulties, that fact comes back to bite us savagely on the arse." The old man frowned and inhaled deeply. "It's an interesting piece. It's the first place, I think, where one really begins to sense her bitterness—all wonderfully understated, of course. And when one considers all the things we've let slip since '89, it's difficult not to agree with her, at least a little. We're such a stupid mixture of the modern and the antiquated, aren't we? So many things have simply stalled. The space program, for instance, the moon landings. That alone…"

"The moon landings, Sir Douglas? Do you mean the moon as in the big round rock in the sky? What on earth do you mean *landings*?"

Sir Douglas glanced at the younger man's anxious face and

sighed. He plucked a tiny piece of meat from one of the quail carcasses and slipped it into his mouth.

"I don't mean anything *on earth*, Tony, that's the point. But don't fret about it. I expect the solution to our little espionage conundrum will be staring MI5 and the BSC squarely in the face, but they're too dim to see it. Either that or they know perfectly well what's going on but they're not telling us because they're hoping we balls up monumentally and fall apart. Neither prospect is particularly pleasant, is it?"

"No, Sir Douglas. Is that what you wanted to see me about?"

The old man giggled.

"Good God, Tony, of course not. This code red is a serious business. It's not for brass-buckles to bother their neatly combed heads about, even ones as conscientious as your good self."

"Oh, I see."

"Don't go all grumpy; it doesn't suit you. Anyway, I have something else for you, something altogether more pleasant."

"Yes, Sir Douglas?"

"Yes, we're going to collect young Samuel Moorcroft the day after Beltane, which will be, let me see, Sunday the third. I'd like you to timetable nine officers for me, please, and arrange an incursion briefing."

"Yes, Sir Douglas."

"Good, put it in the diary. And, come to think of it, three of the officers had better be ghosts so you'll need to sort that out as well."

"Yes, Sir Douglas. Will I be going with you?"

The old man stubbed his cigarette out.

"No, Tony. Samuel's rather precious; I'm going to need people who know what they're doing, I'm afraid."

"I see."

"Yes, I'm sure you do."

Sir Douglas peered at the younger man.

"Tony, what's in that box?"

"Babies, Sir Douglas."

"Babies?"

"Yes. Well, dead ones. At least I think they're dead, or

frozen or something. They've just been withdrawn at Swaffam for the consciousness-upload project, and I've been briefed to take them over to delta block. I was on my way there when you paged me."

"You've been *briefed*, have you? Good lord, how exciting. Still, I suppose one would have to be *briefed* for such important work."

Tony turned red and swallowed hard.

"Well, it's *necessary* work, Sir Douglas."

"Yes, dear boy, I'm sure it is. The proper object of human study is humanity itself and all that. All extremely necessary, I don't doubt. You'd better get on with it."

Chapter Twenty-Two
Beltane

Stanmore prepared enthusiastically for the Beltane festival. The stoutly self-important men of the temple committee—Pereduke foremost among them—recruited a dozen youngsters to take a horse and cart round the local farms and woods to gather logs and kindling for the bonfire. These were built into a ragged pyramid on Sheedy Hill (actually no more than a low rise on the road to Limeport). The young men then took it in turns to guard the site with torches and charms mounted on poles in case tricksters or the demon himself tried to light the fire ahead of time. Soon bunches of whitethorn began to appear on the lintels of Stanmore's front doors, and traders drifted in from nearby settlements, erecting stalls selling sacred trinkets, handwritten prayers and spells, and festive Beltane foods such as duck eggs and cracked corn.

"But don't they have Beltane in their own villages?" Sam had asked Smith when he first saw the traders. She had looked at him as if he were mad.

"Yeah, course they do, but not at the same time, obviously. You couldn't expect the Green Man to wake up at the same time all over the place, could you? It jus' wouldn't work, would it?"

"No, I s'pose not," Sam had replied doubtfully.

Sam was himself on guard duty at Sheedy Hill the night before Beltane and so he slept late the following day. When he finally woke he found the kitchen deserted, and so he helped himself to a large breakfast of pigeon pie left over from the night before. He washed up after himself (Smith was very particular about that sort of thing) and picked up the bundle of whitethorn that had been set aside for him. Then he left the house and walked quickly through the deserted streets to the temple. Incense was spilling from the wide open doors as he approached, and a gang of men were loitering outside at the foot of the crucified man, smoking enthusiastically and drinking cider from a barrel set up on a trestle table. Pereduke was at the centre of the group.

"Hello, young fella," he called out cheerfully as Sam approached. "Old Pereduke's glad to see yer whitethorn's good and green. We wouldn't want it wiltin' on a day like today, now would we?"

The men gathered about tittered and Sam grinned. As he climbed up the steps to the temple entrance, Tom Drake touched his arm.

"Bit full in there, Mick. You might want to 'ave a drink or something first and jus' go in from time to time. That's what most of the blokes do at Beltane. Leave the proper prayin' to the priests and the women. General view is they're better at that sort of thing."

"Fair enough," Sam said. He accepted a tankard of cider and squatted down on the step next to Tom. The breeze was cool and pleasant on his face and as usual the good humour of the local men infected him with cheerfulness. He accepted a second tankard of cider and then a third and fenced easily with Pereduke about Smith and wilting whitethorn and the danger of taking too much drink on a day like Beltane. Pereduke wasn't a bad man at all, he realised lazily. He must tell Smith that. Certainly he could be a bit crude and a bit *forceful*, but basically he was a good sort, like all the men of the settlement. Sam accepted another tankard of cider. He would definitely tell Smith that she was wrong about Pereduke. She couldn't know everything about Stanmore, could she, even if she thought she did? She was trustworthy and funny and he was looking forward to seeing her later, but she didn't know everything. Sam accepted another tankard of cider and talked to Tom Drake about corn prices and the temperature of the outside wind in springtime.

When afterwards Sam looked back on the festival, he could only remember the day as a ragbag of disjointed incidents and impressions, without any feeling of time moving along smoothly from one thing to the next as it was supposed to. He recalled shoving his way into the back of the temple with Tom Drake and nearly being overcome by the shift from the bright spring day outside to the shadowy reverence of the ceremony. Reverend Smythe was standing at the altar rotating the temple's great wheel, which had been bedecked for the day with whitethorn and spring flowers. He was chanting as he did so, softly and slowly, so the sound was almost like moaning, while on the altar steps two boys in glorious green and yellow robes span golden censers through full circles, sending spirals of incense into the nave. Sunlight streamed into the building through its small, high windows, slicing the smoky darkness with blades of brightness. And all around the worshippers followed the priest's chanting with rapt faces or else span small models of the temple wheel, murmuring prayers as the jagged spokes passed through their fingers.

"It doesn't seem like it's the same building on the inside as it is on the out," Sam whispered as he and Tom pushed their way back out into the sunlight. "I mean, you can't help feeling caught up in it, can you? Even though you know it's just the temple with a bit of smoke and singing."

"Aye, well he knows 'is job, does Smythe," Tom Drake grunted as he went to refill their tankards from a new barrel.

Later in the day when the temple ceremony was over and the procession around the village fields had begun, Sam recalled joining the other young men in a game of dyke-leaping between Billy Shoes' allotment and the Robinsons' wood yard. The competitors took it in turns to attempt the jump with a shorter and shorter run up until they all ended up floundering in the water and mud, ducking each other and splashing the cheering onlookers with their dripping whitethorn.

Later still, Sam found himself in clean dry clothes—although he had no recollection of going home to change—playing a game that stretched over three fields and involved dozens if not hundreds of festival-goers. The game was a bit like football except the ball was one of the censers from the festival, now badly dented, and the teams were enormous and ill-defined. Also, there didn't seem to be any rules or any real end to the game. Sam was never sure who won, but he ended up with a bloody nose and black bruises down his arm.

And finally, without any dusk that Sam could remember, the day moved from afternoon to nightfall and the crowd gathered on Sheedy Hill around the leaping flames of the bonfire. Tables had been erected along the edge of the field and set with large pans of stew, loaves of bread and baked potatoes. There was no cutlery so you had to scoop out your food with the bread, or with your fingers. It was messy, painful work, and quite a lot of the food got thrown around, particularly by the younger people, but that seemed to be accepted as part of the fun. There were also dozens of barrels of cider, as well as blackberry juice for the children who were still up. Everywhere Sam looked there were excited faces, flushed with drink and firelight, chattering and laughing as the night darkened and the stars pierced the sky. Reverend Smythe sat enthroned at the top corner of the field beneath a high arch of whitethorn that was crowned with a new model of the Green Man. He held court there with Pereduke and some of the other temple committee men, receiving gifts from local people and laughing extravagantly at whatever it was Pereduke was whispering in his ear.

Sam himself stayed near the cider barrels chatting with his friends from the King's Head. When the time came they went forward to the fire and tossed their whitethorn high onto the flames. Then they retreated to their drinks, glad of the night breeze that cooled their overheated faces. From time to time Sam remembered vaguely that he wanted to see Smith that day and considered walking round the field to look for her. But the crowd was big and the night was dark, and if he wandered too far away from the barrels there was the possibility that he might find himself without cider, which would be disastrous, so he stayed where he was.

Eventually, it was Smith who found Sam. The bonfire flames had sunk down almost to the blackened wood and some of the older people had begun to drift away to their beds when he felt a tug at the back of his jerkin. He span round unsteadily and there she was, half her hair flowing freely from its tie and a smudge of soot on the end of her nose.

"You been avoidin' me, Mick Randall?" she asked. "You hopin' to sneak off when I ain't lookin' and find someone to jump through the fire with and think I won't find out?"

"No, no, nothing like that. I've jus…just been…"   Sam

began.

"Good, because I told you before, there ain't much that goes on in Stanmore I don't know about. You can't escape me that easily, you know."

"Well, that's all right then, be…because I don't really want to escape you anyway."

"So what are you gonna do, Mick, stay 'ere boozing with yer mates and then go home all sad and lonely by yerself, or *are* you gonna find a girl to go through the fire with? Yer a rich man and that counts for a lot round here; you shouldn't have too much trouble findin' someone."

"Yeah, well, I might be rich, but no…nobody knows that 'cept you, do they? And I can't really tell anyone. So that ruins my … my chances a bit."

Smith tucked her escaping hair back into its tie and grinned at him.

"Well, if I'm the only one you can impress with yer big bag of Royal Crowns, you might jus' have to go through the flames with me, mightn't you? If there's no one else available, I mean."

Sam emptied his tankard in a single bold gulp and wiped his lips with the back of his hand.

"All right, I … I will," he said.

Smith grinned again, but more shyly, and took the tankard from him, placing it on the nearby table. Then, ignoring the smirks and rude comments from the drinkers, she took his hand in hers.

"Good. But don't go drinkin' any more of that stuff. It'll just be embarrassin' if you trip and toast yerself when yer head's s'posed to be full of thoughts of love and suchlike."

Smith led Sam to the far side of the bonfire where a group of younger people were gathering in couples. The atmosphere here was more sober; people kept their eyes on the dying flames and only spoke in whispers to their partners. Smith held tight to Sam's hand, her fingers intertwined with his. She leaned in close to his ear so that he could feel her breath against his skin.

"Can you feel the Green Man wakin' up, Mick?" she murmured. "All through the day 'ave you been able to feel him?"

"I dunno, I think I've had a bit too much drink to f…feel anything much, really. But it's been a good day, all right. All w…wild and sort of, sort of *free*."

"Well, that's the Green Man, ain't it? At Beltane he's all to do with drink and wildness. That's why everyone likes the festival so much, I suppose. You ain't quite yerself for the day, are you? And people like that."

A loud cheer erupted from the crowd. Sam looked up and saw that the first of the couples had successfully jumped the flames. Now they were embracing on the far side of the fire while the spectators laughed and whooped and punched the air. One by one the other couples followed suit until, finally, it was Smith and Sam's turn.

"Are you sure yer ready for this?" Smith asked doubtfully as she rolled up her skirt at the waste so that it rose high above her knees. "I don't want to look stupid."

"Yeah, ok, I mean, I … I think so. Of course I'm ready. Do we, you know … hand holds … sorry; I mean *hold hands* as we do it?"

"Yeah, course we do."

"Just might make it a bit more difficult to get a good ru…run up, that's all."

Smith shook her head in disbelief.

"Of course we bloody well hold hands; it's Beltane and we're jumping through the bloody flames. Now come on." And with that she was off, sprinting towards the fire with Sam running as fast as he could alongside her.

At the edge of the flames they hurled themselves into the sharp, wood-smoky darkness, and then there was just the rush of flight, with the fire glowing hot below and the blackness of the sky surging all around them. They landed in a shower of sparks at the fire's edge and stood facing each other, gasping for breath, half laughing, half serious, their hands still clenched.

"Well done, Mick; I wouldn't have said you had it in you," Smith said eventually.

"Nor would … would I, really." Sam shook his head slowly from side to side. "Nor would I, Smith. Do you know I can s…see three of you, by the way?"

Smith smiled and rubbed her nose so that the smudge of soot disappeared.

"Well, then, Mick Randall," she said quietly, "which one of me is it that yer gonna kiss? You better get the right one, hadn't you, or you'll end up kissin' smoke and air and what'll yer boozy friends make of that?"

"I think … I suppose … well, I think I'll just kiss the one in the middle," Sam murmured and suddenly Smith's face was very close to his with her mouth slightly open and her eyelids fluttering closed. Sam closed his own eyes and a moment later felt her dry lips pressed against him, moving insistently against his own.

"I wouldn't have thought you had that in you, either," Smith whispered when they parted. "I wouldn't have thought you had that in you at all. Yer all sorts of things mixed up, you are, and I still can't work you out. Come on, let's go home."

They picked their way through what was left of the crowd, taking care to avoid Pereduke, and wandered back, hand in hand, through the quiet streets. Sam stumbled from time to time so that Smith had to yank his hand sharply to stop him from falling over. When they arrived at the shop, she turned to him and put her finger over her lips.

"I put dozy-meal in me mum's milk," she whispered, "so she shouldn't hear anythin', but we ain't gonna take any chances. Try and forget that yer drunk for a few minutes and go in on yer tip toes. And don't say anything' till we get up to yer room, ok?"

Sam nodded dumbly. Smith giggled and kissed him quickly on the cheek.

"And don't look so bloody nervous, Mick; you ain't goin' to yer hangin', you know. We're jus' gonna 'ave a bit of fun, which I reckon we both deserve."

She let go of Sam's hand and unlocked the shop door. He followed her inside and on through the little gate in the counter. She paused and gestured for him to wait at the door of the mixing room, and then disappeared inside, reappearing a few minutes later clutching a small brown bottle, a knife and a white porcelain tile. Sam crept upstairs behind her to his room where she pushed the door open with her shoulder and set the bottle, tile and knife down on the bedside table.

"Close the door and switch on one of them lamps," she whispered. Sam did as she asked while she carefully tapped three dried leaves out of the bottle and set about chopping them finely on the tile.

"Come and sit down next to me," she said. When Sam perched on the bed she ran her hand quickly along his thigh.

"It's nice to be with you, Mick. You see this stuff; it's called witch's touch. You bung a bit of it up yer nose and it makes … well it makes things better. You'll see."

"Why? What does it do?"

"When someone touches you it makes the feeling go right down inside you and spread out over yer whole body." Smith chopped faster at the leaves. "Like every bit of you is connected up straight to every other bit. It's almost like it hurts, except it doesn't hurt at all."

"Is this the sort of thing you do with all your blokes, then?"

Smith frowned.

"I don't 'ave any blokes, Mick. You've lived with us for long enough, you know that. I don't trust most blokes."

She gathered a portion of the chopped leaf and placed it carefully on the thin stretch of skin between her thumb and forefinger. Then she held her hand to her nose and sniffed it sharply up her left nostril. Her eyes watered and she pinched the top of her nose.

"But I sometimes take a bit when I'm by myself," she said shrilly. "You know if I'm havin' a bath or somethin'. Life's not easy, you 'ave to take yer pleasures where you can."

Smith took another pinch of the leaf and sniffed it up her right nostril then handed the tile to Sam.

"The trick is not to take too much. … No Mick, you need less than that. … That's more like it. … And then sniff it right up, as quick as you can."

Sam held the pinch of grey dust to his nostril and sniffed. His nose suddenly felt extremely hot and then ticklish. His eyes ran and he sneezed explosively.

"That's all right," Smith murmured, stroking his shoulder. "You always do that the first time. Now take another bit up the other nostril quick, but this time sniff harder. Trust me, you don't sneeze as bad if you do it fast."

Sam wiped his face with the back of his hand and took another pinch of the chopped leaf, inhaling it as hard as he could. The burning feeling came again, but this time the tickling wasn't quite so strong and he managed not to sneeze. Smith grinned at him lopsidedly, and then took the tile and placed it on the floor. She extinguished the lamp and lay back on the bed.

"Come on then, Mick, lie yerself down."

Cautiously, Sam lay down next to her.

"I don't feel very much yet, except I want to pick … pick my nose," he said. As he spoke he was surprised at how far away his voice sounded, as if its speaking didn't have much to do with him.

"Give it a chance," Smith murmured. A minute or so later she went on: "Yer shakin' like a leaf."

"So are you," Sam whispered. Then suddenly, out of the darkness, a hand brushed gently against his face. He gasped as the tingling sensation of the touch rippled across his cheek and down his neck, then on through the rest of his body.

"How does that feel?" the darkness asked softly.

"Very nice."

"And so how does this feel?" asked the darkness. Suddenly there were lips working against Sam's face again, seeking out his own. And the weight of a body pushing hard against him.

"Very ni..nice indeed," Sam whispered harshly when the kissing stopped. "Like … like it's the only thing in the world."

From a long way away the darkness giggled softly.

"I told you it were good, didn't I?" There was a rustling and then the darkness was pressed against Sam again, but more keenly than before. And when he reached out his hands were shocked and thrilled to touch smooth, bare skin. He pulled away and shuffled to the edge of the bed, tussling clumsily with his own clothes. When he was stripped he threw them onto the floor, then pushed himself urgently against the darkness's warm flesh, shivering uncontrollably.

"Like it's the only th…thing in the world," he stuttered again.

"That's right," the darkness said quickly as their bodies moved jerkily together, "I reckon that's jus' about absolutely right, Mick Randall, or whoever you are."

And after that the darkness didn't speak again for a long time.

Later, as dawn broke, Sam and Smith lay quietly side by side. One of Smith's hands rested delicately on Sam's chest. Presently, he turned his head to examine her silhouette in the half-light. He was surprised to see that her eyes were open.

"How come everyone calls you Smith, apart from your mum?" he asked. Smith frowned.

"They never used to. I was always Lou until my dad went away. I mean, that's my proper name. But then after he went I had to be, you know, in charge of things in the shop and that. And everyone jus' started callin' me Smith. It's what they all used to call me dad."

Sam was quiet for a while, watching Smith's chest rise and fall slowly with her breath. Then he said, "What actually happened to your dad?"

"The demon," Smith said flatly. Sam waited for her to go on but she showed no sign of doing so. He propped himself up on his elbow.

"What do you mean, the demon? How do you know it was the demon?"

Smith sighed.

"I don't know what sorta place you come from, Mick, honestly I don't, but it ain't like anywhere I've ever heard of. Listen, no one ever talks about it, right, so don't go blabbin' or anything, but there are some nights, they don't happen very often mind, when we get visited from the beyonds. I've only known them twice in my life and I can't remember much about either of them. Both times it sorta felt like a dream, with the sky over to the west full of fire, and people rushin' around and panickin', and a sorta queer yellowy light in the streets that made you feel sick and lose yer balance if yer were caught in it for too long—except it wasn't a dream because both times there was damage done to the fields and the Green Man had been set on fire up at the temple. Also, there were demon marks cut on some folks' front doors and inside those houses people had been took." Smith swallowed hard and went on quickly. "Mostly it were babies, of course, because that's what the demon likes best, because they're innocent, ain't they? But there were some adults went an' all." She pushed a strand of hair back from her face. "Anyway, that's what happened to me dad."

"I'm sorry," Sam said.

"It's all right, Mick. Well, in a way it is. I'm used to it by now, but it's why I have to be so careful, you see. I come from what they call a *troubled family*. We're a family that has a bit of history with the demon. No one knows why. Perhaps somebody cursed us once, or maybe someone walked out to the beyonds and made a pact or somethin'; Reverend Smythe says that can happen. But whatever the reason, we ain't quite safe. My great-uncle was took and my dad's mum lost a child when it were only three months old. Then there were a cousin over in Oxwick that went an' all. And there may be others before that, for all I know." Smith sighed. "That's why I 'ave to keep meself sharp with tallis root and take care who I let into the house. My mum hasn't been the same since my dad went, and I ain't gonna let them get her, too. I gotta look after me and me mum, that's all that matters."

Smith closed her eyes and Sam lay back onto the bed. For a long time the pair of them were silent, and then Smith gently flattened her hand against Sam's chest.

"I can feel your heart beat, Mick."

"That's probably just as well, isn't it? You'd be upset if I didn't have a heartbeat."

"The demon hasn't got a heart."

"Well, that proves I'm not the demon then, doesn't it? That's a relief for us both."

Smith turned her head to look at Sam. Her eyes were open very wide.

"Look, you know this place yer from, that you don't ever talk about, that's ... that's even further away than Walsingham?"

"Yes."

"Would you say it were *safe*?"

"What do you mean by safe?"

"Well, is it somewhere where the demon never gets and where people don't just vanish and where you can think as far as you like in any direction without yer mind getting so tangled and frightened that you end up hardly rememberin' yer own name?"

Sam scratched his head.

"Yeah, I s'pose in that way it's safe. But it isn't perfect. In lots of ways it's horrible, much worse than here. I mean, it's…"

"Well, would you take me there one day? Just for a day, I mean. If you can. And if me mum's all right and everythin'. I'd like to spend just one day somewhere safe, you see, somewhere I don't 'ave to *think* all the time."

Sam was quiet for a long time and then he said:

"If I can. I will if I can, Smith."

"D'you promise?"

"I promise."

They lay together in silence with Smith's hand still flat on Sam's chest, until her eyes fluttered closed and Sam supposed her to have gone to sleep. He was startled when she said softly:

"Your heart's beatin' faster now, Mick Randall. Your heart's beatin' like a lark's wings and I dunno if that means yer lyin' to me again."

Chapter Twenty-Three
A Game Lad

When Sam woke the sun was streaming into his bedroom and he could hear the cats squabbling in the yard. He was alone and had a headache, the kind that felt as if someone were banging a rubber mallet slowly between his eyes. He also badly needed water.

Heaving himself out of bed, he untangled the pile of clothes that lay on the floor and pulled them on. Then, without bothering to wash, he trudged down to the kitchen. He was surprised to find both Smith and her mum sitting at the kitchen table drinking coffee.

"Who's looking after the shop?" he asked.

"No one; it ain't open," Smith's mum replied. "Nothin' much opens after Beltane, except the pubs, of course. An' it's a good job an' all, with all the mud and ash the pair of you tramped in last night. I were just sayin' to Lou, wasn't I Lou, that it's gonna take me most of the day to scrub it up nice, and I'm supposed to be swabbin' down me tubs of elderflower-hearts this afternoon. Well, that's gone out of the window now. I don't know when I'll get it done, to be honest. And it needs doin' an' all because they're absolutely filthy. I had a look at them on Thursday, didn't I, Lou? D'you remember me telling' you how filthy they were?"

"It's all right, Mum," Smith said gently. "I'll sort out the shop. It was us who made the mess. We were late back so we just didn't think about it." She turned to Sam and grinned. "Did you sleep all right in the end then, Mick?"

"Um, yeah, I did. In the end I did. Er, could I have some water, please, and perhaps a bit of bread or something?"

Smith giggled.

"You don't feel like summat fried, then? Fancy that. All right, sit yerself down and I'll sort it out."

Smith sliced and buttered the bread and placed it in front of Sam, together with a mug of water and a pale blue pill.

"There you are, Mick. That tablet's lantern-ease; it's good

for what ails you this morning. Now you better hurry yerself along, hadn't you? Or you'll be late for yer meeting."

Sam swallowed the pill with a big gulp of water.

"What meeting?"

"With his nibs, down at the King's Head. It don't do to keep Master Pereduke hangin' around."

"Oh no. I'd forgotten all about that. The last thing I want is a drink with Pereduke. I feel bad enough as it is."

Smith's mum pursed her lips.

"Now, don't you say things like that, Mick. Mr. Pereduke's been good to you. He's an important man. How will it look if you keep him waiting? You get along there, young man, and make sure yer polite to him an' all."

"Yeah, yeah, of course I'll go," Sam said. "I just don't feel like drinking anything this morning, that's all."

"Well, you don't 'ave to drink anything, do you? You can jus' 'ave water or summat. He can, can't he, Lou?"

"Not when you're with Pereduke, Mrs. Smith," Sam said wearily. "It's just not possible, I'm afraid. I tried it once and he got furious. He pretended it was a sort of joke, him being cross. But it wasn't really a joke at all. In the end he got a bunch of the lads to hold me down while Robby Larkin farted on my head." He shook his head sadly. "No, you just have to drink when you're with Pereduke."

When he had finished his breakfast Sam splashed some water on his head at the kitchen sink and allowed Smith to fetch him a clean shirt. He left the shop and walked to the King's Head. There were some indications of the previous day's festivities in the streets: a few half-dismantled stalls, bunches of whitethorn still hanging at odd angles from lintels, cartons of festival food thrown in the gutter. The few people who were about looked tired and vacant. Mostly they wandered past Sam without speaking.

The pub itself was almost empty. The only customers were a group of six men clustered around Pereduke, none of whom Sam recognised. Nevertheless, they nodded greetings as he approached.

"Ah Mick, good of you to join us," Pereduke chortled. "Especially as you look as rough as a hedgehog's arse. Let's get this man a drink, shall we? Old Pereduke don't like to see his fellow creatures suffrin'."

A pint of beer was produced for Sam and he sipped it slowly. Pereduke peered at him and licked his lips.

"I'm guessin' you might 'ave a story to tell us, Master Mick, concernin' a certain young lady. It goes without sayin' that I love to hear it and in due course no doubt I shall. But for now, it'll 'ave to wait. Myself and these gentlemen have a proposition for you. Bonny, I wonder if you would be so kind?"

A large man with a weather-beaten face and scrawled tattoos of the Green Man on his knuckles detached himself from the group and shut and bolted the pub door. Sam was aware of another of the men moving casually behind him.

"That's better," Pereduke purred. "Some matters are best kept private, ain't they, Mick? You're the kind of man who'd appreciate that, I'm sure."

Sam nodded and sipped his beer again.

"Now then, you don't know these fellas and I'll save the introductions till you've heard what I've got to say and decided whether you want in with us or not. All you need to know for now is that they're trusted associates of mine from Limeport who turn a shilling in import-export." Pereduke leaned close to Sam and winked. "But not the sort of import-export you'd want to talk to the magistrate about, if you get my drift."

"I ... er ... I think I understand," Sam said. The beer was making him feel sick and his hands were shaking.

"Good lad," Pereduke said. "I told 'em you weren't no slouch, Micky. Quick on the uptake, that's how old Pereduke described you, and I believe I was right to do so. Well, anyway, these lads are on the lookout for someone to do a bit of fetchin' and carryin' for 'em round about. Nothin' dangerous, of course, but it might involve a bit of travelin' up near the beyonds. Now then, when they came to me and asked me if I knew anyone local who might be available for a bit of that, who did old Pereduke think of but Mick Randall. Like I said to these fellas, the very first time I met you, you was wanderin' around bold as brass, practically on the demon's doorstep."

"What is it that I'd actually be doing?"

"It's simple enough," the tattooed man said. "All we'd be wantin' is fer you to do a bit of collectin' from such and such a place for us. Or perhaps meetin' a certain person and handin' over certain moneys as we'd direct. Nothin' too taxin' and nothin' too dangerous. And you'd find the remuneration very satisfactory."

"So what do you say then, young fella?" Pereduke asked. "Will you take a bit o' work with these gentlemen or not?"

Sam was sharply aware of the men's waiting faces. They looked rough and challenging. He desperately wanted to be back at home with Smith, or back in bed. In fact, he wanted to be anywhere but in the pub. His shaking hands had got worse.

"All right, yeah, I'll do it," he said quietly.

Pereduke smiled and clapped his pint glass down on the bar.

"Bravo," he said. "I told 'em you were a good bet. Didn't old Pereduke tell you lads, eh? I said you were a brave boy with a bit of adventure in you, and I was right. Yes, yer a game lad and no mistake, Samuel Moorcroft. I've thought that since the first moment I saw you."

For a full minute no one said anything. Sam stared at Pereduke open-mouthed and Pereduke returned his look evenly, a thin smile playing round his lips. And then the light around Sam began to ripple and fret as if it were disturbed water and gradually three human forms appeared out of the shimmering air. They were clad entirely in purple overalls, their faces covered with masks of the same colour. They carried what looked like hand guns, trained on Sam. Pereduke glanced at them approvingly and said, "Now then, Samuel, there are two ways we can do this. One hates to speak in clichés but either you *come quietly*, in which case this can all be over quickly and painlessly, or else you make a fuss, in which case we'll all be slightly inconvenienced and you'll risk being rather badly hurt. It's up to you."

"You're … you're not Pereduke anymore," Sam whispered.

"Well, in a way I am. But you're quite right, I'm not *only* Pereduke, thank goodness. To be honest, though, I think deep down you may have known that all along. You're not stupid;

you know as well as anyone that the Project is thoroughly policed. I told you when we first met that I make connections. In your case, dear boy, the connections really weren't that difficult to make."

"So why didn't somebody do something before? I've been here for … for ages. I mean, why not just…"

"Samuel, these are interesting questions but this really isn't the time or the place to discuss them. Still, I'm glad you're not trying to do anything heroic. You're not the only one who's hung-over this morning. I'm not sure I'd enjoy a fight."

The man who wasn't only Pereduke nodded to the person standing behind Sam. Sam heard a click and felt a sharp prick, like a nettle sting, on the back of his neck. There was a moment of bright colour and then nothing at all.

Chapter Twenty-Four
Sede Veritatis

"Come on, Samuel, time to wake up. Up you come, dear boy. Up, up, up."

Sam wondered vaguely if the voice was addressing him. He didn't think it could be; it was coming from too far away. Realising that he was lying almost flat, he tried to sit up to investigate but found that his body wouldn't do as it was told. He tried to open his eyes but found that he couldn't do that, either. Perhaps under the circumstances it would be better to go back to asleep. Yes, sleep was a good idea. After all, there didn't seem much point in waking up at the moment. He let himself relax again.

"No. No, Samuel. I'm afraid I'm not going to let you go. You and I have work to do, dear boy. Now then, let's see if this doesn't pep you up a bit."

Sam felt his heart race and a wave of energy ripple through his body. The wave reached his head and he suddenly felt wide awake and alert.

"There we are. That's knocked a few cobwebs off, hasn't it, Samuel? Eh? Don't forget to breathe. Now then, dear boy, the technician chaps tell me that you *should* be able to speak. So will you try and say something for me, please?"

"What w…would you like me to say?" Sam said slowly. His mouth tasted foul.

"Oh, I don't know, how about something like, "I understand that by compromising the boundary I have broken bylaw 36 for which the maximum penalty is chemical curtailment. I take full responsibility for my crime and whilst I am not particularly looking forward to spending the rest of my days trussed up and drooling like a baby, I recognise that this is no more than I deserve.""

"I'm not … I'm not sure I can remember all that."

The voice giggled and Sam heard the sound of a match being struck. A moment later the smell of cigarette smoke teased his nostrils.

"No, I don't suppose you can, but at least we've established that you can talk. That's the important thing. Now then, I expect you're wondering where you are and what's going to happen to you."

"Yes."

"Well, I'm afraid I'm not going to tell you. I'm keen that things should be rather up in the air at the moment, as far as you're concerned. You won't like that, of course, but you don't really have any choice in the matter. All I will tell you, Samuel, is this: at present you're sitting in the *sede veratatis*. Do you have any Latin by any chance?"

"Um ... not really, no."

"You don't surprise me. We only use the bits we do in deference to our founder. She didn't think a chap was properly educated unless he knew something of the ancient tongues. *Sede veratatis* means 'seat of truth.' Over the next few days you and I are going to have a number of conversations, and you are going to have to tell me the truth. Do you understand?"

"Yes. Yes, I understand."

"Actually, dear boy, you don't—or not entirely. When you succeed in telling me the truth you will be rewarded with pleasant feelings such as this one." The voice paused and a wave of pleasure rippled through Sam's body. "When you lie," the voice went on, "and I'm afraid that you *will* lie, Samuel, the consequences will be rather less pleasant. Is that clear?"

"Yes."

"Excellent. Now then, don't worry about food or drink, that's all been taken care of by the technician chaps. We're actually rather keen to keep you alive, so we're not going to let you starve."

There was another pause while the voice stubbed out his cigarette. Sam was amazed at how loud the cigarette end sounded as it was ground into the ashtray.

"And don't worry about toilet business, either," the voice went on amiably. "That's all been sorted out as well. You don't smell in the least."

"That's a relief."

"For both of us, dear boy, I can assure you. The only other thing I should mention is that you really shouldn't try to move.

The techies have buggered about with the bit of your brain that's responsible for movement and so if you *do* try and wriggle about you'll only end up whizzing the wrong kind of messages around your bonce. You'll get confused and panicky, which isn't at all what you want in your situation. Is that clear?"

"Yes."

"Excellent." The voice suddenly sounded bored. "Well, to be honest, Samuel, I think I'm done with you for today. I'm going to put you to sleep again. Not too deeply, though. I don't want you forgetting what we've talked about or imagining it's all been a rather unpleasant dream. I'm afraid that I'm horribly real and when you wake up you and I will have things to do."

Sam tried to nod his head but couldn't move it. He opened his mouth to speak but the words never came. He slept.

"Nice snooze, Samuel?"

Sam heard the voice before he even realised he was awake. He felt fresh and curious.

"Yes, th … thank you."

"And how do you feel now?"

"Very well."

"Excellent, and you remember what we spoke about last time?"

"Yes."

"Good. Any questions?"

"Um … yes," Sam said. "Could you … could you tell me who you are, please?"

The voice giggled.

"Goodness, that's rather forward of you, Samuel. Still, I suppose I did ask. Let's just say that I'm rather a lot of people. You knew me as Pereduke. He's one of me, but there are several others. Maybe you'll meet them one day, maybe you won't. That rather depends on you. And I think that's all I'm prepared to tell you for now."

"Oh."

"It's all a bit muddling, isn't it? Still, I'm afraid that's what you get for breaking the law. Your little escapade has created rather a lot of muddle for us too. But we shan't worry about that at the moment. Today we're going to talk about why you made your spectacular decision." Sam heard the sound of liquid being poured into a glass and someone drinking. The voice went on: "I'm referring, of course, to your decision to slip through that ridiculously heavy door in the Stanmore installation and set yourself up within the enclosure as Mick Randall, leather worker's son from Walsingham. You did the unthinkable, Samuel; something like that needs real drive as well as a certain amount of courage...'

"I'm not brave," Sam broke in.

"Well really, I see no sign of cowardice, but forget that for now. What I want to know is precisely *why* you found yourself on the other side of the door."

Sam struggled to think clearly. It was important that he told the voice something that sounded coherent and, most of all, truthful. He knew instinctively that it would be dangerous to be caught lying. A sweat broke out on his forehead.

"Take as long as you want," the voice said gently. "You won't be punished for taking your time. And don't worry too much about trying to make it all sound neat and tidy. Real lives are never neat and tidy, at least the interesting ones aren't. Just say what you remember, in whatever order it comes to you."

"I went ... I went to Ely for my birthday, when I was 16," Sam said slowly, "and I got the chance to go up into real-space. There was this man, he was a friend of Jen's—she's my brother's girlfriend—and he knew people in the Project. He's a cadet, doing something in Swaffam, I think he said. Anyway, he arranged for me to go up into real-space and I ... well, I just loved it up there, even though there wasn't really much to see. I mean ... I liked the rest of the Project as well. I liked it a lot: you know the holographs and the double pubs and the Oval Chamber and everything. But ... but to be in real-space, to hold the soil and feel the wind—there was a bit of rain even though it was Summer—that was just fantastic. I felt ... well, I felt like I *belonged* up there, somehow."

"Good lad," the voice said tenderly. "You may find this difficult to believe, but I really do know exactly what you mean. Keep going, dear boy. Please keep going."

Sam talked in detail about his visit to Ely and his conversation with Rachel later that evening. He mentioned *Soul Freedom* by Hilary Lynch and as many of his other Ely books and downloads as he could remember. He described the hours he had spent in his room studying and day-dreaming about the Project, the charts and print-outs he had made, and how his parents had begun to worry about him. From time to time the voice would light a cigarette or pour himself a drink, and occasionally he would interrupt Sam to offer encouragement or ask for clarification. But most of the time he stayed quiet, his presence marked only by his soft, wheezy breathing.

Finally Sam arrived at the point in his story where he had discovered his brother and Rachel on the sitting room floor.

"And I looked through this tiny gap in the curtain and … and there they were. At first I thought it was Jen with Roger, but of course it couldn't have been because she was at the restaurant dealing with those alphas, who Roger had booked on purpose, by the way, to keep us all away from the house."

"That's a low trick," the voice murmured.

"Yes, it was. Anyway, then … then I saw that it wasn't Jen, it was Rachel. But she didn't really look like Rachel at all. Not like I'd always known her. Her face looked different and her shoulders looked thin and … I mean … well, obviously she wasn't wearing knickers or anything …"

"Oh dear boy, I'm so very sorry," the voice said softly. And immediately Sam felt a soothing feeling spread through him, beginning at his heart.

"Take as long as you want, Samuel. We're not in any hurry. Just remember to breathe; that's the trick, as I recall."

The backs of Sam's eyes tingled as if he were about to cry but no tears came. He sniffed and continued.

"Well, anyway, Roger came out to talk to me. And he tried to be *nice* about it all. He said that they were sorry if they'd upset me and they shouldn't have been so careless and … and I *hated* him then … I absolutely hated him—more than I'd ever hated him before…"

"Good lad, Samuel," the voice purred.

"And after that I went out for a walk for ages. I don't really know how long. I just didn't want to be inside, not with Roger.

I walked and walked, and the only thing that made me happy was thinking about how much I hated Roger. That made me feel sort of ... excited, I suppose, but in a dark, horrible way. And apart from that I felt ... well, just completely awful. And I kept remembering what I'd seen through the window, although obviously I didn't want to, and it was the worst feeling you could ever have."

Sam halted. The voice stubbed out his cigarette and lit another.

"What did you just say, Samuel?"

"I ... er ... I just said how horrible it was when I was walking around. That I kept thinking about what I'd seen and that it was awful."

"What phrase did you use exactly?"

"Um ... I think I said that it was the worst feeling you could ever have."

A wave of pain flowed from Sam's thigh. He screeched and instinctively tried to grasp the spot but was unable to move. He felt dizzy and sick, and then terrified. Eventually he passed out but even then his unconscious mind flashed with panic and agony. When he came round, he had no idea how much later, there was a smell of burning. His thigh still ached alarmingly.

"Now then, Samuel," the voice said pleasantly, "how would you say the feeling of discovering Roger and Rachel compares with the feeling of a simple cigarette burn on your leg? Which was worse? Think carefully now, my cigarette is still glowing nicely."

"What you ... what you just did was worse."

"Good lad. I'm sorry to put you through that. Please don't think that I am unmoved by your story, because I am. The image of shy, sensitive Samuel peering through the window and watching his dullard brother tupping *the one* is actually rather affecting. But I'm afraid that I can't have you going silly and sentimental on me. For one thing it's dishonest, and for another, it's frankly embarrassing. The worst feelings in the world are the ones that occur in nerves and synapses, not airy fairy nonsense about love and loss. Is that clear?"

"Yes, that's per...perfectly clear," Sam said.

"Good," the voice said more gently. "Now then, we must

almost be at the point in your narrative where you return to Ely. Was it witnessing the sex that finally shoved you over the boundary, would you say? Oh, Samuel, I'm so sorry, where are my manners? Have a little bit of this for your pains, and don't forget to breathe."

The ache immediately melted from Sam's thigh and he felt calm and happy again. He smiled dreamily into the darkness.

"No, it wasn't just the sex," he murmured. "When I got back from my walk I went on the clip and read a bit of *Soul Freedom*. I did it every night, but that night especially I wanted … well, I wanted comfort, I suppose. Anyway, it happened to be the bit where Hilary says how much she enjoyed crossing over when everything got difficult or complicated at work. I can't remember exactly what it said but it was something about everything feeling…"

"…*each trip across the boundary felt like a minor rebirth*," the voice broke in quietly. "*Things felt peaceful and possible when I was on the other side.*"

"Yeah, yeah, that was it. Peaceful and possible. Peaceful and possible, that was it. Well, suddenly, when I read that, everything seemed absolutely obvious. I know it was against the law but I didn't think about any of that. It just didn't *matter*. I felt really awake and alive and well … happy, I suppose. I mean, I … I didn't even want to be on the clip anymore. I … I just knew what I was going to do. It all seemed so natural."

"So Hilary saved the day, did she? Well, isn't that extraordinary. Excellent, dear boy, absolutely excellent."

Sam heard the click of the voice placing his glass on the table, more forcefully than normal. The noise sounded final. "Well, you've worked well today, Samuel, apart from that moment of idiocy at the end. It's been a pleasure spending time with you. Have a jolly good sleep now and we'll talk again soon."

Sam's heart swelled with pride and then he lost consciousness.

"Rise and shine, dear boy. How do you feel?"
"Not … not too bad, thanks."

"Excellent. And do you remember what we discussed last time?"

"Yes, we talked about why I crossed over."

"Good. And do you remember that I had to hurt you?"

"Yes."

"Good. Please keep it fixed in your mind. I'd much rather speak to you than hurt you, Samuel; you're an interesting chap. But I will hurt you if you tell me any more lies. Now then, today I want us to consider your time within the enclosure. I wonder if you could pick up your narrative from the morning after your awful experience with Roger. What sort of preparations did you make for your adventure, I wonder? For what it's worth, you did very well indeed inside—considerably better than average."

"What, do lots of people cross over, then?"

The voice sighed and Sam heard him light a cigarette.

"You'd be surprised, Samuel, really you would. Maybe we'll get to talk about that one day, and I certainly hope so. But forget it for now. Today I want to know about you."

"Right, Samuel, today I want us to consider Roger."

"Roger? You mean my brother? Why?"

"Because he writes an awful lot of the script, doesn't he? Your whole story so far has been full of his stupid sarcastic quips, he's the one who first takes you to Ely, he's the one who gets you *Soul Freedom* for your birthday, and he's the one who makes love to the delightful Rachel, sending you bonkers enough to break the law in the most serious way imaginable. Would you have reacted quite so madly if you had seen anyone else with her, I wonder?"

Sam was silent.

"Consider this, dear boy," the voice went on. "Of the cover story you concocted to explain your arrival in Stanmore, the only detail that was true was the name of your evil brother. What's your first memory of him, Samuel? Start from there and keep going."

* * *

"Feeling ok, Samuel? Excellent. Then tell me some more about luscious young Smith. What attracted you to her? And when precisely did you begin to feel attracted to her?"

"Wake up, Samuel. Come on, have a spot of this to blow the cobwebs away. That's right, dear boy, don't forget to breathe. Now then, tell me more about your dad. From what you've told me so far he seems a strange sort of chap.

"Let's revisit the fight in the barn, Samuel. You actually acquitted yourself rather well there, didn't you? You beat the little toe-rag off and then dealt with a knife wound without melodramatics. All a bit un-Sam like, wouldn't you say? A turning point perhaps?

Chapter Twenty-Five
Rather a Lot to Give Up

Sam had no idea how long his interrogations lasted. He didn't know if it was day or night, or how long had passed since he had been apprehended. He had no idea if he was taken away somewhere to sleep between sessions or if he stayed in one place and the voice came to him. He was never hungry, never hot, never cold, never in any pain except for the dreadful pain the voice inflicted on him. He was burnt twice more for telling lies. After that he answered all the voice's questions truthfully. He spoke about his home and family, his knowledge of the Ely Project, his experiences in the enclosure. The voice probed, queried, challenged and encouraged. It was insistent and unhurried; under its examination Sam described incidents he had completely forgotten about and revealed truths about his own motives that he did not know were true until he heard himself speak them.

Finally—Sam had no idea when—he woke up with the flesh of his face and hands feeling tingly and alive as it hadn't done for a long time. He took a while to consider the sensation and realised it was the movement of fresh air over his body. It was a good feeling, Sam decided, a very good feeling indeed.

"Come on Samuel, wake up. Last time, I promise you. Up you come. Come on, dear boy. Come on. Up, up, up. That's the way. Now then, how are you feeling?"

"Not too bad. A bit … different. A bit sore."

"Yes, well, I'm afraid I've no potions to give up here, so you're going to have to come round the old-fashioned way. Take your time now."

Sam yawned and stretched, and then realised that the back of his head was itchy. He scratched it and the itch shifted to his thigh. He scratched there too and then froze.

"I can … I can move my hands."

"You certainly can, dear boy, and your legs and your head as well, I hope. But I'd take your time with all that if I were you. Everything's probably going to be a little bit wobbly for a while. Don't forget to breathe."

"Can I open my eyes, please?"

"Of course you may, Samuel. I dare say they'll be a bit gungy, though. Careful how you go."

Sam tried to force his eyes open but discovered that, although the eyelids flexed, they wouldn't rise. He gently prised the right lid up with his fingers. Bright light dazzled him.

"Ouch. Ah. Ooo, that hurts."

"I'm not surprised. You haven't seen sunlight for quite some time. If you turn to your left you'll be facing the wall and it might not sting quite so much."

Sam shuffled round on his seat and slowly opened his eyes. The light was still painfully strong but it wasn't as bad as it had been. He blinked several times and shapes emerged from the brightness until he was able to make out a rough stone wall, pitted with ragged patches of shadow. The wall's only decoration was a small black and white photograph of an old woman holding a cat. Someone had fixed a bunch of yellow flowers to the picture's top corner. Squinting about, Sam found that he was sitting at a table in a low room. There were some cupboards and an oven in one corner and a ladder reaching up to the floor above in another. A short man was standing in the blaze of sunlight by the room's door, studying him. He approached Sam slowly out of the glare until Sam could make out that he was quite elderly. He had an untidy mane of white hair, bright blue eyes and a firm, slightly cruel, mouth. He was dressed entirely in black and was carrying two small metal cups.

"Here you are; have a sip of this stuff. It will help to sharpen you up. For your information, it is twenty past nine in the morning on Thursday 16th May. It's 10 days since we picked you in Stanmore."

Sam nodded, taking the cup and lifting it carefully to his lips. The drink warmed him.

"It's port. Non-vintage, I'm afraid, but it's still rather early for anything decent. Anyway, it's nice to meet you properly at last, Samuel. My name is Sir Douglas Latch, but don't bother with the 'Sir'. Not many people do."

The man extended his hand and Sam shook it gently.

"Are you the person I've been talking to?"

"Yes, I'm your debriefer. That's interesting, isn't it? Does it make you hate me, I wonder?"

"No, I ... I don't hate you. I don't know what I think of you, really. I think I sort of *enjoyed* talking to you in the end, if that doesn't sound too stupid." Sam paused, "So does that mean that you're Pereduke as well?"

"Yes, it does."

"It's just you don't look like him. You're thin for one thing. And I thought ... well, I thought you'd be younger."

The man drank deeply and giggled.

"Not me, dear boy, I'm afraid I'm just about as old as sin. Now do come and have a look at the view. Go carefully, though, or you're likely to tumble."

Sam tottered behind the man to the door and looked around, shielding his blinking eyes against the sun. The landscape was green and lush, rising gently to a near horizon. There was a tang of something sharp and exciting in the air that he recognized.

"We're near the sea," Sam said abruptly.

"About half a mile away, depending on the tide. We're eight miles south of Limeport on the enclosure coast. This place is called Faggle End. You may recall reading about it in Hilary. The cottage was one of her favourite retreats later on in her life. She came here the night before she died, in fact. It's been a rather special place for people in the Service ever since. Oh, that reminds me."

Sir Douglas dropped to his knees and rooted around in a tatty rucksack that was propped up by the door. He produced Sam's copy of *Soul Freedom* and handed it to him.

"There you are, dear boy, retrieved from *Smith's Potioners*. I'm afraid we had to leave the rest of your gear there for continuity, but I thought you might want this back. I got the impression it was rather special for you."

Sam took the book and Sir Douglas refilled their cups from a bottle on the floor. He lit a cigarette.

"Do you fancy trying one of these things, Samuel?

Sam shook his head.

"Suit yourself. I find a fag and a mug of port go rather well together first thing, but perhaps that's just me. The Service gives one funny tastes in all sorts of ways."

The old man continued to smoke and drink while he stared keenly into the landscape, occasionally tilting his head back and sniffing, like an animal scenting the air. Sam watched his profile in silence and then said quietly, "You're an interlander."

Sir Douglas giggled as he exhaled.

"You know, I said you were a bright boy and I wasn't wrong, was I? I wasn't wrong at all. You're absolutely right; I am an officer of the Interland Security Service, licensed by the Guardian's Office, no less, to walk freely in two worlds. Legally, Samuel—licensed to *cross over legally*. Imagine that, now."

The old man giggled again and walked past the table and chairs to an open black metal hatch that Sam hadn't noticed before. He peered into it thoughtfully for a moment and then flicked cigarette ash down it.

"Yes, we certainly guard our great privilege. Not even the Guardian can turn up at the Project and cross over without our permission and escort. Although, in point of fact, I often think the real joy of being in the Service isn't actually our right to walk freely in the enclosure and on the outside. I think the real joy is to be able to linger in places like this."

"Well, it's … it's certainly a nice spot," Sam said.

"Not what I meant, dear boy, not what I meant at all." The old man walked back to the door and gestured vaguely up the path that led away from the cottage, inland. "Look, from here I could, if I so chose, get changed and walk two miles into Lower Thraxton where I could catch old Bobby Morton's Limeport coach—assuming his horses aren't glue by now, of course. I could be in Limeport by midmorning and spend a fun day pissing it up, or gaming, or ambling round the market or the dock, or whatever takes my fancy." Sir Douglas gestured back towards the hatch. "Alternatively, if I chose to, I could nip back through the boundary lock and down the ladder to the access corridor, 20 feet below us. I could follow the corridor to a minirail platform, take the minirail to the Oval and catch the monorail from there to London. I could be in town in just under half an hour and spend a pleasant day taking advantage of all the delights the capital affords. I should add that the pleasure would be considerably enhanced by the fact that Service members get free admission and privileged access to theatres, galleries and so on, but forget that for now."

Sir Douglas ground his cigarette out on the doorframe and tossed it outside. He put his arm round Sam's shoulders.

"My point is this, dear boy: although I *could* perfectly happily spend the day wandering in either world, I very often choose not to. I find I am actually happiest precisely here," the old man stamped his foot on the cottage floor, "and in places like this, where I am perched on the line, as it were, neither quite in one place nor the other."

Sir Douglas shivered violently and withdrew his arm. He returned to the table and sat down, pouring himself another drink.

"I believe in the old folklore the line between parishes and the moment between days was regarded as magical, a place that wasn't quite a place, a time that wasn't quite a time, a space that slipped through the net of conventional reality. Well, I think I understand that nonsense a little when I hang around here, between the worlds, as it were. I feel sort of weightless, Samuel, almost selfless, although not in any virtuous sense, obviously. It's really rather wonderful, especially as I get older. I feel *light*. You might have experienced something similar yourself up in that old observation trench at Stanmore."

The old man looked at Sam expectantly. Sam walked to the table and sat down opposite him. He poured himself another drink and sipped it.

"What's going to happen to me?" he asked.

The old man sighed.

"Sorry. Sorry. Here I am wittering about my odd little fancies when, you're quite right, we're here to speak about you. You know the maximum penalty for violating the boundary, of course..."

"Yes, it's ... well, it's chemical curtailment, isn't it?"

"Quite so. But the government does not always *enforce* the maximum penalty. It rather depends on why we believe the particular person has crossed over."

Sam opened his mouth to speak but Sir Douglas Latch waved him into silence.

"For God's sake, don't bother trying to defend yourself. You should take it as read that I know rather more about you and your reasons for being here than you do."

Sam subsided and the old man went on, "Whether the government curtails someone depends on their particular reason for crossing the boundary. If a malefactor has crossed over intending to harm the Project in some way or destabilise the state—that's known as a red/black boundary breach, by the way—then chemical curtailment is normally a matter of course. If, on the other hand, someone has crossed, not out of ill will as such, but out of a spirit of adventure, or escape, or just because they feel somehow drawn to the enclosure as you were yourself, well, that's known as a blue/green boundary breach and the consequences are rather different. In such cases the state is considerably more lenient, particularly if the law-breaker is a teenager, as most are."

The old man lit another cigarette and smoked it for a while, observing Sam carefully as he did so. Eventually he said slowly, "Now Samuel, how would you feel, I wonder, about the opportunity to cross over as often as you wished, without any secrecy or fear? How would you like to be licensed to do it by the state? How would you like to be paid to do it?"

Sam felt his heart pound.

"What … what do you mean?"

"I think you know perfectly well what I mean. The ISS recruits officers exclusively from the pool of blue/green boundary transgressors. That's why we allowed you your lengthy playtime within the enclosure. We wanted to see precisely what you were made of, and you did exceptionally well. If you choose to join us, you'll work bloody hard, I promise you that, but you'll get, well …" The old man gestured vaguely towards the door where sunshine still streamed into the cottage. "I always think there's a particular clarity of light on the enclosure coast," he murmured. "It's vastly superior to anything on the outside. I don't know if it's the absence of heavy industry here, or what it is, but I swear it's true. There's a freshness, I think."

"What happens if I don't agree?" Sam said flatly. The old man shrugged.

"Oh, in that case we just bung a hefty injection up your bum so that you won't remember too much about the last six months and send you back to Mum and Dad. You'll have a sore arse and a scrambled head for a bit but eventually you shouldn't be any the worse. Oh, and you won't be able to visit any Project installations again, of course. But there'd be no question of any punishment, as such. We don't blackmail people into the Service. You're making a free choice, remember that."

Sam stood up and walked back to the cottage door. He leant on the rough wooden doorframe and felt the warmth of the sun and the salty tang of the air sweep over him. A family of rabbits were playing nearby, tumbling and clambering over one another as they rolled down a bank.

"It's rather a lot to give up, isn't it?" Sir Douglas said. "And of course, as an ISS officer you wouldn't have to limit yourself to this country; we work in every installation on the planet. There's no reason why you shouldn't end up operating in the enclosure in Siberia (that's the biggest in the world), or in Tennessee, or Alaska, or New South Wales, or on the continent, or just about anywhere, if you put your mind to it. You're a bright, daring boy. You could do very well indeed." When Sam didn't answer, Sir Douglas coughed softly. "And of course, your brother could never, ever follow you inside, Samuel, because it would never occur to the poor blockhead to try. You really would be free of him."

Sam swung round to face the old man.

"I don't know why you have to drag Roger into everything," he said. "He's got nothing to do with it. Anyway, you know perfectly well that I'll do it. I love it here. And I don't want to go to Siberia or Tennessee or anywhere. I want to stay in Ely."

Sir Douglas smiled.

"In which case, dear boy, welcome aboard. Let me say how very pleased I am. And, believe me, I understand your wanting to stay at Ely; it's special for people like us, isn't it? Now then, much as I'd love to let you enjoy the view all day, I'm afraid I have a couple of things to do to get you sorted out as a postulant. First of all, we need to get you installed in your new digs of course. How does that sound?"

"Um, look, it sounds good, obviously, but … well, would it be possible to get a message to my mum and dad. I wouldn't have to see them necessarily, but I'd like them to know that I'm ok. They'll be worried."

Sir Douglas Latch stubbed his cigarette out and finished his drink. He looked suddenly irritated.

"That's all very touching, but isn't it rather late? Shouldn't you have thought about poor old Mum and Dad before you buggered off without so much as a note?"

"Well, yes, I know, but … I didn't really think about them while I was on the other side. I was completely cut off from them, you see, so I couldn't even feel bad about running off. I couldn't feel anything about them, really, nothing *reached* me. But since I've spoken to you and everything …"

"Samuel, your parents have been informed that you are in state custody and that you are safe and well. They probably suspect rather more than that, to be honest. But you won't be able to contact them, or anyone outside, until you finish as a postulant. In fact, you won't be able to leave the Project at all. Frankly, dear boy, soon you'll be too busy to think about Mum and Dad very much."

Sam shrugged.

"What's a postulant?"

Sir Douglas placed both cups in the rucksack together with the bottle. He hoisted the rucksack onto his shoulders.

"More Latin, I'm afraid. A postulant is someone who is in formation for the Service. Don't worry about it. I've every confidence you'll do brilliantly."

"Oh, I see. Well, thanks. So when does this training, or formation, or whatever it is, start?"

"Well, there's the thing. As it happens, we're briefing a new intake tomorrow. You're rather last minute, I'm afraid. We could have nabbed you before, of course, but for various reasons I was keen you should have your Beltane." The old man smirked at Sam as he lowered himself into the hatch. "For which I hope you're bloody grateful. Now come on, dear boy, but do be careful on this ladder; I'm still not sure if your legs are quite up to snuff."

Chapter Twenty-Six
Hilary's Victory

The following day found Sir Douglas Latch standing in front of Sam and 17 other new ISS postulants in a parlour deep beneath the enclosure. The postulants were seated around a highly polished table. They were fidgeting and studiously avoiding one another's eye while Sir Douglas checked his notes at an imposing lectern. Occasionally the old man glanced at his wrist watch. After several minutes he cleared his throat.

"Well then, let's begin," he murmured, "and if our latecomer turns up we will just have to exercise charity. The poor chap has rather more to cope with than the rest of you."

He looked up and his blue eyes slipped quickly around the table, taking in the 18 faces that were staring at him, and the empty chair. They all looked so terribly anxious and innocent in their crisp new blacks, with their neat piles of note paper and their biros arranged in front of them. Hair was smartly combed, teeth nicely cleaned and cheeks well-scrubbed. You could practically smell the fresh scent of soap and toothpaste wafting off the little dears. The old man smiled lazily, moistening his lips with his tongue. Perhaps he was getting sentimental in his old age. After all, the last thing you could call this lot was innocent. He'd read their files thoroughly and they weren't bloody innocent at all. It was their lost innocence that made them so exquisitely desirable.

"Welcome all of you to Interland Security Service, Great Britain Division," he said. "You have joined one of the most exclusive organisations in the world, with the most exacting entry requirements. You are all here because you are exemplary law-breakers, liars and cheats. To be specific, each of you has crossed the boundary into the enclosure, thus breaking the single greatest taboo our society maintains— arguably, it's *only* real taboo. And, having crossed over, you all subsequently lived on your dishonest wits with great imagination and skill. None of you are decent or responsible people, none of you are good citizens, and if I had children I certainly wouldn't want any of you to marry them. You are, however, clever, resourceful and imaginative people, and capable of tremendous endurance. And these qualities might make you into excellent ISS officers one day. Anyone who fancies one, by all means, help yourself to a bun."

The buns were arranged on delicate china plates. No one helped himself to one as Sir Douglas lit a cigarette. He sighed with pleasure as he exhaled and then removed a large tabby cat from his lectern, kissing it on the head and placing it gently on the floor.

"Now then," he went on, "in crossing the boundary and surviving within the enclosure you have already passed the most difficult stage of selection for the Service. We allowed each of you your run on the inside in order that you could *transform yourselves into interlanders*. You are, therefore, already Service members and as such you are fully entitled to wear the uniform, with brass buckles, of course. You may enjoy all our privileges except the great privilege of crossing the boundary unsupervised. That particular right is reserved for *commissioned* officers, and before you can become one of those there is a final stage of selection to pass through." Sir Douglas looked round the table again and his voice became grave. "That test will be extremely personal in nature, designed to test your moral ingenuity, integrity and commitment. If you pass, you will receive your silver belt buckles. You will then be commissioned ISS officers, free to come and go as you please across the boundary, *to walk in two worlds*, as we put it. If you fail you will be given the choice of either going home with a suitable injection up your arse, or of staying on as permanent brass-buckles. If you elect to remain, you will be fully part of the Service, but you will never work alone within the enclosure. Brass-buckles support commissioned officers operationally and, under supervision, they participate in operations themselves. There is absolutely no shame in being a brass-buckle, eh, Tony?" Sir Douglas glanced at a smartly dressed younger man who was standing to attention at the door. The young man opened his mouth to speak then blushed and shut it again quickly. The older man smirked.

"You see, Tony agrees; there's no shame at all. Now then,

are there any questions?"

The young people around the table shook their heads quickly.

"Thank God for that. Well, thanks to your debriefings I already know all of you extremely well—rather better than your own mothers do, if truth be told, but not all of you know me. My name is Sir Douglas Latch, but please don't bother with the 'Sir'; not many people do. I glory in the title of Operational Director of the Interland Security Service, Home Division. That means that I'm ultimately responsible for all Service operations in Great Britain, and for obvious historical reasons I'm also *primus inter pares* amongst Service O.D.s around the world. Much more importantly, however, the moniker means that I get first crack at the booze and ciggies when they come down to the mess. Excuse me."

The young people laughed nervously while Sir Douglas poured himself a glass of port and sipped it. He nodded to the young man by the door who stepped forward and tapped a series of buttons on a holograph machine at the bottom end of the table. The blurred figure of an elderly woman, about a metre high, materialised slowly on the tabletop. She was somewhat stout and slumped in an ancient rocking chair. There was an exhausted looking cat stretched across her lap and a pipe in her hand. The young man marched to the wall and dimmed the lights, lending definition to the sagging folds of the woman's face and the creases in her black cardigan. Sir Douglas surveyed the group through his cigarette smoke.

"Now then, I wonder if any of you would care to hazard a guess as to who this might be."

A thin-faced girl with freckles and wire-rimmed glasses thrust her hand into the air. Sir Douglas smiled at her kindly.

"No need for hands up here, Ruth. You're not at Cheltenham Ladies anymore; we're not that sort of place. But anyway, my dear, please do tell us, who is it?"

"It's Dr. Hilary Lynch," the girl said, blushing furiously. "She was...'

"Excellent, Ruth," Sir Douglas interrupted. "You're absolutely right. This is Dr. Hilary Lynch. Now then, I wonder if anyone could tell me who Dr. Hilary Lynch *was* exactly."

The thin-faced girl put her hand up again and then pulled it down quickly. Sir Douglas looked round the table.

"Let's give someone else a go this time, shall we? One of the chaps perhaps. Samuel, I know you're a fan. Tell us about Hilary Lynch, dear boy."

Sam had been craning his neck to get the best possible view of Hilary since the holograph had appeared; now he shrank back in his seat and stared at the tabletop.

"Well, she was um... you know, she was Sebastian Randall's colleague and the founder of the ISS, wasn't she?" he said slowly. "She ... she was one of the very first Ely people. She knew Randall before it all started."

"Excellent, Samuel," Sir Douglas purred. "Absolutely excellent. Doesn't do to keep your light hidden under a bushel here, dear boy. If you know something, let it be known that you know it. And you're right, of course. You wouldn't know it from the official histories, but Hilary was one of Sebastian Randall's earliest collaborators. She was also the founder of the Interland Security Service and she remains an extremely important figure for Service people. Much of her personality, her enthusiasms, what I suppose we must call her *style*, although I've no doubt she would absolutely bloody hate the word, linger in our culture to this day. We owe her an awful lot, as you'll discover.

"The footage you're about to see was taken in the last months before Hilary's death when she was spending more and more of her time alone within the enclosure, and was communicating less and less with even her closest colleagues. There was a feeling, I think, that her life was beginning to unravel in some way and, with that in mind, a group of senior ISS people thought it would be valuable to have some of her private recollections on record for posterity. She was already working on her biography, of course, but that was going to be a public document and so even someone as significant and powerful as Hilary had to tread carefully. As any of you who have read it will know, *Soul Freedom* gets a bit naughty in places but it never actually crosses the line. The idea was that these recordings would belong exclusively to the Service, and in fact to this day no one outside has ever seen this material. In consequence, Hilary speaks extremely freely, as you'll see. Tony, I wonder if you would be so kind."

The young man marched forward again and pressed another button on the top of the holograph machine. The holograph figure flickered and then twitched into life. A moment later a man's voice echoed into the parlour.

"Hilary, last time we met, we spoke about the first years of the enclosure and the struggles involved in the birth of the Service. Today I'd like to shove things forward a bit to 1989 and the Revolution. What are your recollections of that period, I wonder?"

The old woman drew deeply on her pipe and exhaled holograph smoke which drifted to the top of the shot and then vanished. She scratched her chin and grinned mirthlessly at her invisible interviewer.

"Absolute bloody terror and chaos," she said slowly in a tired, precise, tobacco-stained voice. "This isn't something people care to talk about too much today, of course, but it's true all the same. One Nation was the campaigning group that opposed Ely, and very soon after the Project began they commanded a significant minority in the House of Commons. And attached to them, deniably of course, was their armed wing: the Fen Liberation Front. Now, they were vicious buggers, often attacking the boundary or putting car bombs under our people. They even issued mocked-up wanted posters for all the top Ely figures, myself included. It was fashionable in the Project to laugh at those posters and it even became a sort of badge of honour to have one's head on one. I believe Seb even has one of the damn things framed in his loo. But the effect on me personally was profoundly unsettling, to say the least. You have to bear in mind, Colin, that I regarded myself as a *good* person; in fact, I regarded the whole project as fundamentally *good*. I didn't like the idea of people with bloody big guns and bombs pegging me as a baddy. I didn't like it one little bit. It ... well, frankly it upset me."

The old woman frowned and poked around in the bowl of her pipe with her yellowed thumb. After a moment the invisible interviewer said gently, "How about the '89 election itself, Hilary, could you tell us about that please?"

"Well, it was Seb's great triumph, of course, but for me and for many of us in the Service it was pretty ghastly. One Nation campaigned harder than ever and their tone was increasingly confrontational and nasty, and the FLF were extremely active. The Service lost half a dozen excellent people to assassination in the run-up to the voting. And then, as everyone knows, the election was a dead bloody heat. One Nation had 152 seats in the House of Commons and so did the parties that were sympathetic to the Project. Both sides were very broad churches, bear in mind. The only real dividing line in British politics at the time was Ely. Were you pro- or anti-Project; modern or trad; progressive or reactionary? It was a line that ran through the old political affiliations of left and right, through social classes, through regions, even through families. Perhaps … perhaps even through individual consciences."

"So, how did the election result actually *feel*? Do you remember your own responses on the day itself?"

"It felt jolly unnerving, to be honest. The king couldn't form a government, Parliament couldn't meet, laws couldn't be passed, the army couldn't be commanded. For a moment it looked as if we were on the edge of civil war, facing the abyss, as it were." The old woman shrugged wearily. "But of course, Seb was always rather good with abysses; I don't think the opposition had reckoned with that."

Out of the shot Sam heard the sound of papers being ruffled.

"You're referring to the 14th of July, I assume," the interviewer asked eventually. Hilary inclined her head so that her helmet of grey hair sagged over her face.

"Of course I am. The 14th of bloody July. I can still see Seb clambering up onto the altar in Ely Cathedral to address the faithful, the great visionary, the great daredevil, in his moment of triumph. He'd put on a bit of weight since I first knew him and he was a little grey at the temples by that time, but he was still a striking-looking man, I don't think anyone would disagree. In some ways, you know, I think he'd actually improved with age. Dressed in that rumpled old corduroy jacket of his, he looked like an excited sixth-former on a day trip, fizzing with enthusiasm and desperately wanting everyone's love and approval—and yet still with that same *noli me tangere* quality about him. Let's face it, he was extraordinarily brave in 1989 and … well … there was a kind of splendour about him. I remember that…"

Hilary tailed off, her eyes distant, and stroked the cat softly so that its fur stuck up the wrong way.

"But what about the *events* of the day?" the interviewer prompted.

"Oh, the events? Well, I think most of them are fairly well-known, aren't they? The 14th was the day after the election. At six o'clock in the evening Seb ordered the BSC into the airports, television studios, government offices and so forth all over London. He had the city locked down by seven-thirty and, really, whoever holds London holds the country. Then he went to see the king at Windsor and explained to him our position that the five constituencies covered by the Project should not be denied their representation in the new parliament simply because they were within the enclosure. As the fenlanders themselves could not be expected to participate in the election, Seb argued that their votes should be exercised as a block by the Ely Project itself. And obviously this gave our side the necessary seats to obtain an overall majority. It was all absolutely bloody ridiculous, of course, but what could the king do?" Hilary sighed. "The official histories have Seb travelling to Windsor by himself, neglecting to mention the party of 80 BSC men he took with him. I think Seb rather likes the image of himself going to face the massed ranks of ignorance and reaction alone, armed only with the moral force of his courage and the rapier of his reason. But that simply wasn't the case. It was the king who was alone, absolutely alone, and so in the end I don't think he really had any choice but to accept Seb's terms. It can't have been easy for him to hand over the country to someone like Sebastian, though. Even at the wrong end of 80 BSC guns, it really can't have been an easy decision. I thought about that rather a lot afterwards … poor chap. The king was rather a kind man, actually—a bit ineffectual, but kind—the precise opposite of Seb."

The old woman trailed off again and sat in silence. After a minute the interviewer said gently, "It must have been a relief to be free of all the conflict at last, I imagine?"

Hilary stared at him blankly and then threw back her head and laughed out loud so that the pouches of fat wobbled alarmingly on her cheeks and neck. Finally, the laughing drowned itself in a coughing fit that turned her face pink and made her whole body buck and quiver like a terrified animal. The cat whined and jumped from her lap, slouching out of the holograph shot.

"Well, it would have been a bloody relief," Hilary stuttered, wiping the tears from her eyes, "except that we then started fighting each other. Consider, before 1989 the Project had functioned as a state within a state: we had our own security and intelligence services, our own administration, our own basic government. But now, literally overnight, Colin, the Ely Project had become sophiocracy. Now we *were* the state and so there was an immediate rush for influence and power. Read your history; this sort of thing always happens after revolutions. And, believe me, it was just as awful as the fighting beforehand, more so in some respects: at least one knew who the enemy was before the election."

"And how did the Service fare in this infighting?"

"How did we fare? That's a jolly good question. How *did* we fare?" The Hilary holograph frowned and licked her lips, glancing at her watch. "Look here, Colin, the sun's more or less over the yardarm, is there any chance of a G and T before we go on, do you suppose? You'll find the stuff over there in the sideboard. I'd make it myself but it would take me about 20 minutes to lever my carcass out of the sodding chair."

"Yes, of course, Hilary."

"Splendid. Help yourself to whatever, obviously. And don't forget, pour the gin over the ice. Tonic and lemon afterwards."

There was a pause in which it was possible to make out the faint sounds of glasses clinking and drink being poured, and then the holograph figure of a young man appeared on the table top. He had blond, shoulder-length hair and was dressed in black jeans and a black, open-neck shirt. He had a clipboard under one arm and a glass in the other hand. He handed the glass to Hilary, and then faded out of the image to the left. The old woman sipped the drink and sighed appreciatively.

"Lovely Colin, you're a credit to the Service. Now then,

where were we? Oh yes, the squabbling after 1989. Well, you see, our first problem was recruitment. Seb was determined to expand and ultimately export the enclosure and so the Service had to grow rapidly if we were to maintain our position. We had to recruit good people extremely quickly and to our credit we managed to do so by selecting blue/green boundary transgressors. Now, at the time, that was a tremendous innovation, although in retrospect it seems obvious—who better to recruit to the Service than those courageous, unsettled souls who have already crossed the boundary? As a system, it continues to work extremely well, as you know. But beyond that we faced the greater issue of securing our position as *the only people entitled to enter the enclosure*. That was the real struggle and it was one we absolutely had to win if we weren't going to fade into irrelevance, or worse."

Again there was the sound of papers being shuffled out of shot.

"I'm not aware of any record of this particular issue," the interviewer said. Hilary sipped her drink again.

"Well, of course you're not bloody aware of any record of it; it's the one fight Sebastian bloody Randall lost so you're not likely to find any record of it, are you? Consider this: the Service had no influence whatsoever in the machinery of the new state. We were small even after our expansion and we only operated within the boundary. We had no clout at all outside the Project and yet our right to walk within the enclosure made us intensely enviable to just about everyone involved at Ely. Well, it was obvious from the start that lots of the bright young things who rose to prominence following the Revolution resented us. And I've no doubt Seb feared our power as well; he was *dependent* on us, you see, and he didn't like that. So it was clear that we had a fight on our hands if we wanted to hang on to our great privilege. And obviously as head of the Service, most of the fighting fell to me."

"What exactly did you do?" the interviewer asked.

"I invited Seb to dinner," Hilary said simply. "I've no doubt he disliked the prospect of eating with me, but I dropped large hints that I wished to negotiate the surrender of the Service's privileges and so obviously he agreed to meet. We went to a little Italian place in Cambridge that we used to visit in the old days. It was all rather intimate, actually, or it would have been if it weren't for the dozen or so security people Seb brought with him. Big buggers they were, with dark glasses and horrid bulges under their armpits—rather intimidating, I don't mind saying."

The old woman gulped the last of her drink. She held out her glass.

"Any chance of another, Colin?"

The interviewer's arm reached into the holograph shot and took her glass, and a few moments later returned it half-full. Hilary sipped the drink.

"Well, you see, I'd been clever. Ever since the very first days of the Service I had insisted that our people keep a precise paper record—paper, mark you, not electronic—of everything they encountered in the enclosure every time they crossed over. It became something of a discipline for us to keep our logbooks up to date and, of course, we circulated our experiences freely amongst ourselves, but shared nothing at all with outsiders. In consequence, it was only Service people who knew the physical geography and what one might call the *psychological geography* of the enclosure. We knew how to get in and out of each settlement, where the trouble spots were, how the various communities functioned. We knew the strong figures, the problem people, the nutters. We knew absolutely everything there was to know about the enclosure, such that the place couldn't function without our goodwill. Well, I didn't bother to pull my punches; over dinner I made it crystal clear to Seb that unless he enshrined the Service's unique right to cross over in the new constitution I would make his precious project ungovernable."

"Rather a dangerous game. How did the Guardian react?"

The old woman waved a plump hand dismissively at the interviewer and gulped at her drink again. A thin stream of the liquid leaked from her mouth and wove its way through the course tufts of hair that sprouted on her chin.

"A wise man once said that if you have a chap by his balls, his heart and mind will follow. Seb is a pragmatist before all else, you see. He knew he was beaten, so he decided to be amicable. Well, what choice did he have? Over coffee, he even spoke about how much he missed the old days and how little time he had for some of the new Ely people: 'too many damn square heads these days, Hillers, if you ask me, half of them don't even drink.' That sort of thing. He was quite convincing really, at least superficially. But I have no doubt whatsoever…" Hilary frowned, the flesh of her face seeming to sag further under the weight of memory. "Colin, I … I have no doubt whatsoever that if he could have had me killed that night he would have done. I have no doubt about that at all. Our dear Guardian really doesn't like being thwarted, you see. He doesn't like it one little bit."

Sam felt the silence thicken around the table and the postulants' attention suddenly deepen. To suggest that Sebastian Randall willed murder was treasonable by anyone's standards, and it didn't matter that the person making the accusation was an elderly holograph figure, long dead, with gin dribbling down her chin. It was the sort of thing that could simply never be said. At the top of the room Sir Douglas Latch continued to smoke peacefully, an amused smirk playing round his lips.

"But … but it was a triumph for yourself and the Service?" the interviewer asked in a shaky voice.

"Oh God, I've upset you, haven't I, Colin? Sorry about that, but I've been asked to tell the truth in these recordings, you see, and that's what I've determined to do. Yes, to answer your question, I suppose it was a triumph for the Service, although I can't say it particularly felt like one at the time. Frankly, I just felt bloody miserable. But the next day the Guardian's Office issued bylaw seven, confirming that the right to cross over was reserved to the Service alone, and whomever we agreed to escort. So I'd made our people safe, constitutionally speaking. After that we settled into the uneasy relationship with the Guardian's Office that continues to this day." The old woman dabbed at her chin with a grubby hanky. "And actually it *was* quite an exciting time, in a way. A new *esprit de corps* flourished amongst us. We adopted our blacks, largely to distinguish ourselves from Marcus's boot boys. And just when the rest of the nation was being enjoined from every available horizontal surface to *Know Thyself*, we opted for a motto of our own."

"*In Duobis Mundis Ambulare*," the interviewer murmured reverently."

"Quite so. *In Duobis Mundis Ambulare*: To Walk in Two Worlds. That was our unique privilege and our responsibility, you see. Absolutely wonderful, despite everything. And it's *still* wonderful, isn't it?"

"Yes, of course, Hilary. Of course it is. But what a painful ending to your relationship with the Guardian. Perhaps not the last supper you might have wished for with your old friend?"

Hilary swilled back the rest of her drink and leant forward to slam the glass down on an invisible tabletop. Years later the sound echoed round the parlour like a pistol shot. Sam and several of the other postulants jumped.

"Well, actually, Colin, you're quite wrong there. I believe that my last supper with Sebastian Randall is yet to come. And I can't say I'm particularly looking forward to it." Hilary grimaced and went on lifelessly, "I'm still fond of him, you see. I know it isn't rational or reasonable, and I know jolly well that I'm more hideous than ever now, and we're hardly friends anymore. But still, I can't help myself. The damn feelings don't go away, you see. They just don't. If I could cut the love out of my heart, I would have done it years and years ago. But I can't. So, no, I'm not looking forward to my last supper with the man one little bit. I think it will be a pretty poisonous affair, to be honest."

Hilary gazed at her interviewer with a look that flickered between defiance and defeat. Then her eyes dropped to her lap.

"Look here, Colin, I'm afraid we're going to have to leave things there for today. Mendel will want his supper, you see."

The figures on the tabletop froze.

Chapter Twenty-Seven
Latecomer

"You're all looking rather shocked, bless you," Sir Douglas murmured when the lights had been switched back up, "and to be honest, I'm glad, because if what you've just seen has shocked you, you're unlikely to forget it." His gaze slithered round the table. "As interlanders you will of course be loyal to the sophiocratic state. You will preserve the psychological and physical integrity of the enclosure, what we call its *continuity*; you will co-operate with government officials in their research; you will remove subjects for experiment; you will deal with boundary breaches; and you will do all of this to the highest standard. But your first loyalty *will be to the Service itself* and to the great privilege that Hilary won for us. We have enemies within the state and beyond it, some of them very dangerous and powerful. You will do nothing whatsoever to assist them."

The old man poured himself another glass of port while the postulants glanced nervously at each other. Sam noticed that the glasses-girl had covered three pieces of paper with notes during the holograph presentation.

"Well, then," Sir Douglas went on, "perhaps we should consider what you'll actually be doing in your time as postulants. Fifty per cent of your time will be given over to operational work, the rest of it to study and assessment. We all work pretty hard, but I hope you'll find ..."

The old man halted as the door swung open and banged against the wall. All the postulants turned to look as another boy half ran, half stumbled into the parlour. He was dressed in the same black uniform as the rest, but his shirt was untucked at the back and he had damp patches under his arms. He looked wildly round the room and sagged with relief when he saw Sir Douglas.

"Sorry I'm so late, Sir Douglas," he panted, "I got lost, did'n' I? I went wrong by the Horbury Junction Barrack Block, I think. There's a fork there, in't there? And I think I musta gone left instead of right like I should've done. Then I got lost for ages 'til I ended up at that food place you showed me. In the end one of them stewards found me and brought me here."

The boy tossed a pad of paper onto the table in front of the empty chair and shrugged. "Sorry," he said again.

"Ah, Simeon," Sir Douglas said soothingly. "Delighted to see you, old chap. I was getting a little concerned about you, to be honest. Now then, don't worry yourself; you've missed nothing vital, or nothing that you can't see another time. You just sit yourself down and get your breath back. Did you bring your pen as I told you?"

The boy flopped into the empty chair and nodded, pulling a biro from his top pocket.

"Excellent. And you remember how it works?"

The boy blushed and nodded again.

"Good. Somebody give the poor chap a cigarette, please. Thank you, my dear. Simeon, the little china dish on your right is an ashtray. Do grab a bun if you fancy one. Ok? Excellent. Now then, where were we? Oh yes, the syllabus. It's only fair that you all understand what you're letting yourself in for."

Sir Douglas talked about the formation that the new postulants would receive and the opportunities that awaited them when they were qualified. He described hours of hard study and physical training; hair-raising night exercises within the enclosure and restful summer days spent on reconnaissance duties in isolated observation trenches; he mentioned the possibility of participating in exchange schemes with foreign branches of the Service and much more in a similar vein, until even the glasses-girl gave up taking notes and cupped her head in her hands to gaze at him wide-eyed.

But Sam remained oblivious to it all. He sat and stared as the newcomer smoked his cigarette in sharp, urgent breaths, while his other hand twisted the biro through his fingers. His hair had been cut and his teeth repaired since Sam last saw him, but the darkly violent eyes were exactly as he remembered them, as was the brownish shade of his skin and the restless movement of his tongue over his lips. Sam shuffled his feet nervously under the table and, of its own accord, his hand drifted beneath his shirt and traced the thin scar that reached from his shoulder almost to his navel. He continued to watch as the newcomer stubbed out his cigarette and slumped back in his chair, studying the contours of the boy's sticky shirt to see if he could detect the outline of another knife. (Surely they wouldn't have let him come here with a knife!) As Sir Douglas showed holograph footage of enclosures across the globe, from Siberia ("bloody big and bloody cold") to the Galapagos Islands ("tiny but wonderful. The locals have the most beautiful skin tone. I spent my two weeks there in an erotic haze."), Sam found himself back in the dust and terror of the dilapidated barn where he had fought for his life. The parlour became oppressively hot and a film of sweat broke out on his forehead. The boy himself remained oblivious to Sam's attention; he slouched in his chair and stared unblinkingly at Sir Douglas, a vein throbbing in his forehead.

"And so," Sir Douglas said half an hour later, "it really only remains for me to introduce you to your tutors. On my right is Deborah Hershwitz, from Tucson, Arizona, and on my left is Kevin Spark from Wigan. I wonder if the pair of you would care to make yourself known."

The sigh of wonder which followed finally drew Sam's gaze away from the newcomer. He swung round in time to see the air on either side of Sir Douglas become unsettled, like disturbed water. The light gradually thickened and swayed, and then washed away from the spaces beside the old man, exposing two human forms. They were dressed from head to toe in purple overalls, with purple masks covering their faces. The pair pulled their masks off revealing an attractive woman with flowing blonde hair and lively, blue eyes, and an intense-looking young man with a finely sculpted beard. Both of them were grinning at the postulants' amazement.

"Some of you are already familiar with our Cognitive Interrupter Concealment Outfits," Sir Douglas said, "and the rest of you will be before long. It's a silly trick, I know, but it tends to wake everyone up after my bit. Esteemed colleagues, introduce yourselves."

"Hi guys," said the blonde woman. "I'm Deborah, and as Sir Douglas says I'm from near Tucson, over in the States. So what else can I tell you? I grew up in farm country and crossed over when I was 18 years old, just a coupla' days after my senior prom. I had a blast for three months and then got my ass hauled in and got recruited into the Service. I cut my teeth herding rednecks out in Tennessee, in the Dixie enclosure, and right from the first day I loved it. I figured I'd found my place, if you know what I mean. I've been over here in England for two years now and I still can't believe my luck that a dumb country girl like me should end up working at Ely, instructing postulants. I guess I owe the Service just about everything. Anyway, I'm going to be teaching you guys field craft, communications, phys. ed. and combat." The woman shrugged. "And I think that's all I've got to say for now."

On the other side of Sir Douglas the young man cleared his throat.

"Hello," he said. "I'm Kevin from Wigan. I studied Law in Edinburgh for seven years and crossed over into the highland enclosure when I failed to receive my doctorate. So I'm what they call a late-crosser. I've been working with postulants for 18 months, and I teach constitutional law and enclosure structure; that's the psychology, sociology, geography and politics of the enclosure, all the things that Hilary insisted the Service keep to itself. With that in mind, you'd all better grab one of these." The man took a pile of slim red books from the table and handed them round the room. Sam flicked his open and found that its pages were blank.

"These are your logbooks," the man went on. "Starting from today, whenever you cross over, whether it's on your own or in a group, for business or for pleasure, you make sure you fill in your log when you get back safe-side. Everything that might be even the slightest bit significant goes in them and once a month you'll have a cross-over review with a senior officer where you'll work through the book together so that anything useful can get passed along. It's all very Hilary, really: nothing on computer, nothing missed out, nothing kept to yourself. And the cross-over reviews tend to be done over a bottle of wine, so that's pretty Hilaryish—or would the word be Hilarious, I don't know—as well. You're also going to need these." The man handed round a pile of blue books. They were filled with dense typescript, divided into elaborately numbered paragraphs. "This is the ISS rulebook. It contains the fruit of 90 years' worth of crossover meetings, which basically means 90 years of cock-ups and near misses in the enclosure. It also contains the legal stuff about how we relate to the BSC, the Guardian's Office and so on. I hope you'll become intimately familiar with it in the months and years ahead. It's a great treasure." The man clenched his hands into fists and cracked his knuckles. "That's me done," he said.

"Thank you, Kevin," Sir Douglas said gravely. "I hope you all come to fill in many, many logbooks. Youngsters often resent taking the time, but believe me, quite apart from the absolute operational necessity of completing them, it is one of the great comforts of old age to be able to review one's best years in the enclosure. Now then, to be honest, I'm thoroughly fed up with all of you staring at me bright-eyed and sober. Why don't you get yourselves along to the junior mess for something to drink and a spot of lunch? Get to know one another, flirt a bit, entertain one another with tails of derring-do in the enclosure." He glanced at his watch. "We don't need you back here until half one, when, all being well, you'll have your first *legal* trips across the boundary."

A hum of excitement passed round the room at this and the postulants gathered up their belongings and began to shuffle to the door, followed by the two tutors. Sir Douglas folded his notes and glanced up from the lectern.

"Ah, Samuel and Simeon, I wonder if you two would hang on for a sec. I want a quick word. Won't keep you long, I promise."

The late arriving boy glanced round from the door. He looked at Sir Douglas and then noticed Sam for the first time. His face twisted in shock and anger. The two boys stared at each other for a moment and then trailed to the front where Sir Douglas drained his glass and lit a fresh cigarette from the stub of an old one.

"Rather an awkward situation, isn't it?" he murmured. "Having a couple of chaps who've tried to kill each other in the same class. In point of fact, I'm not sure it's ever happened before in the history of the Service. Of course, you'd have to check that with Kevin; he's much more the Service history buff than I. Samuel, undo your shirt please."

"What, Sir Douglas?"

"Undo your shirt," the old man said firmly. "I want Simeon here to see his handiwork."

Sam slowly unbuttoned his shirt and held it open. The scar was clearly visible: a fine red line, sharp against his pale flesh.

"There you are, Simeon, that's what you did. A good long cut, isn't it? Run your finger along it, please."

The boy glanced uncertainly at Sir Douglas, then reached out and drew his finger gently along the wound. Sam felt sick. He stared at the floor.

"Excellent," Sir Douglas said. "Now then, Simeon take Samuel's hand please and show him where he hit you. There's a good lad."

The boy's lips parted in a sneer, but he took Sam's hand and placed it palm-downwards on the left side of his head, towards the top. His hair felt damp and coarse, like an animal's. He pressed Sam's hand into his scalp and Sam felt a spot where the skull was flattened and smooth. He was aware of the boy's quick breath close to his face. After a moment he pulled his hand away.

"You gave him quite a wallop, didn't you, Samuel?" Sir Douglas said gently. "Yes, you practically did our job for us with young Simeon."

"I'm sorry," Sam said quickly as he re-buttoned his shirt. "I had no idea you were from outside the enclosure. I thought you were a subject. I mean, you looked ... well, you looked like a fenlander. I thought you were about to kill me."

"I am a subject," the boy said dully. "At least I was. I grew up jus' outside Cromer."

"But ... But ... Well, I mean, what are you doing here? I thought ..." Sam turned to Sir Douglas. "You said that people could only join the Service if they had crossed over."

"That's perfectly true," said Sir Douglas. "But what makes you think that everyone crosses over in the same direction? Simeon here belongs to that very select body of men and women who cross over from the inside out. These people tend to make exceptional officers," he glanced at the other boy and smiled, "or else I'm afraid they're absolutely bloody disastrous, Simeon. But don't worry, I'm sure you'll be in the former category.”

“I was hidin’ in that barn till it was dark,” the boy said. “Then I was gonna make a run for it westwards and jus’ see what happened. I was half-asleep when you found me; I thought you were the demon or somethin’, you see.”

“No,” Sam said. “No, I … I didn’t want to hurt you. I just wanted to get some money, well, *steal* some money, really. That’s all.”

“Now listen, gentlemen,” Sir Douglas said. “My experience of people who’ve tried to kill each other and failed is that they either finish the job one day or else they become firm friends. I think honours are about even between the pair of you, so let’s try and keep you both alive, shall we? I see no reason why you shouldn’t get on. Now off you go for some nosh. The junior mess is down the main corridor on the left. Just follow the noise.”

Sam and Simeon left the parlour and walked along the corridor in silence, Sam occasionally stealing glances at his companion. The boy still looked tense; he stared straight ahead and kept swallowing hard. Suddenly, without planning to say anything, Sam found himself speaking.

“What’s it like crossing over and thinking you’re going to find the demon or something and then discovering all this? I mean, how do you cope with something like that? What does it feel like to discover that everything you grew up with is, well, *a lie*? That you’re, sort of, a lie, yourself?”

Simeon frowned and then spoke quickly, without looking at Sam.

“When I were young I used to play in me uncle’s barn. You know, swingin’ round off the roof with ropes and climbin’ and suchlike. Well, one night I got stuck danglin’ off the end of a bit of gutterin’. I knew I couldn’t climb back up because I were too weak, but I didn’t know exactly how far I were from the ground either, see? In the end I jus’ had to let go, didn’t I? D’you understand?”

“Yes.”

“Well, I fell for a while, further than I were expecting, and when I hit the ground it hurt like hell and I broke me ankle. Anyway, that’s kinda what I were expecting when I crossed over. I thought I'd go out into the beyonds for a bit, I didn't know exactly how far, and then I'd meet the demon or whatever and that would be it. It'd hurt, but it'd all be over. But instead of that it's like I'm still fallin' into the dark and I'm never gonna stop. I'm alive and nothin' really hurts but I can't *think* about anythin' cos if I do my mind sorta goes cold and gives up." The boy shrugged. "I jus' gotta get on with things one day at a time, Sir Douglas says."

They walked in silence again until they reached the highly polished mess door. Inside Sam could hear the soft clink of cutlery and the glasses-girl saying loudly, "Actually no, I don't agree. I think he's an absolute sweetie. And, I mean, he's *so senior*. Do you know what I mean? I believe the Guardian actually has to make an appointment to see him. *The Guardian*, can you imagine that?"

The pair of them halted.

"So look," Sam said. "What made you … you know, *why* did you actually cross over? I mean, it's pretty much unthinkable from your side, isn't it? Literally. So how come…?"

"I thought I'd killed someone," Simeon said quietly. "Turns out I hadn't, but I thought I had. And after that I didn't care about anything much. I jus' wanted to be out in the beyonds where there's nothing but the demon. I wanted the nothingness of it. I sorta felt that I belonged there." He turned and looked at Sam. "You were lucky an' all. I would 'ave killed you if you hadn't've hit me. I really would 'ave done. I'd 'ave slit you open like you was an old sack or somethin'. I jus' didn't care, you see."

Chapter Twenty-Eight
Night Errand

Mick Randall had gone and Smith didn't care anymore. She didn't care about the shop, either, or about her stupid, feeble mother, or the town, or the temple. But most of all she didn't care about Mick bloody Randall himself, or whoever he was, with his bag of Royal Crowns and his easy promises and his lies.

She still looked as though she cared about things. Carried by momentum and routine, she worked conscientiously in the shop and the house, turned up at the temple services and involved herself in the normal round of Stanmore life. She did not know how to *stop* doing these things. But the world she walked in was muted and grey. When people spoke to her she felt as if she were listening to them from a great distance and had difficulty concerning herself with what they were saying. She could feel a hard, hollow space forming inside her. It wasn't a pleasant feeling, but she didn't care about that, either.

As she slipped out of her bedroom at midnight two months after Mick's disappearance, Smith paused for a moment to listen at her mum's door. There was only the sound of heavy, regular breathing. Good. She didn't want to be disturbed on her errand. She still cared a bit about small, silly things like embarrassment and making a fuss.

When Mick had first vanished she had cared horribly. She had stayed up all night waiting for him to return and the next day she had gone out hollow-eyed with fatigue to search for him in the streets of Stanmore and the surrounding fields and footpaths. Eventually, she had mustered her courage and approached Pereduke himself, but when she had told him of Sam's disappearance he had burst out laughing so hard that the matted strands of his hair had bounced around his face like quivering rats' tails.

"He never turned up at the pub, the little bugger," he had said when he had calmed down sufficiently to speak. "Pereduke himself was stood up by him, my dear. I reckon that young Master Mick is something of a wanderer, the likes of us was never going to tie him down." He had winked at Smith and thrown an arm over her shoulder pulling her close to his side. His clothes smelt of cigarette smoke and stale sweat. "Still, if you're missing something that he was supplyin' I dare say old Pereduke can step into the breach, so to speak, noble self-sacrificin' fella that I am."

Smith had wriggled out of his grip and gone home to get on with her work. The days had passed and, without really intending to, she had found herself counting them as she had once counted the days following her father's disappearance. She knew it was ridiculous, *she absolutely knew it*, but still she couldn't help herself. Mick Randall had only been in her life for a few months but he had needed her desperately and in his neediness he had burrowed into her affections further than she liked to admit. He had also made her laugh and been good company around the shop, and he had listened to her when she had spoken of her worries about the business or her mum. He had broken into her narrow, dutiful world from somewhere unspeakable, somewhere *outside*, if one could imagine such a place, and had stirred wild hopes in her that she hardly knew how to name. In fact, she had not dared to name them, because they were the sort of hopes that fluttered away if you tried to cage them in words. And then there had been Beltane night when they had shared a bed and Mick had cried and clung to her like a child. And afterwards, when they were calm, she had finally dared to speak of what she hoped for, and he had promised to take her to his home one day. He had *actually promised* to take her to his mysterious home beyond Walsingham where the demon never reached.

"Well, bugger that for a devil's tale," Smith muttered as she crept down the landing. "And bugger Mick Randall too." She wouldn't be taking young men to bed again, not ones she cared about anyway. And she certainly wouldn't be asking them for stupid, impossible things afterwards, just to have them lie to her and then vanish without a word. And as for Mick Randall himself, well, he would simply have to be forgotten. It wasn't going to be easy. In fact, it was going to be complicated and horrible to get Mick Randall out of her life forever. But certain things just had to be done no matter how horrible they were, and that was that.

She padded downstairs and felt her way to the mixing room, slipping inside and pulling the door shut behind her. Carefully, she lit the oil lamp and hung it from its hook above the mixing bench, then placed a stool beneath the potioner's cupboard that covered the whole of one wall. She eased the cupboard open, climbed onto the stool, and reached above her head for two unmarked black jars that were tucked away on the top shelf. These were hardly ever touched; they were only taken down when a young woman presented herself shamefaced in the shop with a certificate signed by Reverend Smythe confirming that the correct tithes had been paid and the appropriate prayers said to transform the requested procedure into an *acceptable oblation, fit to be received by the Green Man who is sole lord of living and dying and living again, through the spokes of the Sacred Wheel*. With her privileged position, however, Smith needed no such certification and she felt herself completely free of any obligation to Reverend Smythe, or even to the Green Man himself. On impulse she unhooked the crucified figure from inside the door of the potioner's cupboard (where he guarded the ingredients' innocence and vigour) and tossed it face down onto the floor.

She took down the two jars and placed them on the mixing bench. Lighting a spill from the oil lamp, she melted their wax seals and then unscrewed their lids and examined the contents of each one in turn. The first was full of coarsely chopped purple leaf mixed with white seeds. It smelt of wild flowers and aniseed and something else, something dark and extraordinarily sweet that she couldn't identify. The scent was pleasant for a moment but quickly became cloying and slimy at the back of Smith's nose and throat. The second jar contained grey powder, as fine and as dry as dust. It smelt sharp and distant, of rain and dying bonfires. Its tiny grains were disturbed by Smith's breath, flying into her eyes and hair. She pulled her head back quickly and reached for a mixing dish and a candle.

And then she stopped and listened. There was a tiny scuffling sound, almost undetectable, coming from the corner of the room. Laying the dish and the candle aside, she took the oil lamp from its hook and dropped to her knees, peering into the narrow gap between the potioner's cupboard and the stone floor. A small, dark shape twitched and whimpered at the light, then shuffled rapidly forward and flustered into the air. It flew crazily around the little room for a few seconds before coming to land on top of the equipment rack. Smith clambered to her feet and stared at the rumpled little bird, sighing in frustration.

This was happening increasingly often. One window in the mixing room was kept permanently open to allow the more sensitive ingredients to breathe and to keep them in fellowship with the turning seasons. There was meant to be a piece of steel mesh over the window to prevent uninvited guests from getting in, but it kept coming loose. More than once recently Smith had left a potion on the candle, only to return five minutes later to find it ruined by the unwanted contribution of some loose-bowelled bird or other. She didn't want to risk being interrupted in this way tonight. And anyway, it didn't seem quite right to do what she had to do with an audience, even if the audience was only a bird. She pulled the stool across the room and climbed onto it slowly, reaching for the little creature.

Just as she was closing her hands around it, however, the bird flew off. Smith made a grab for it and dislodged a pile of sieves, sending them clattering to the ground. The bird flew past her face, so close that she felt the breeze on her cheek, and settled on the windowsill. She stepped off the stool, clambered onto the mixing bench and reached for it again, but once more the creature flew away and this time, as Smith span round after it, she upended one of the black jars, spilling purple leaf and white seeds all over the bench and floor.

For 10 minutes Smith and the bird did chaotic battle. The flickering light of the oil lamp sent small shadows fluttering around the walls and often Smith found herself clutching wildly at air. More than once she tripped and fell, dislodging more equipment and medicines. Finally, when the mixing bench was knocked halfway across the room and the floor was strewn with jars, bowls, meshes and spoons, she cornered the creature, with the help of two sieves, between the wall and the door. Slowly she laid one of the sieves aside and reached stealthily through the shadows, grabbing the bird from behind.

"Got you! You nasty little bugger!" she hissed. As she drew the creature to her chest, she went on more softly: "I wasn't gonna hurt you. I jus' don't want you messin' up my remedy tonight. It's important tonight, you see."

The bird felt ridiculously light and delicate in her fist, as if she would only have to twitch her hand to squeeze the life from it completely. Its heart was beating impossibly fast and its black eyes were wide open and very still. Smith felt the terror pass from its shivering body into her own, speeding her own heart in response.

"There ain't no need to be afraid," she murmured. "I ain't gonna eat you or anythin'. I only eat big birds like pheasant and woodcock, you see. Not little ones like you. You wouldn't even make a mouthful. I'm gonna let you go."

She climbed awkwardly back onto the stool and opened her hand next to the window. Rather than fly away, however, the little bird stood still on her palm, watching her intently. Without warning, moonlight flooded the mixing room. It bathed the creature in its glow so that Smith could make out the delicate mottling on its underside and the soft movement of the breeze through its feathers.

"Go on, then, go ... go away," she said urgently. "You're free, ain't you? You can go anywhere you like. Jus' go away."

The bird hopped from Smith's hand to the windowsill. It twitched its head back at her and then launched itself into the night. Smith stood on tiptoe and watched as it careered haphazardly across the yard. It swerved past the wood pile, cleared the back fence by a hair's breadth and was swallowed by the moon shadow cast by the house opposite.

"Fly quick," she whispered into the darkness. "And don't let anyone else eat you neither. No cats or anythin'. Jus' keep goin', you understand? And don't stop for no one."

She stared into the yard for several minutes and then, when her heart beat had returned to normal, she stepped down from the stool and examined the mess. Just as she was bending down to pick up two canisters of Thyme and Blueberry syrup an unhappy voice sounded from upstairs.

"Lou! Lou! What's goin' on? What you doin'?"

Smith frowned. She wiped the tears from her cheeks and went quickly back upstairs and into her mum's room. An oil lamp had been lit and her mum was sitting up in bed with her hair unkempt and her nightshirt rucked up awkwardly round one shoulder. She looked terrified.

"It's all right, Mum," Smith said softly. "It was only me. I was jus' gettin' a little bird out of the mixin' room before it crapped all over everywhere. That's all."

"I were dreamin' that you'd gone off somewhere, Lou," her mum whispered. "I were dreamin' that some people were breakin' in and I could hear 'em all bangin' around but I didn't know what to do 'bout it and you weren't there to sort it out. Then I woke up and there really was bangin' and I was frightened. You hadn't gone away anywhere, had you?"

Smith sat down on the edge of her mum's bed. She eased her night shirt around her shoulder so that it was smooth and straight, and stroked her hair gently back into place.

"I suppose I have sorta been away, Mum," she said quietly. "But don't worry, I'm back now. And I ain't gonna go away again. Yer jus' about stuck with me I'm afraid. Forever."

"I'm glad about that, Lou. I'd be quite miserable if you weren't around, with the shop and everythin', you know. I think I'd find it all quite difficult—even if there weren't anybody breakin' in."

Smith continued to stroke her mum's hair until her eyes closed and her breathing became slow and heavy again. Then she extinguished the oil lamp, crept out of the room and went back downstairs. She tidied the mixing room as best she could without risking making more noise and cleared up the purple leaf remedy with the white seeds. She resealed both of the black jars and replaced them in the potioner's cupboard. Finally, she retrieved the figure of the Green Man from the floor, kissed it softy and hung it back on the cupboard door.

"I wouldn't really have done it without the certificate and everythin'," she whispered. "At least, I don't *think* I would. Even if you hadn't sent the bird to wreck everythin' and spill the ingredients, I wouldn't have done it. I do know what's right."

She closed the cupboard and slipped out of the mixing room, then went back to her bedroom and climbed onto her bed. There she sat for a long time in the moonlight with her knees drawn up to her chin and a frown fixed on her face. And as the hours slipped by she thought hard about all sorts of things and felt wide awake and uncertain of herself. She thought about unhappy mothers with unkempt hair; and deceitful boys with funny underpants; and little birds whose hearts beat as if they were going to explode; and all the other sharp, sudden and unfair things that have the power to pierce your heart.

Finally, she undressed and slipped under the covers, pulling the blankets up tight around her chin.

"I'm back," she whispered. "I'm definitely back, Mum, and I'm not gonna go away again. Honest, I'm not. Yer jus' about stuck with me, I reckon."

Chapter Twenty-Nine
Ghost

The young fisherman picked his way carefully down the gangplank of his boat and wove through the crowd on the Limeport quay. Round about him fat fishmongers and boat owners haggled energetically over barrels of gleaming fish, packed with ice. They sealed their deals with brutal handshakes and a dash of chalk on the barrels' sides. A little further back, women in filthy shawls and stout boots yelled obscenities at one another as they gutted fish with raw, blood-stained fingers. And all around the chill wind battered the quay, whipping the words from everyone's salt-dry lips and whirling them off to the inland country, which the Limeporters despised, where the elements and the people were altogether more gentle. The quayside itself was slippery with ice and water as well as the dark fish innards that the shouting women discarded, but the young fisherman had the steady step of a man used to keeping his footing in the sudden squalls of the outside sea, where the wind blew up gales from nowhere and sent boats bucking like stallions. He plodded carefully over the uneven stones and on towards the main street. He caught no one's eye.

On the main street he turned right and pushed his way along the cobbled pavement until he reached a pub called *The Swan*. He paused and glanced both ways before ducking quickly through the open door.

Inside, the atmosphere was thick with liquor, damp garments, smoke and sweat. Sawdust covered the floor. Two men were hunched silently over the bar while five more, obviously fishermen, were playing cards round a table stacked with piles of money and empty glasses. The leader of the group was a stocky, unshaven man with a leathery, wind-bruised face. He had a young woman balanced on his knee and kept one hand resting protectively on her exposed thigh. The other hand, with two fingers missing, held his cards.

"All blacks apart from the lady. I needs the bloody lady to set me right," the man growled. He grinned and glanced up at his companions. "Or do I? Maybe I'm havin' you lads on a piece and you ain't gonna know no different. Then again, maybe I'm speakin' truth. Who can say?"

The man guffawed and slapped the woman's thigh, making her wince. He laid two cards face down on the tabletop.

"Twist," he said.

A thin man with half an ear missing slid two cards across the table. The unshaven man lifted their corners and smiled.

"The black lady hasn't let me down. She's come home to her daddy, lads, jus' like she always does." He guffawed again. "Or 'as she? Who can say, boys, who can say, eh?"

Around the table the other men laughed and consulted their cards, scratching their heads and tugging at their ear lobes (those who had them). Gradually the little group became noisy.

The young fisherman studied the card players discreetly and then bought himself a brandy and placed himself directly behind the unshaven man. The table slowly fell silent.

"If you're 'ere do me harm, young fella, you'd better see about doin' what you come for so I can rip yer lungs out for you and we can get on with our game," the unshaven man growled. "And if you've come for anythin' else you can shove off now. We don't need an audience."

"I haven't come do you harm, Amos Half-Hand," the young fisherman said. "I'm not stupid. I'm here because I've got some information for you."

Amos Half-Hand sniggered.

"He's got some information for me, fellas, well fancy that." He swung round to look at the newcomer and spat onto the floor, an inch from the other man's foot. "Listen 'ere, young 'un, the only information I want at present is what that devious little weasel, Billy Salt-Cheeks over there, has got in his hand, and perhaps which way the cod is running out in the east. If you can advise me on either of them matters please go ahead, and if not, you'd better hop it quick before I forget me good nature."

"I don't know either of them things," the young fisherman said quickly. "But I know this, that Tom Woodman is presently drinkin' in the back room of the *Moon and Sixpence* and he's tellin' all who will listen that Amos Half-Hand is a liar and a cheat, and that he ain't even got the guts to meet for a fair fight."

For a moment no one spoke and then Amos Half-Hand brought his fist crashing down on the edge of the table. The wood splintered, sending glasses and coins tumbling everywhere. The woman on his lap jumped and squealed.

"Who are you?" Amos Half-Hand growled. "You're no friend of mine that I can recall. And I remember my friends."

"No, I'm n…not your friend, at least not yet," the young fisherman stuttered. "But I'm no fr…friend of Tom Woodman's, either, least ways not since he cheated me out of half shares in a boat, a few weeks ago."

"What boat would that be then?"

"The Boy Blue."

The other man considered for a moment and his tone softened fractionally.

"The Boy Blue's a handsome craft. I s'pose I'd be a little annoyed if some snot-nosed thief like Tom Woodman had cheated me out of half shares in summat like that."

"He lost it at cards fair and square and now he won't answer for it. He laughed in my face when I said I wanted what was mine."

Amos Half-Hand pushed the woman off his lap so that she went sprawling to the floor and stood up. He stepped towards the newcomer and suddenly there was a knife in his hand, pushed delicately against the other's heart.

"Now listen 'ere, young 'un. You and I have this in common it seems to me—we both 'ave just cause to hate Tom Woodman. So what we're gonna do is this. We're gonna take a little stroll down to the *Moon and Six* and if that lying, thieving little bastard is there like you say he is, then there'll be a spot of bother and blood and you'll have made a friend of Amos Half-Hand for life. And I can be a useful friend to have, as I'm sure you'll appreciate."

"I do, I … I appreciate that."

"Good. But if he ain't there, well then, there'll still be a spot of bother and blood. I don't like havin' my time wasted, do you understand?"

"P…perfectly."

Amos Half-Hand smirked and stowed his knife inside his shirt. He yanked the woman off the floor by her wrist. She flushed with pleasure and scrambled to brush the worst of the sawdust of her skirts.

"Right then, fellas," he said, "you can deal me out of the next hand, but no bugger pinch my seat. One way or another this ain't gonna take long."

With that he gestured to the young fisherman to follow and strode out of the pub, tugging the woman behind him.

"Is it a good idea to bring 'er along?" the young fisherman said, nodding to the woman as they walked back towards the main street. "It could get a bit rough, couldn't it?"

The other man laughed.

"She's a little Limeport whore, young fella, she's seen worse in her time, haven't you, Molly my sweet?" He turned to the woman, who grinned and nodded. "Anyway, I purchased her services for the whole day. Like as not, if I leave her alone she'll run off and I'll be left with no one to wash the blood off me knuckles and solace me after me battles. D'you know what I mean?"

"Don't say such things, Amos Half-hand," the woman said breathlessly. "I wouldn't leave you. You know I wouldn't."

The man grunted by way of reply and led the little party left onto the main street and left again onto a side road. They hurried down narrow roads and passages until they arrived at a pub whose faded sign displayed a crescent moon and a silver coin. The pub front was extremely narrow, scarcely wider than its front door, and its thin windows were grimy with salt. Amos Half-Hand let go of the woman's wrist and pulled the knife out of his shirt again, his damaged hand flexing gently on the handle.

"And you're sure this is the place?" he growled.

"Yeah. He was here 10 minutes ago anyway, in the snug at the back."

"Well, in you go first then, young fella. I ain't sayin' I don't trust you. But until yer my friend I want you where I can see you."

The young fisherman man nodded and entered the pub. He walked quickly through the main bar, ignoring the barman and two elderly women who were sipping stout by the fire, and pushed open the door to the back room. There was a man in oilskins sitting in shadows at the room's single table, a pint of dark beer and a block of cheese set on the table top in front of him. He was reading a newspaper and glanced up at the sound of the door.

"He's brought a woman with him," the young fisherman hissed as he entered the room. "Sorry, I tried to stop him but he insisted. Also, he's got a knife."

"Bloody hell, he's not supposed to be armed. It's meant to be a fist fight. I thought we agreed..." the man in oilskins began. Before he could go on, however, Amos Half-Hand strode into the room. When he saw the man in oilskins he stopped dead, causing the woman to bump into his back.

"What's goin' on? You ain't Tom Woodman," he roared. For a moment no one moved and then the young fisherman jumped at Amos Half-Hand and clambered onto his broad back while the man in oilskins struggled to pull something that looked like a hand gun from deep inside his pocket. He lifted it to aim it at Amos Half-Hand but before he could fire the young woman picked up his beer and flung it in his face and then smashed the glass on the side of his head.

"I'll 'ave you," she screamed. "No one hurts Amos Half-Hand when I'm with 'im. No one hurts my man, got that?"

"Good work, Molly my sweet," Amos Half-Hand roared. "When I've settled these two jokers I'll see you right for that. I don't forget my friends, my darlin'."

For several seconds the little room was in chaos. Amos Half-Hand staggered from wall to wall, bellowing and slashing the air with his knife while the young fisherman clung grimly to his back, his hands clamped over the other man's eyes. At the same time the man in oilskins struggled to fend off the woman's wild blows while blood streamed from his head to mix with the spilt beer on the tabletop.

And then, without anyone in the room noticing, the door to the bar opened again, apparently of its own accord, and the light in the doorway began to shift and move like ripples in water. The outline of a human form with its right arm extended shimmered into view and suddenly Amos Half-Hand froze and crumpled to the floor. A moment later the woman did the same. The man in oilskins lowered her body to the ground and gingerly prodded at his temple.

"I don't know why it is," he said to the young fisherman, "but I always seem to get smacked in the head when I'm out and about with you. Couldn't you 'ave separated him from the woman?"

The young fisherman disentangled himself from the prone form of Amos Half-Hand.

"Sorry, Sim," he said as he scrambled to his feet. "He insisted she come along and I didn't want to make him suspicious by protesting too much. I didn't think she'd be any bother, to be honest. I didn't think she'd give a toss about him, really; he didn't seem particularly fond of her. Anyway, if you'd been a bit quicker with the immobiliser we'd have been ok."

Simeon opened his mouth to reply but before he could say anything an arc of light began to glow gray-blue in the corner of the room. Five white-coated men carrying medical apparatus rushed through the arc, apparently from nowhere. They knelt next to Amos Half-Hand and one of them produced a pair of tiny electrical scissors from inside his coat. He switched them on so that they hummed like an angry wasp and used them to cut Amos Half-Hand's thick waistcoat and shirt back from his chest. Without pausing, the man cut on through his damp skin, revealing a network of silver struts and a web of wiring where his ribcage should have been. Another of the men removed a pale cloth from a sealed plastic packet and wiped the cavity before applying a steel instrument with a digital display to the wires above Amos Half-Hand's heart. The man studied the instrument's flickering numbers and grunted.

"I don't *think* you've done any significant damage," he said. "But I'll be putting in my report that you were more than a little heavy-handed. This is a new generation cyborg, you know? It's a prototype and it's sensitive bloody stuff. These things are supposed to be rolled out over the next five years to replace a lot of the older drones. That's if you lot don't smash them all to bits." He shook his head in irritation and glanced anxiously at the steel instrument again. "Yes, I'll definitely be putting something about you in my report."

"Put what you like in your damn report, sunshine," said an American voice from the door. The men in white coats swung round and took in a blonde woman dressed from head to toe in purple. "You got your man and I have an interlander postulant injured. So why don't you pack your subject into your hover-tube and get on your way while I get my guy treated and see about arranging some continuity here." The woman turned to the injured man. "You ok, Sim?"

"Jus' about."

"Good enough. Let's get out of here. We'll get some duty men down to clean up."

One of the white-coated men pulled a floating chrome tube through the blue arc and three more of them heaved Amos Half-Hand into it. The man with the scissors was pulling some forms from a pocket at the end of the tube when the image froze.

"Ok then, guys," said the same American voice, sounding considerably more cheerful. "There we have it. Let's begin by figuring out what went *right* with the operation, shall we?"

A hum of conversation rose from the 19 postulants. They were sitting, with Deborah their tutor, in semi-darkness, around a platform where the pub fight had been just been played out by life-size holograph figures. Ruth, the girl with the glasses, stuck her hand in the air.

"No need for the hand, Ruth, but go on."

"Well, Sam got the subject to the light-portal, didn't he? You know he *actually got him to the right place*. I mean, that's the main thing."

"Yeah, but with a knife and a woman in bloody tow," interrupted Simeon, who still had a plaster fixed to the side of his head. "That weren't part of the brief, if it hadn't been for ..."

"Ok, ok, Simeon," Deborah said soothingly. "We'll come to the goof-ups in a minute. Right now we're thinking about what *went right*. And Ruth's correct; we got our guy to the pickup point. So that worked. Anything else?"

"Well, Sam got Amos away from the group," said a fat boy with ginger hair. "And he got him knocked out and in the tube eventually."

"Yeah Trev, but only because Deborah were ghosting us," Simeon said. "If she hadn't been there we'd have been buggered, wouldn't we?"

"That's not *entirely* my fault," Sam said. "If you hadn't got that immobiliser stuck in your pocket ..."

"Well I were gonna put it behind the cheese but then when it came, the block were smaller than I expected so I had to improvise, didn't I?"

"Well, you can hardly blame me because you didn't order a big enough chuck of cheddar."

"Guys, guys, guys," Deborah said, "come on, this isn't helping. We're all on the same side, remember? Can anyone tell me why we have someone on ghost for this kind of operation?"

"Ghosts are ISS officers trained in the operation of Cognitive Interrupter Concealment Outfits," Ruth said automatically. "They're practically invisible to most enclosure people, unless they've had prolonged exposure to CICOs in the past, that is, and they're provided for back up in retrieval operations. By the rulebook—I think it's module TS1 but I'd have to look that up—you're not actually *obliged* to have ghosts on an incursion, but they're recommended in case ... well ..." She gestured at the frozen holograph figures of Sam and Simeon who were still poised, and in Simeon's case bleeding, on the platform.

"Quite, in case things mess up," Deborah said quickly. "Now listen, guys, you did pretty well, believe me. Sam, you were dealing with a very dangerous subject and I think you basically handled him pretty smartly. But when things did go a little goofy I was there to do my job and wrap things up. As a ghost, that's what I was *for*. And by the way, don't worry about those asshole techies. An interlander never apologises or takes crap from those guys. They need us, we don't need them. Remember that." She turned to Simeon and grinned. "Now then, Sim, before you wet your pants in frustration, what could Sam have done differently? How could he have lost the woman or the knife?"

"Well, he could have said summat in the first pub, *The Swan*. Like he could have told Amos that the other fella wanted a fist fight and he had people with him to check no knives. Or, better still, he could 'ave had an immobiliser himself to back me up."

"He's not permitted to carry an immobiliser on an incursion," Ruth cut in. "You're not allowed one in real-space more than fifty yards from a portal or a boundary lock, unless it's a possession. It's in module T1A, Sim."

Simeon opened his mouth to reply but before he could say anything the door of the holograph theatre opened and bright light streamed in. The postulants span round in their seats to see the squat figure of Sir Douglas Latch silhouetted in the doorway.

"Deborah, my dear, so sorry to interrupt," the old man murmured. "I wonder if I might have a quick word in private, please."

"Yes, of course, Sir Douglas," Deborah replied, frowning. "Ok guys, get on with your plans for Friday's incursion down at Lower Emberton. And I want you to think particularly carefully about where you're gonna locate your ghosts, because it ain't gonna be me ghosting next time, it's gonna be two of you, got that?"

A couple of the postulants nodded and Deborah stood up and left the room. Two minutes later she stepped back in and switched the lights on. The postulants groaned and crinkled their eyes at the sudden brightness.

"Sorry guys, sorry. But I'm afraid we're done for the day. Something serious has come up. You're all free for the afternoon, but you've gotta keep your pagers on, you understand? And you're not to go above level three unless and until you're told otherwise."

An inquisitive murmur rose from the group. Deborah put her hands in the air for silence and when she spoke there was an edge in her voice.

"Guys, I *cannot* tell you anything else. Use the time to get your logbooks up to date and I'll see you all tomorrow morning, if not before. Now off you go."

Chapter Thirty
Emergency Possession

Twenty minutes later Sam was sitting at his desk in his apartment with his logbook open in front of him. He had a cigarette in his hand and a mug of Badger's Snout beer at his elbow (the Service had it piped directly from the brewery). He was staring at a line of his own handwriting which began: *I proceeded from the Service ship* Osprey *at zero nine fifty hours and made my way to* The Swan *public house on the main street in Limeport. I noticed nothing of consequence on the quay or in the town.* It had been five minutes since Sam had written the sentence. He sucked at his cigarette and glanced round the room for inspiration.

As always, since the day six months before when Sir Douglas had shown him round, he felt a surge of pleasure as he took in his apartment. It was by far the most luxurious accommodation he had ever lived in, and part of him still couldn't believe that it was really his. The main chamber was approximately twice the height of a normal room, the walls made of red brick, the floor of smooth, well-fitting, floorboards. As well as the desk, there were two sofas arranged around a fireplace at one end of the room and a table with four chairs at the other. At present half the table was covered with an antique car-racing set. There was also a drinks cabinet, a sideboard and a bookcase, which already had three red logbooks on the top shelf, as well as the ISS rulebook and Sam's old copy of *Soul Freedom*. A metal balcony projected from the left hand wall, halfway up. It was reached by a spiral staircase and bounded by a waste-high fence of woven steel and copper.

"You kip up on the mezzanine," Sir Douglas Latch had said when they had arrived at the apartment. He had nodded at the balcony. "There's a bed and a table and so forth up there and a wardrobe full of new civvies for you, as well as a couple of sets of blacks. There's also the door through to your bathroom: you get a bog, shower and jacuzzi, if memory serves. I think there may even be a bidet; God knows why we feel that our postulants must all have spotless backsides, but apparently we do. Over there," Sir Douglas had pointed to a small door beneath the balcony, "is your holograph room with 24-hour access to all holographed real-space, and beyond that is the kitchen. Do you cook much, Samuel?"

"Hardly at all. I can boil an egg and make a sandwich but that's about it. Sometimes Smith made me cook a bit while I was at Stanmore. But even then she'd supervise me pretty closely."

Sir Douglas had giggled.

"Shame on you, dear boy, what would your mother say? Anyway, there's no reason you should cook at all if you don't want to. You can take all your meals in the junior mess, or alternatively have them bring your grub up here; it's entirely up to you. If you do decide to cook, you pick up your food from the mess stores; they get outside goods and enclosure produce absolutely fresh, obviously."

Sam had nodded and Sir Douglas had glanced at him and smiled.

"Yes, we do ourselves pretty well," he'd murmured. "No point in slumming it unnecessarily, is there, dear boy? That's a fairly well-established Service principle, as a matter of fact."

In the intervening months, Sam had taken the principle to heart. He had eaten excellent food—practically none of it cooked by himself—and continued to drink a good quantity of Badger's Snout ale as well as wine and port. At the end of the first week he had accepted a cigarette off Simeon and hated it, and then he had accepted another the next day when he was drunk and liked it. Now he smoked about 20 a day, more if he was studying hard or socialising with the other postulants. To offset the effects of the drink and the rich food, he visited the mess gym each morning before breakfast, as well as attending Deborah's phys. ed. classes. The muscles he had begun to develop in Stanmore had grown taut and hard, and his stomach had flattened off. Whenever he caught sight of himself, his new shape pleased him immensely; although he privately conceded that he still couldn't match Roger's physique, he certainly wasn't a skinny little boy anymore, either.

When Sam wasn't eating or working out, there was the whole of the Project to enjoy with the other postulants. Often a group of them would take the minirail to the Oval Chamber or to one of the installations and spend time shopping or visiting exhibitions or just hanging around in the cafés and pubs laughing at the more ridiculous tourists. (They had all been issued with ISS currency cards on their first day, so money was no object.) There were also tutorials to attend each day and, best of all, the regular trips across the boundary to assist in small operations. The thrill of crossing over had not left Sam. More than anything he delighted in striding down a Project corridor in full enclosure costume, shivering with anticipation, to arrive at the hazy back-glow of a light portal or the steel door of a boundary lock. There he would receive his final whispered briefing from the accompanying ISS officer before slipping through the sheen of grey-blue light or the door and finding himself within the enclosure: in the back room of a shop, or the disused galley of a moored ship, or an abandoned pig sty. The rush of shock and delight that accompanied the moment of crossing was like diving into deep water and surfacing into bright sunlight in the same instant, except it was more intense, more spectacular, more free. Nothing could ever compare with it, of that Sam was certain. The only problem was that when you got back you had to write it all up in your bloody logbook.

I proceeded from the Service ship Osprey *at 09:50 and made my way to* The Swan *public house on the main street in Limeport. I noticed nothing of consequence on the quay or in the town…*

Sam squashed out his cigarette and moved a framed picture of Hilary Lynch from the left to the right-hand side of his desk. He picked up his pen and was about to bring the nib to the paper when a loud banging sounded from the door.

There was a pause and then a voice called gruffly, "It's me, let me in."

Much relieved at the distraction, Sam tossed his pen down on the desk and called out, "It's not locked. I always leave it open in case some uncouth ex-subject takes it upon himself to kick in for me."

The door swung open and Simeon marched into the room. He was carrying a bottle of port, two glasses and a notebook.

"Rude git," he snarled at Sam as he dumped everything on the table. He picked up a racing car controller and began to race one of the cars around the track.

"Lovely to see you too, Sim," Sam said politely. "Anyway, what do you want, apart from an opportunity to insult me, of course?"

"I'm stuck on my notes for Kevin's tutorial, ain't I?" Simeon said without taking his eyes off the speeding car. "I can't work out the difference between a patrol, an incursion and a ... what's-it-called ... a possession. I keep searchin' through the bloody rulebook but all the bits are scattered all over the place, ain't they? I can't get it all together in my head."

Sam sighed. Up in real-space, on patrol, Simeon was easily the best of the postulants, but he just couldn't get the hang of books and studying. Privately he'd explained to Sam that schooling in Cromer was pretty basic, and the small amount that was available had mostly passed him by because he had skipped classes whenever he could. Since crossing over he had also learnt that he had been the subject of a "feral child' experiment when he was very young, which probably hadn't helped. The other postulants tried to be sympathetic.

"Sim, look, it's really not that complicated. A patrol is just wandering about in real-space with your eyes open; it's what duty men do all the time, right? No one actually does anything, they just gather information and they're there in case things kick off. But an incursion is different; that's when Service people do actually *do* something in the enclosure, like repairing a bit of continuity or getting Amos Half-Hand out like we did this morning,"

"What you messed up completely."

"Yes. Well, no. Well, whatever. Do you see the difference, though? Patrolling is just walking about, but an incursion is when something actually *happens*, although it's supposed to happen covertly and enclosure life is meant to go on as usual all around.”

The toy car hit a curve too fast. It skidded off the table and slid across the floor. Simeon, threw the controller down in disgust and poured two glasses of port. He handed one to Sam.

“Enclosure life wasn’t going on normally in that pub room, were it? Not with me head all cracked open.”

“Do you want me to help you or not?”

“Yeah. Go on.”

“Ok. Now a possession is different again. That’s when a lot of work needs doing, either major continuity stuff, or setting up some big experiment, or removing a whole street of subjects, or something. And so the Service takes over a settlement completely; *we possess it*. Then, obviously, we don’t bother with any of the secrecy stuff; all the subjects know that something scary is going on, but they don’t know what. Have you got that?”

Simeon nodded and gulped his port.

“Demon days.”

“Yeah, that’s right, demon days, although they’re almost always at night, for obvious reasons.”

“Yeah, yeah, I get all that. I’ve actually lived through ’em, remember. But what about all them rules about how you can set up a possession or an incursion? And where did Ruth get that stuff about personal immobilisers and fifty yards from the portal and stuff?”

Sam stared at Simeon blankly and then got up and went over to his bookcase. He pulled down the rulebook, returned to his desk, and began flicking through it, marking pages with scraps of paper as he went along.

“It’s ridiculous havin’ all these bloody rules,” Simeon growled as he retrieved the car. “If anyone here actually knew what it’s like inside, *really knew*, I mean, not jus’ visitin’, they’d know that no one’s got a clue about the Service, or the Project or the outsides or anythin’ else. You jus’ can’t *think* like that if you’re a subject; yer mind doesn’t stretch that far.”

“Yeah, yeah. I’m sure that’s true.”

“Right. So why can’t we jus’ get on with stuff without havin’ to check a massive bloody rulebook to see if someone ages ago said it’s ok? It’s stupid.”

"I think Sir Douglas would say that no one in the enclosure knows about us *because* we have the rulebook," Sam said quietly, without looking up. Simeon made a rude gesture at him and replaced the car on the track. He was reaching for the controller again when his and Sam's pagers bleeped simultaneously. Simeon groped in his pocket while Sam reached for his off the desk. He squinted at its screen and then read the message aloud.

From the Refugium Peccatorum: an emergency possession has been ordered. All postulants to report immediately to parlor three. Dress code is ad libertas. *This is not a drill. Message ends.*

For a moment neither of them spoke, and then Simeon said, "Heck, that sound serious. It must have been what Sir Douglas was talkin' to Deborah about. I thought she looked bothered afterwards."

"Yeah, well she certainly looked something."

Sam returned the rulebook to the shelf and headed for the door.

"Come on, we'd better get going. Maybe taking part in your first possession will clear up your muddle."

"It wasn't jus' me who was muddled," Simeon said. "You didn't know either, remember."

He drained his glass and hurried after Sam.

The Project corridors were normally quiet and calm, but this was far from the case today. Interlanders, BSC officers and technicians rushed up and down in a variety of clothing: uniforms, lab coats, enclosure costume, even pyjamas. The walls echoed with anxious murmuring and the occasional barked instruction: "You need to get those restraint bags to the western barracks, the quicker the better."

"I believe we're going in at Thetford. Confirm that with the *Refugium*, will you: Thetford for unit B. Got that?"

"Apparently we're rendezvousing with 20 BSC at the double pub at Bolton Brow at 15:30. Sort out immobilisers and

CICO's for the ghosts, will you. And get a move on, yeah? Time is short."

Sam and Simeon pushed through the bustle (there was a rule that you should walk on the left in the Project corridors, but that seemed to have been forgotten today as well) and entered a lift where they met Ruth and her friend Laura. Both girls were in dressing gowns and Ruth had green ointment smeared over her face.

"Bloody typical, isn't it," Laura said. "We plan a nice evening with a bottle of wine and a couple of holographs and, wouldn't you know it, a great big emergency happens. I mean, we're not exactly dressed to defend the Project and the state, are we?"

Simeon stared at Ruth in fascination.

"Yeah, yeah, it's bad, innit, it's typical," he said vaguely. "What's that crap all over your face, Ruthie?"

"It's not crap, Simeon," Ruth said patiently. "It's called moisturiser. And when you finally get to see the outsides you'll find it's quite popular, especially if you've spent half the day getting your face blown off somewhere like Limeport. God knows where we're off to now, but I bet it's somewhere windy."

"What do you think's going on, Sam?" Laura asked.

"No idea," Sam answered as the lift hissed to a halt. "But it must be serious if they're having to involve us. I don't think they're really meant to do that, are they?"

"Actually, they *can* use postulants in a possession," Ruth said. "But the book says it has to be *in grave and extraordinary circumstances*. I don't know what that's supposed to mean, but it doesn't sound good, does it?"

The four of them hurried the short distance from the lift to parlor three and discovered that most of the postulants had already arrived. They were sitting in silence around the table while Kevin and Deborah stood at the front with their arms folded, looking tense. Kevin nodded at them as they entered.

"Good, get sat down, please. We're just waiting for Sir Douglas; he should be here any time now."

As Kevin was speaking the door opened again and the remaining postulants hurried in, followed by Sir Douglas himself. Everyone took their seats and the old man slotted a holograph disc into the machine at the head of the table. It hummed into life and a three-dimensional landscape flickered into focus along the table top.

"Right then," Sir Douglas said. "For those of you who don't know, this is the south-eastern portion of the enclosure around the town of Bentham, on the coast." He unclipped a pointer from the side of the holograph machine. "The situation is extremely serious; approximately half an hour ago we received confirmed reports of a code red boundary breach, which we're expecting to go black within the next 20 minutes. Details are a little hazy but it seems clear that the terrorists will enter the enclosure in two places: west of Stump Cross and by sea near Bentham. The BSC have already taken significant casualties on land and the Navy has lost a patrol boat a couple of miles out to sea."

There were gasps of dismay around the room. The old man held up his hand for silence.

"Now, any of you who've kept up with the weekly operating notices will be aware that we've known for some time that a red/black breach was coming, but this is considerably more than we were expecting. I shouldn't have to tell you that a double boundary breach is unheard of and would seem to imply that the numbers involved are considerable. The opposition are extremely organised this time. They seem to be jolly confident, which is worrying."

"Where are the terrorists from, Sir Douglas?" Ruth asked. The old man's face twitched in irritation.

"Cambridge, Ruth, always Cambridge. The town has something of a history in fen-lib matters. If the other security agencies were halfway efficient I would be able to give you more details, but for now I'm afraid that's all I know. Now then, in consultation with the Guardian's Office and the Department of Boundary Security, I declared an emergency possession at 1800. I will be PICOP, that's Person in Charge of Possession, for anyone who is still a little shaky on the rules. And, in accordance with standard operating procedures, the Project has been cleared of tourists. The gravity of the situation means I am having to put every single officer, every brass-buckle and even yourselves into the field. It's not what I would wish to do, but I don't feel I have any choice."

The old man indicated a stretch of coastline just east of Bentham.

"You will enter the Project by sea here, with a unit of fifty BSC officers and a support group of 20 technicians. There's a footpath here through sand dunes that you'll follow into Bentham itself. When you get there, *and I can't emphasize this enough*, your job is not to engage the terrorists. Leave the nasty stuff to the BSC. It's what they're for and if a few of them end up with bullets in their thick skulls, frankly, it doesn't matter too much. Your job will be to immobilise subjects, to attend to emergency continuity and to escort the techies to anyone who might need to be withdrawn. *Is that clear?*"

Around the table the postulants nodded quickly.

"Good. You're all rather valuable; we don't want to lose any of you in silly fits of heroism. You will be under Kevin's command with Deborah deputising, and they will be in contact with me through the *Refugium*. I'll be ghosting about myself, so don't be surprised if I pop up. Now listen," the old man looked round at the postulants, "you are all excellent operatives and I expect you to conduct yourselves in accordance with the highest standards and traditions of the Service. These red/black boundary breaches are the sort of thing that can make Service careers. They can also break them. I think that's all I want to say; are there any questions?"

The postulants were silent.

"Excellent—in which case I'll leave you. Forgive the brevity, but my time is not my own today, as I'm sure you'll appreciate. Good luck, all of you."

Sir Douglas replaced the pointer at the side of the holograph machine and removed the holograph disc, making the map dissolve. He patted Kevin and then Deborah on the arm and marched out the room. For a moment there was silence and then Deborah cleared her throat.

"Ok guys, we can complete the briefing *en route* as we get more information. For now, why don't you go and get changed into your ops blacks and we'll meet back here in 15?"

Around the table the postulants nodded but still no one

moved.

"Come on guys, *it's time to lock and load*. And let's do it right today, shall we? This isn't a drill, remember."

There was a rush for the door.

After regrouping, the postulants hurried to the nearest minirail platform, where they crammed into cars, five at a time, to take them to the Oval Chamber. Here, Kevin and Deborah counted heads before hustling them across the darkened chamber floor and on through the Eden Gate. There followed a short journey by lift and coach to the monorail terminal, where the group stood silent and watchful while Kevin spoke urgently into his radio. Columns of grim-faced BSC officers and other Project personnel marched past them onto the platform where they boarded a train with blanked out windows. Eventually a very senior-looking BSC officer marched through the terminal gates. She approached Kevin and Deborah and spoke to them briefly. Kevin frowned and nodded, then raised his arm for the postulants' attention.

"Ok then, this is Major General Geraldine Stag, and she's here to brief us about the journey. Now, it sticks in my throat to say this, but during an emergency possession the BSC have constitutional priority over us while we're travelling outside the Project, so make sure you listen to her. Major General..."

"Thank you, Mr. Spark," the officer said curtly. "In a minute you lot are going to entrain into carriage one of the trains behind me, where seats 6 to 26 have been reserved for you. You will detrain at a military hover-port in London's South West zone, and from there you'll be taken out to the SS Fortuna by hover-copter. After that you will be in the Project's territorial waters, technically within the boundary, which means you will no longer be my responsibility. While you *are* my responsibility, however, you will obey any order given to you by a BSC officer immediately." The officer peered round the group, as if daring anyone to contradict her. "You shouldn't see any civilians, but if you do you must make no effort whatsoever to communicate with them, and if anyone attempts to communicate with you, you must report them to a BSC officer immediately. Is that clear?"

The group nodded.

"Good. Now then, let's see just how well the old rascal's got you trained. Can anyone tell me the penalty for compromising operational security during an emergency possession? Yes, you at the back with your hand up."

"Depending on the gravity of the offence, it's chemical curtailment or death," Ruth said.

"Very good, young lady. And when is the penalty applicable?"

"Depending on the circumstances it's … well, it can be immediate."

"Can you give me the rulebook reference for that?

"Module T3, section 4.8."

A tiny smile twitched across the Major General's lips.

"Well, at least one of you seems to know what she's doing, and I'm not in the least surprised she's a woman. So remember, ladies and gentlemen, if you mess around while you're my responsibility you're likely to get yourselves promptly killed. That said, of course, at times like this we all have to put our little squabbles aside and pull together for the good of the Project and the state." The officer smiled more kindly. "My goodness, you all look so terribly young. Keep your precious little heads down and the very best of luck to all of you. Now off you go."

The postulants trooped somberly onto the train and settled themselves in their seats. The doors hissed shut behind them. No one spoke for a few minutes, and then Simeon leaned across the aisle and whispered to Sam, "You'd think they'd want to get us shiftin', wouldn't you? You'd think there might be a bit of urgency."

Deborah swung round from the seat in front.

"We've been going since we got on, Sim. You don't notice a monotrain moving unless you look at the scenery and well…" she nodded to the plastic covers over the carriage windows.

"Bloody typical, int'it?" Simeon said. "My first visit to the outsides and I don't get to see a thing. It's gonna be a boring trip, this is."

"Trust me, Sim, I don't think you're going to be bored for

long," said Deborah gently.

During the journey Kevin kept murmuring into his radio headset and relaying snippets of information to the postulants.

"The terrorists have gone ashore at Bentham just as Sir Douglas predicted. Apparently they've left a small squad on the beach."

"We've got Service people and BSC approaching Bentham from the west and north. The *Refugium* advise that we're encountering heavy resistance."

"It seems there's still an opposition presence at sea. The navy is engaging them, but it could affect us getting ashore, obviously."

And then with particular delight and savagery, "The subjects in Bentham are resisting the terrorists themselves and a number of them are already down. That'll show the toffy-nosed brats what's what."

After half an hour, without any indication that the train had been slowing down or stopping, the doors slid open and bright light spilled into the carriage. Deborah and Kevin leapt to their feet and counted the postulants out onto another platform. It was set within a cavernous steel building which was open to the sky at one end. There were dozens of other platforms on either side, all of them bustling with Project staff, and there was a row of hover-copters near the open section. A young BSC officer stepped forward smartly.

"Are you the chaps for the Fortuna?"

Deborah nodded.

"Thank goodness for that—something's actually working as it should. Are you all here?"

"Yes," Deborah said. "We're meant to be hooking up with a bunch of your guys and some techies before we go ashore."

"What, haven't you travelled down with them? It would have made sense for you to set off together, surely?"

Deborah shrugged.

"Go figure."

Frowning, the officer pulled a computer from his pocket and tapped at it quickly.

"Yeah, yeah, I've got it. I've got it. It's ok. You're right. You're meeting our men from Sierra Bravo Unit and some technical chaps from ops. But they're already aboard the Fortuna. They're waiting for you. Obviously they can't land without you lot."

"Bloody right they can't," Kevin said. "So what are we supposed to do next?"

"Your hover-copter is waiting," the BSC man said as he tucked his computer away. "Come on, I'll take you straight over."

Afterwards, whenever Sam told the tale of his first possession, he struggled to recount the time between arriving at the hover-port and finally going ashore at Bentham. He remembered the sudden disorientating roar of the hover-copter taking off and the low, sweeping journey out to the Fortuna. The copter's doors were left open so the postulants could see the white caps meters below them and feel the rush of salty wind that made their eyes water and set their hair whipping around their faces. Sam could never quite recall the hover-copter landing on the Fortuna's flight deck, but he remembered being led down a steel stairway by a young naval officer with red spots on the back of his neck. There followed a final briefing by Kevin and Deborah in the ship's mess, where the postulants were joined by the BSC unit and technical officers who were to go ashore with them. Sam couldn't remember anything he was told at the briefing, but he remembered Kevin's pale, tense face and his barked instructions, which kept changing every two or three minutes as new reports crackled through the radio. Finally, Deborah laid a hand on his arm.

"I guess that's about all we can tell them, Kevin. We gotta move out."

"Yeah, yeah ok. Let's get immobilisers issued and get going," Kevin answered. "And BSC and techies, remember you're now within the enclosure, so you're under ISS control. Once we're ashore, unless you're actually involved in combat, you do what we tell you. Clear? And that's module T3 section 4.2 in the blue book if anyone cares to look it up."

The postulants trooped to the ship's galley where an interlander brass-buckle with a clipboard issued them with immobilisers and personal communications units. Then the whole group—interlanders, BSC, technicians—were led back up to the deck. Afterwards Sam had no memory of descending the scramble nets slung over the side of the ship to enable them to reach the inflatable dinghies that would take them ashore. But he vividly remembered nestling between Simeon and Ruth in the front of his dinghy, and the exhilarating thrust as the craft sped over the sea towards the smudge of coastline. He remembered, too, Simeon cursing and growling to no one in particular on his left, while on his right Ruth fiddled with the microphone of her personal communications unit, her eyes bright with excitement. He remembered laughing wildly and leaning forward to dip his hand into the waves as the line of boats swung in towards the beach.

Then a shot rang out and Sam abruptly stopped laughing.

Chapter Thirty-One
You Are Not Free

"It's all right, it's one of ours," muttered a BSC officer behind Sam. "Better get your heads down, though. It could get a bit hairy."

Sam, Simeon and Ruth all hunched forward as the dinghy picked up speed for its final run in to the beach. There was the rattle of more gunfire and then the earpiece of Sam's personal communications unit spluttered into life.

"Ok, ladies and gents, this is it," said Kevin's strained voice. "The shooting was from the terrorist rearguard on the shore. Captain Horsham tells me they've been neutralised so we're going in as planned. The two BSC assault boats will land first. We'll go in behind with our escorting officers and rendezvous by the top dune; that's point 36 on the standard Service positioning system. Techies will come in last. Keep your wits about you and good luck."

As Kevin finished speaking, Sam felt the bottom of his boat scrape on the sand. The BSC officer at the back lifted the outboard motor out of the water and the dinghy ran on up the beach. While it was still moving, the BSC men scrambled into the surf and ran towards the sand dunes, sighting their rifles as they went. There was another brief burst of shooting.

"Better get out, too," Simeon said softly as the gunfire died away. Sam and Ruth nodded and the three postulants clambered out of the dinghy. They hauled the boat a little way up the beach and then headed for the large sand dune where Deborah and Kevin were already crouching in the shadows. When all the postulants had arrived Deborah addressed the group.

"Take a look round, guys, and tell me if anyone from your boat is missing."

There was silence.

"Good enough. Anyone hurt?"

More silence.

"Ok. There are three of the opposition dead on the beach

and two more in custody. Our BSC unit is pushing on towards Bentham as we speak, and another group is coming in from the west. The plan hasn't altered; we're gonna' follow this path here," she gestured to an opening in the dunes behind her, "and then fan out and move into the town. The idea is that the BSC will focus the opposition in the main square—that's point 81— so we can clean up the streets without interruption. But that may change, of course. Any questions?"

Trevor raised his hand; he was grinning.

"Yes, Trevor."

"Are there any decent places to eat in Bentham, when we're finished, I mean? Sea travel always makes me peckish."

The group giggled, breaking the tension, and Deborah poked Trevor in his bulging stomach.

"A little bit of rough and tumble will do some of us no harm whatsoever, Master Milner. But listen, buddy, I'll buy you dinner in Bentham when it's all over, and then I'll take you dancing to slim you down again. That's a promise. Now let's go."

The opening in the dunes led to a shallow path that deepened into a trench about two meters high. The postulants moved along it swiftly, occasionally passing BSC officers standing guard against the trench wall and scanning the surrounding country with night vision binoculars. Sounds of gunfire and the occasional louder explosion came from inland, and after a few minutes the evening sky in front of them began to turn a smoky yellow colour.

"Devil sky," Simeon whispered. "Makes you feel sick and turns everything blurry and difficult to see—bloody horrible stuff. Scares the hell out of everyone."

A moment later Kevin's voice came through their earpieces.

"Ok, the eastern group are putting up *lux obscura,* so it's goggles on time, fellas. Don't forget, if you look directly at the stuff with the naked eye for any length of time you'll lose your bearings for a good 10 minutes, so don't."

Sam unzipped his pocket and pulled out his goggles. He tugged them on and flicked a switch on their frame. The world turned fuzzy and pink for a few seconds and then clicked back into focus. He, Simeon and Ruth had reached the end of the trench and were now facing a stretch of open ground leading to the outlying buildings of Bentham. Deborah was crouching at the trench mouth with a rifle in her hand and an immobiliser stuffed into her belt. She gestured for them to join her.

"Right, you three; everything ok?"

They nodded.

"Good. You're going off to the left. Keep low next to the hedge until you get to that old cowshed; it's point 25, in case you get lost. There you'll find a lane that'll take you right into the square. Most of the subjects should be inside now we've got *lux* up, but if you do see any, take them down and radio their position through to the *Refugium* immediately. When you get to the square, Kevin will give you new instructions. Got that?"

The three postulants nodded.

"Ok then, repeat it back please."

Ruth repeated the instructions in a shaky voice and Deborah grinned.

"You've got it, girl. Now go and kick some ass!"

Sam, Simeon and Ruth set off at a crouching run. When they arrived at the cowshed, they edged along the side wall towards the path, holding their immobilisers in front of their faces. Sam was the first to reach the corner of the shed; he glanced round it quickly, then jumped round and slithered down the bank to the path. Moments later Ruth followed him.

"You all right?" Sam whispered.

"Yeah, yeah, I'm fine. I'm excited, really. I don't know if you *should* be excited but it's impossible…"

A loud groan cut Ruth off. She and Sam span round in time to see a fenland man slump off the cowshed roof and onto the path in front of them. His crossbow clattered to the ground after him and discharged itself. The bolt hissed past Sam's head.

"It's not that excitin'," Simeon said gruffly as he emerged from behind the barn, his immobiliser still trained on the roof. "Let's keep the chit chat for afterwards, shall we, so we don't all end up with our 'eads split open?"

"Sorry, Sim. God. Sorry. I mean, thank you. I mean … I mean, you're right, we've got to stay focused," spluttered Ruth.

"They think they're being attacked by the demon," Simeon said slowly. "Now you two dunno what that feels like, but it's horrible, honestly. It's terrifyin'. They won't think nothin' of killin' you if you give them a chance. They don't know that yer on their side, do they?"

Ruth nodded and knelt next to the fallen man, feeling for his pulse, while Sam and Simeon scouted quickly round the shed and up and down the path.

A moment later Ruth whispered into her microphone, "*Refugium*, this is Postulant Garvey, presently engaged in emergency possession C145, at Bentham. Password domino. I am speaking from point 25." She paused. "Oh for goodness' sake, you know perfectly well how to spell domino. Don't waste my time. Now look, I wish to report an immobilised subject, a male in his early forties, possibly with a broken wrist, at point 25." She listened for a moment, still crouched over the unconscious man, and then said, "Ok, understood," and clambered to her feet.

"There'll be someone out to the subject as soon as possible. We've got to keep going."

Simeon nodded but showed no sign of moving. Instead he tugged off his gloves and knelt next to the fenlander. He pulled off his black ops jacket and removed the body warmer he was wearing beneath it. This he folded and tucked under the man's head.

"They're not jus' subjects, Ruthie," he said as he stood up. "They're people as well, you know. Well, in a way they are."

"I know they are, Sim."

"Yeah. It's jus' that it's hard sometimes. It's difficult 'cos … well, 'cos … you know…"

Ruth touched his arm.

"I understand."

"You don't. You might think you do, but you don't. No one does, really." Simeon shook his head and adjusted his immobiliser. "Oh look, forget it, it doesn't matter. Let's jus' get goin', shall we, before we miss all the fun?"

The three postulants moved swiftly and skillfully through the shadows and doorways of Bentham, the gunfire still sounding sporadically ahead of them. They kept their immobilisers drawn and communicated with one another through hand signals or by whispering directions into their communications units. Soon, however, their precautions began to feel unnecessary. All the fenlanders had apparently retreated to their homes where they had drawn the curtains and locked (and sometimes barricaded) the doors. The only people they saw were two dead terrorists, one man and one woman, who were sprawled in the gutter close to the town square, their camouflage tops sticky with blood. The man looked as if his face had been stamped on; his nose was flattened and his mouth was a pool of gore and shattered teeth. Simeon stopped and nudged the corpse's head with his foot; it sagged backwards, revealing a deep gash across the throat. He whistled softly.

"Hell, they're not messin' around, are they?" he said.

"Apparently not," Ruth said quietly. "I suppose these red/black breaches are what the BSC live for, really. They're in charge for a while, aren't they? Come on, let's get on."

Ahead of them the street curved sharply to the left and then opened onto the square. Here a row of barrels had been placed across the road and Sam could see Kevin crouching behind them. He was speaking animatedly to a BSC officer and a senior-looking interlander whom Sam didn't recognise. When he caught sight of them, Kevin gestured for the postulants to come forward.

"You lot ok?" he asked.

"Yeah, fine," Sam answered.

"See any opposition?"

"None living."

Kevin nodded and gestured towards the square. It was dominated on the far side by the temple, and Sam could see at least a dozen camouflaged bodies of terrorists, as well as two BSC men, lying under the building's walls. What appeared to be leaflets were strewn on the ground and bullet holes scarred the temple front and surrounding buildings.

"As far as we know all the terrorists are now in the temple where they seem to want to make a last stand," Kevin said.

"Captain Horsham here is going to tickle them with stun grenades and then assault the place. Time is of the essence now, of course, because we have a massive continuity job on and it's only going to get worse the longer it's left. The complicating factor is that there may well be some subjects in the temple as well, whom the terrorists have taken as hostages. That's ironic when you think that they're supposed to be liberating them, but there we are. I don't suppose the little brats are particularly clear thinkers. The point is, as soon as the BSC have the temple secure, we have to get in after them and take down any subjects who might be there. Clear?"

The postulants nodded and Kevin span round to the BSC officer.

"Ok, how long till we go, captain?"

The officer glanced at his wrist watch.

"Four minutes."

"Good. Now then, this is Harry Pollit ..."

Kevin stopped talking and ducked low behind the barrels as a loud cry of *Freedom!* echoed from the temple, followed by a rattle of gunfire. For half a minute the square was filled with the sound of shooting and bullets ricocheting off stone. Kevin shook his head in irritation as the noise died away.

"Bloody hell, some people just don't know when they're beaten, do they? Anyway, as I was saying, this is Harry Pollit, who commands the Service group that's come in from the west. His people are over on the far side of the square. They'll go into the temple from the back; we're going in the front."

The interlander officer smiled cheerfully at the postulants.

"Good to meet you, chaps. Glad to see you all bearing up. All this while you're still only postulants, eh? Marvelous really. I wish I'd had your opportunity. I really do."

"Yeah, well anyway," Kevin went on, "you three follow that alley on the left, Chapel Street it's called. A hundred yards down you'll come to a white building with a thatched roof that backs onto the square. Hold your position there, in cover. And when you receive my order you get to that temple door as quick as you can. Got that?"

Sam, Simeon and Ruth nodded.

"Repeat it back, please."

This time Sam repeated the instructions. When he had done so Kevin said:

"That's more or less it. Off you go, then."

The three of them scuttled away from the line of barrels and moved quickly down the road Kevin had indicated. When they arrived at the white house they crouched in its doorway, breathing hard, well out of view of the temple. Nearby there were several of the leaflets that Sam had seen scattered in the square. He picked one up and smoothed it out on his knee.

People of Bentham
We are your friends.
We are not demons or pirates.
We are here to help you, not to harm you.

The society you live in is not what it seems. You believe that you are free, but you are not. Every aspect of your lives is manipulated by a government that you know nothing about, functioning in what you call *the beyonds*.

This government has technology at its disposal that, through no fault of your own, you cannot hope to understand. This technology is used to control your minds and your bodies, in the same way that the demon controls some people's minds and bodies in the stories your priest tells you. The government we speak of is a thousand times more powerful than the demon you believe in.

In the same way that your farmers experiment with livestock, cross breeding different lines to get the best results, so you are experimented upon by the wicked people in *the beyonds*. These experiments can lead even to your death.

It does not have to be this way. The system that controls you is only powerful while it is hidden from you. If you recognise it and challenge it, it can be defeated. You have supporters in *the beyonds* who hate the system and care for you. We who have come to your homes today represent those people. Join with us to march into *the beyonds* and liberty. You will find no demon there, only a handful of wicked men and women, and beyond them a great number of friends.

You have nothing to lose but fear and illusion. You have a whole wide world to win.

You are not free. You are not free. You are not free.

Sam elbowed Ruth in the ribs and handed her the leaflet. She read it quickly, chewing her lip and then handed it back.

"Bloody hell, they're not exactly *sophisticated*, are they?" she whispered. Sam grinned and stuffed the leaflet into his pocket. As he did so a dull boom echoed from the square, followed by the tinkle of smashed glass. A column of black smoke rose into the sky and then came the sound of running feet and shouting, and more gunfire. There was a moment of silence, and then Sam's earpiece crackled into life, *"Interlander units move in. Go. Go. Go."*

The three postulants scrambled to their feet and sprinted out into the square. All around, Sam could see other small groups of interlanders racing towards the temple with their immobilisers drawn. He leapt over the body of a terrorist, skidding wildly in a pool of blood as he landed, then ran up the temple steps three at a time. Two BSC men were crouched at the door, cradling their rifles and squinting round the surrounding buildings. Sam charged past them and burst into the temple with Simeon and Ruth just behind him.

The walls inside were scarred black in several places, all of the windows were blasted out and the acrid smell of burning lingered in the air. At the far end, next to the altar, Sam could make out a small group of unconscious fenlanders and, beyond them, black-clad interlander officers with their immobilisers leveled. Around the walls groups of terrorists were held at gunpoint by BSC officers; their hands were on their heads while BSC men secured their feet with plastic shackles.

Sam raised his immobiliser and approached a large wooden figure of the Green Man embracing the moon. He scouted round it carefully, and then moved on past a group of terrorists who were lying on the floor under the rifles of two BSC men. Several of the prisoners were injured and at least two of them seemed to be crying. They all looked very frightened and also, Sam was shocked to notice, very young. They were hardly older than he was himself. It seemed indecent to stare at them.

Grateful for the goggles which obscured his eyes, Sam turned away and continued past.

Then he stopped. He span round, tugged off his goggles and peered at the group again. He felt his body turn very hot and then very cold. He had not been mistaken. There, lying in the centre of the group, in full camouflage gear with blood oozing from his thigh, was Roger.

Sam approached the group slowly. One of the BSC men, a sergeant, leveled his rifle at him.

"What do you want?" he growled.

"I wish to speak to one of the prisoners," Sam answered. As he spoke Roger jerked his head round to face him. His lips moved painfully, without any sound.

"I don't think the prisoners are really any of your business yet, sunshine," the sergeant said. "I don't think you look old enough to be dealing with prisoners, to be honest."

"If I want your opinion, Sergeant, I'll ask for it. I am a postulant in the Interland Security Service, operating in an emergency possession. We are no longer in a combat situation, which means you are under my authority. And I wish to speak to one of your prisoners, so you will let me through."

The sergeant stared hard at Sam and then lowered his rifle and nodded him past. Sam knelt next to Roger. The stone floor around him was sticky with blood and the beat from the CV chip in his wrist was weak and intermittent. Roger smiled faintly.

"I'm delighted you've become m…more assertive, Sam," he whispered, nodding at the BSC man. "I used to worry that you didn't stand up for yourself enough, especially when you were talking to me. Now, I must admit to *a few* reservations about your career choice, but if it's helping your self-confidence, that can only be a g…good thing, I suppose."

"Shut up, Roger. What on earth are you doing here?"

"Fighting for l…liberty, Sam. Not making an awfully good job of it, as you can see, but there we are. That's what I'm s…supposed to be doing anyway."

"What happened to your leg?"

"Shot by a fenlander as I hopped over his garden wall."
Roger smiled feebly. "I expected them to be *nicer* somehow. I
think I even expected them to be *grateful*. It's great propaganda
for your lot, isn't it? We were attacked by the bloody
p...people we were trying to help, before your gang even
turned up."

"But I don't understand," Sam said. "You're not *political* or
anything. You don't really *care* about things."

"I don't care about *many* things, Sam. But I care about a
few very im...important things quite a lot. I know that I'm not
always..."

Roger's eyes opened wide in astonishment. He writhed
backwards on the floor, jerking his injured leg as he did so and
gasping in pain. Sam turned round and saw the light behind the
BSC men shift and quiver like disturbed water. After a few
seconds it rushed away from the space, revealing a short figure
dressed in a purple concealment outfit. The figure lifted its
mask and smiled pleasantly at Sam.

"Samuel, dear boy, lovely to see you. Good work so far.
Jolly proud of all of you and so on. Now look, I'm afraid I've
rather startled your terrorist friend. One forgets how shocking it
must be to see someone turn up in a CICO. Why don't you
introduce us?"

Sam blinked and stared, his mouth open.

"Come on, Samuel, I'm rather busy today. Who's your
friend?"

"This ... this is my brother Roger, Sir Douglas," Sam said.

Sir Douglas's blue eyes sparkled with pleasure. He pushed
past the guards and crouched next to Sam. He took hold of
Roger's face and turned it gently towards him, "Goodness me,
Roger Moorcroft. Is it really? I've heard an awful lot about
you, old chap, one way or another. In point of fact, I've seen
you rowing once or twice. It's absolutely splendid to meet you
at last. I wonder if you know who I am."

"You're Sir Douglas Latch," Roger said, and Sam was
taken aback at the contempt in his tone. "I've h...heard a little
bit about you, too."

"Frankly, I'd be disappointed if you hadn't, dear boy. Now
then, what have you done to your leg?"

"Crossbow bolt," Sam answered. Sir Douglas frowned and leaned forward, probing the flesh around the wound with his finger. Roger groaned again and even in the poor light Sam could see the blood drain from his face.

"There's still something in there," Sir Douglas said matter of factly. "It needs looking at urgently." He stood up and approached the BSC officer who had spoken to Sam.

"Sergeant. I am Sir Douglas Latch, Operational Director of the Interland Security Service and PICOP of this possession. Do you understand what that means?"

The officer straightened.

"Yes sir, I do."

"Excellent. This man possesses intelligence that may be of crucial significance to the Project and the state. I wish him to be evacuated to London immediately for medical treatment. Is that clear?"

"Perfectly, sir."

"Very good. Now then, you will organise his escort yourself and you will be personally responsible for his safe conduct. If he comes to any harm you will answer to me."

The sergeant opened his mouth to object, but Sir Douglas waved him into silence.

"I'll speak to your senior officer, Sergeant, don't worry about that. Now get moving please. We don't have time to waste."

The sergeant shrugged and marched off across the temple. Sir Douglas turned back to Roger.

"That's the best I can do, I'm afraid. At least no one will harm you now, you have my word."

"How reassuring," Roger grunted.

Sir Douglas smiled. He reached into the front pocket of his concealment outfit and withdrew a silver hip flask. He took a gulp from it and then held the bottle to Roger's lips. Roger turned his head away. The old man shrugged and offered the bottle to Sam who took a gulp and handed it back. A minute later the sergeant reappeared with another BSC man, dragging a hover tube. They lifted Roger into it and strapped him down. He raised a hand weakly towards Sam.

"Not much to say, is there?" Sam said flatly.

"Not much, no. But look, S…Sam, if you ever get the chance, do write to Mum and Dad. They miss you dr…dreadfully, you know. So does Rachel, as a matter of fact. I don't know if that means a…anything now."

"It doesn't mean a great deal, to be honest."

"I'm sorry, Sam," Roger said softly. "I really am sorry, you know, more than you can understand, I am. But look, you must realise that there will be a r…reckoning." He gestured shakily round the temple. "All this can't go on forever. One day, it will bring a reckoning, Sam. You have to grasp that."

Sam flushed. He reached into his pocket and pulled out the crumpled leaflet he had picked up. He waved it towards Roger.

"Yeah, well it won't be today," he said. "Not if you're relying on crap like this. It's hardly going to…"

Sir Douglas placed a hand on Sam's wrist, silencing him. The old man nodded at the BSC men and they began to manoeuvre the hover tube towards the temple's back door.

When they were alone, Sir Douglas turned to Sam, his face grave.

"Now then, Samuel," he said, "something like this is bound to be upsetting. But you have work to do and so you must simply get on with the job. Plenty of time to *reflect* on things afterwards. For now you just have to keep going, d'you understand?"

As he spoke he reached into the front of his concealment outfit again and retrieved a packet of cigarettes. He took one for himself and handed another to Sam. Sam lit it and wiped a smear of blood from the handle of his immobiliser with his handkerchief.

"I know perfectly well that I have to get on with the job, Sir Douglas," he said. "And I'm not upset in the least. Not in the least."

Sir Douglas smoked silently and then smiled.

"Of course you're not upset, dear boy. Of course you're not, how stupid of me. Sorry, I was forgetting."

He patted Sam on the arm and stubbed out his half-smoked cigarette on the end of a pew. For a moment he looked as if he were going to say something more but instead he shrugged and replaced his mask. He touched a button on the control pad mounted on the concealment outfit's cuff and began to fade until all that was left of him was a tremor in the dark air.

Sam jammed the cigarette between his lips and went to rejoin his friends.

Chapter Thirty-Two
A Very Senior Officer

Storming the temple had ended the fighting in Bentham, but there was still much work for the interlanders to do. Portal points had to be secured; disturbed and injured subjects had to be immobilised and adjusted; builders had to be escorted as they repaired settlement infrastructure; prisoners had to be evacuated. In wasn't until half past five the following morning that the postulants received the order to withdraw, by which time Sam was exhausted. He slipped through a light portal in a tomb in the town's graveyard and headed back to his rooms in a weary daze, twice falling asleep on the minirail so that he had to be shaken awake gently by Project staff. Back in his apartment, he staggered up the spiral staircase to the sleeping area where he slumped on the bed and tugged off his boots with feeble fingers. The effort drained the last of his strength. Fully clothed, he crawled under the bedcovers and slept.

Sam's sleep was so sudden and so deep that it seemed to be the next moment that he was woken by the sharp beeping of his pager. He fumbled for it in his trouser pocket and read the message through bleary eyes:

Samuel Moorcroft—Report to Sir Douglas Latch's office (Level 18, 273a) with immediate effect. Dress code is smart civvies. Message ends.

Sam was suddenly wide awake and uneasy. It was extremely rare for a postulant to be called to see Sir Douglas in his office and, as Sam understood it, such encounters were not normally very pleasant. They were commonly referred to as "meetings without port." A sequence of his recent training mistakes paraded through Sam's mind: there had been a remote boundary lock left ajar; a courting couple whom he had failed to notice stealing towards the beyonds; the business with Amos Half-Hand and the knife. None of these errors had been disastrous, but they certainly weren't examples of good practice. Perhaps Sir Douglas had learnt of them and decided that Sam deserved a warning about his performance. As the events of the previous night clicked into focus, however, Sam grinned with relief. The meeting was going to be about Roger. It had to be. It was, after all, an extremely serious and delicate situation—just the sort of thing Sir Douglas would want to discuss in the privacy of his office. Sam, an interlander postulant, had a brother who was in custody as a declared enemy of the Project and of the state. He and Sir Douglas now had to decide how to deal with him. *He and Sir Douglas had to deal with Roger.* Sam chuckled and jumped out of bed.

Ten minutes later he was standing before Sir Douglas's office door. He took a moment to compose himself and get his breath back before knocking firmly on the rough wood.

"If that's you, Samuel, do come in. If it's anyone else, shove off," Sir Douglas called out.

Sam pushed the door open and walked in. Sir Douglas was sitting behind his desk drinking from a chipped mug. A three-quarters empty bottle of port was at his elbow. He smiled broadly at Sam.

"Ah Samuel, dear boy, dearest of dear boys. Thanks for coming. Now then, would you like drink? Or a cigarette perhaps?"

Sam sagged with relief. His instinct had been correct; it wasn't going to be a meeting without port.

"Um yes. Um … Both please, Sir Douglas."

The old man giggled and fumbled in his desk drawer, pulling out a glass tumbler that was smeared with ink around the rim. He wiped it with his cuff, slopped port into it and handed it to Sam, then reached into a wooden box on his desk and withdrew two cigarettes. They were unlike any that Sam had seen before: oval and made of very dark tobacco, with two gold rings near the tip. Sir Douglas lit both of them and handed one over. It tasted rich and strong, and made Sam's head spin.

"Splendid things, aren't they?" Sir Douglas purred, examining his own cigarette at arm's length. "I have them flown in directly from the Turkish enclosure. Pricey though, so I tend to save them for special occasions, of which this is definitely one. Don't know if you've heard on the grapevine, dear boy, but the bother is basically finished. Our people had a rather harder time of it over at Stump Cross than you lot did at Bentham, but the fighting's over and the opposition are all very satisfactorily dead or in custody." Sir Douglas drew deeply in his cigarette and sighed contentedly, smoke flaring in twin streams from his nostrils. "We're not out of the woods yet, of course; there's a massive continuity job still to do, but we've put the brats from Cambridge back in the box, that's the main thing."

"Is that what you wanted to see me about, Sir Douglas? You know, about Roger?"

"Oh yes, that particular brat. Well, in a way I suppose it was, but before we get to that there's someone I'm rather keen for you to meet."

"Yes, Sir Douglas?"

"Yes, a very senior interlander officer—very senior indeed. Tipped for the top of the Service at one time."

"Oh, will he be able to help us? With the Roger situation, I mean?"

Sir Douglas giggled and sipped his port.

"Not in the least, I'm afraid."

"Oh."

"Probably be the other way round, actually."

"Oh."

The old man grinned at Sam, his blue eyes sparkling. Eventually Sam said, "The other way round, Sir Douglas?"

"That's what I said, Samuel."

Sir Douglas lapsed into silence, broken a minute later by a loud banging on the door. Sam jumped and Sir Douglas tapped at his computer, leaning forward to examine the screen. He clapped his hands in delight and called out, "Been waiting for you, old chap. Come straight in."

The door swung open and Arthur Moorcroft strode into the room.

To begin with he didn't notice Sam. All his attention was focused on Sir Douglas. He stood before the old man's desk, swallowing hard and shaking with emotion. A layer of sweat glistened on his bald head. Sir Douglas smiled cheerfully at him.

"Arthur, how splendid of you to visit. When the *Refugium* buzzed me to say you were after a chat, I didn't hesitate. "Send him straight through," I said. Strictly speaking, I shouldn't have done, of course. You shouldn't really be anywhere near the place, as you know. But I just thought, "Sod it, let him come." After all, I am the boss. I was *excited*, you see, Arthur, really I was. It's been so very, very long."

"I'm...here...about...my...son." Mr. Moorcroft said in a slow, strangled voice. Sir Douglas raised his eyebrows in feigned surprise and then shrugged.

"Fair enough. We don't really *do* parents' evenings here, as I'm sure you'll recall. But I'm happy enough to fill you in on how he's doing." The old man leaned back in his chair and pursed his lips, staring thoughtfully at the ceiling. "Let me see … Samuel is making excellent progress in both his enclosure work and the more theoretical aspects of his studies. He relates well to his fellow postulants and has won the affection and respect of serving officers. He lies well and, although he isn't what one might call a natural fighter, he is making sound progress in that area, too. He has all the wit, guile and courage to make an excellent officer one day. In point of fact, he reminds me rather a lot of another Moorcroft postulant I knew once."

"I WASN'T TALKING ABOUT SAM," Mr. Moorcroft bellowed. Sir Douglas raised an eyebrow.

"Did you hear that, Samuel? Your father wasn't talking about you."

Arthur Moorcroft span round and stared at Sam. He opened his mouth to speak and then shut it again and turned back to face Sir Douglas. His shoulders sagged.

"That's not fair," he said quietly. Sir Douglas shrugged and stood up. He made his way unsteadily round his desk and settled himself in one of the armchairs by the fire.

"I don't know anything about fair," he said. "But it certainly seems *appropriate* to have Sam along. The Moorcroft men are all involved in this together, one way or another, aren't they? I don't believe Roger got messed up in the fen-lib nonsense without some idea about his old man's past."

Tears welled up in Mr. Moorcroft's eyes. He dabbed at them with his sleeve and then span round and hugged Sam, so tightly that the buttons of his jacket dug painfully into Sam's chest. For a long time he didn't speak, and then he said, "Sam, we were desperate when you vanished. It was absolutely awful, honestly, the worst time in my life, like a wound that wouldn't heal or … or a part of me that was missing. I woke up every morning knowing vaguely that something was wrong but not sure what it was. Then I'd switch the clip off and remember, and after that I'd just feel, I don't know, *horrified*, all day. But you see, once we'd heard from Douglas here, at least we knew you were safe. We still worried like mad, of course, but we knew you weren't actually going to be hurt. The Service looks after its own. But … but with Roger, it's different. Anything could happen to him …" Mr. Moorcroft hugged Sam even more tightly to himself, "… anything at all. He could be chemically curtailed or shot at any time. I know that he's arrogant and insensitive, but he really was devastated when you left…"

Mr. Moorcroft tailed off and Sam wriggled out of his embrace. He was blushing.

"You're not stuttering, Dad," was all he could think of to say.

"Oh, Arthur never stutters when he's at home," Sir Douglas said. He was watching Sam and Mr. Moorcroft closely, his cigarette dangling out of the corner of his mouth so that the smoke curled up into his hair. "That only started when the woman got her claws into him, didn't it, Arthur?"

"Which woman?"

"He's talking about Angela, Sam," Mr. Moorcroft said quietly. "Well, Douglas, are you going to tell him or am I?"

Sir Douglas flicked the butt of his cigarette into the fireplace and smiled.

"It's your story," he said. "Why don't you sit down and tell it?"

Mr. Moorcroft and Sam both sat down and Mr. Moorcroft took a deep breath.

"I used to be an interlander, Sam," he said.

"You were rather more than that, Arthur."

"All right, I used to be a *very senior and successful interlander*. I was Douglas's deputy and his protégé. I clocked up hundreds of hours of crossover time, supervised dozens of possessions, pulled out God knows how many subjects for adjustment, experiment or termination, and arrested more than my fair share of boundary transgressors. For 10 years that was my life.

'Oh,' was all Sam could think of to say.

'Yes. But then I met your mother when she was working here as a catering manager. Angela gave me a different perspective on things." Mr. Moorcroft's voice assumed a hard edge. "Before I met her I hadn't really been able to view the Project in the round. I hadn't had the opportunity to, frankly. Anyway, I … she and I … well, she became pregnant with Roger fairly soon after we met and so I had to leave the Service, and the rest you know. Your mother's so strong, you see, Sam, she gave me the courage to do what I'd wanted to do for some time."

"So, you see, the infant Roger was your father's savior, Samuel," Sir Douglas said quietly. "He was the compelling reason to get out—although you didn't actually leave us, did you, Arthur?"

Mr. Moorcroft sighed.

"Technically no, I didn't leave, Sam, because it's constitutionally impossible for an officer to leave the ISS. I'm what they refer to as a *stood down* officer, but it amounts to the same thing. I don't work as an interlander anymore, and that's what counts."

"Some people refer to you as a stood down officer, others just call you a traitor—but not to worry. The point is, it's not just *constitutionally* impossible to leave us, is it? Tell me a day goes by when you're peeling spuds in that café of yours or making love to your fat wife, when you don't miss the thrill of the boundary? Look me in the eye and tell me you don't ever regret the lost joy of your youth? You walked in two worlds like a god, Arthur; you were carefree once. Tell me you don't weep for all that and I shan't believe you." Sir Douglas lit another cigarette and winked at Sam. "We don't really bother punishing our deserters, Samuel, because the act of desertion is itself far worse than anything we could ever do to them. You can stand down from the Service, but once you're an officer you can't ever really leave it. The Service leaves scars, doesn't it, Arthur?"

Mr. Moorcroft turned red and stared at the fire. Sam glanced at him.

"So you're like me, Dad,' he said slowly. 'You crossed over into the enclosure, just like me. We're ... I mean we're sort of the same."

"No, Sam," Mr. Moorcroft said. "We're not the same at all, I'm afraid. I didn't cross over *into* the enclosure, you see. I crossed over out of it. I was born a subject of the Ely Project in the village of Farnley Fen, just south of Cromer. And I *don't* regret crossing over because if I hadn't, I never would have met Angela, and I *don't* regret standing down from the Service, either, because if I hadn't I would never have had you and Roger. And the three of you are the most important things I've ever known. Of course there are times when I miss the Service, Douglas, of course there are. Absurd as it sounds, I also miss you. You were always kind to me in your own way. After all, what was I but a ragged fen kid whom no one had ever taken much notice of before? But, you see, at least I'm decent now, even if I'm not particularly *strong* anymore. Nothing else matters half as much as that."

There was a long pause and then Sir Douglas coughed politely.

"Well, that was beautifully put, Arthur. I must say you've lost none of your talent. I confess myself to be rather moved. But, without wishing to be indelicate, you don't actually *have* either Roger or Samuel at present, do you? In point of fact, I have both of them, in different ways."

Mr. Moorcoft shook his head angrily. He pulled an envelope from the inside pocket of his jacket and handed it to the old man.

"This is from Roger's girlfriend, Jennifer Catesby," he said. "She's from a staunch Ely family and she's a very committed sophiocrat herself. I don't know why I'm telling you this; you'll know it all already. Anyway, she asks that you communicate what she has to say to the Guardian's Office on Roger's behalf. She's … well, she's convinced that Roger simply fell in with the wrong sort of people at university. He's such an enthusiastic boy, you see; perhaps his enthusiasm doesn't always serve him very well." Mr. Moorcroft swallowed hard. "Please help us, Douglas. I … I need you."

Sir Douglas smiled. He opened the envelope and read the letter, then looked up at Mr. Moorcroft.

"I told you that you wouldn't ever be free, didn't I?" he said, so softly and silkily that the words came out in a single low hiss. "I told you that one day you'd come back. But even I didn't imagine you'd bring me your children. I never expected that, Arthur." He surveyed Sam and his dad through half-closed eyes, still smiling, then stood up and moved back to his desk. He went on in his normal voice: "Now, look here, you know perfectly well that I have no power to release Roger myself. That privilege belongs to the Guardian's Office, and they guard their rights quite as jealously as we guard ours. But I'll send them a note and make the case on your behalf. The Catesby name and Samuel's record might help us a bit. That's all I can say."

Mr. Moorcroft wiped the sweat from his scalp and shrugged helplessly while Sir Douglas began tapping at his computer, occasionally glancing at the letter from Jen. He typed for 10 minutes, his thin tongue protruding slightly from his lips, the cigarette forgotten in his ashtray. Finally, he murmured, "Oh dear," and swung back in his chair.

"Too late, Arthur, too late, I'm afraid. His case has already been adjudicated and, as one would expect, he's been sentenced to curtailment. The Guardian's Office doesn't hang around after a red/black breach, as I'm sure you recall."

Mr. Moorcroft inhaled sharply and tears welled in his eyes again. Sir Douglas went on, "Oh come on, old chap, brace up. It's not as bad as all that. Most of the curtailed people I've met seem to be reasonably happy, as far as one can tell. And I imagine you and Angela would be entitled to all sorts of support with feeding and changing and so on. You might even get a domestic drone out of it. The state isn't vindictive. Who knows, you may actually enjoy having one of the boys back at home."

Mr. Moorcroft's fists clenched.

"Is there nothing at all we can do?" he growled. "There must be something, Douglas, please. I'll ... I'll do absolutely anything."

The office was very quiet. The only sounds were the flames crackling in the hearth and Sir Douglas's quick, excited breathing. The old man peered at his computer again and said, "Well actually, just possibly there is. It seems that the sentence has not yet been confirmed, whatever that means. If Roger agrees to co-operate with the authorities and if he consents to be fitted with a mind tag, there's just a chance it may be suspended."

"What's a mind tag?" Sam asked.

"New Fruit of Sophia, Samuel. I think the techies are keen to test them, actually, which may be why the Guardian's Office is being so uncharacteristically merciful. They're little gizmos that they bung behind your ear if you're a baddy. Don't ask me to explain the science of the things but, as I understand it, they detect and read the pattern of one's brain waves and then relay them to the Home Office or the Department of Boundary Security. Some poor bugger has the job of staring into the thoughts of all the crims and the perverts and the brats from Cambridge, 24/7. If your brother has so much as a grumpy thought about the Guardian's choice of socks when he's got one of these things fitted, he'll be automatically paralysed. Then he'll be lifted and shot before you can say *personally, I blame the parents.*"

Mr. Moorcroft leapt to his feet.

"Well, look Douglas, let's ... let's tell them that we agree. And Roger *will* agree, you know, I'm absolutely certain he will. I don't doubt his courage, but it's the sort of courage that expends itself quickly in dramatic gestures. He'd love the romance of landing in the enclosure by sea to bring liberty to the captives and all that, but I'm sure he won't be able to face curtailment. He's too vain."

Sir Douglas held up his hand.

"Not so fast, Arthur. The Guardian's Office is prepared to be generous with Roger but it's not about to be reckless. It says here that before Roger's sentence can be suspended, they require credible testimony in support of the defendant's appeal. Specifically, they want to know that with appropriate safeguards the defendant may be trusted to amend."

"Well, there's Jen's letter," Mr. Moorcroft said. "And I can vouch for him. And I'm sure there are people at Randall who would vouch for him as well. Roger's tutors all think highly of him, as far as I can tell."

"I don't doubt it. I'm sure Roger's a very popular and persuasive young man. But that's not going to be enough, I'm afraid. Be honest, Jennifer will say anything to defend him because the silly girl thinks she loves him, and so will you— not that your testimony would count for very much. And his tutors would no doubt say nice things about him because he's polite and he rows well and he looks pretty around the college." Sir Douglas poured the last of the port into his mug and sipped it thoughtfully. "No, no, no, the Guardian's Office has left the decision in the hands of someone who knows Roger intimately, but isn't so enamored of him as to be blind to his very serious faults—someone who grew up with him. Someone whose loyalty to the Project and to the state cannot be doubted. I think they're jolly wise in their choice, actually."

Mr. Moorcroft stopped pacing. Sir Douglas giggled and reached into the cigarette box again, retrieving two more cigarettes and tossing one to Sam.

"Well, dear boy," he murmured, "It's all down to you. Is the heroic Roger Moorcroft going to be curtailed? Or are we going to give him another chance? The Guardian's Office will act on your recommendation; they're quite clear about that."

Sam felt himself blush. He lit the cigarette and inhaled deeply, avoiding his dad's eye. His head swam again and the image of Roger naked on top of Rachel drifted idly through his mind like smoke. He considered the picture for a moment and found that he could do so without pain. He felt detached, anaesthetized.

"Well, I don't know, Sir Douglas," he said softly, "there's no doubt Roger is a silly, self-indulgent young man. No doubt at all about that. But I'm not convinced that he's fundamentally wicked. All things considered, I think this mind tag thing might be the best way forward—with appropriate safeguards, of course."

"Very good, Samuel," the old man said as he began to tap at his computer keyboard. "Very, very good indeed, dear boy. I shall communicate your decision to the Guardian's Office directly.

The sky in the Oval Chamber had been switched on again and tourists had already returned to throng the shops and restaurants. Sam and his dad had made the journey there in silence, but now, as they approached the Eden Gate, Mr. Moorcroft turned to Sam.

"I don't s...suppose you can come any further."

"No, Dad, not yet."

Mr. Moorcroft extended his hand.

"Well, th...thank you very much for your h...help, Sam."

Sam took his dad's hand and shook it.

"It's been a pleasure."

A paper seller approached them. *The Insider*'s front page carried a photograph of five battered and shackled rebels beneath a six-inch high headline that simply read POINTLESS. Mr. Moorcroft dismissed the man with a curt shake of his head.

"Why do you h...hate Roger so much?" he asked. Sam frowned.

"I don't care enough about him to hate him, Dad. If I hated him I wouldn't have bothered saving him, would I?"

"He told me all about Rachel. That must have b...been dreadful, and it was unkind. Yes, it w...was unkind. But look, Sam, there are lots of dreadful, unkind things in life. You just h...have to accept them. You have to face them and learn to stay ch...cheerful and carry on caring for p...people and hoping for the best. You really do, or else you end up b...becoming unkind yourself. I know it's complicated, b...but that's how things are. You m...must believe me."

Sam glanced up at the sky. Dawn was breaking into the Oval Chamber, turning the windows of the boutiques and cafés into sheets of gold.

"I'll bear it in mind, Dad," he said quietly.

Mr. Moorcroft stared at the floor.

"Look. I can't t...talk about why I crossed over. I just c...can't."

"It's all right, Dad, you don't have to."

"But I w...w...want you to un...understand, before it's too l...late."

"What is there to understand?"

"What I was s...s...saying about unkindness and..."

Mr. Moorcroft stuttered to a halt and shrugged helplessly. He scratched his head, then, without looking at Sam, turned and made his way to the Eden Gate.

Sam watched as his dad was retina-checked and searched by a BSC officer before being ushered through a turnstile and out of sight. As he turned back to the minirail terminal his pager beeped. He pulled it out and read the message.

Dear boy, many, many congratulations. I have often thought that mercy is one of the most eloquent expressions of contempt and today you have proved it beyond measure. Whatever will the old man think, eh? Poor old Arthur! It may interest you to know that, together with the rest of your gang, you have been released from duty for 24 hours—a fitting reward for services rendered. I believe that a party is already underway in the junior mess. Dress code is ad libertas. *Whatever you wear will end up covered in puke anyway. Fondest Regards, Douglas. Message ends.*

The thought of drink and the company of his fellow postulants was suddenly very attractive to Sam. He walked quickly to the minirail terminal and slipped past the queue, flashing his pass at the BSC officer as he went by. He showed his pass again on the platform and a car was immediately made available for him. Three minutes later he arrived at the junior mess. He yanked the door open and stood still on the threshold, taking in the scene.

The main lights had been dimmed and sheets of various colours had been arranged over a number of lamps, sending swathes of red, blue and green around the mess walls. The furniture at the far end of the room had been pushed to one side, creating a dance floor where a number of postulants and junior officers were jumping around wildly to loud rock music. One end of the bar was stacked with food and bottles of port and beer, which the interlanders were helping themselves to freely. Sam spotted Trevor winding his way from the bar carrying three bottles in one hand and a plate of steaming pies in the other. Ruth (Ruth!) was dancing on the bar at the other end. Her glasses were gleaming like neon and she had a bottle clutched in one hand while the other punched wildly at the air above her head. Below her Laura was kissing another postulant whose face Sam couldn't make out, her hands gripped tightly around the man's bottom. Other people were kissing, or wrestling, or just laughing together, all over the room.

Ruth caught sight of Sam and waved. Sam waved back and was about to approach her when he was struck by a heavy blow just above his ear, making him stagger back against the door frame. Stars and dark clouds played before his eyes and he felt himself sink towards the ground. Someone grabbed him, however, and pulled him close, kissing him roughly where he had just been hit. Sam wiped his eyes and found himself staring at Simeon. His face was flushed and his dark eyes were sparkling. He was holding his belt in his hand, thrusting the brass buckle towards Sam's face.

"Got you back!! Got you back!!" he half yelled, half sang at Sam. "They pack a fair bleedin' wallop, these little things, don't they, eh?" He bit the buckle and pulled Sam's head towards him, kissing him again. "We'll soon be rid of 'em, though, jus' you wait and see. We're *all* gonna be officers now. We've handled a rebellion, haven't we? No more brass for us. We're heroes, Sammy."

Ruth arrived and slipped her arms around Sam's and Simeon's shoulders so that all three of them were locked together in a tangled embrace.

"Welcome to the interlander bacchanal, Sam," she shouted. "We're all going to get drunk and snog each other and then go off to our rooms and … bloody hell, what happened to your head?"

"It's him," Sam said. "The stupid arse hit me with his belt. Gotta remember he's a bit of a barbarian, Ruth. He's just a barbaric fen kid, isn't he? Gotta make allowances for him."

Ruth stared at Simeon unsteadily then leant over and kissed him on the cheek.

"He *is* a bit of a barbarian," she said, "but in a *nice* way. I like him, Sam, and I think he may have saved our lives last night. And now we're all going to be interlander officers together and it's all going to be brilliant forever."

Sam burst out laughing.

"Yeah, yeah, that's right, Ruth, it's going to be absolutely brilliant forever. Now let's get drunk."

Chapter Thirty-Three
A Certain Significant Piece of Silver

"So ladies and gentlemen, to recap the entry arrangements: unit alpha under Sergeant Marshal will go in from the boundary lock at point 36, taking advantage of the lie of the land provided by the dyke path between points 21 and 38. Unit beta under Sergeant Graves will go in from the light portal in Lewis's barn—that's point 22. And units gamma and delta under Captain Fairfax and Sergeant Bush, respectively, will go in from the free-standing light portal at point 29, which is approximately 6 chains west-by-northwest of Tom Drake's mill. All of that is as published in the weekly operating notice and I don't anticipate any amendments. May I assume that everyone is clear?"

Sam looked up from his notes and glanced round the briefing parlour at the assembled BSC officers. There was some shuffling of papers and whispered comments, not all of which sounded particularly friendly. He had expected that. The tough, cynical faces of the Boundary Security Corps men indicated that they were veterans of hundreds of possessions; naturally they resented being commanded by someone like Sam, whose boots were still stained with the mud of his very first. But, resent it or not, they had to put up with it. As Kevin had said to him before the briefing began, "It doesn't matter how much stuff they've done in the enclosure, kid, they've only ever done it *under orders*. You've walked on the other side as a free man and that puts you in a different league from them. And they know it. You're a child of Hilary, Sam, so don't go taking any crap from them. Just do your job."

Now Kevin was sitting quietly at the back of the parlour observing the proceedings. When Sam caught his eye, he winked and then stood up and slipped out. Sam cleared his throat.

"Ok. Perhaps we could move on to look at evacuation strategies. You'll find the relevant material on page six."

There was another round of disgruntled whispering, but

Sam could see the group turning to the correct section of their briefing documents. They might dislike taking instructions from him but they did not know how to disobey; in that respect they were no better than a bunch of drones. Sam felt a wave of confidence surge through him. Who cared what the BSC thought? Kevin was right; he was an interlander, a child of Hilary, a walker in two worlds. And not only that—he was an interlander on the brink of receiving his commission.

In fact, several of the postulants had received them already. Ruth had been the first; she had vanished in the night, six weeks after the fight at Bentham. The following day a brief note had appeared on the notice board in the junior mess:

Colleagues will be pleased to learn that Ruth Garvey has been granted her commission. Miss Garvey received the silver buckle at 2115 hours on Wednesday evening and has been given a month's home leave with immediate effect. She is incommunicado to postulants. She sends her best wishes to the rest of the cohort. DL

Three days later another note appeared informing the postulants that Laura had received her commission, and two days after that another note was pinned to the board informing them that Michael Swale had received his. Four more notices followed in quick succession, and then, a week later, a rather different message had been posted:

Colleagues will be sad to learn that Trevor Milner has failed to attain his commission. Trevor has elected to remove from the Service and, after adjustment, has been returned to his family home. He is incommunicado to postulants. He sends his best wishes to the rest of the cohort. DL

"I was bloody sure he'd get through," Simeon grumbled to Sam as the pair of them slipped through the somber group gathered around the notice board. "I mean, I know he was fat, but he was a bright lad, wasn't he? And everyone seemed to like him. He was good on his rules an' all, and he weren't bad up in the enclosure."

"I'm not sure the commission assessment is about being clever or popular," Sam said. "It's more to do with *commitment* or *morals* or something, isn't it?"

Simeon shrugged.

"Well, we don't really know what it's about, do we, 'cos no one ever talks about it. The officers get all quiet and mysterious if you ask 'em and our own lot vanish as soon as they get through. Anyway, I hope they get round to us soon. I'm sick of wearing brass."

Sam nodded glumly. Since the emergency possession, a restlessness had spread among the postulants. Tutorials had become shorter and more informal, and they were given increasingly responsible roles in operations. It was clear that everyone was itching to be finished with the training. And each time a postulant received his commission, the feeling intensified, more so now that Trevor had actually *failed*. Sam shuddered. What would it be like to fail to get your commission and so have to choose whether to hang around the Project as a permanent brass-buckle, or else go home with a cocktail of drugs inside you so you would only have the vaguest, muddled memories of your time as an interlander?

"I'm sick of wearing brass too, Sim," Sam said quietly. "Whatever happens, I just want to get on with it."

Fortunately Sam did not have much longer to wait. Ten days after the conversation with Simeon he found a bundle of papers in his pigeonhole in the junior mess. There was a note attached.

Dear Samuel,

Please find enclosed the details for a proposed possession (C189) at Stanmore. Given that it covers your old stamping ground, it seems sensible to let you run this one. As you will see, Kevin Spark is named as the person in charge, but he will function only as a "paper PICOP'. The real responsibility will rest with you. I have no doubt whatsoever that you will acquit yourself with your usual brilliance.

You will see that the possession is booked for the end of next week; it goes without saying that you are excused from tutorials and operations during the planning period.

*Also, Samuel, please don't worry that you are being
overlooked in relation to a certain significant piece of silver. I
know you will be worrying, but please don't. The order in
which people receive their commission is of no significance
whatsoever. When you come back from Stanmore, we will have
a conversation about your own commissioning.
Fondest Regards,
Douglas*

The attached documents detailed the possession timing and
limits, the work to be undertaken, the personnel available,
possible entry and exit points, budgeting, catering
arrangements and a hundred other administrative details that
Sam had never considered before. He had hurried to his
apartment and spent the following days hunched over his desk
with a pile of maps and holographs stacked in front of him,
calculating the precise arrangements for the operation: which
units should enter where and when, their routes through the
settlement and the particular tasks each would be assigned.
Occasionally, Kevin would look in to see how he was doing
and make the odd suggestion, but basically Sam was left alone.
He banned Simeon from visiting and had food brought up from
the mess at odd hours, which he often forgot to eat. He smoked
almost non-stop until his clothes and hair stank of tobacco. And
he slept only a few hours of shallow, dream-filled sleep each
night.

When the arrangements were completed to his own
satisfaction, Sam took them to Kevin for final approval. The
tutor had read through them, then slapped him on the back and
grinned.

"Great job, kid. You're thorough, I'll give you that. Now
you've just got to explain it all to the morons you're taking
with you."

And so, less than 48 hours before the possession was due to
start, the briefings had begun. Sam had meetings with ISS
colleagues, technicians, first aid units and retailers in the
Stanmore installation. He emailed a short memo outlining the
possession plans to the Guardian's Office and had it returned
immediately, marked *approved*. He even had a short meeting

with a weasel-faced woman from *The Insider*, who scrawled on a tatty notepad as Sam outlined the possession arrangements, "Pretty routine stuff," she had grunted when he had finished. "We might give you a couple of paragraphs somewhere on the inside, assuming there's no decent sex or violence between now and then."

And finally, of course, there were the miserable-but-obedient men and women of the Boundary Security Corps to instruct…

"So, are there any questions about any of the material we've covered?" Sam concluded an hour later. The BSC officers stared at him sullenly. "Or is there anything that I may have missed?" More silence. "Very good—in which case you may as well go. Please be at your muster points tonight by 21:30 hours at the latest."

There was the noise of belongings being gathered up and a low hum of conversation as the BSC hustled quickly out of the parlour. None of them wanted to be left alone with the young interlander. Sam watched them go and then gathered his papers together and tossed his empty polystyrene cup in the bin under the lectern. He paused to stroke a large, ginger cat that was sprawled on the floor by the door and then headed for the junior mess. There was nothing he could do now but wait, and after the last few days' frantic activity the prospect of enforced idleness was not pleasant. A drink or two—not too much, obviously—would help to make the day go by a bit more quickly. Maybe Simeon would be around somewhere and they could play cards or pool or car racing or something.

When Sam arrived at the mess he found a single envelope waiting for him in his pigeonhole. He took it into the bar, where he ordered a pint of Badger's Snout ale and a round of squirrel and cranberry sandwiches from the elderly steward on duty. As the man phoned the food order through to the kitchen and set about pouring the drink, Sam opened the envelope. He scanned the letter quickly and then drew it close to his face and re-read it, slowly and carefully. The paper began to shake in his hand. Sam staggered and gripped the bar, then turned on his heel and ran from the room.

By the time the steward returned with the pint of beer, Sam

was nowhere to be seen. The old man rolled his eyes—how typical of the arrogance of these young postulants, so different from the great old gentlemen of the Service—and tipped the beer down the sink. He didn't cancel the sandwiches, though; they would make a nice lunch. Stewarding for the ISS had its perks.

Sam ran all the way to Sir Douglas Latch's office, shoving people out of his way as he went. He hammered on the door while he fought to catch his breath. When there was no reply he beat harder at the door and then flung his shoulder against it. Eventually, it was opened calmly by Tony, Sir Douglas's adjutant. As usual, he was immaculately turned out, his shoes and brass belt buckle gleaming in the harsh light of the corridor. He was carrying a plastic tray overflowing with documents.

"It's Samuel, isn't it?" he said. "Samuel Moorcroft."

"Yes, that's … that's me," Sam answered, still breathing hard. "Look, I need to see Sir Douglas urgently."

"Ah. Well, that's going to be rather tricky, I'm afraid, Samuel, because you see…'

"I don't care how bloody tricky it is, I need to speak to him immediately."

A murmur of conversation and footsteps echoed down the corridor. Tony glanced anxiously towards the noise.

"You'd better come in," he said.

Sam followed Tony into Sir Douglas's office. There was a fire burning fiercely in the hearth and a bottle of wine open on the desk. Piles of red logbooks and documents were stacked around the floor. Tony cleared a space for the tray of papers he was holding and turned back to Sam.

"As I was saying, it's going to be difficult for you to see Sir Douglas because he isn't here."

"Not here! What do you mean he's not here? Where is he then?"

"Siberia."

"*Siberia!*"

"Yes." The adjutant sighed importantly. "Look, what I'm

going to tell you is just about as classified as it gets, but I understand that you and Sir Douglas have something of a special bond, so I suppose you can be trusted. A squad of interlanders has gone native in the eastern Siberian enclosure. I believe they've even started worshipping Elk or something. Sir Douglas did tell me the details, but I'm afraid I've forgotten most of them. Anyway, the point is they've taken guns in, so obviously it's caused a hell of a stink—questions asked in the Kremlin and so on. You can imagine."

Despite himself, Sam was appalled.

"Guns! They've gone native with guns? Bloody hell."

"Quite. So Sir Douglas has had to go straight out there as an emergency consulter. It's very hush-hush, of course, so make sure you keep it to yourself." Tony gestured vaguely round the office. "I'm just catching up on some filing while the old rascal's away."

"Well, look, is there any way I could contact him? There must be a phone link or something."

Tony poured himself a glass of wine. He didn't offer Sam one.

"Of course there's a phone link. I have to speak to Sir Douglas every day to keep him briefed. The point is no one else may, because no one else is supposed to know that he's there. Sir Douglas was absolutely clear about that. Anyway, what was it you wanted to see him about?"

"This." Sam pulled the letter he had found in his pigeonhole from his pocket. He handed it to Tony, who studied it briefly.

"Of course you're PICOPing the Stanmore possession, aren't you? I believe Sir Douglas mentioned it. But look here, this is just a list of some additional withdrawals. It's a bit last minute, I suppose, but it shouldn't cause any practical problem for a man of your talents."

"Of course there's not a bloody practical problem," Sam spluttered. "It's just I'm not ... I'm not sure ... Look, there must be *some way* of contacting him. I'm certain he wouldn't mind speaking to me."

"There's no way at all. I don't know what sort of difficulty you have with the instruction, but whatever it is I suggest you forget about it. You'll just have to grit your teeth and get on with the job. Either that or have yourself removed from the operation, of course. But that would look very bad, wouldn't it? Especially with you so close to your commissioning." Tony passed the letter back to Sam. "Sorry I can't be more help, but there we are."

"Yeah, I'm sorry about that as well," Sam growled. He turned and marched out the door.

Sir Douglas left a decent interval before he materialized. He was sitting in the chair behind his desk. When he lifted the mask of his concealment outfit he was giggling.

"Elk, Tony?! Where on earth did the Elk come from?"

Tony shrugged.

"Don't know really, Sir Douglas. I just thought of it. I thought it might be good to add a bit of local colour."

"But do they actually have Elk in Siberia?"

Sir Douglas continued to giggle as he retrieved his glass from behind a pile of books and topped it up with red wine. He lit a cigarette.

"Well, anyway, you were absolutely bloody magnificent. Once again I find myself entirely in your debt. Really, I mean it. Young Master Samuel isn't the only interlander with whom I would claim a special bond. Do you understand?"

"Yes, Sir Douglas. Thank you."

"Not at all, dear boy, praise where it's due and all that. Now then, I wonder if you'd be so good as to tidy these logbooks away. I can hardly see my own feet."

"Yes, Sir Douglas." Tony flicked a speck of dust off his uniform shirt. "Um, Sir Douglas?"

"What now, Tony?"

"Do you think he'll bite?"

The old man peered into his glass and smiled. He took a sip of wine and whirled it luxuriously round his mouth before swallowing. He licked his lips with his reddened tongue.

"One can never be sure of these things, as you know only too well, but on the whole I rather think he will. Samuel came to us as a fragile child, Tony. The adult in him is our creation, entirely our creation. And it's also extremely brittle. So, yes, I think he probably will bite. I don't think we've left him with many options."

Chapter Thirty-Four
The Demon

Some potioners, the less conscientious ones, would think nothing of gathering the ingredients for their evening remedies in the morning or at noon, when the day was young and impatient and the healing elements ran turbulently through the seeds and stems of the necessary plants. Smith was not one of these. Fiercely proud of the tradition she belonged to—her family had, after all, been potioners to the magistrate since 1752—she was determined to do her work properly. And this involved collecting evening time ingredients in the evening, obviously. And so at dusk on the night when the demon returned to Stanmore, she was to be found crouching next to a clump of wild fox-balm in a ditch by Sheedy Hill, sucking juice from the plants' roots with a needle and a straw.

She sucked three, four, five, six droplets of the milky liquid into her tincture bottle, then sealed the root's wound with her own spit, reburied it, and clambered to her feet. She took a moment to steady herself and get her breath back, and then moved on and crouched awkwardly next to another clump. She couldn't afford to waste time; she had berries from lovers-loss and bark from devil-ease to gather as well. And she mustn't be late home or else her mum would panic and begin re-arranging the shop again.

Smith was happy that evening to be away from Stanmore. For the last weeks the settlement had been alive with rumours of violence and devilment in the coast towns and in the villages to the north, and such talk was deeply disturbing to her. The news had come first from the lively mouths of the traders, whispered down the back roads like leaves scuttering before the autumn wind. It was said that the demon had come as legion from the sea, in alliance with savage pirates from the outer east, wherever that was. It was said that he had come with great spite: stealing children, salting the land and desecrating the temples, leaving them scorched and knee-deep in human blood. It was said that those who had actually seen the demon still could not speak of what they had witnessed, so grotesque had he appeared.

Not long after the rumours had begun to circulate, Reverend Smythe had been summoned to a special conclave of the clergy and had returned solemn-faced and fearful. His sermons since had been littered with references to *the abiding closeness of the evil one* and *the needfulness of constant obedience* and *tithing as the spiritual stockade that guards our hearts and hearths.* All this had lent substance to the traders' tales and darkened the clouds of anxiety and conjecture that hung over Stanmore. Little wonder, then, that Smith was glad to find excuses to wander away from the settlement now and again, to escape all the murmuring and the worry.

She sealed the root, placed the tincture bottle in her satchel and clambered back to her feet. Next was lovers-loss. You had to be careful with the berries: if you snatched at them too vigorously they would bruise and the healing elements would flee off into the air and back to the stars. Smith reached tenderly into a bush and loosened a spray of the purple berries with extreme care until they came away from their branch with a tiny click. She withdrew her hand slowly and wrapped her prize in tissue before placing it in a brass flask. This she fastened and tucked into her satchel before scrambling out of the ditch and skirting the edge of Sheedy Hill to reach a copse of elms where devil-ease grew thick among the tree roots. When she reached the trees, she removed a knife from her satchel and carved a crude depiction of the Green Man onto the largest of the elms. This was necessary to protect the plants from evil inclinations in the air as she wounded them. She paused for a moment with her head bowed to reverence the carving, and then began slicing strips of soft bark from the devil-ease, never taking more than one cutting from each plant and murmuring prayers all the time she was working.

It was not only the disturbing talk of the demon that made Smith happy to be away from Stanmore. There was also the question of her child, now only weeks from being born, and the effort involved in keeping it hidden. She had never gone to Reverend Smythe for the necessary temple certificate to offer it as an oblation, nor had she returned to the black jars at the top of the potioner's cupboard. Since the muddled night when she had rescued the bird from the mixing room, something living and sore had reawoken in her, which made such things impossible. The world had become vivid again in its demands and its joys and, cautiously, Smith had accepted all of it, including the child that was growing inside her. She had taken potions to keep the baby small in her belly and worn her clothes loosely, and so had managed to keep her condition a secret. With her time so near, however, the deception was becoming more and more difficult to maintain. It was a relief to be away from inquisitive eyes and clacking tongues, if only for half an hour.

After much agonising, Smith had decided that she would give birth alone (there were potions to help with that, too) and then leave the baby outside the temple before the Sunday ceremony. After all, she had been a devout and obedient child of the Wheel her whole life, faithful in her tithes and hearth offerings. Surely, she reasoned, her child would be safe in the shadow of the Green Man. She had heard talk of temple foundlings being taken and trained as acolytes. If the child were a boy, it wasn't completely impossible that he would one day be a priest.

It wasn't a good solution, of course. It made Smith ache with unhappiness whenever she thought about it. She knew that if she were brave she would keep the child and put up with all the nastiness and gossip. But she did not consider herself to be brave, or at least not *that* brave. Also, what would the baby's sudden arrival do to her mum? That had to be thought about, too. All things considered, the temple solution was the least dreadful of the options available.

A burst of shouting from the outskirts of Stanmore disturbed Smith's thoughts. She glanced up from her work and her eyes narrowed and then opened vey wide. She stirred sharply like an animal sensing danger and her hands fell protectively to her stomach. There was a smudgy yellow glow in the western sky that seemed to be rising, smoke-like, from the earth itself. As she watched, the light thickened and swirled in shimmering eddies, and then drifted slowly towards the settlement, twisting the landscape as it went. Smith felt the first twinge of sickness in her throat. That light was known to everyone in Stanmore and roundabout. Children had it drummed into them as soon as they could talk that if you saw yellow light rising from the fen, you said a prayer and ran home as quickly as you could with your eyes fixed to the ground. Pastor Smythe called the light *mental luminance* that broke from the demon's imagination when he stirred himself against decent folk. Smith had seen it twice before herself; it meant only one thing.

Another burst of shouting reached her through the still evening air.

"Devil sky," Smith breathed. "Oh no, he's coming. Mum! Mum! Don't worry, I'm on my way."

She slung her satchel over her shoulder and ran as fast as her condition would allow back round Sheedy Hill and along the road into Stanmore. By the time she reached the outskirts of the settlement she was gasping for air and clutching her side in pain. She leant on the parish boundary stone for a full minute, struggling to regain her breath, before continuing.

The streets were mostly deserted, but here and there a householder could still be seen securing shutters over his windows or erecting hasty barricades in front of his door. A group of younger men, armed with knives, flails and cross bows, clustered around the temple steps. They had handkerchiefs tied round their mouths and wore improvised goggles made of smoked glass and wire against the devil sky. Despite these precautions, however, a couple of the younger ones were already being sick in the gutter. The leader of the group urged Smith forward with his crossbow. She nodded at him and hurried on.

The settlement was now bathed in deep yellow on every side. Buildings twisted in the glow, making them unfamiliar and sinister. Twice Smith lost her way and had to retrace her steps before she finally arrived at the shop. She flung herself through the door and dropped to her knees, retching and sobbing.

"Oh, look who's finally come 'ome," said a familiar voice. "And not before time, young lady, I must say. Now listen, Lou, you can't jus' lie around there all day. Not today you can't, you'll be in the way. I'm givin' the whole shop front a good goin' over, see. I'm getting rid of all the stock that's too filthy to be saved and I'm givin' everythin' else a scrub down with Rogerson's Patent Fishbone and Lime."

Smith slowly opened her eyes and looked around. The shop was littered with medicine bottles and tubs of ointment. Several of the shelves were bare and there were piles of broken glass and scatterings of herbs and powder on the floor. One window was shuttered but the other was left open to the street and devil sky was spilling into the shop. Her mum was standing by the counter with a cloth in one hand and a jar of Rogerson's Patent Fishbone and Lime in the other. She had vomit splashed down her front and gray powder under her nostrils. She was smiling proudly.

"M...Mum, look, it ain't really the day to be tidying," Smith stammered. "The demon's comin'. We gotta get the shop sealed up and get ourselves hidden away in the cellar. Honestly, Mum, we gotta do it quickly."

"Don't be so silly, young lady. The demon ain't comin'. He never comes 'ere, does he? I don't know, Lou; the things you'll say to get out of a bit of work!"

"He does come here, Mum. Please, let's close the shutters at least. *Please.*"

"But why would we want to do that, you silly girl? It's lovely is this bit o' sun. No Lou, I ain't gonna shut it out for you or anyone."

Smith's mum moved towards the un-shuttered window until she was bathed in the devil sky. Her skin glowed sickly orange. She sighed contentedly.

"You see, Lou, it's lovely, is this. All warm on me old bones. Gives the shop a bit of colour an' all, for when yer father fetches home. He likes a spot of sun, does ..."

A torrent of vomit gushed from the old woman's mouth, splattering onto the window display and down onto the floor. She bent double until she had finished being sick and then wiped her lips and chin with her cuff and stepped back into the darkness of the shop. Lou levered herself to her feet.

"You see, Mum, that ain't sunlight. It's devil sky. The demon's comin'."

"IT'S SUNSHINE, LOU," her mum screamed. "It's sunshine and the demon ain't comin' because the demon don't exist. He don't exist and he don't come anywhere near here anyway. Do you hear me, young lady?"

Smith felt tears prickle in her eyes. She fought to control herself.

"Ok, Mum. Ok. Ok. Look, I'll jus' go and get us both a nice cup of tea, then I'll come back to help you clean up. Yer right—the shop *does* need it and you know I ain't really afraid of a bit of work."

Smith's mum calmed a little. She nodded approvingly and concentrated on wiping the sick off her dress as Smith made her way through the counter and on into the back of the shop. She went first to the kitchen where she closed the shutters and boiled the kettle, making two cups of tea. These she placed on a tray together with a plate of biscuits. Next she went to the mixing room. She took a bottle of clear liquid from the potioners' cupboard and tipped three drops from it into one of the cups before returning to the front of the shop. Her mum was now scrubbing vigorously at the brass till while her other hand wound a lock of hair tighter and tighter round her fingers. The room smelt appallingly of vomit and spilt medicine. Smith handed her mum one of the cups and said, "You've brought that up nice, Mum. I think you've earned yerself a bit of a tea break."

"Reckon I have, Lou," her mum said. "Bit of elbow grease is all it takes." She sipped the tea and frowned.

"Bitter, this is Lou, love, you sure the cup was clean?"

"Yeah, Mum, I cleaned it myself. But the tea was right from the bottom of the caddy. Maybe a bit old, I suppose."

Lou's mum nodded.

"Well, it's wet and warm, at least. Set us up for ... for ..."

The old woman's eyelids fluttered and her chin sank to her chest. She staggered and grabbed the counter, lowering herself to the floor. For a moment, as she sat down, she looked surprised and then suspicious. "Lou, this ain't right," she mumbled. "What you done to me, Lou?"

Then she rolled over and lost consciousness.

Smith bent down and felt her mum's pulse before picking her way quickly to the window. She groped for the shutters and slammed them closed, then removed two of the emptied shelves from their racks and wedged them against the door.

"I'm sorry, but I ain't gonna be able to get you into the cellar, Mum," she murmured, "so I'm afraid we're jus' gonna 'ave to make the best of things here."

She rolled her mum onto her back and arranged her cardigan under her head, making her as comfortable as she could. Then she sat down next to her with her back propped against the counter. There was nothing to do now but wait and listen—and pray. Smith slipped her hand into her pinafore pocket and her fingers closed over her old model of the Sacred Wheel. She spun the wooden spokes quickly through her fingers, murmuring *Thorn and Bloods*, *Turning Earths* and other ancient, familiar prayers as she did so.

After about an hour, Smith heard the distant sound of regular, disciplined footsteps. She shuffled forwards and checked that the shelves were still firmly wedged against the door. Satisfied, she returned to her mum and held her breath as the footsteps clattered down the street, relaxing as they went past. Other noises sounded from outside: breaking glass, splintering wood and then the terrible sound of screaming. Gradually, the street grew quiet again until, sometime later, more footsteps sounded on the cobbles. Once more, Smith held her breath and waited as the steps drew level with the shop. Instead of continuing past, however, the footsteps seemed to stop directly at the potioner's doorstep. There was the sound of murmured conversation followed by silence, and then a heavy blow crashed into the shop door, splintering the frame and sending one of the shelves clattering to the floor.

Smith cried out and shrank back against the counter, pulling her mum closer to her and shielding her as best she could with her own body. A second blow struck the door, and then a third and a fourth. At the fifth blow, the door shattered and fell inwards. Devil sky spilt into the shop like a pool of bright poison.

Smith pushed herself still further against the counter as the devil sky surged around the room, making the furnishings lively and chaotic. As she watched, terrified and fascinated, the yellow light in the doorway began to move and ripple faster than the rest, like disturbed water. The rippling grew more and more urgent and then the light washed away from the space entirely, leaving only a dark and smudgy emptiness. For a few seconds nothing happened, and then the emptiness itself seemed to flash and quiver, and slowly contort itself into a specific shape. The shape gradually acquired colour and definition. It glanced from side to side and stepped unhurriedly into the shop.

All at once Smith was completely calm. She felt lightheaded and detached from the scene, as if she were viewing it all through water or thick glass. She was intensely curious about the figure before her, so curious that even the sickness caused by the devil sky subsided a little. She had heard stories about the demon since she was a child. She had dreamt of him, listened to sermons about him and imagined him thousands of times. He was the dark background to her every calculation, the pressure at the back of her skull that never quite went away, and now here he was in her own shop, standing next to an upended box of honey and cowslip suppositories. It was much too extraordinary and unbelievable to be properly terrifying.

The demon was human shaped and reddish purple from head to toe. That made sense: it was a cruel, demon-like colour. His face was smooth and featureless. That made sense too: Reverend Smythe often talked about the *blank evil of the devilish visage.*

As she watched, the demon took another step towards her then reached up to his face and slowly pulled it away from his head. It came away in a single sheet of stretchy, purple skin that wrinkled up on his forehead, revealing another face underneath. Smith gasped and hauled herself to her feet, using the counter as support. The second face was familiar. It was a bit thinner than she remembered, perhaps a bit sterner, but familiar all the same. Its cheeks were wet with tears.

She took a step towards the demon but it lifted a long, cruel finger towards her, halting her. It swallowed hard.

"I've come to take you away," the demon said softly. "To the place that's safe, beyond Walsingham."

Smith nodded and as she did so she felt understanding pour into her like icy water. In a rush she knew that Reverend Smythe had got most of it wrong. The demon was not just the being that you hated and feared; he was also the thing that in the deepest, darkest places, you desired. Certainly he was the bleak power slouching through the beyonds, but he was also the spark of danger and delight in every human face and meeting. He was always present: half known, half unknown. You couldn't ultimately defeat him with prayers and tithes and amulets; she understood that now. You had to recognise him, suffer him, accept him. Finally you could only defeat him by *welcoming him.*

She swallowed a stream of vomit that rose in her throat and took another step towards the demon, raising her arms shakily to hold him as once she had held him before. She opened her mouth to explain all that she now understood but the words never had a chance to come. The demon twitched his cruel finger and the world flew away from her in a blaze of colour.

Sam pulled his goggles out of his trouser pocket, yanked them over his face and switched them on. The *lux obscura* was so intense now that he risked being seriously incapacitated if he was exposed to it for any length of time. Smith was apparently suspended in mid-air directly in front of him; as he watched she sank gently to the ground while all around her the light rippled and twisted.

"Good catch," Sam said.

"Just doing my job, sunshine," a disembodied voice replied. "Do you want me to hang around for the hover tube?"

"No need. I'll wait for a bit. You go and join Sergeant Graves; he should be working on the holograph relays outside the King's Head by now. Is she all right, by the way?"

The air above Smith rippled jerkily, implying a shrug. "Seems to be. Nice looking bird really, well, nice body, anyway. Not sure about her face. I wasn't expecting you to materialise, by the way."

"It was important. I wanted her to see me."

"What, do you know her then?"

"Used to. Now get along to Sergeant Graves, please. We're on a timetable here."

The pillar of swirling air brushed past Sam and left the shop. Sam closed the door after it, then went to examine Smith. She was very pale but she seemed to be breathing evenly. Her swollen stomach was more pronounced now that she was lying on the ground. He stared at her for a long time without moving, then pulled the microphone of his personal communications unit down to his mouth.

"Hello, *Refugium Peccatorum*; this is ISS Postulant Moorcroft engaged in possession C 261 at Stanmore, password hunger. You spell hunger: hotel, uniform, november, golf, echo, romeo. Do you receive me?"

"Receiving you loud and clear Postulant Moorcroft," a bored voice answered. "Please state your message."

"I have subject 915, L. Smith, immobilised and ready for withdrawal at point 437, *Smith's Potioners*. I request immediate removal team."

Sam heard some murmured instructions and then the voice said:

"The team's on its way. Will there be anything else, Postulant Moorcroft?"

"No, that's all," Sam said. "Thanks for your help."

The line went dead and a few minutes later Sam heard clattering from the back of the shop. The door behind the counter opened and three technicians came in, dragging a hover tube. They eyed the two prostrate women for a moment and then one of them pulled a document from a pocket at the end of the tube and studied it. He kicked Smith gently.

"I take it we're after this one," he said. "Female, 19 years old, pregnant."

"Yes, you're here for her," Sam said.

The man nodded to his colleagues, who lifted Smith into the tube. Her hair fell free of the plastic head piece so that one of the men had to gather it up in fistfuls and stuff it in the side beneath her cheek. The leader turned to Sam.

"Nice job," he said. "What do you want us to do with the other one?"

Sam turned to Smith's mum and shot her with his immobiliser.

"That'll keep her quiet for a bit. You can leave her be. She's not on the list."

"Fair enough, mate—in which case, can I just trouble you for your signature?"

He handed the document and a biro to Sam, who leant on the counter and signed it in the spaces the man indicated. The man took the document back, slipped it into a laminate pocket and fixed it to the top of the tube. The three men pushed the tube back through the counter and on into the rear of the shop.

Sam listened as the back door open and shut, and then walked through the little gate in the counter himself. He glanced up and down the corridor before slipping through the door opposite and climbing the stairs. At the top he pushed open the door to his old room and stood on the threshold. The bed was neatly made, the floor swept, the Green Man statue honoured with a spray of fresh grasses.

Sam walked to the window and looked out. There were technicians working on two subjects immediately outside the shop, while further down the road another group were crouched around a pinhead holograph camera mounted in a doorstep, their tools spread out on the pavement. Sam glanced at his watch and nodded; everything was as it should be. Further off, he could make out a deep, reddish glow spreading within the yellow of the *lux obscura*. That would be the fire from the temple mauling. The demon always damaged the temple when he visited a settlement. In his great malice he could never resist it. The BSC expected it; it was an accepted perk of possession work.

Sam pulled a packet of cigarettes from the pocket of his concealment outfit. He lit one and smoked it slowly, watching as the technicians went about their tasks and the glow from the temple grew stronger. Several minutes later he yanked the window open, stubbed the cigarette out on the windowsill and tossed the butt into the street. He glanced round the room and shrugged, then pulled off his goggles and tugged the mask of his concealment outfit back over his face. He touched the control panel on his wrist and slowly dissolved.

Devil sky oozed undisturbed around the little attic room.

Chapter Thirty-Five
Animacide

Everyone agreed that possession C 261 at Stanmore had passed off extremely well: holograph maintenance work had been successfully completed; all the subjects who needed to be withdrawn had been withdrawn and those requiring adjustment had been adjusted, with minimal fuss; two new light portals had been installed in the settlement and successfully tested. All units were finally pulled out just before daybreak, and then all the personnel involved in the operation—interlanders, BSC, technicians, support staff—enjoyed breakfast in the King's Head double pub in the Stanmore installation (the installation was still closed to tourists and would remain so for at least a week following the possession). Post-ops breakfasts were traditionally occasions where inter-agency feuds were briefly forgotten, and this one was no exception. Burly BSC men laughed and joked with technicians as they munched bacon sandwiches together; interlanders span exaggerated tales of their enclosure adventures to wide-eyed catering assistants who had never been near the boundary in their life. The breakfast soon became raucous. Drinking games began in which interlanders and BSC men competed to see who could drink the most glasses of eye-watering enclosure brandy without falling off their stool (you were allowed to stop and be sick after every four glasses). Music was supplied and soon a number of younger staff were dancing while another group spilt out of the pub and began an improvised game of rugby in the installation plaza. And time and again, above the hubbub, people remarked on the exceptional interlander postulant who had supervised the whole operation.

"Credit where it's due, he knew his bleedin' stuff," said tough BSC men as they absentmindedly scratched the faded tattoos on their forearms.

"Absolutely brilliant," white-coated technicians agreed in between mouthfuls of beer.

"Incredibly calm when things got hairy."

"Knew the place like the back of his hand."

"So bloody calm."

"Bloody young as well."

Whoever he was, the young man clearly had a golden future ahead of him.

The young man was not present to receive his praise, however. Sam had waited in the shadow of Tom Drake's mill until he had it confirmed from the *Refugium Peccatorum* that all personnel were safely withdrawn; then he crossed the adjacent field to the light portal at point 29. He slipped through the pool of shimmering blue light and took the minirail directly to the Oval Chamber.

Despite the early hour the chamber was busy with tourists. Sam took the lift to the lower balcony and paced round it until he reached a small pub called *The Outside Inn*. It was designed to look something like a Limeport tavern, with coils of rope and pictures of old fishing boats on the walls. The tables were made of upended barrels, the lighting came from electric lights concealed in oil lanterns, and a ship's bell above the door tolled mournfully as Sam entered. He settled himself at a barrel-table near the window and studied the menu until a waitress came over. She was young and attractive, dressed in neat fenland costume with her hair arranged, enclosure style, in long plaits.

"Hi, welcome to the *Outside Inn*," she said. "We have a full range of authentic enclosure breakfasts or outside food if you prefer. We also serve a range of alcoholic and non-alcoholic drinks from inside and outside, and the lunch menu is available from 11."

Sam looked up at the young woman and smiled unpleasantly.

"What do you suppose the people thought who designed this place?" he said. "Do you think they thought, 'bung a few bits of rope on the walls and get some barmaids dressed in fen smocks to talk funny; then it'll be just like the enclosure and the punters will come flocking'? Do you think they thought something like that?"

The woman blushed.

"Yes, well, I don't think it's meant to be exact, is it? It's just meant to give you, you know, a flavour."

"Yeah, I know. A *wonderful, authentic*, enclosure flavour."

"Um, yeah. So, do you want anything to eat or not?"

"You don't do this full time, do you?"

"No, I'm a student, although it's none of your business. Now what do you want?"

Sam lit a cigarette and smoked it thoughtfully.

"Where are you a student?"

"Cambridge."

"Of course. You would be. Eight and a half minutes away by monorail. What a convenient way to earn a bit of cash through college, dressing up like one of the poor prisoners on the other side and serving expensive drinks to the idiots who get their kicks from leering at them. I bet you've got a boyfriend who works here as well. You have, haven't you? And at the end of the day you go home together and have a cuddle on the sofa while you laugh at all the pitiful morons you've had to deal with."

Sam stubbed out his cigarette out in the shell-shaped ashtray and looked up at the waitress. To his horror he felt his eyes begin to fill with tears. The waitress eyed him warily.

"Um, are you *all right*?"

"No, I'm not in the slightest bit all right." Sam wiped his eyes. "I've had a crap night, but that's not your fault, is it? Just get me coffee, please, black coffee, and keep it coming. But don't do anything to make it seem like it's from the enclosure. Just give it to me in a normal, outside, cup, ok?"

Without answering the waitress returned to the kitchen. She came back a couple of minutes later with the coffee and placed it on the table without a word. Sam drank it quickly so that it scorched his mouth and peered out of the window. He followed individual faces around the general swirl of the Oval Chamber: a fat woman with a limp and a pot plant; a short man with an enormous floppy hat who vanished into pornographic holographic show when he thought no one was watching; a BSC man who desperately wanted to look stern but who obviously had a very itchy buttock.

As soon as Sam's cup was empty the waitress returned with a second and then a third. When she had cleared away Sam's fourth cup she hovered at his elbow.

"Look ... um ... I don't think it's good to drink this much coffee, at least not without something to eat. Are you sure you don't want some food? It doesn't have to be enclosure stuff; we do ordinary food as well."

"I think I'd be sick if I tried to eat anything at all, but thanks for being kind." Sam frowned. "Actually, I'd better go; there's something I've got to do."

He handed the woman his currency card. She swiped it, and then returned it to him.

"Ok, well, good luck with it, whatever it is."

"Yeah, and good luck with Cambridge and everything." Sam made an effort to smile. "My brother was at university there, actually, I used to visit him with my mum and dad. I liked it."

"Oh right, so are you a student yourself?"

"No."

"Are you going to be?"

"No."

"Oh. Well, do you *want* to be?"

"That's not really relevant anymore. Sorry I was so rude before; like I say, I've had a rotten night. And thanks for the coffee."

Sam left the pub and returned to the minirail station. He waved his pass at the BSC officers and went quickly down the steps, speaking briefly to the member of staff on platform duty. The next car was made available and Sam buckled himself in as the man tapped the keypad on the wall.

The journey was one of the longest Sam had ever taken by minirail—about 15 minutes—and when he arrived at his destination, the platform was unlike any other minirail platform he had ever seen. It was silent and brilliant white, and smelled strongly of disinfectant. As soon as the car roof slid open a drone in white overalls and face mask stepped forward and sprayed Sam with a fine blue liquid from a pipe that extended from a cylinder on his back. When Sam's front was entirely covered the drone unbuckled him, allowing him to step onto the platform. The drone then sprayed his back before withdrawing to his stool and playing with a set of building bricks.

"What's your name, please?" asked a man sitting next to the platform's control pad. He was also dressed from head to foot in white overalls, but a blue armband with three gold stripes indicated that he was a sergeant in the BSC. He had been studying a copy of *The Insider* when Sam arrived.

"Samuel Moorcroft, postulant ISS."

The BSC man studied the small computer screen in front of him.

"You're late, sunshine. We were expecting you an hour ago."

"Um, I think there may have been a mistake. I don't have an appointment or anything. I've just come here because there's someone, well a subject, I want to see—sort of visit."

"No mistake, young man. We don't make mistakes down here in techno-surgical. Now come and do your eye, please."

Bemused, Sam applied his eye to a scanner in the wall. It flashed twice and then beeped.

"Good, you are who you say you are," the BSC man said. "That always makes things easier. Here, you'll need these."

There were some drawers set into the wall next to the sergeant. He reached into one of them and handed Sam a transparent plastic bag containing a set of white overalls. Sam shrugged and pulled them on.

"I'm here to see someone who came in after last night's possession at Stanmore," he said. "Um, obviously I'm not actually technical staff. But I'm ... well, *involved* in the situation so I wonder if you could help me out. Sort of as a favour ..."

"She's in room 33. Through the door at the end of the platform and then eight doors down on the left. If you try to go anywhere else, the system won't let you. If you try to take anything away with you, the system won't let you leave and you'll be immobilised. Clear?"

"Perfectly."

The BSC man nodded and went back to his paper leaving Sam more baffled than ever. There didn't seem much option other than to do as he had been told, however, so he approached the door that the man had indicated. It slid into the wall with a soft hiss as he drew near. The corridor beyond was also entirely white, its light coming from thousands of brilliant pin-pricks in the ceiling. The only noise was a low hum that seemed to come from every side at once. Sam made his way down the corridor, counting the left hand doors as he went along. 27, 29, 31, 33. As he approached the eighth door it also slid noiselessly into the wall, revealing another brilliantly-lit room beyond. Sam took a deep breath and stepped inside.

Smith was lying on her back, unconscious, on a trolley in the centre of the room. She was dressed in a green gown which lay smooth on her flattened stomach. Her hair was pulled back tightly from her face and her skin was so pale that Sam could see the blood pulsing through the veins at her temples. Her lips were drawn back, snarl-like, from her gappy teeth.

She looked so unspeakably ugly that, for a moment, Sam's courage failed him and he was possessed by the urge to run. He leant on the wall to steady himself and slowly counted to ten. Then he gritted his teeth and shuffled forwards to the trolley, extending a shaking finger to touch Smith's cheek. There was a cough from behind him.

"Probably best if you don't actually fondle her in here, dear boy. The techies can get a bit sniffy about that sort of thing. And it goes without saying that we're being watched."

Sam snatched his finger back as if it had been burnt and span round.

Sir Douglas was perched on a steel chair in the corner of the room. He had a delicate china cup in his hand and a matching tea pot at his feet, next to his rucksack. He was also dressed in white overalls but had left them undone, revealing his black uniform beneath.

"What are you doing here?" Sam asked. "I thought you were in Siberia."

Sir Douglas smiled lazily.

"Oh yes, my little sojourn among the elk. Do you know, I'd quite forgotten about all that? Well, Samuel, if I ever was in

Siberia I am now well and truly back, as you can see. I'm here to keep a promise."

"What promise?"

"I wrote you a note saying that when you got back from Stanmore, we'd have a conversation about your commissioning." Sir Douglas sipped his drink and smiled. "Well, here I am. You did extremely well, by the way. A difficult job in some ways, I appreciate that, but you absolutely excelled yourself. We're all very proud of you."

Sam swung away from the old man and looked at Smith again. There was a smear of blood on the side of her neck, about the size of a man's thumb print. He hadn't noticed that before. He felt sick.

"Um, Sir Douglas," he said in a small voice. "I don't think I can talk about my commissioning at the moment, and I'm pretty sure I'd fail any assessment you might set me. I think I've got what Deborah calls *motivational issues* today."

Sir Douglas chuckled.

"I'm sure you have. But you misunderstand me, dear boy. I don't wish to *set* you any assessment, I wish to congratulate you on *passing* one, or at least passing most of one. You're four fifths of the way through your commissioning procedure, Samuel. May I be the first to offer my congratulations?"

The old man produced a second tea cup, wrapped in tissue paper, from his rucksack. He unwrapped it, then filled it with greenish liquid from the teapot and handed it to Sam.

"Well done."

"I ... I don't understand. What's this, by the way?"

"Jasmine tea. Really rather soothing, just the thing for you this morning. It's not quite the moment for a proper drink, is it?"

"I don't understand," Sam said again.

"No, dear boy. No one ever does straight away." Sir Douglas took a packet of cigarettes from his pocket and lit one; the smoke drifted darkly around the bright room. "Samuel, do you know how Hilary died?"

"Hilary Lynch, you mean?"

"Yes, of course I mean Hilary Lynch."

"Um, she died just after Randall, didn't she? Didn't she have a heart attack or something? It was all very sudden, I think, which is why *Soul Freedom* was never properly finished. She died before she wrote the last chapter."

The old man giggled and flicked ash onto the white-tiled floor.

"Yes, I expect a heart attack seemed like the most plausible story. Hilary wasn't exactly healthy, was she? Much as we love her, we can't claim she was any sort of athlete. And in her day you only had one, or possibly two, sets of lungs to get you through, and they were natural." Sir Douglas thumped his own chest appreciatively; it made a hollow, tinny sound. "Yes, I suspect I'd probably have gone for a heart attack as well."

"What do you mean?"

"I mean that she killed herself, Samuel. Our noble founder did herself in with rat poison the day after Randall had his stroke. The heart attack story was a cover-up. What do you think of the tea, by the way?"

Sam sipped the tea again. It tasted soft and sharp at the same time, and filled his throat and nose with a smoky smell.

"Quite nice. Why ... why did she kill herself?"

"Because she knew she'd lost." Sir Douglas ground his cigarette out and flicked the butt into the bin. "When Randall was still alive I think the poor woman believed that she could use her connection with him to mitigate the dreadful excesses, as she saw it, of the Project. She thought that even after '89. She was a romantic old soul in some ways. With Seb dead and gone, however, the Project and the state were firmly in the hands of the next generation. They were ruthless people who hated Hilary's guts because of the privilege she'd won for the Service. Well, the poor woman couldn't live with herself. Think about it: she'd helped create the Project, she'd believed in it devoutly, and now it was entirely out of her control and pursuing a path she regarded as utterly corrupt. In the end the disillusion and the guilt became unbearable so she took the only route open to her and gobbled pills." The old man shrugged. "I know it's tasteless to say it, but it doesn't seem like an unfitting end, does it? There's a chord of melancholy running all through her writing. One might expect the misery to kill her off eventually."

Sam stared at the floor to cover his confusion.

"But look, what has this got to do with my commission?"

"Think, Samuel. Hilary was committed to Anthropology and Posthumanism. She was disillusioned and bitter about the Project's excesses but she still fundamentally believed in *Know Thyself* and *Humanity Refashioned* and so on. As far as we know, she remained a pious sophiocrat until the day she died. Now if *she* was troubled by the work she had to undertake for the Service, she wasn't likely to be the only one, was she? After her death, senior Service officers had to think very hard about how they could stop our people from following her path."

"And how did they do that?"

Sir Douglas sipped some more tea and glanced at Smith. Then he stared straight at Sam.

"Animacide."

"What?"

"Last bit of Latin you've got to learn, dear boy. Animacide means soul murder; it's the moral test you go through before you can receive your commission. In the long run it's animacide that will save you from suicide." The old man paused. "To be blunt, you have to kill your own soul before you can be a commissioned interlander."

"I don't know what you mean."

"The silent place deep inside you, Samuel, where you still secretly believe in good and evil, where you still cling to the idea of virtue and the notion that life somehow *makes sense*: that's what I mean by *soul*—the secret, tender spot where you are still vulnerable to guilt, and unhappiness, and *seriousness*."

Sam opened his mouth to speak but the old man waved him into silence.

"Don't bother protesting that you don't believe in these things. You might say that you don't, but secretly you do. Please don't forget I know you rather well. Now, of course, this *soul* is completely artificial; it's human, it's made up. It wasn't breathed into us by God or spun into us by the Sacred Wheel and it certainly isn't inherent in us as the will-to-progress or whatever the sophiocrats might call it. As interlanders we sense this because we walk in two worlds and feel the power and falsity of both in turn. Within the enclosure we assume an enclosure soul, as it were, and *feel* that the enclosure world is true and meaningful. Outside we assume the souls of good sophiocrats and *feel* that sophiocracy is true and meaningful. We have to, or else we wouldn't be able to do our jobs. But as we slip between the two worlds it gradually dawns on us that both souls are false and artificial. The only moment of truth we know is the moment of crossing over where we are between worlds, where there are no values, no great truths, no meanings. Is any of this making sense, Samuel?

Sam thought for a moment.

"A bit. I mean, I always love crossing over, in either direction. I love the shock of it, and ... and the freedom. And sometimes ... well ... I sometimes wonder whether I ever actually stop pretending, or performing, or whatever, on either side. I'm never sure when I'm actually speaking as myself, from the middle of me. Is that what you mean?"

"Sort of, dear boy. Now, of course, the poor subjects haven't got a clue. As far as they're concerned, their lives are moral and meaningful and they never for a moment suspect that their meaning and morality are entirely artificially constructed. But, Samuel, the great sophiocrats are equally deceived. They're so fascinated by their own power to recast the human spirit that they can't begin to turn their mighty science back on themselves and see that *Know Thyself* and *Humanity Refashioned* and all the rest of their tosh are just as constructed as the Green Man and the Wheel—less *deliberately* constructed maybe, but constructed nonetheless, equally without foundation, equally malleable, equally human." The old man giggled. "Incidentally, do you know how long it took our chaps to legitimise baby cannibalism over in Faylsham in the fifties?"

"No, I didn't know they ..."

"Two and a half months. And this wasn't in famine conditions. Two and a half months to shatter the strongest of conscience's supposed taboos. And the good folk of Faylsham didn't do it regretfully, either. They were roasting and frying and even pickling bits of kids in the end. They even produced a recipe book; I think I still have a copy somewhere."

"But ... but, what was the scientific benefit in that?"

"Oh nothing, that one was just a bit of fun. In fact I think it was to settle a bet. But do you see the point? Human beings will always cling to their sense of morality and meaning, their little illusion of eternity, their soul, even though it changes like the wind. And this applies to Service postulants as much as anyone else. So our forebears' task after Hilary's suicide was to find some way to shake their recruits out of the dangerous illusion of *soul* before any more of them reached for the tablets." The old man sipped his tea delicately and sighed. "It really is delicious, isn't it? The trick is to have the water slightly less than boiling. Remember that. Now then, the solution that the Service came up with was animacide. It's some specific act, tailored to the individual postulant, which forces him to embrace the moral liberty of the boundary in its entirety. It's an act that so directly contradicts one's sense of goodness, that so violates one's imagined meaning, that it becomes almost impossibly painful to maintain such notions. At one quick stroke our successful animacides face the harsh reality that their so-called souls mean rather less to them than a small piece of crafted silver. Our poor brass-buckles don't manage to do the deed, of course. They fall at the final hurdle and so, although they might be excellent postulants in every other respect, we can't let them wander free in the enclosure. They still believe in right and wrong, you see; they hang on to the idea that what we do somehow makes sense. And that makes them irrational and dangerous." Sir Douglas smiled. "But we shouldn't be talking about brass-buckles today, Samuel, because you are most certainly not of their number. You animacided yourself last night with great verve and elegance when you immobilised young Smith here."

Sam's breathing had become quick and shallow. He could not look at Sir Douglas.

"I'm still not sure that I *completely* understand."

"And I rather think that you do. Last night you shot and paralysed the woman who loved you, the woman who gave you food and shelter, and ultimately her own body. Not only that, you exposed her to great terror and then delivered her into the hands of her enemies so that the child you conceived together could be removed from her womb. And you did all of this absolutely freely and in the coldest of cold blood. It was a class animacide by anybody's standards, dear boy, one of the best I've ever constructed, a moment of great beauty. And, notwithstanding poor old Tony and his Elk, you mustn't think I had abandoned you. I was with you every moment in that shop, Samuel, every step of the way. When you pulled the trigger on that immobiliser I felt ... I felt ... well, I felt almost *paternal*."

Sam swallowed hard several times. Finally, he said, "Is she going to be ok?"

Sir Douglas shrugged.

"Smith? I doubt it. She'll get drugs, of course, so she won't remember any details, but she'll know that she's lost her baby and she'll know that something dreadful and demonish has happened to her, and so will the good folk of Stanmore. So no, her life certainly isn't going to be pleasant. I don't know if you're interested, by the way, but the foetus is going to contribute to an alpha child for the Brazilian ambassador." The old man's voice dropped. "Apparently, his Excellency is keen to have something of a rather lighter hue than is generally available at home, although we mustn't speak that aloud, of course."

Sam felt himself begin to sway. He groped his way along the trolley and sat down heavily on the steel chair, his head in his hands.

"At present you feel sick and distressed," Sir Douglas went on gently, "because currently your animacide is a weakness rather than a strength. But that can change, Samuel. In fact, it must change. The final part of your commissioning requires that you *choose* to live your animacide, intentionally and professionally. And for that you'll require this."

The old man took Sam's hand and pressed a small paper packet into it, the size of a sticking plaster. Clumsily, Sam ripped it open. A thin piece of silver-coloured rubber fell into his palm.

"What is it?"

"It's a liberty patch, arguably the most potent Fruit of Sophia ever created, and the one that we keep exclusively for our own officers. It works in conjunction with your animacidal act. Stick it on your arm and, providing you make some small effort to guard your thoughts, you'll have no further trouble with conscience—no guilt, no clinging pointlessly to notions of meaning or goodness. On the contrary, your animacide will come alive within you; you'll come to delight in the common emptiness of both the sophiocrats and the Wheel-worshippers. You'll see through both with increasing clarity as you see through your own self. Your life will be mask upon mask upon mask, dear boy. It will be skipping over differences and knowing the truthlessness of all things. It will be pure freedom and pure, boundless PLAY—play in two beautiful worlds. Now isn't that a wonderful gift?" The old man grinned. "I'm buggered if I can explain the science, of course."

Sam stared at the little patch, then slipped it back into its wrapper and put it in his pocket.

"And is there any way back from this?" he asked quietly. "If ... if I don't put the patch on, can I ever be, you know, *normal*? Or what happens if I put it on but later decide to take it off again?"

Sir Douglas considered for a moment, his head cocked on one side like an owl, his eyes flickering from Smith to Sam and back again.

"Samuel," he said finally, "please look at what you have done to Smith. Really look at her, I mean. Look at the fear on her face and the ugly stains on the bottom of her gown. In truth she's just a little bit repulsive, isn't she, dear boy? That's your handiwork and none of it will ever, ever be undone. Do you understand? Now, of course, you *could* try to muddle on without the patch, you could turn your back on the Service and try to make yourself good and purposeful again, and it goes without saying that we would let you go. Or you could put the patch on and later decide to take it off—such things have been known. But you should know this: the patch is an organic composite. It self-settles into your skin so that it becomes part of your body as well as your mind. We certainly wouldn't let you leave us with such a valuable piece of technology on your person, but neither would we provide a surgeon to remove it. You'd be left alone in the mess with a bottle of whisky and a knife; the pain and the disfigurement would be considerable— just a little something to ensure that you were serious, you see, a leaving present, you might say, a goodbye kiss. But let's suppose you went through with it; you should know this, too: the greater your success in distancing yourself from the Service, the closer would poor Smith draw to you. She'd be waiting for you in every quiet moment, Samuel, every pause in the day, every dream. Rather than being your great strength, your animacide would become your wound and weakness once again. You'd become a miserable, miserable ghost of a man. It takes a very particular sort of foolishness to embrace that level of suffering." The old man sniffed delicately. "But don't take my word for it; think of your own father."

For a long time Sam didn't speak. Then he said, "I don't really want to think of him."

"No."

"In fact, I don't want to think of him at all."

"Dear boy, why on earth would you?"

"He's got a scar on his arm. It's all ridged and twisted. He says he got it from hot oil in the kitchen."

"Does he now?"

Sam reached slowly back into his pocket and withdrew the patch. He stared at it in his palm for a moment, then peeled the paper off its back and rolled up his sleeve, pushing the patch's adhesive side onto his upper arm. For a moment nothing happened and then Sam felt his skin begin to tingle. It dimpled and rolled, and the patch sank slowly into it. When it had sunk about two millimetres the skin spread over it again until only a fine strip of silver was visible at the bottom of a shallow valley in his flesh. There was a burning smell and the tingling had been replaced with a dull ache. The skin of his upper arm now glowed red.

Sir Douglas had looked away as Sam had applied the patch. Now he turned back to him and said gravely:

"Well done, Samuel, very well done. You'll find that it begins to work surprisingly quickly. It's much more than an enhancement; it's a new sort of life. And now I have other presents for you."

The old man reached into his bag again and withdrew a slim envelope and a belt with the familiar two-faced belt buckle, cast in silver. He handed them to Sam, who buckled the belt on and tore open the envelope. Inside was a card embossed with golden gothic script and decorated with a beautiful young woman. She was dressed in a simple robe and had a dove hovering above her head—the goddess Sophia:

"Bloody hell," Sam murmured when he had read the card. "Bloody hell, I wasn't expecting that. It's a wedding invitation." He glanced up at Sir Douglas. "Will I be able to go?"

"Of course you will. You are a commissioned officer of the Interland Security Service. As of now, you're free to send and receive mail, communicate with whomever you wish and travel where you want, inside and outside the enclosure. Obviously we'll have to give you another job for excursions; only your closest family will ever know your real career, but that's easily done. Perhaps one day soon we could have a day in London together. We could go to the theatre and get drunk in dubious pubs, and I could show you where I get my tea. Would that be nice?"

"Yeah, yeah, that would be nice," Sam said. And, unexpectedly, he meant it.

Chapter Thirty-Six
A Perfect Ely Day

Romantic Rush for Reformed Randall Rebel

The talk was of love rather than of politics at the Sophiocratic Temple yesterday as ex fen-libber Roger Moorcroft (22) married his longterm girlfriend Jennifer Catesby (22), a cadet administrator at the Ely Project. Thanks to a special dispensation from the Guardian himself, the happy couple exchanged vows before the Altar of Progress in the temple's central chamber, the first time the altar has been used to solemnise a marriage since Sebastian Randall's own niece tied the knot there forty years ago. The bride, who wore an ivory gown and carried a bouquet of lilies from within the enclosure, was delighted with the arrangement. "We're obviously both thrilled and extremely grateful," she told The Insider. *"My mum and dad are both professionally involved in the Project and know the Guardian a bit, and of course Roger and I now have our own connections with Ely, but, even so, I was flabbergasted when I learnt that we could have the temple. It's my dream come true. It's the icing on the cake of a perfect day—a perfect Ely day."*

The couple met when they were both studying at Randall College, Cambridge, and began dating in their first term. "We realised early on that we had a tremendous amount in common," the groom confirmed. "We both like reading and sport, we enjoy discussing current affairs and we tend to laugh at the same things. It just seemed natural that we should get together."

Current affairs were very nearly the couple's undoing, however, when Mr. Moorcroft allowed himself to be inveigled into last year's rebellion at Bentham and Stump Cross, which left 156 dead. "There are some extremely nasty and manipulative people in the so called fen-liberation movement," Mr. Moorcroft told us. "They are skilled at selecting victims who are likely to be vulnerable to their schemes, perhaps because they're a little thoughtless or naïve, or even a bit lonely. I was suckered in at the last minute to serve as cannon fodder. I suppose I was quite mixed up emotionally at the time. I was certainly very, very foolish. It's something that I bitterly regret and I can only express my gratitude to the Guardian's Office for giving me a second chance." So what does Mr. Moorcroft now think of his former views? *"Infantile and extremely dangerous. Just think of all the Fruit of Sophia: alphas, drones, enhancement technology, longevity technology, mind-monitoring, various degrees of curtailment and so on. And this is only the beginning. Consider the human species we have yet to create, how wise, how strong, how free we are yet to become. How could we possibly throw it all away? And, ironically, having spent a little bit of time in real-space, albeit illegitimately, I know better than most people just how happy the subjects really are. In fact, I wonder whether the fen-libbers aren't actually motivated by envy of enclosure life. I'm just very glad that the rebellion didn't do any lasting damage."*

It was clear from his wife's kisses that any damage done to the relationship has already been thoroughly repaired. "Roger was only very peripherally involved in it all," she explained. "Of course, when I first heard about his involvement I was furious and extremely frightened for him. But now I'm relieved that he has managed to sort himself out, and I'm looking forward to us building a future together. We hadn't planned to get married for another couple of years, but we brought things forward to mark a fresh start—for both of us. After all, even good people do silly, rash things occasionally. It's time to move on."

Mr. Moorcroft has recently been appointed as a history teacher and deputy housemaster at Gormley Independent School for boys, Cambridge, where the couple will make their home.

The marriage party of 500 enjoyed a sumptuous wedding breakfast in the soaring grandeur of the Randall Rooms, adjacent to the temple. Catering costs were no object to the happy couple as Mr. Moorcroft's restaurateur parents undertook to provide the food themselves—a five-course banquet including outside dishes and enclosure delicacies.

"We were determined to do our very best for Roger," an emotional Arthur Moorcroft, the groom's father, said yesterday. "My wife and I are both unspeakably proud of our son. I don't think people realise quite how proud we are, actually."

In a final, ironic twist to the unlikely tale, the groom's younger brother, Samuel Moorcroft (18), is a cadet with the Department of Boundary Security, giving the Moorcrofts an ex-poacher and a trainee gamekeeper in the same family. Samuel told us yesterday: "Roger's obviously been a complete prat but, credit where it's due, he's seen the error of his ways and made efforts to amend. And he's obviously doing something right if he can attract someone as bright and as lovely as Jen."

The journalist finished writing in her note book and glanced up at Sam. She was chewing her pen and frowning.

"I wonder if we should lose the *arse*," she said. "It's not good to refer to someone as a *complete arse* in a piece about his own wedding, especially as this is meant to be about everything settling down again after the rebellion. *Arse* seems too contentious. Could we put something a bit milder? How about *prat*?"

Sam shrugged.

"Put what you like. He's more of an arse than a prat, but if you've got to make everything smooth and lovely, then you'd better do what you've got to do. It doesn't make much odds to me."

"Yeah, I think we'd better have *prat*. Thanks for the quote."

"Pleasure."

The journalist snapped her notebook shut and tucked it in her pocket, then made her way across the dance floor to the bar. There were a few flesh and blood guests dancing, as well as a large number of holograph fenlanders who were being projected into the Randall Rooms from a contemporaneous wedding at Swaffham. The music came alternately from a holograph folk band at the enclosure wedding and a proper, outside disco. At the moment it was the holograph's turn. They were singing about a foolish groom who drank too much beer on his wedding day and ended up being thrown out of bed by his wife and sleeping in the cow shed. The song was provoking great hilarity among the women—holograph and real. Sam stared gloomily at the band and hoped that the disco would start again soon.

"Hello you."

Sam span round.

"Oh, hi Rache. You all right?"

"Yeah, I'm fine. I don't feel that I've seen you all day."

"I know. I'm sorry. It's just there are loads of people here who I haven't spoken to since I got myself in trouble. I've had to go around reassuring all my aunties and cousins and everyone that I'm respectable again. Anyway, have you enjoyed it all?"

"Yes, I suppose so. Well, in a way." Rachel frowned. "It's all been ever so posh and ... well ... establishment, hasn't it? I don't know if it feels quite *Roger* somehow. You know, the ceremony..."

"Yeah, I know, was it really necessary to have 'My Guardian's Heart' *and* 'Song for Sophia'?" Sam smiled. "I suppose they feel they have to make it clear just what loyal sophiocrats they are."

"But Roger can't actually *enjoy* that sort of thing, can he? A couple of years ago he'd have sung all the rude words to the songs and had a laugh at this bloody folk band as well. And now he's got it all at his own wedding! People don't change *that* much, do they?"

"I don't know. He did have a very lucky escape, Rache."

They were silent for a couple of minutes. Then, as the band finally flickered off and the music stopped, they spoke together:

"Sam, I just wanted to say..."

"I've been meaning to ask you, Rache..."

They both stopped and giggled, and then Sam said, "Go on, you go first."

"Look, Sam. I haven't properly seen you since that awful night with, you know, Roger and me. And, to be honest, I haven't really spoken much to Roger since, either..."

"I didn't know that."

"Yeah," Rachel said lightly. "He more or less ended it, whatever *it* was, as soon as you vanished. He couldn't face seeing me after that. Anyway, that doesn't matter now. The point is, I felt guilty about the whole Roger thing anyway. You know I'm not a complete cow and I really do like Jen, so obviously I felt dreadful about it all. But that was nothing compared to how I felt after you left. I felt absolutely horrible, I really did. I can't describe how awful it was. I had to spend ages on the clip before the guilt even began to fade. I just ... I just wanted to say that all that stuff I said on your birthday about, you know, liking you, or loving you and everything. Well, I meant it, Sam. The last thing I wanted to do was to hurt you. Honestly."

"It all seems a tremendously long time ago," Sam said slowly. "I know I felt crap at the time. But an awful lot's happened since then. Nothing's the same. I'm fine, really."

Rachel grinned at him.

"I'm glad about that. Because I'd hoped we could be, well, *friends* again. Life's less interesting without you around to boss about. I miss you, Sam. I mean, I know you're very busy and important now with the Department of Boundary Security or whatever it is, but..."

"It would be nice to see a bit more of you, Rache, even though I *am* so busy and important. I think I've missed you, too, in a way."

"Good. So come on then, let's start as we mean to go on. Have you met anyone on your adventures? You've turned into quite an attractive bloke, in a weird, aloof sort of way. And you're a bit dangerous as well now, aren't you? You're an ex-outlaw. I should think they're flocking."

Sam lit a cigarette and frowned.

"There was someone for a bit, but it ended. Well, I ended it. And now I'm not really with anyone. They're certainly not flocking. There's a woman at work called Ruth and sometimes we do things together. She's all right; she's quite posh, actually, a bit intense. But basically I'm quite happy on my own."

"Fair enough. I don't believe a word of it, of course, but I've got plenty of time to grind you down and find out the truth."

Just then the disco started again. Rachel leaned in closer to Sam and shouted into his ear, "What was it you wanted to ask me?"

"Oh yeah. You know that bloke you came with?"

"Bartholomew? Yes, he's over there talking to your brother. What about him?"

"Is he actually your boyfriend?"

Rachel smiled.

"Well, let's just say we *do things* together. And for various reasons I didn't fancy coming to this on my own, so I brought him along."

"He's very big, isn't he?"

"Yeah, I suppose so."

"And he's got lovely broad shoulders and strong-looking legs and a nice bum."

Rachel began to blush. "Yeah, yeah, he has."

"And you'd have to say he was a handsome chap, wouldn't you?

"Well, obviously *I* think so, Sam."

"Is he an alpha by any chance, Rache?"

Rachel's blush deepened and she giggled into her drink.

"He bloody is, isn't he?"

"Yeah, all right, he is. But he's ok; they're not all arrogant idiots, you know. He doesn't belong to any of those horrible dining groups or anything, and he doesn't look down on standard people. He's got quite a few standard friends."

"Bloody hell, Rachel, an alpha! Where did you meet him?"

Rachel glanced around.

"There are websites where women who, you know, *like* alphas can get together with alpha men who fancy standards. I use the biggest one, *Standard Honies - Alpha Guys*, but there are several others. It's not really approved of because of all the genetic stuff. But no one ever seems to get into trouble. I believe that even some government people are alpha-chasers."

"But what's in it for them? I mean, you're nice looking, Rache, but you're not exactly alpha quality, are you?"

"Thanks very much Sam; I just said you were attractive!"

"Well, you said I was *quite* attractive in a weird, aloof way!"

"Still counts." Rachel smiled and shook her head. "I dunno why they do it, really. Power? Superiority? Wanting something rough and imperfect for a change? Perhaps they even feel a bit guilty about who they are. It's not something you go into, Sam. You just email each other, then send pictures and talk a bit on the phone or the holograph, and if you think you might get on, you meet up. It's more common than you'd think."

"What do you mean you talk on the phone or the holograph? What do you talk about to an alpha before you've even met him?"

Rachel rolled her eyes. She hooked her hair behind her ear and drained her glass.

"Bloody hell, do I have to spell it out? Look Sam, I don't want to marry any of them. I just want a bit of fun. I think I'm entitled to that after all the crap with Roger and then you disappearing. At least it's all honest and straightforward with Bartholomew, even if it's technically not quite legal. Now stop asking embarrassing questions and dance with me before that stupid folk band start again."

"Are you sure Bartholomew won't mind?"

"I doubt he'll even notice, and if he does he won't give a toss. Trust me, it's really not that kind of relationship."

Later on, when Sam was standing near the bar, a pair of drones on glass-collecting duty bumped into him, causing him to step backwards onto someone's foot. He span round and found himself face to face with his mum. Now that the meal was over Mrs. Moorcroft had finally abandoned her chef's whites and was wearing a purple dress that flowed over her like a crumpled parachute. An explosion of white and yellow flowers was pinned to her chest.

"Sorry, sorry. Oh, it's you, Mum, hi. Sorry about that. You look nice."

"I don't, Sammy, I look ridiculous, but it's kind of you to lie." Mrs. Moorcroft shoved her glasses up her glistening nose and gulped her drink. "Anyway, are you enjoying yourself?"

"Yeah, it's not bad. The food was really nice. How about you, are you having a good day?"

"Oh, it could be worse when you consider that I'm spending it in a place that makes my flesh crawl, watching my son marry a woman I dislike, who comes from a family I detest and who regard me as a fat nonentity. *And* I have to pretend to bloody like them. God knows what he sees in her but there we are. Yes, considering all that, Sammy, it's not been too bad a day." Mrs. Moorcroft took another gulp of her drink. "Sorry, I probably shouldn't be saying that to you, should I? You can blame it on the Malibu."

Sam was quiet for a moment. Then he said:

"It doesn't matter, Mum. I don't think we have to please each other anymore, do we? All that's finished with."

"Yes, I suppose it is."

The pair of them stood in silence as the party flowed around them. Eventually Sam said, "I haven't seen much of Dad, by the way. Is he ok?"

"Your father is embarrassed about speaking to you, Sam. He thinks he's let you down. In fact, he thinks he's let both you and Roger down. He won't admit it, of course, but I know him too damn well for him to keep it secret. Whenever the subject of you, or Roger, or Ely comes up the poor man's stutter gets worse and worse, until eventually he finds some excuse and changes the subject. It's just like the days after he left all over again. It's absolutely awful for him." Mrs. Moorcroft frowned and stared at her feet. When she looked up again her eyes were glistening with tears. "It's not bloody true, though, Sammy. It isn't true at all. Your father is an incredibly brave man, and he's a very, very good man. And he hasn't let anybody down. Whatever lies you might swallow, don't you dare believe any different."

"Nobody's suggesting that Dad has let me down, Mum."

"Aren't they? Not even that poisonous little man in charge of you all? What does he say about Arthur these days, I wonder?" Mrs. Moorcroft shrugged helplessly. "Oh, there's no point in talking to you about it, is there? Look Sammy, you're my son and you'll always, always be welcome at home. I'll do literally anything I can to help you, particularly if you want to *change course*. But don't ever, ever, ever ask me to betray any of the people I love, even in thought. Do you understand?"

"I've never asked you to betray anyone, Mum," Sam said. "And Sir Douglas Latch, who I assume you were referring to, is not poisonous. He's given me gifts that you and Dad could never give me. And he's never made me feel small or pathetic or ... or *overwhelmed* me. He's treated me well. You might not approve of that, but it's true all the same. He also made it possible for me to save Roger, incidentally."

Mrs. Moorcroft stared at Sam. She opened her mouth to speak and then closed it again. She shook her head fiercely, wiped her eyes with her purple sleeve and turned on her heel.

Later still, as the music became louder and the dancing more furious, Sam nestled himself in a dark corner where the towering glass and chrome of the Randall Rooms abutted the warm stone of the temple. He sipped his beer and allowed his gaze to sweep up the glittering columns to the glass ceiling high above. There were stars glimmering in the cold winter sky, no street lights to dim them in Ely, of course. The city was surrounded on all sides by the enclosure, so it had to stay dark.

"Spectacular building, isn't it?"

Sam looked round and saw that the voice belonged to Jen's dad. He was carrying two pints of beer, one of which he held out to Sam.

"A little bird tells me that you enjoy this stuff. Nothing wrong with that of course, especially for someone in your line of work. Almost *de rigueur* for you lot, isn't it?"

"Oh, thanks." Sam took the beer. "Um, which little bird told you that?"

Mr. Catesby tapped the side of his nose self-importantly.

"The same one who told me what a splash you've made with the powers that be. The old rascal himself thinks highly of you, I believe."

"Yes, well, I generally enjoy life at the Department of Boundary Security," Sam said formally. "Obviously it's pretty busy, but there are plenty of rewards and, you're right, we all play hard as well as work hard."

The older man surveyed Sam with twinkling, confident eyes and then burst out laughing. He was still laughing a minute later when Jen glided over.

"Well, I'm glad you two are getting on so well."

"Indeed we are, Jen," Mr. Catesby said. "Your brother-in-law and I were just chatting about how much he enjoys his work with the Department of Boundary Security."

Jen grinned.

"Oh, I see. Sam, I really hope we might get to work together before too long, you know, on a possession or something." She leaned in closer to him. "My lot work quite closely with the *Department of Boundary Security* from time to time." She made little quotation marks with her fingers as she spoke the department's name. "Obviously we all regard you with absolute awe. I never tell anyone that I've got a relative who's actually a member of *your lot*, but often I'm itching to."

Sam smiled.

"It would be great to work with you, Jen. I'm still grateful to you for taking me to the Project in the first place, and getting me *Soul Freedom*, of course. I've never really said thank you, have I?"

Jen hugged Sam.

"Oh, you're such a lovely man, Sam, I'm so glad you're my brother. Come on, put your drink down and dance with me." Her voice dropped almost to a whisper. "Dance with me like you've danced on the *inside*. Daddy can find one of his government friends to talk to, can't you, Daddy?"

Mr. Catesby nodded and beamed, and Sam followed Jen out onto the dance floor where the folk band was playing again. Jen danced with great energy, her arms flying in all directions, her whole body twisting and swaying to the music. Opposite her, Sam jigged about self-consciously.

"So solemn, Sam," Jen said as she twirled towards him. "Ever since I met you, always so solemn, even today." She span away from him, clapping her hands high above her head and kicking one leg into the air.

"I'm not really solemn," Sam said as she span back towards him. "I'm just a bit of a crap dancer, that's all."

Jen shook her head. She placed her hands on his shoulders and wriggled up to him.

"Two years ago you were a solemn little boy, Samuel Moorcroft, and now you've turned into a solemn young man. There's no need, you know; we're through all the horrible stuff with you and Roger. We're done with all that. Things are ok now."

She span away again, faster this time, so that her skirt whirled up almost to her thighs. Then the tune abruptly stopped and she stepped back to Sam, slipping her arms round his waist and pulling him close.

"Don't be solemn today," she whispered. "Be happy for me. It's my wedding day, Sam, please be happy for me."

After midnight the music slowed and, fearful that he might be cajoled into a slow dance, Sam slipped through the high silver doors at the north end of the Randall Rooms. The outside air was sharp and pleasing against his skin and his breath drifted up into the darkness in white clouds. He turned up his jacket collar against the cold and lit a cigarette, enjoying the solitude and the soft sounds of the night. Presently he heard the doors swish open again. He turned round.

"Oh, it's you.

"I'm afraid so, Sam. You've done jolly well to avoid me so far, but now here I am. The proverbial bad penny. Awkward of me, isn't it?" Roger breathed in deeply and slipped a thin envelope from beneath his jacket. "I suppose I should say thank you for saving my neck. The Guardian's Office made it clear that it was ultimately your decision. And thanks for coming today, I know it's made Jen very happy."

"I was surprised to be invited, frankly."

"Well, you are my brother, Sam, despite everything. Blood's thicker than water and all that." Roger looked sideways at Sam, who continued to smoke silently. He went on,

"Strange to think we've made Ely an island again—all those subjects hemming us in on every side; talking or sleeping or making love while we're perched, unimagined, in the middle of them all, like ghosts. It's a funny feeling, isn't it?"

"Shouldn't you be inside with your wife, Roger?"

"Oh, don't worry about her. She's perfectly happy. She's got important government people to schmooze, friends of Mummy's and Daddy's. It's important for an ambitious cadet to make the correct impression. And to be honest, since a certain incident with a crossbow, I'm not much of a dancer. Anyway, I wanted to speak to you."

"I don't know why you wanted to speak to me. I can't think of a single thing we have in common."

"Well, I can think of something: we're both rather fond of the same woman."

Sam opened his mouth to protest but Roger waved him into silence.

"I'm not talking about Rachel. If you think I'd even look at a woman who's happy to have sex with an alpha you're very much mistaken. Do you know how they make those things?"

"Yes, actually I do."

"Yeah, I suppose you would. I thought better of Rachel, frankly."

Roger was overtaken by a bout of coughing. He struggled to catch his breath, and then said quietly, "No, I wasn't talking about Rachel. I was talking about Hilary Lynch."

"Hilary. What do you mean Hilary? What on earth do you know about Hilary?"

"Rather a lot, Sam." Roger gagged and shuddered then spat on the floor. "For instance, I know that she was one of us."

"I don't know what you mean."

Roger didn't speak for a few moments. He stood staring into the darkness, breathing quickly, with his hands clenched at his sides. Finally, he said in a rush, "She was one of us, Sam, or rather she was one of me. She came to hate sophiocracy and the Project with absolute conviction, and she wasn't afraid to take up arms to resist them. She was a brave, brave woman. Believe me, I admire her just as much as you do, probably more."

By the time Roger had finished speaking he was visibly shaking and his head kept nodding forwards.

"Are you ok?" Sam asked flatly, "because you aren't supposed to be talking like this. You know perfectly well that your thoughts are being monitored; if you carry on they'll paralyse you and you'll be lifted at your own wedding."

"Not true, Sam," Roger mumbled. "Our people have drugs that help you isolate selected thoughts in one part of your brain. If you think them quickly and keep them in one place you can confuse the sensor." He tapped the small cylinder that was fixed beneath the skin behind his right ear.

"What do you mean *our people*?"

"Rebels. Fen-libbers. We have our own techno-surgical people and they're just as good as the government ones. In fact, some of them *are* government ones. They've been helping me since I was fitted with the tag so that I can keep some of my thoughts private and carry on working for the organisation. It's not easy to do. Apart from anything else you feel bloody sick and lose your balance whenever you try it."

Roger stopped speaking abruptly and screwed his eyes tight shut. His breath was quick and shallow and his face was covered in sweat.

"But why, Roger? Why are you bothering with this crap anymore and ... and why are you telling me about it?"

"Read this," Roger croaked. He thrust the envelope that he was carrying into Sam's hand. "It's the final chapter of *Soul Freedom*. There are very few copies around, and they're only circulated privately, among sympathisers—all on paper, of course. I hope it might help you see things differently."

Sam waited for his feet to begin walking back towards the Randall Rooms where he could speak to security and arrange for Roger to be arrested. It was his duty to do so immediately. If he hesitated he would become an accessory to treason. He waited and waited, but his feet failed to move. Instead, he watched as Roger's breathing returned to normal and he stopped shaking. Finally, he said, "Roger, I know you always think you understand absolutely everything, but just for once accept that you might have got something wrong." Sam's voice dropped to a whisper. "*Soul Freedom* was never finished because *Hilary killed herself* straight after Randall died. That's not generally known but, trust me, it's true. So whatever this rubbish is, it's not the last chapter of *Soul Freedom*. Now for God's sake, try and think normal, happy stuff and in a minute we'll go back inside. I'll chuck this away and we'll pretend the conversation never happened."

Roger wiped the sweat from his face and glared at Sam.

"Did you believe it when they told you that Hilary committed suicide?" he spat. "Knowing what you know about her, did you really believe that she killed herself because she couldn't face the thought of the world without Sebastian Randall, a man whom she held in contempt? Are you so convinced that Sir Douglas bloody Latch knows everything?"

"*Hilary died at the same time as Randall, Roger.* Everyone knows that. Now for God's sake, pull yourself together. It's your wedding day!"

"Just read the chapter, Sam."

The strength drained from Roger. He collapsed against Sam, who stumbled and lowered the pair of them slowly to the floor. Roger moaned and curled up on his side. He closed his eyes again.

"Do you know what I'm thinking about to ... to try and control my th...thoughts?" he whispered after a couple of minutes.

"No, of course I don't."

"I'm thinking about the night you caught me with Rachel. I'm thinking about how *empty* you looked when I spoke to you, sort of hollow, as if I could have flicked you and you'd have drifted away into the dark. And I'm also thinking about how sick Rachel looked the next day when I spoke to her, and how worried she was about you. You two made a great pair of friends, didn't you, and I buggered that up completely." Roger levered himself into a sitting position and smiled crookedly. "I find that shame is pretty good for concealing seditious thoughts. I don't suppose it's an emotion the sophiocrats recognise—puts the monitors right off the scent."

"That's all extremely touching," Sam said sharply. "But if you're still somehow anti-Ely, we're on opposite sides. I've made my choices. You know that."

Roger shook his head violently.

"No, Sam, not your choices. I drove you crazy enough to run away and become ... become ... what you are. I owe you the opportunity to change. You'd be a great asset to us."

"But I'm *not going to change*," Sam said. "It's your wedding day and you're outside, shivering on the grass and facing arrest because you're still stupid and arrogant enough to think you can make me do what you want."

"Believe me, Sam, I'm doing my very best not to be arrogant. Please read the chapter. You admire Hilary; if she helps you to see what I can see, perhaps we can talk about it again."

"*But there's nothing to talk about.* I'm an officer in the ... well, you know what I am. And you're a respectable teacher who's married to an Ely cadet." Sam tapped the envelope, "Even if this stuff is what you say it is, you don't believe it anymore."

Roger leant forward and spat onto the floor again, then he began to hum *Humpty Dumpty* softly with his eyes closed. When he had finished, he turned to Sam.

"I've married Jen because she can't help herself from passing on classified material to me. She's rather coy about it now, which makes me want to puke: 'you aren't going to be naughty again, are you, dear?' that sort of thing. But in the end she always tells me what I need to know. She's so self-important she can't help it. That's why I went out with her in the first place, Sam. She's one of the best-connected sophiocrats of her generation, so she's extremely useful for the organisation I work for. It's also why I couldn't let you tell her about Rachel and me, incidentally. It was a critical time; then more than ever I needed the silly cow to think I loved her."

"Don't you love her?"

"Of course I don't love her! How could I possibly love a monster like that? Oh, I suppose I used to feel a bit of sympathy for her before she actually started work at Ely. After all, she couldn't help her family any more than we could. But that's long gone. Sometimes when she touches me and I think about what her hands have been doing at work that day, it's all I can do not to break her wrists." Roger smiled grimly. "Still, I suppose I've got off lightly. There are worse things to do for the organisation than go to bed with a pretty woman. I'm not faithful to her, of course. That helps."

Roger had begun to shake again as he was speaking and now he leant forwards and vomited onto the grass. He remained with his head between his legs, shivering.

"You're not much of an advert for your cause." Sam said.

"I know I'm not," Roger mumbled. "I wish I were, but I'm not. I'm selfish and shallow. You know that better than anyone. But even I know that I have a duty to resist evil. And I know that all that," Roger jerked his thumb towards the temple, "is the most evil thing that humanity has ever devised. And because I love you, Sam, I'm not prepared to give up on you. I'm afraid that I'm not going to let you go." Roger levered himself to his feet and closed his eyes again. Then he said very quickly: "Look, you've got the chapter. It's up to you what you do with it. If you get caught with it, you'll be tortured and curtailed. If you turn me in, I'll be tortured and then killed. If you choose to read it, you might just find a different perspective and a bit of courage. Now if you'll excuse me, I have to rejoin my beautiful and talented wife."

He wiped his mouth with his handkerchief and stumbled back towards the Randall Rooms. Sam followed him.

"But you must know that you can't win," he said. "You can't possibly beat them. You'll just cause more pain."

"I used to think it all was about winning," Roger said. "But since that fiasco at Bentham I've come to see that winning's not quite the point. A rising in each generation, that's all we aim for, Sam, enough to show them that love and decency and rebellion are not quite dead and buried. That's the real reckoning. And as for causing pain," Roger shrugged, "well, let's just say that in this context I don't think that causing pain is necessarily a bad thing."

The brothers had reached the high silver doors to the Randall Rooms. Roger paused with his hand on the door handle and steadied himself.

"How do I look, Sammy?"

"Ok."

"Not too sicky?"

"No, you look pale and shaky, like you might be a bit drunk."

"Excellent." Roger smiled. "What is it you lot say: *In Duobis Mundis Ambulare*? I know you all regard it as a great big thrill, but, personally, little brother, I just find it a total pain in the arse."

And then, without waiting for a reply, he straightened his tie and pulled the door open wide, flooding the pair of them with light and music.

Sam quickly slipped the envelope under his jacket.

Chapter Thirty-Seven
The Final Chapter

"Trepanning."

"What?"

"Trepanning, it's an old Anthropology and Posthumanism procedure." Sam gulped a mouthful of beer and leant across the table, lowering his voice. "I read about it in the paper library. But when I say old, I mean it's *really old*—not just before the Project, but before Randall and Hilary, right back in the earliest days. What they'd do is drill a hole in a subject's skull and monitor his behaviour and brain activity before and after."

"Bloody hell fire!" Simeon's hand drifted to his head where Sam had struck it. "I didn't think they could get away with stuff like that back then."

"They could, Sim," Ruth said gently. "Right from the start they could do almost anything. Back in empire days they had people from the colonies to use as subjects, after the war they had the camp inmates, and then they had the Project. One way or another they've always had heads to drill into." She turned to Sam. "Anyway, what happened to people who got, whatever it was, trepanned?"

"I know it sounds bizarre, but apparently most of them liked it. It was like their minds got lighter, or *fizzier*, some of them said—something to do with reducing the pressure on the brain. Some of them asked to have it done again and again, so that they ended up with skulls like sieves."

"And you honestly reckon that's what your animacide feels like?" Simeon asked quietly.

Sam lit a cigarette and nodded.

"Well, it feels more like that than anything else I've ever heard of. I seem to have more energy than I did before and I feel as if I'm less anchored to the earth somehow, like gravity's eased off me a bit. And although things still irritate me, nothing ever hurts right inside anymore. Do you know what I mean? Everything's sort of *cool* or *numb*. It's a bit like the clip, I suppose, only more subtle and about a thousand times stronger. What about you?"

Simeon helped himself to one of Sam's cigarettes and glanced around the mess. It was Saturday evening and the place was filling up with interlander officers as well as some of the new intake of postulants. Beer and the conversation were flowing freely.

"Remember the first time we met?" he murmured to Sam.

"Yeah, we tried to kill each other."

"No, not that; we didn't really meet then, did we? I mean after the meetin' with Sir Douglas, when you asked me what it was like crossin' over outwards."

"Yeah, course I remember it."

"At the time I said it was like fallin' into the dark. Well, that's changed since my animacide. I don't feel like I'm fallin' anymore. Now I feel like I'm flyin', and I sort of like it. It's still dark and there's still nothin' to hold onto, but now I don't expect to land anywhere and I'm sort of happy with the darkness. I didn't feel like that straightaway, of course, not after..."

Simeon stopped abruptly and gulped his beer. It wasn't done to discuss animacide too freely. ISS officers had all sorts of ways to speak about the procedure: *the black gift, the silver gift, the change, the welcoming, getting made, getting the key to the door.* The proper term was used sparingly. Also, no one ever mentioned the form of their own animacidal act, and it was considered extremely offensive to pry into anyone else's, however obliquely. An officer's animacide was deeply personal, to be guarded with a mixture of shame and pride. "We try to respect one another's darkness," as Sir Douglas had put it to Sam.

The mess door swung open and Laura strode in. She glanced around before hurrying over to the three friends. Like Sam, Simeon and Ruth, she was dressed in enclosure costume.

"Sorry I'm late," she said. "We had a code green over at Cromer. Obviously I had to hang around."

"Gosh, who was it? Are they getting a run?" Ruth asked.

"No, nothing to get excited about. It was just some mad old bloke who'd got funny about a teenage lad over there. He's already been picked up and curtailed. Anyway, are you lot ready?"

"Yeah. Well, Sim and I are. Sam still insists he's not coming."

Laura glared at him.

"Oh, come on Sam, don't be such a misery. We've all been working hard. We deserve a bit of fun. And Lincoln's brilliant on a Saturday night. There are loads of bands and food stalls round the temple close, all lit up with torches. And there're some great inns just down the hill as well, with dancing and gaming pretty much all night. Deborah said she might bring a couple of the best new postulants over later on, so we can show off a bit. Oh, please come. You'll like it. I swear you get a better class of subject up among the Lincoln folk. The gene pool is just a little bit deeper than hereabouts. Husbands and wives actually look dissimilar. It makes all the difference."

Simeon growled softly and Ruth reached out and stroked his arm.

"She only says it to annoy, Sim, don't give her the satisfaction. Are you sure we can't persuade you, Sam?"

Sam stubbed out his cigarette.

"Sorry, not tonight. Normally I'd love to, you know I would. But tonight there's something else I've got to do."

"Gosh, look at him go all mysterious," Ruth said. "This something else wouldn't have anything to do with a woman, would it?"

"Yes. Sort of."

"Well, then, we won't pry. Come on, Sim, drink up and let's get going."

Simeon drained his glass.

"Have a good night, mate. I hope this woman, whoever she is, is worth missing an evenin' with your friends for."

"So do I, Sim. Have a good time."

Sam watched as his three friends left the mess. He lingered over the rest of his drink and then, 10 minutes later, he also slipped out. He took the lift to the nearest minirail platform where a single attendant was on duty:

"Limeport Southwest, please," Sam said. "Just me."

"Fair enough. You can hop into that one there, if you like."

Sam clambered into the car and buckled himself in. The attendant punched the keypad on the wall and the car shot into the tunnel. Three minutes later, it hissed to a halt at an empty platform. Sam climbed out and walked down the echoing concrete to the lifts. The doors of one of them opened automatically on Sam's approach. As Sam stepped inside, the doors slid shut again and the lift ascended quickly. A minute later, the doors opened and Sam found himself in a whitewashed chamber with four low passages leading off it. At the centre of the chamber was a BSC guard post where two BSC officers, a man and a woman, were playing cards. They glanced up as Sam stepped out of the lift:

"Good lord," the man said. "We've only gone and got ourselves a customer, Judy—and on a Saturday night as well. Wonders will never cease. Now then, young man, what can we do for you?"

"My name is Samuel Moorcroft," Sam said casually. "I'm an ISS officer. I'm going up to Faggle End for the evening."

"You are, are you? And what you planning to do up there?"

"Just going to have something to eat and maybe go for a walk on the beach. I fancy being on my own for a bit. '

"The young lad fancies being on his own, Judy," the BSC man said. "Says he wants to go for a bit of a walk or something. And on a Saturday night as well. Seems a bit odd, doesn't it?"

"ISS *are* a bit odd, Sergeant," the woman giggled, "even the sweet-lookin' ones like this kid."

"Yeah, but this is *really* odd, wouldn't you say? On his own, on a Saturday night. Doesn't seem quite right, does it?"

Sam's throat suddenly felt dry. He was sharply aware of the slim package tucked into his trousers beneath his shirt. It was unheard of for the BSC to detain or search an interlander at the boundary, but technically they had the authority to do so. And jurisdictional issues were always sensitive...

"It's not really that odd," Sam said quickly. "I've spent all week in the company of my brilliant colleagues; the last thing I want is to be stuck with a bunch of them on Saturday night, especially when they're drunk. There're only so many stories of adventure and heroism on the inside that you can listen to without wanting to throw up."

The man stared hard at Sam and then grinned.

"I think you might be in the wrong team, young man; that was spoken like a true boundary man. Through you come, then; just do your eyes for me and bung your signature down here, if you don't mind."

"Happy to, Sergeant."

Sam allowed himself to be retina-checked and then signed the logbook where the sergeant indicated.

"You know the way?" the sergeant asked.

"Yeah, I've been once before."

"Well, have yourself a good night, then. And remember, if you ever decide to swap your black uniform for a blue one, I reckon there's definitely a place for you."

Sam smiled weakly and set off down one of the passages, taking care not to rustle the papers beneath his shirt as he went.

It took 15 minutes to reach the vertical tunnel and iron ladder that led to the Faggle End cottage. When Sam arrived, he stopped and listened to check that he wasn't being followed, then climbed upwards as quickly as he could without looking down. The locking wheel on the boundary lock's outer door was well-greased and span easily. Sam swung the door to one side and climbed through, pulling it back into place and re-locking it behind him. The upper door opened equally easily; Sam scrambled through and hoisted himself up into Faggle End.

Evening sunlight was streaming through the west windows, bathing the cottage in soft gold. Sam closed his eyes and felt the warmth playing on his face. He breathed deeply for few moments while he adjusted to the fact that he had once again crossed over. Then he secured the boundary lock behind him and pulled the bundle of paper from under his shirt. He uncrumpled it and placed it reverently on the table in the centre of the room before walking to the small cooking area. There was a faded, hand-written note pinned to the door of the larder.

*Faggle End cottage is maintained for the use of **all** commissioned Service personnel. Therefore, please think of* *others. Clean up after yourself, and if you use any food, make sure that you arrange with the householder committee to have the stores restocked.*

Also, if the flowers on Hilary's photograph are dead or dying, please replace them. Fresh flowers are the very least we owe our founder; without her courage and guile we would not be free to enjoy Faggle End's beauty and tranquillity at all.

Inside the larder there were some vegetables, pasta, cheese, bread, butter, lemonade and beer. Sam made a cheese sandwich, added a thick layer of yellow pickle from the jar he found on a shelf above the sink, and poured himself a pint of shandy. He took his food back to the table and sat down.

He contemplated the pile of paper in silence. The first sheet read simply *Soul Freedom, Chapter 36: At Faggle End. In which the author outlines her death.* They were the only words of the document Sam had read so far, and they made him queasy about continuing. In the months since the wedding he had twice retrieved the papers from their hiding place beneath his mattress and taken them to the fire in his room. He had got as far as holding them over the flames, but had found himself unable to burn them. In his mind Hilary was something between parent, tutor, friend and heroine. The thought of destroying any of her writing revolted him. The thought of reading Chapter 36 disturbed him almost as much, however.

Finally, and quite unexpectedly, the idea had popped into his head that he should read the papers at Faggle End. It seemed fitting to read the document at the place where it was supposed to have been written. Also, things that were illegal or distressing on the outside never seemed quite so threatening inside the boundary. If the document was too dangerous or too dreadful to be contemplated, he could simply destroy it at the cottage and cross back over. The whole incident would then belong within the enclosure and could be forgotten. Certainly he would never raise the topic again with Roger.

Sam glanced around the little room and noticed that the flowers attached to the picture of Hilary were dry and brown, their petals scattered on the rough floor. That was bad. He half stood to attend to them and then sat down again. He picked up

his sandwich and lifted it to his mouth, and then put it down
untouched. He patted his pockets until he found his cigarettes.
He lit one and smoked it quickly to the butt. Finally, he turned
over the first page and began to read:

*Mendel III is dead, so I know that the poison works. I have
buried him in a shallow grave in Turner's Field immediately
behind the cottage. He used to love the field in summer, rolling
around on his back among the dandelions and coarse grass
until his eyes glazed in delight and the fur on his stomach was
soft and dusty with heat. I hope he is at peace there.*

*Good Lord, dear reader, listen to me. My journey into
sentimentality and folly is complete. Hilary, my dear, Mendel
III is neither at peace, nor is he at unpeace (or whatever the
word is). He is dead; he is carbon; he has ceased to be.*

*I bought a trowel for the internment but my wrists are now
too weak to wield the thing effectively. For a moment, kneeling
over Mendel's little corpse with my wrists aching, I nearly
wept. But then I pulled myself together and scraped out the
hole with my hands, scrabbling away like a demented mole.
Now there is dirt under my fingernails and my hands smell of
damp soil. If the manuscript becomes smudged, dear reader,
forgive me.*

*This is my final testimony, the last chapter of my
autobiography,* Soul Freedom. *The rest of the work is arranged
in my rooms where it will be discovered by Service colleagues
when they receive my suicide note. There are instructions that
it should be published as soon as possible.*

*This chapter will not be found in my rooms, however.
Instead, it will reach certain persons at Cambridge whom I
believe may be receptive to its message. There is a female don
whose smile conveys only contempt for me when I occasionally
return to dine (and how I love her for it!); a professor whom I
once spotted smirking when a pigeon defecated on the statue of
Sebastian that now graces Randall's main court; another
whom I believe I once heard humming* One Nation Once Again
*after the port had flowed rather too freely. Do these people
recognise some spark of dissent in one another, I wonder? Do
they ever meet in secret to speak the unspeakable? Do they*

perhaps identify undergraduates who might sympathise with their views? I cannot know. I can only hope that my reflections might galvanise them in some way. Since 1989 the fen-liberation movement has been moribund; perhaps a call to arms from the heart of the sophiocratic establishment will help to inspire a new generation to resistance. I certainly hope so. It gives me tremendous satisfaction to think of Seb's own city, his own college, incubating opposition to his grand design.

One does not have to be a distinguished thinker to appreciate that human society has always been divided on the basis of social position or class. A cursory reading of the history books makes the fact plain enough. In Greece and Rome there was slave and free, in feudal Europe there was lord and vassal, in modern Europe there was bourgeoisie and labourer. The sultans had their emirs, slaves and eunuchs. The great cultures of the East had their administrative class, their merchants and their serfs. Within any given society there will always be groups who enjoy great power and privilege and other groups who enjoy less or none. These are the facts of life. The poor and the powerless are always with us.

What has been true of every preceding society is self-evidently also true of the sophiocratic system. Under sophiocracy, there are the subjects who live within the various enclosures around the world, submitting unknowingly to the programmes and experiments of the sophiocrats; and there are the outsiders who benefit from the life-enhancing technologies and the dubious entertainments that the enclosures provide. However, the sophiocratic system differs from every society that has preceded it in two key respects: firstly, in the degree of separation between the two groups, and secondly, in the absolute power that the sophiocrats wield over the subjects.

In earlier ages, oppressors and oppressed at least shared the same world. Slave and free, vassal and lord, labourer and bourgeoisie, although they enjoyed vastly different degrees of wealth, power and prestige, at least knew of each other. They spoke to each other, fought with each other and occasionally, when they thought no one was looking, had sex with each other. They honoured the same ideals and worshipped the same gods. Under sophiocracy, this is not the case. The subjects cannot imagine a world beyond what they know as the beyonds and so they cannot imagine a class of people who might live there. The enclosure represents the most complete social separation in human history.

The nature and extent of the power exercised over the subjects follows from this radical separation. Free men have always coerced and abused slaves, lords have always coerced and abused vassals, the bourgeoisie coerced and abused the labourers whom they held in wage slavery. But in each case, the coercion took obvious and identifiable form. It was the lash; the slave galley; the aching, empty stomach. Being invisible to the subjects, however, the sophiocrats exercise their power invisibly and internally. Theirs is the power of the gentle injection, the obscuring light, the adjusted water, the false fable, the corrupted mind. The sophiocrat does not force the subject to act against his will; rather, he shapes the will of the subject to serve his own ends.

If you wish to picture the power of sophiocracy, therefore, do not picture the law court, the lash or the boot in the face. Imagine instead the cold gaze of the ambitious scientist (imagine my gaze), imagine knowledge without love, imagine a stream of pure power reaching into the depths of the human soul to shape and re-shape it at will.

This is the vilest evil imaginable, and yet it is undertaken for the best of intentions. The sophiocrats do not regard themselves as monsters. On the contrary, they see themselves as excellent people. According to their book, they are working "to refashion humanity in a nobler form, free from the tyrannies of ignorance, superstition and nature itself." They seek "to recreate humanity as its own artifice and possession." What cause could be more noble, what vocation more altruistic? But the brutal fact is that humanity is not meant to be its own artifice and possession. We are not capable of it. We are weak, contrary, mortal creatures who struggle to do the good that we know we should do and often fail to catch hold of the joys that are legitimately ours. To recreate humanity as its own artifice and possession, therefore, does not mean the general emancipation of humanity; rather, it means the limitless extension of some people's power over the lives and souls of others. This is the great truth that the sophiocratic system proves beyond doubt, and which its practicioners resolutely refuse to acknowledge.

I have just taken a short break to fortify myself with a glass of port (not from the special bottle, of course; that remains untouched at my elbow, waiting its moment). The fact is, it is extraordinarily painful to think of sophiocracy and humanity in these terms because in doing so I have no option but to cast myself unambiguously amongst the baddies. I agreed to work for the Ely Project because I genuinely believed in the principles of Anthropology and Posthumanism, and because I loved Sebastian with the obsessive, unhappy love of a middle-aged spinster. I gave my ongoing consent to Ely and then to the sophiocratic state because I was too busy to take stock and consider precisely what I was involved in. That sounds disgusting even to my own ears, but it is nonetheless true. I had reports to write, budgets to manage, training programs to devise, personality clashes to smooth out and departmental battles to fight. Surfing a tide of administration I have absent-mindedly become one of the most evil women who has ever lived. (Sometimes when I am bored I measure the extent of my own wickedness against that of other wicked women from literature and history—does Lady Macbeth beat me, does Herodias? Perhaps they do in terms of the depravity of their motives, certainly not in terms of the consequences of their actions.)

There is precious little I can do to correct the evil I have done. My biography is written to communicate as much discontent with Ely and Sophiocracy as one may and still hope to avoid the censor's list. My suicide note to colleagues in the Service, while making no mention of murder, outlines my grievous moral concerns with the Project. It may give the best of them pause. And this text may yet stir my "enemies" in Cambridge to renewed action.

I have resolved to do more than write, however. I have also arranged to meet Sebastian for a drink to discuss my retirement. He is happy to keep the appointment, regarding it as an opportunity finally to relieve the Service of its great privilege. (In his arrogance and self-delusion he fails to learn from his past mistakes. The man really has no sense of history at all.) I will supply the port at our meeting and neither of us will leave the room alive. I hope that the Guardian's death may destabilize the system sufficiently to make renewed resistance possible. At the very least, it might serve as an example to future generations.

The above paragraph makes me seem extraordinarily selfless and rather daring and gung-ho. Please do not be deceived, dear reader; my motives for killing the Guardian are far from pure. Certainly I wish him dead because his death may harm the state, but it also pleases me immensely to be the agent of his demise. I hate the man quite as much as I love him. It will give me great pleasure to watch him drink and then tell him what I have done and why.

I certainly do not wish for, or expect, any honour for the deed. The best I can hope for is that history will forget me, although I know that being forgotten is itself an honour that I do not deserve.

There must be a reckoning for all that has gone on. There simply must be. There must be a reckoning. Or else everything really is meaningless.

At any rate, there will be a reckoning for Sebastian.

Sam put the papers down and sat back in his chair. While he had been reading, the light had faded to dull grey and the wind had picked up. The sandwich was still untouched on its plate and there were now three dog ends in the ash tray. Another cigarette, smoked down to the butt, smoldered in his hand. Sam stubbed it out and stretched, then gathered up the papers and walked to the picture of Hilary. He bent down, picked up the fallen petals and tipped them into his trouser pocket. Straightening, he pulled the withered stalks from behind the photograph and pushed them into his pocket as well. He ran his finger softly over the faded print, then turned on his heel and walked quickly out of the cottage.

There was a narrow path leading across the dunes to the beach. It was sandy and overgrown, occasionally skirting pools of clear water. Sam followed it as if in a dream, clutching the papers to his chest while the wind whipped at his hair. Where the dunes finally gave out and the beach began, he found a spot partially sheltered by rock and knelt to dig a pit in the damp sand. He scrunched each of the papers into a loose ball and dumped them in the hole, then applied his cigarette lighter to the base of the pile. For several moments the fire fought with the wind, and then it suddenly caught hold and papers burst into flame. Fire and smoke leapt high out of the pit, making Sam jump backwards. He wafted the smoke from his face and watched as the blaze roared and then died quickly away. When it was out he shuffled forwards again and kicked sand back over the ashes, stamping it down and then scraping fresh sand over the top so that there was no indication that the ground had been disturbed.

When he was satisfied that the spot could not be found, Sam turned and walked down the beach to the sea. He crouched in the surf and splashed water on his face, relishing the gritty cold against his skin. He shivered and blinked, and as he did so the image of an old woman—a murderess—drifted uninvited into his mind. She was kneeling over a dead cat with soil under her fingernails, a trowel discarded at her side. She was trying not to weep. The image disturbed Sam. His breathing quickened and his heart raced, and for a fraction of a second he felt a spark of warmth and pain flash inside him. It was a new sensation to him, or perhaps it was a very, very old one. It was threatening and tempting. Instinctively, he scratched his arm over his warming liberty patch, willing it to extinguish the feeling. As he did so, however, other thoughts clustered into his mind, drawn by the power of the old woman, spinning around her like planets orbiting a fading sun. He thought of his own father, whom he had always considered weak, but who still had the courage to confront Sir Douglas Latch and an alpha for the sake of his family. He thought of his ridiculously fat mother who had told him a few months ago that she would not betray those she loved, even in thought. He thought of his stupid, insensitive brother who somehow still knew the art of feeling shame and the duty to battle evil. And, finally, he thought of a red-headed girl with a gap between her teeth who, not so long before in a chaotic shop, had opened her arms wide to welcome him and hold him.

The thoughts span and span in his mind until the spark of warmth and pain fired inside him with new intensity and the liberty patch grew hot on his arm.

There were tears in Sam's eyes as he clambered to his feet and lifted his face to the darkening sea. But whether they sprang from grief or just from the buffeting of the outside wind that blows from nowhere to nowhere, not even he could say.